PHANTOM SHADOW

As I swung my feet to the floor of the dark room, I saw him. I knew it was Adam. Standing by my window, he remained perfectly still, almost as if he hoped I wouldn't notice him.

"Adam," I said, trying not to sound surprised and frightened, "how in the hell did you get up here?"

Climbing to my second floor window requires some tricky maneuvering. It can be done. I've done it. But for Adam, it must have been pretty difficult.

When he didn't answer me, I figured he was upset or something.

"Just a second and I'll turn on the lights," I said.

I took about two steps and the shadowy figure of Adam raised one hand.

My bedroom light blinked on. The small fan roared like a jet plane.

I squinted at the floor because the light seemed much brighter than usual. And when I glanced up, the shadow-Adam became a phantom outline, a perfect ghostly image of him.

And then it dissolved.

HAUNTING TALES OF UNSPEAKABLE EVIL
BY RICK HAUTALA!

NIGHT STONE (1843, $3.95)
Their new house was a place of darkness and shadows, but with her secret doll, Beth was no longer afraid. For as she stared into the eyes of the wooden doll, she heard it calling to her and felt the force of its evil power. And she knew it would tell her what she had to do.

MOONBOG (1845, $3.95)
From the murky depths of the swamp it arose to claim its human sacrifice. But one child wasn't enough. It needed a second, a third—and then nothing could stop the raging bloodthirst of the MOONBOG!

"AN IMPRESSIVE NOVEL OF SUSPENSE AND DARK HORROR . . ."

—STEPHEN KING

LITTLE BROTHERS (2276, $3.95)
The "little brothers," hideous forest creatures who feed every half-decade on human flesh, are about to emerge once again from their underground lair. And this time there will be no escape for the young boy who witnessed their last feast!

NIGHT TOUCH

Stephen Gresham

ZEBRA BOOKS
KENSINGTON PUBLISHING CORP.

ZEBRA BOOKS

are published by

Kensington Publishing Corp.
475 Park Avenue South
New York, NY 10016

First printing: December, 1988

Printed in the United States of America

PART ONE:

ADAM'S WORLD

CHAPTER 1

My name is Rob Dalton. I am fifteen years old and I live with my older sister, Leah. I have always lived in Warrior Stand, Kansas. So have Andrea and Adam. My best friends.

Thing is, this story's about them, especially about Adam, about something that happened to him last year. Something very strange. To begin with, I've got to say that I never expected the darkness. None of it. Adam and Andrea and I, we were just three kids who had played together since we were in diapers. We thought we understood the world.

Boy, were we ever wrong!

All this started late last summer in the Warrior Stand Cemetery, which has been one of our favorite haunts for as long as I can remember. Well, from here the story gets weird. So hold on. . . .

Andrea's bright yellow blouse flapped out at her waist. I could see the soft, brown tan on her belly from suntanning at Summer's Pond and up at Council Grove Lake. The wind played tenderly with her strawberry blond hair. But she was frowning. She was worried.

Over to the west, a thunderstorm was building, painting the sky blue-black with pockets of green promising hail and high winds and maybe a tornado.

"We can't wait too long for him," I said, dreading the thought of my new motorbike getting soaked, but also

9

wondering how I might capture the storm-touched, lightning-edged blues and greens and dark grays of the clouds.

You see I love to paint. It's my dream. To be a painter. Last Christmas Andrea's grandfather, Doc Newton, gave me a book called *Christina's World,* a collection of Andrew Wyeth's drawings and paintings and now I've got my heart set on being the "Andrew Wyeth of Kansas." Like I said, it's my dream. Andrea's is to be a country western singer like Reba McEntire, and Adam's dream is . . . well, that's hard to say.

"Is that him?"

Andrea was pointing across a pasture toward Summer's Pond and the old Dodd place beyond it. She looked good in that yellow blouse and those white, runner's shorts—the ones that cut way up on her thighs.

The wind kicked in my face as I squinted.

"No, it's Blackie. You know that dog always comes up when we're around. Your grandfather says he likes to dig up bones around here."

Andrea merely rolled her eyes at my attempt at humor. Doc Newton's Labrador retriever eventually lumbered into the small cemetery, red tongue lolling; he sniffed about and promptly urinated on a leaning headstone.

"Hey, Blackie," I exclaimed. "Damn your hide. Don't you have any respect for the dead?"

Dogs don't.

Maybe I wouldn't either except that over in the far corner are three plots where my parents and brother are buried. I try not to think about them too much.

Down on the road leading into town, a shiny red Camaro slowed, and Andrea waved at the guy driving because she knew I get jealous when she does that.

"What do you see in that scumbucket Brian Gunnellson?" I asked her. "You like him because he's a senior?"

Andrea wheeled. Her "anger wrinkle," a tiny fingering up from the bridge of her nose, came to life.

"Robert Dalton, why don't you grow up? You believe I'm in love with any boy I even look at. You forget that

10

we vowed a long time ago—right here in this cemetery—that we'd get married when we got out of school. I don't break promises, mister."

She's really steamed when she calls me "mister," and she's right about breaking promises. She won't.

I tried to cool her down some.

"Remember the night you and me and Adam stayed out here way past midnight and told ghost stories? Adam—he told that story about the girl who drove a stick into one of the graves to ward off evil spirits and she accidentally drove it through her skirt and got trapped right there on the grave. She died. Died of fright trying to pull away."

Adam can make up the weirdest stories. I think he ought to be a writer someday. The guy has a wild imagination.

Well, Andrea didn't respond. She kept watching for the first sign of Adam.

"Remember what else we did that night?" I coaxed.

She turned. The anger wrinkle had fled.

My strategy was working.

She smiled shyly.

"We were thirteen," she said, "and it was the first time you ever kissed me full on the lips."

That's not exactly right. As I remember it, *she* did the kissing and I sorta kissed back. The kiss was wet and clumsy and rimmed with some awkward, heavy panting and some giggling, but the memory of it was taking her mind off Adam.

Andrea and I have gotten some better at kissing. Practice. That's what it takes. The cemetery and Pudge's Auto Salvage are the main places we go for practice sessions.

"You got grounded for two weeks for staying out so late," I added.

A pretty dumb comment because it seemed to return her attention to Adam. Mine, too.

"Why did Adam want us to meet him here?" she asked. "What's going on?"

11

"Said he had something he wanted to show us."

"Probably some gadget," said Andrea. "He spends hours taking radios apart and connecting all those little colored wires every which way. My daddy says Adam's a whiz with gadgets. That's like a genius, I think."

I agreed.

"Andrea, listen, he didn't say he was in trouble or anything. Just wanted to show us something."

The wind whipped a lock of hair down to a corner of her eye and she brushed it aside.

"Adam's *always* about to get into trouble," she corrected me. "Trouble with his dad. Or at school. Wherever. That's why we look after him. To keep him out of trouble."

"God almighty, Andrea, he's fifteen years old, same as us. He'll be a sophomore in high school same as us. He can take care of himself."

Andrea stabbed me with her best dagger stare.

Thing is, you see, Adam's sorta the little brother Andrea never had. She has two older brothers, but they're married and off to parts unknown and never show their faces in Warrior Stand. Years ago, Andrea took it upon herself to tend extra to Adam. She felt sorry for him. Because of his face and all. And the way kids in town and at school would make fun of him.

Off in the distance, thunder rumbled, crawling closer. Those clouds were gathering darkness in bushels, providing an even muddier backdrop for the occasional strokes of lightning.

I reached down and petted Blackie and tasted a bitter thought about school starting next week. I wasn't ready to let go of the tail of summer, wanting the hot but freedom-filled Kansas days to romp on forever.

I hated change.

And my life was about to change in ways I couldn't have imagined.

"There he is," Andrea exclaimed, bouncing on her tiptoes to get a clearer view down the slope from the windy perch of the cemetery. She waved both hands at the approaching figure, and then something super strange happened.

The figure returned her wave.

Andrea's hands seemed to melt in the air. They fell to her side. Then she pressed them to her cheeks and looked at me.

"Did you see *that?*" she squealed.

I felt a chill all the way to my groin.

"Yeah . . ." I stammered. "I think I did."

We stood as still as the headstones around us and watched as Adam struggled up the slope. Blackie barked a few rounds, then settled on his haunches to survey the intruder.

"Andrea," I half-whispered, my mouth dry, "wave again."

She did.

And the figure, then about forty yards from us, waved back once again.

"God almighty," I murmured. "God almighty damn."

You see, Adam is blind. Has been since he was six. Can't see a thing. Not a blessed thing.

I swallowed a mouthful of saliva the consistency of gravel.

Andrea had her fingertips pressed to her lips.

Neither of us took much notice of the thunderstorm for the next half hour.

A satchel slung over his shoulder, Adam rambled toward us, his wandlike walking cane barely touching the pasture grass as he moved. He was smiling. Almost laughing.

Andrea started to giggle nervously. I couldn't tell whether she was happy or scared. Or both.

"What is it, Adam? What is it?" she cried out, but the wind snatched her words and flung them into the sky like lost birds.

"Don't you guys leave," Adam shouted. "I got stuff to show you."

He slid his cane up into his armpit and held his hands out in front of him, palms out. It was a curious gesture; it was as if he were saying, "See. See this. I'm not hiding anything."

Andrea and I huddled around him, careful not to step on a grave—bad luck, you know. Adam dropped to his knees and we followed suit. He cackled as he swung the satchel from his shoulder, but I couldn't help hearing a tiny tremor of fear in his apparent joy.

Beside herself with curiosity, Andrea leaned close to his face, a couple of inches from his eyes, cocking her head first one way and then the other. When she spoke, her question tailed off into a whisper.

"Adam . . . Adam, can you *see?*"

He bobbed and pivoted his head and grinned so broadly I thought he would injure his face. That face. What a face. Bushy black eyebrows rainbowed, touching between his dark eyes; the rest of his face—the wide nose, lipless mouth, and the low-set, shell-shaped ears— well, I had to admit that Adam did resemble a chimpanzee somewhat, though I would have busted anyone (and have a few times) who called him that. He was an ugly kid, but he was our friend.

"Can I see?" he echoed. "In a way. In a way I can. But donchoo tell anyone, Andy. You neither, Rob."

"We won't," I answered, "if you don't want us to. But, hey . . . what's going on? You been to the eye doctor or something?"

He gritted his teeth.

Adam hates eye doctors. After a half dozen unsuccessful operations, he has a right to, I guess.

He rummaged around in his satchel and pulled out a small, red transistor radio.

Andrea shoved at my shoulder.

"I told you. I told you he had some gadget to show us."

"See this?" Adam muttered.

He held up the transistor and deftly removed its back cover. Truth is, I saw nothing special about it. Didn't even have a battery in it. I glanced at Andrea and shook my head. She continued to stare at Adam's eyes as if she had overlooked an obvious answer to the apparent return

14

of some of his vision.

"I'm not really impressed," I shrugged.

Blackie nosed in a second, then bounced away.

"Try to turn it on," said Adam.

He was baiting me and enjoying it.

"Adam . . . you call us up here to look at a broken transistor radio?"

Rocking back and forth, he cackled some more.

"*I'll* try it," said Andrea, snatching the radio and thumbing the on-off dial.

"It's dead," she exclaimed matter-of-factly.

"No shit?" I responded, injecting the comment with as much sarcasm as I could muster.

"Watch it, mister," she shot back, swatting at me pretty hard.

"You guys," said Adam. "Hey, you guys, hey . . . let me show you something. Crazy stuff's been going on. Let me show you."

Andrea and I silenced our tiff.

Adam's hands took over. You'd have to see his hands to understand what I mean. You see, they're real long and thin and the two middle fingers on each hand are the same length. Andrea measured them once. And the backs of his hands sport a jungle of thick black hair just like his bushy eyebrows.

Anyway, Adam clamped the plastic parts together and smiled, lifting the radio aloft and squeezing it with those long fingers. Next thing you know we could hear the radio station in Emporia blaring away.

"Turn it down," Andrea squawked, jamming her fingers in her ears.

Blackie barked his disapproval, and I frowned at Adam.

"So what," I said. "It's just some kind of trick."

Adam's face fell like a house of cards.

"No. No trick. All I did was . . . I . . . *touched* it just right. Stuff like this has been happening ever since . . . here, you guys, let me show you something else."

Animation returned to his face.

I couldn't tell what Andrea was thinking as Adam

15

pawed through his satchel again. But it was obvious the radio trick hadn't exactly dazzled her.

"Adam, stop a second," she insisted.

"Sure, Andy."

He glanced up from his satchel and grinned. His dark eyes rolled lazily, one up and down and the other from side to side. You could tell he was still blind. No doubt in my mind except . . . well, I'll describe what happened then.

Waiting like a smart dog for his owner's next command, Adam appeared to gaze at a piece of infinity just above Andrea's head.

"Adam," Andrea continued, her cheeks flushed, " . . . can you tell me what color my blouse is?"

I caught myself suddenly holding my breath.

Tentatively, Adam reached out with his right hand. Andrea wet her lips and pushed a bottom corner of her blouse toward him the way I've seen her cautiously push a saucer of milk toward a stray kitten.

It was an oddly electric moment when his fingertips touched the material. I watched him. He never looked at the blouse, keeping his eyes, instead, glued to the threatening skies.

His head bobbed. He was concentrating.

Then he grinned mischievously.

"It's solid black 'cept for purple moons and green stars and a red cow jumping over one of the moons, and there's a blue dish and an orange spoon and they're running away."

He cackled.

Andrea jerked back and issued some half-strangled cry of surprise and maybe disgust at being toyed with.

I laughed, too. Adam toppled over on his side, spasms of laughter shaking him. Andrea's face reddened and her anger wrinkle danced.

When the yuks began to subside, I said, "You had us going there. Fooled us damn good."

Andrea shoved my shoulder again.

"Don't get after me," I said. "Adam's the one who

fooled you."

There was a warm hesitation then as Andrea reluctantly allowed a smile to creep in at the corners of her mouth.

Lightning bathed us in a sudden and prolonged camera flash, and I grabbed for Andrea's hand and squeezed it. But she wouldn't look at me.

Adam leaned forward. He shut off his grin.

"*Yellow*," he exclaimed.

His word hung in the air like a piece of ripe fruit begging to be picked.

He leaned so close to Andrea's face that he could have kissed her.

"*Yell-low*," he repeated, exaggerating the word.

"You can *see!*" Andrea exclaimed. "You can really *see!*"

She was overjoyed. But I felt funny.

Even as Andrea celebrated, I could tell that Adam wanted to say something and to show us something more. He grew frustrated as Andrea squealed and giggled.

"No!" he shouted, pulling the plug on her jubilation. "You don't understand."

Andrea just stared at him, then blinked rapidly, then glanced at me with that silly, confused look she wears every so often.

"I can't exactly *see* it," he explained. "It's more like I *feel* it. My hands. My fingers. It's kinda crazy."

He paused to listen for some indication that we halfway understood. Receiving none, he dug into the satchel. This time he wrestled free a yellow legal pad and a medium point Bic pen.

"Watch what I can do," he murmured. "Just watch this."

Andrea folded her arms against her breasts and frowned. Blackie nuzzled at my shoulder, and I stole a peek at the storm which was scudding a little north of town. Someone was getting heavy rain.

"It doesn't happen every time," said Adam, shifting my attention back to him. "Not every time."

17

Pen poised an inch or so above the paper, he steadied his gaze at the sky. There was a crack of thunder; Andrea and I jumped, but Adam didn't even flinch. He was concentrating. He appeared to be controlling his breathing.

And then he began to write.

In a clear hand—ornate letters perfectly on line—he wrote the following:

> *March will search, April will try,*
> *And May will tell if you live or die.*
>
> *March will search, April will try,*
> *And May will tell if you live or die.*
>
> *March will search, April will try,*
> *And May will tell if you live or die.*

It's an old Kansas saying about the mysteries surrounding death. I'd heard my grandparents use it, but seeing it written there . . . by Adam . . . or something controlling Adam's hand . . . well, I was freaked. So was Andrea.

"Unreal," Andrea whispered. "That's just . . . unreal."

Adam settled back as if relieved. But his face blanched. He seemed pleased with himself and yet scared.

I couldn't think of anything else to say, so I asked, "You been around old Willa?"

Willa Snagovia is a strange, gypsylike woman who lives with her brother in a big, dilapidated house down from the Dodd place. When anything out of the ordinary happens around Warrior Stand, someone invariably maintains that Willa's responsible for it. Truth is, she's just a nutty old woman who keeps to herself.

It wasn't really a serious question, but Adam shook his head solemnly as if it were.

"I got an idea about it," said Andrea, recovering somewhat. "It's like this man I read about in *The*

18

National Enquirer. He got struck by lightning and when he's around appliances they go haywire. It's something like that, isn't it, Adam?"

Andrea and her mother read *The National Enquirer* religiously. They also devour Harlequin Romances—so you get the picture of their literary tastes. Well, anyway, Adam poo-pooed Andrea's kooky theory.

"Nothing like that, Andy," he said. "But something . . ." Then he turned to me and said, "You worked the evening shift at Arrowhead Saturday, didn't you?"

Funny he should ask that because he knew I did. He and I always work Saturday evenings at the Arrowhead Truck Stop out on the highway. Andrea's dad owns and runs the restaurant out there and is part owner of the service station. Pudge Wilson is the other owner. He lets me work as a pump jockey and gives me any little pissant job nobody else wants to do. Adam, you see, he works at a small candy and gum counter Pudge set up by the main register. And you ought to see how well Adam can find what a customer wants and how he can make change and keep everything straight.

"Yeah," I said. "It stayed ninety degrees that night till past ten o'clock. 'Bout melted the asphalt."

"There was a Greyhound bus pulled through. You remember it?"

I did.

"You remember any of the people on it?" he continued.

"Not particularly. Just bored-as-nails people. Like all bus riders."

"Well, there was this one guy . . . ," said Adam.

He told us about a man "with a hollow voice" who bought a package of salted peanuts.

". . . and when I held out my right hand for his money, he took hold of my fingers and said, 'You have an unusual hand. May I see your other hand?' And so I let him, but I thought about calling for Pudge because I figured this guy was gonna turn a trick on me. You know, a flim-flam, maybe."

19

"Sounds like 'the phantom hitchhiker,'" Andrea interrupted. *"National Enquirer—"*

"Let him finish, would you?"

"I can talk if I want to, mister. You can't tell me when to talk."

We hissed and spat at each other awhile before Adam could get back to his story.

"He looked at my hand, and for a pretty long time he didn't say nothing. And then you know what? I heard him make a noise like he was real relieved. And . . . and he pressed my hands with his . . . you know, squeezed them, and then he said—this is what he said—'God forgive me, the night touch is yours.' That's what he said. He left and didn't even take his package of peanuts."

We all mused silently about his story until finally I said, "Probably just some weirdo . . . like that busload heading out west the other day to get in harmony with the universe when all the planets lined up. Remember them?"

I didn't like the seriousness on Adam's face, so I tried to lighten things up. Andrea accidentally helped when she said, "That's how much you know, mister. Adam might've come into contact with an alien. He's lucky he wasn't kidnapped and sterilized and stuff."

I laughed, and Adam began to grin and then he held out his hands and said, "Maybe it'll make me rich and famous. The 'night touch.' Yeah, it could . . . and . . . I could help Andy be a country western star. Buy her some fancy clothes, sequins and all, you know—and a brand new guitar. And I could build Rob a studio so he doesn't have to set up and paint in the old empty hardware store."

He touched the right nerves.

I hate to admit it, but we all got kinda silly and excited, speculating on what Adam might do with his wild talent. Boy, we got carried away, talking about television shows and nightclub acts and *The Tonight Show*. Andrea started singing "On the Road Again"—who knows why—and took Blackie by the paws and danced with him—dogs hate for people to do that. We continued to disregard the storm and the white light streaming low to the horizon beneath the dark throat of blue-black clouds until the wind gusted and a dead limb tumbled from the King.

That's our tree. Not *our* tree exactly. Just the only tree around the cemetery. It's a mammoth old cottonwood which we've always called "King Cottonwood," pretending over the years that it possessed magical powers. Mainly it anchors the southwest corner of the cemetery and draws lightning. Whole tree's dead as a doornail.

Funny how quickly the mood began to change when that big limb fell.

"We better all get our butts home," I said, surveying the angry swirl above us.

I can't recall precisely what happened next—not precisely—but it was something like this:

Blackie, who as I said didn't much want to dance with Andrea anyway, wrestled free of her and ran to me and I boxed at his big, friendly head. Andrea was standing there, an imaginary microphone in one hand, deep into the second or third chorus of "On the Road Again," and I was about to holler at her to sit down before she attracted lightning, when Blackie snuggled up to Adam. He used both his hands to scratch the dog's ears and then he crooned some silly dog talk at him the way people do sometimes.

And Blackie went nutso.

I don't know any other way to describe it.

I couldn't believe it. Neither could Andrea.

We watched and Adam listened as the dog uncharacteristically yelped and growled and acted like he'd been shot with rock salt or something. He rolled and jumped and wheeled around, sometimes chasing his tail, sometimes biting at his front paws.

Andrea screamed.

Confused, Adam stood up and started muttering Blackie's name.

Finally the dog jerked and flopped until he wedged himself up against a headstone and I could close in on him.

"Do something, Rob!" Andrea cried. "Do something! What's wrong with him?"

I had no idea.

But I know it scared the hell out of me. It was like riding in a car when you just miss having a bad accident. I felt a shaky coldness all over.

"Blackie," I said, stepping warily toward the dog, "what is it, boy?"

That dog was trembling, shivering like it was forty below zero.

Strangest part, though, he was totally disoriented. Acted like he didn't know me.

"Damn," I whispered.

I looked back helplessly at Andrea. Then I glanced at Adam and he was staring down at the palms of his hands.

"What'd you do to Grandpa's dog?" Andrea yelled at him.

Adam worked his mouth, but no words came out at first.

It was all so weird. I got away from the dog because I thought he might bite me. Next thing I remember, Adam was crying. I hadn't seen him cry since the first grade so that threw me for a loop. Andrea, too.

"Help me, you guys," he sobbed. "Something's wrong. Come here, you guys."

We drew up to him and he had his hands out away from him as if they were diseased or something.

"Don't touch me," Andrea warned him.

"I won't. I won't," he said. "Just promise me. You guys, promise me something. Promise you won't tell *nobody* about this. Specially my dad. Please. Promise me."

He was really upset and so I said, "Sure . . . sure, Adam. We promise, don't we, Andrea?"

She was crying, too.

"Yes," she mumbled. "I'm sorry, Adam. I'm sorry.

22

What can we do?"

He groped around for his walking cane, repositioned his satchel, and scrambled away without saying another word. We watched him feel his way down the slope, watched him stumble, then right himself, and eventually disappear into the storm-ridden twilight.

CHAPTER 2

At first, I was mad at Adam.

I can't really explain why. But there I was, storm coming, Andrea crying, hugging me, wanting to be consoled, and her grandfather's dog acting like he had rabies. And Adam had trotted off home leaving us to tend to the animal.

All my momentary reflections turned against my friend.

The transistor radio trick seemed more and more just that—a trick. As for writing on that legal pad, well, maybe he'd been practicing. And maybe knowing the color of Andrea's blouse was simply a good guess.

The story of the man from the bus and his comment about a "night touch"—that's the kind of wild tale Adam's an expert at concocting.

Blackie? Yeah, well, that one had me puzzled. The dog was behaving very strangely. Had Adam affected him somehow? Or could it have been that the lightning or thunder had scared him real bad?

While I was discounting everything that had occurred, Andrea pulled away from me and started toward the dog.

"Be careful," I cautioned. "He might bite."

"No, he won't," she responded. "I've been around Blackie since he was a pup. He would never hurt me."

She swiped at a stray tear skating down her cheek and held out her hands to show the dog she meant no harm. She got to within maybe ten feet of him when he suddenly rolled up from the headstone and lunged at her, teeth flashing, a deep, I-mean-business growl coming from his throat.

She shrieked, and I ran and grabbed her.

"Damn it, I told you!"

She was trembling and got real quiet.

Twilight softened the scene. But scattered drops of rain began to pelt us.

I kept hold of Andrea's shoulders as she stared at the dog, his blackness thick and solid there in the dwindling light.

"Blackie, it's me—Andrea," she whispered.

The dog growled low, and then the growl became a pathetic whine.

"He doesn't recognize me, Rob. Blackie's . . . what's *wrong* with him?"

"Come on," I said. "Let's go get your grandfather. He'll know what to do."

Helmets in place, we climbed on my motorbike, and just as I started to kick-start it, Blackie gave out a long, eerie howl that we could hear even through our headgear.

A shiver jagged up my spine.

We rode out of the cemetery, nerves pin-balling.

Normally I enjoyed giving throttle to my bike and feeling Andrea's warm and well-endowed figure pressing against my back, but not that particular evening. So many thoughts were waging battles in my head I could barely concentrate on dodging the big flint boulders which dotted the pasture below the cemetery.

But we made it to the town road and roared over the railroad tracks that mark the entrance to Warrior Stand. Main Street, deserted as usual except for dust devils spun to life by the wind, added to the curious sense of uneasiness I was feeling.

I banked left and accelerated. Darkness coming on, I reasoned that Doc Newton would be at home, so I swung into his driveway, and as we bounced up to the door of his small, red-brick home, I whispered to Andrea, "Don't say anything about Adam."

Not sure why I said that except maybe my old

26

allegiance to Adam couldn't be compromised very easily.

Andrea said nothing; she appeared to be in shock.

Poor old ghostly Alma greeted us, smiling broadly, her hair spiraling off in unruly gray wisps.

She had no idea who we were. That made me think of Blackie.

Alma's Doc Newton's wife. She has Alzheimer's.

"Grandma . . . is Grandpa here?"

Andrea knew better than to ask; she pressed her nose up to the screen, but her grandmother just kept smiling blankly until Mrs. Tenney scurried up behind her.

"Hi, kids," said Mrs. Tenney. "No, Doctor Newton isn't around. I expect he'll be back shortly. He went off this afternoon to paint or whatever it is he does when he goes off."

Mrs. Tenney looks after Alma most days.

I nodded.

Seeing the distress in Andrea's face, Mrs. Tenney added, "Is there something wrong? Someone sick?"

Andrea shook her head.

"It's Blackie. He's acting real funny."

"My lands. Well, try the hardware store or the Arrowhead. Aren't too many places a body can be in Warrior Stand."

Mrs. Tenney smiled sympathetically and guided Alma away from the screen.

So Andrea and I scrambled onto my bike again, but the image of Alma Newton remained in my thoughts like the after-flash of a camera. They say she's getting worse. It's a horrible thing that's happened to her.

I remember—it was a couple of summers ago—when the Alzheimer's first got serious. Adam and I had been walking the railroad tracks—you know, doing the usual stuff—like laying pennies on the track or putting our ear against it to hear a distant train or speculating on what it would be like to ride a boxcar all the way to California— and there she was. Dressed in a tattered robe and house slippers, there was Alma stepping from tie to tie, glancing from side to side, panic in her eyes.

27

"Grandma Newton," I said, "what are you doing out here?"

She clutched at my arm.

"I've lost my way."

She repeated those words over and over.

Adam and I took her home. And I wondered: Why Alma Newton? A sweet little grandmother. What did she ever do to deserve such a horrible affliction? I still don't understand. But thinking about Alma jolted me into realizing that I wasn't being fair to Adam. I shouldn't have been mad at him—maybe something really terrible had come upon him for no reason—just like his blindness came upon him when he was six—just like Alzheimer's had come upon Alma.

Maybe Adam was losing his way.

I geared up the bike and we rumbled to the hardware store, a big ugly wound in the middle of Main Street. The Ryans used to run the hardware, but they went out of business back in the '60s. Doc Newton bought the place and turned it into a studio for his artwork. He lets me paint there, too. And at that moment, seeing the shadow-filled, deserted hardware, I wanted to be in there under soft track lighting seated before a canvas.

I wanted to pretend nothing was wrong with Blackie.

I wanted to believe that Adam hadn't caused whatever was wrong with the dog.

Fortunately the rain let up as we sped toward the Arrowhead Truck Stop. Lightning and thunder and wind continued, however, and the dust of our tiny, dying town swirled into our faces.

Doc Newton wasn't at the Arrowhead. We could tell just riding by. You see, he has his own booth there—not actually *his*—but he always sits in the far left corner booth by the front window. Everybody knows that's Doc Newton's booth.

"He's at the Snagovias', I bet."

That's what I hollered over my shoulder to Andrea as I slowed to turn around and head out of town again.

I was right.

Out south of the railroad tracks, beyond the cemetery, beyond the Dodd place where Adam and his parents were probably settling down to supper, stood the three-story, graying clapboard monstrosity shared by Willa and John Snagovia. It loomed there on a windy hill, and when we read Poe's "The Fall of the House of Usher" in freshman English last year I couldn't help thinking about the Snagovia place. Willa and John seemed pretty similar to Madeline and Roderick Usher—to me, at least, though I doubted that John would ever bury Willa alive the way Roderick buried Madeline, but who could tell? They're strange folks.

We saw Doc Newton trudging toward his old white-over-aqua Ford Victoria—it's a 1955 in mint condition— runs like a son-of-a-gun. He had a sketch pad under his arm, so I knew exactly what he'd been up to. He's sketched hundreds of angles on the Snagovia place and their barn and even a few dozen of Willa and John. Especially of Willa. That's like what Andrew Wyeth did with the Olsons in Maine. Doc Newton's not quite as good as Wyeth, but he's damn good.

He's taught me a lot about drawing and painting.

I admire the man so much; he seems at peace with himself.

But Andrea and I were about to shake his contentment.

"Grandpa, it's Blackie!" Andrea cried out. "He's been hurt. Up at the cemetery. He's in bad shape."

Jacob Newton, a pipe in his mouth which he rarely smoked, looked from Andrea to me and then back to Andrea. He raised one of his fine, long, slender hands— hands perfectly formed to hold a paint brush—and took the pipe from his mouth.

"He get hit by a car?"

"No," said Andrea, "but he's hurt bad. Isn't he, Rob?"

"Yeah," I followed. "He's suffering."

"OK, I'll drive right up there."

I tried to sneak a peek at his sketch; I could spend hours (and have) studying his work.

As he tucked his tall, thin body into the old Ford, I thought again about Alma. This lonely, warmth-questing man who could create so much beauty on a canvas—didn't he deserve the comfort of a healthy, loving wife in his retirement? I say "retirement"—that's not quite accurate. He's been the only doctor in Warrior Stand for years and years and still has an office in his house, but he only tends to folks with piddling ailments. He'll send you to Council Grove or Emporia if you're really sick. It leaves him plenty of time to paint and, I suppose, be near Alma.

Darkness came on us as we followed Newton to the cemetery. I think Andrea and I were both relieved that he would be looking after the dog. But once we got to the cemetery our discomfort—or at least mine—returned.

Blackie was howling, crying, obviously in pain.

"Can you do something for him, Grandpa? Listen to him . . . please do something for him."

Newton patted Andrea's shoulder reassuringly.

"I'll try, honey. I'll see what I can do."

He paused to let the sound of the animal echo down the slope. Maybe I just imagined it, but I thought I saw the man shudder. The dark shrouded his face, so I couldn't see his expression clearly. My guess is that he was kinda shaken by what he was hearing.

He went to the trunk of his car and got a flashlight and his 20-gauge shotgun. When Andrea saw the gun, she almost flipped out.

"Grandpa, no . . . don't shoot him!"

"Can't you hear, honey? It would be the most humane thing to do."

He started up the slope; we shadowed him a few feet behind. I held Andrea's hand, not really comforting her, I'm afraid.

I'll never forget what a weird scene it was—the small, lonely cemetery up ahead anchored there by the giant, dead cottonwood, its branches reaching ghost-like into a backdrop of lightning to the east. Another set of rain clouds gathered behind us.

And Blackie's cries.

If it's possible for a sound to reflect a sense of being *lost,* hopelessly lost and in deep anguish, it would be the one which filtered down from that dog.

You could see the reddish-amber dots of Blackie's eyes the second we entered the cemetery. He hadn't moved from the headstone where we'd left him.

Doc Newton speared the dog in the beam of the flashlight. Blackie yelped as if the light hurt his eyes, so his owner directed the beam to one side. He didn't approach the dog at first; instead, he half turned and said to us, "Did you see him hurt himself? Did you see a snake? One of those small prairie rattlers? What did you see?"

His voice was calm.

For a moment, I clung to the suggestion that a small rattlesnake perhaps had bitten Blackie. We had seen a few snakes during the summer. Then Andrea started telling all that had happened, leaving out, of course, anything about Adam's apparently renewed sight.

"The only thing any of us did was pet him," she explained. "There was no snake, Grandpa."

Waiting for him to respond, I looked away. Movement near the cottonwood caught my eye, and what I saw there punched the breath out of me. But I tried not to give myself away.

I was glad Doc Newton didn't press us about Adam; I'd always had a feeling that he was suspicious of Adam, or maybe it was just that he didn't like Karl Dodd, Adam's father—a mean man who had no use for doctors of any kind.

"Hold this for me."

Newton handed the shotgun to me and hunkered down in front of Blackie.

"Hey, fella, what is it? You gonna let me get close to you?"

He switched off the flashlight.

I glanced back at the cottonwood and again the breath sucked out of me, tearing at my lungs like a strand of

31

barbed wire.

Blackie howled.

I gripped the shotgun and felt dizzy. Andrea pressed her head against my shoulder. I hoped she wouldn't look toward the cottonwood.

Trailing off into a whimper, the dog's howl seemed to lose all its energy.

"Blackie, . . . hey, fella."

Doc Newton's voice was soothing, but it was pretty apparent that the dog didn't know him, and when Newton reached out to him, Blackie got up and tried to run. Yet, he couldn't. He had no use of his legs. He flopped along the ground until Newton got hold of him and cradled him in his arms.

"I'll run him over to the vet at Council Grove," he said.

"I want to go with you," said Andrea.

Blackie struggled, quivering with fear; Newton held him firmly, and we made our way down the slope.

I turned once to look over my shoulder at the cottonwood.

The dark outline of Adam ducked out of sight.

A light rain began to fall.

Doc Newton loaded Blackie in the back seat; Andrea slid in beside the dog. I could hear him whimpering and crying even as they pulled away. Andrea waved at me but couldn't quite muster a smile.

I jumped on my bike and kicked hard. My plan was to beat Adam home and be there to help him explain to his dad why he was late. Karl Dodd would not tolerate anything like his son not showing up for supper. Adam would catch holy hell.

So I burned a patch of rubber and held on; the rain began to fall more heavily, drifting through the spray of my headlamp. I tried to concentrate on slick spots. I couldn't.

Once or twice I looked toward the pasture, hoping to

see Adam's route home, but it was too dark. When I wheeled up the long, narrow drive to the Dodd place, I felt relieved. Everything would be fine, I told myself. Blackie's on his way to the vet, and I'll tell Mr. Dodd that I asked Adam to help me fix my bike.

Sure, it would be a lie, but . . .

Thunder followed me up the drive; the rain was soaking through my jeans. Leah would probably bitch at me some when I got home. So it goes. I didn't care. I turned off the bike and parked it under a cedar so it wouldn't get any wetter than was absolutely necessary.

It was curious how my feelings had changed so quickly from being mad at Adam to being willing to defend him against his dad. I guess that's the kind of friendship we had.

From under the cedar I could see into the Dodd kitchen. There was the broad back of Karl Dodd at the supper table. Mrs. Dodd to his left.

And Adam to his right.

My whole body went limp.

Who had I seen up by the cottonwood?

I would have sworn to God it was Adam.

Too freaked out to go to the door, I climbed back on my bike, kicked life into it, and wheeled into the rain. Mr. Dodd must have heard me because he stepped out onto the front porch as I made the town road.

Over my shoulder, through the rain-glistened night, I saw him, his hulking body. Just the sight of him scared me, and suddenly I thought of the first time I'd seen him be mean to Adam. The episode had to do with a stray cat and our desire to protect it. For reasons I don't recall, Andrea wasn't involved in the escapade.

You see, one day Adam and I found this cat—I guess we must have been eight or nine—and somebody had dipped this poor cat in kerosene, the result being that he had no fur except for right around his eyes and a tip on his tail. We named the cat "Supernaked"—seemed like a good name for the pathetic, pink-skinned creature.

Adam really felt sorry for that cat. Well, I did, too.

"Too bad cats don't have armor," I said at the time. "You know, something like the armor those medieval knights put on their horses."

That comment clicked for Adam. He had an idea. I'll admit I thought it was a good idea. It was around Thanksgiving, and Adam had felt the tinfoil his mother wrapped leftover turkey in. So . . . yeah, you're right.

You ever try to wrap a cat in tinfoil?

It's not easy.

We used a whole roll of it and wore ourselves out wrestling with that cat, but we were proud of the finished product. Supernaked wore tinfoil on every inch of his body except for a cut-out around his eyes and his private parts—even his tail was neatly wrapped. But when Mr. Dodd got home that evening, he failed to share our sense of accomplishment. In fact, he yanked Adam up by one arm and whipped him hard. Real hard.

After that I was always afraid of Karl Dodd . . . of his hair-trigger temper.

The rain chilled me back to reality. I don't recall the ride home. My bike knew the way automatically. Lost in thought about Adam, I rolled the bike into the barn and wiped it down. My clothes were soaked.

My sister, Leah, met me at the door.

"Robert Wayne Dalton, don't you have enough sense to come in out of the rain?"

What could I say? It was a long story. Not one I felt like telling. And the business with Blackie appeared to be only the tip of a very, very strange iceberg.

I went up to my room and changed into dry clothes, and when I came back down. Leah was spooning some macaroni and cheese onto my supper plate.

"Eat some of these sliced tomatoes, too," she said. "Last ones of the season. From Mrs. Buckley's garden."

Leah and I had tried to grow our own tomatoes, but the summer had been so hot and dry that we lost them by mid-July. We took on the garden because we knew that our folks—if they had been alive—would have put one in. They did every summer.

I ate quietly, stealing a glance at Leah once in a while to gauge just how upset she was. My sister's twenty-three, kind of pretty, and a nurse at the new rest home north of Emporia. She works the graveyard shift—ten to six—and so has to sleep some during the day. She always looks tired. And I think she's sort of lonely. Not many eligible bachelors in a small Kansas town like Warrior Stand. I keep hoping somebody will come along for her. Andrea's mom tried to fix her up with the visiting minister from the Manhattan Bible College, but that was a disaster. So it goes.

I love my sister.

No, I guess I don't show it much. We fight about things. She leans on me too hard at times. But, in a way, we need each other. And I probably wouldn't be living in Warrior Stand—where I really want to be—without Leah. You see, when my mom and dad and my older brother, Drew, got killed a few summers ago—a train hit the car they were in—Leah stepped forward and said she'd take care of me and that we'd keep living in the farmhouse our folks had lived in for years.

Money-wise and in other ways, too, it hasn't been easy. Leah's had to sacrifice, giving up her dream of becoming a doctor. I owe her a lot.

Midway through supper, she said, "Anything wrong? You're awfully quiet tonight. You're usually chirping away about something."

Leah can read me like a book sometimes.

I thought about shrugging it off and then about making something up.

Instead, I said, "It's Adam."

Geez, I surprised myself. I had no intention of saying anything about Adam.

"What about him?" she asked.

"He's been acting kind of funny."

I couldn't believe I said that.

Luckily, Leah gave me an out.

"Probably nervous about school starting Monday. You know what a difficult time he has doing schoolwork.

35

nd socially . . . keep in mind he must feel more and more an outsider every year."

I nodded, thankful to have an explanation handed to me.

"Yeah, I bet you're right. He's worried about school. That's what it is."

"What about you? Ready for another year on the honor roll? Sophomore biology coming up. You know how important that could be."

She was leaning on me. She's real proud that I make good grades, but she's always dropping little hints that I should give up on planning to be an artist and aim for med school instead.

"Doc Newton's dog, Blackie, got hurt. That's why I was late."

I told her about what happened in the cemetery. Not much about it. Just enough to shift the topic from school and Adam and me to the dog.

"I'm going to stay up for awhile and see if Andrea calls," I added. "Maybe they found out something at Council Grove."

We watched some television—a dumb British movie in which nothing really went on—and then Leah got ready and left for work, having reminded me to lock the doors before I went to bed.

I felt really lonely that night for some reason.

I usually don't.

The old farmhouse had never felt so empty.

Andrea never called. I decided not to call her, figuring she would let me know if they heard anything on Blackie's condition.

So I headed up to bed.

The rain had stopped, but the humidity was unbearable. I opened my south window all the way, hoping for some kind of breeze. Because the window had no screen, I had to risk an attack of mosquitos. I positioned a small electric fan on my dresser and aimed it at my bed where I sat and thumbed through an art book.

On the wall to the left of my bed there's a poster, a

36

large print of Wyeth's famous painting, *Christina's World*—it's my favorite. Pillows propped behind me, I found myself suddenly staring at that print: Christina, a crippled and slightly retarded woman, is sprawled out in a pasture looking toward a gray-washed house which always reminds me of the Dodd place.

It must have been some kind of a hallucination.

You see, the longer I stared at that print the more I began to sense that it was *changing*—Christina seemed to move. But when I looked closer it wasn't Christina at all.

It was Adam.

God almighty.

I'd let myself get too worked up about my friend. The solution, I reasoned, was to relax, think about something or someone other than Adam. Naturally Andrea filled the role. Thing is, I have this notebook devoted entirely to Andrea. Mostly sketches of her. Some from school pictures, but some from more informal poses—like one in which she's sitting on top of an old, badly wrecked '58 Plymouth Fury down at Pudge's Auto Salvage and another under the willow tree at Summer's Pond.

She's seen the notebook and all the sketches. Except one.

One of her posed in the nude as if she were modeling for a professional artist.

Of course, I had to use my imagination, having never actually seen her fully naked. She would probably brain me if she ever saw it.

The sketch is like a fantasy. Other guys have copies of *Playboy* or *Penthouse*, but I have my Andrea notebook. And I wouldn't trade it.

Visions of Andrea snuggled close to me, I eventually fell asleep.

And I dreamed. About Blackie. A corker of a nightmare.

Doc Newton and Andrea and I were in the cemetery searching for Blackie. We could hear him: barking, crying, howling. But we couldn't find him. Not until I stepped onto one of the graves and realized that he was below my feet—*underground*.

Talk about weird.

Well, that's not all. When we started digging in the direction of Blackie's howling, I heard another sound down there—Adam. He said he had something to show us.

Kicking the sheet from me, I woke; a trickle of sweat skated down my backbone. I shook off the dream, though Adam's voice lingered on as if recorded on a tiny tape playing in my ear.

I was thirsty.

As I swung my feet to the floor of the dark room, I saw him. I knew it was Adam. Standing by my window, he remained perfectly still, almost as if he hoped I wouldn't notice him.

"Adam," I said, trying not to sound surprised and frightened, "how in the hell did you get up here?"

Climbing to my second floor window requires some tricky maneuvering. It can be done. I've done it. But for Adam, it must have been pretty difficult.

When he didn't answer me, I figured he was upset or something.

"Just a second and I'll turn on the lights," I said.

I took about two steps and the shadowy figure of Adam raised one hand.

My bedroom light blinked on. The small fan roared like a jet plane.

I squinted at the floor because the light seemed much brighter than usual. And when I glanced up, the shadow-Adam became a phantom outline, a perfect ghostly image of him.

And then it dissolved.

CHAPTER 3

I thought maybe I was losing my mind.

Seems like when you get scared enough, something in your brain just shuts down. That's the way it was with me. Nothing made sense. I couldn't come up with an explanation for what I'd seen. I swear I did *not* imagine the whole thing.

I have a burned-out electric fan as proof.

Right after the ghost—or whatever it was—of Adam disappeared, my body began acting weird. Not in the same way that it has since I became a teenager. This was different. I mean, there it was, a hot night in August, and I felt like I was in a walk-in meat locker.

I was freezing to death.

I got blankets out of my closet and piled them on my bed. I shut the window and turned off the light, and then I dived under those blankets and shivered . . . just as I had seen Blackie shiver.

I counted the minutes till dawn because I couldn't sleep. Every shadow in my room shaped itself into Adam or someone or some *thing*. So I lay there, shivering, hiccupping with fear.

First light, I got up and went downstairs and watched television—Saturday morning cartoons. They were loud and mindless. Gradually I got hold of myself. I was absorbed in Daffy Duck when Leah returned from work. Naturally she wondered why I was up so early and I fed her some line about having a touch of flu. She felt my forehead and looked at my face real close, just the way

39

Andrea had stared at Adam's face the night before.

"You don't have a temperature," she said, "but your color's not good. Eyes are a tiny bit dilated. I can give Doc Newton a call. He could probably give you a quick checkup before school starts."

"No . . . no, I'll be okay. Gettin' soaked in the rain last night musta brought on something. I'm feeling better. Really. Don't call Doc Newton."

Leah smiled and tousled my hair.

"All right. I'm going to hit the sack. Had a rough shift. We got bombed again during the night. Mr. Thomas saved everyone and assured me that he'd file a damage report tonight."

I chuckled at that. You see, in the rest home there's this old guy named Harold Thomas who was in London during World War II. He survived a *blitzkrieg* or two and now, forty some years later, he relives the Nazi bombings in the middle of the night, yanking old folks out of bed and hustling them off to imaginary shelter areas. It's chaos city for the nurses and orderlies. And Thomas can make the sound of an air raid siren—man, it's realistic.

Leah went upstairs, and the lingering image of old Harold Thomas swirled in my thoughts. It faded on the third ring of the phone.

"Rob, it's me. Andrea."

"Hi," I said. Her voice sounded funny. "Hey, have you been crying?"

She had and suddenly she was.

It's a real helpless feeling to hear someone crying on the other end of the phone and you're a mile or so away unable to reach out and hold them or anything. She sputtered and snuffled and let go a loud, heavy sigh, and then she said, "They had to put Blackie to sleep."

The curiousness of that expression hit me pretty hard. *Put to sleep.* Seems like something you would do to little kids who had been up too late.

"What'd they find was wrong with him?"

"Oh, . . . I don't know. Something about damage to his nervous system. They really couldn't tell. They

40

hadn't seen anything like it . . . they couldn't do anything to cure him, so . . ."

"I guess it was best," I said, not knowing what else to say.

"I remember when Blackie was a pup," she stammered.

I was afraid she was going to start crying again, so I said, "You want me to come over?"

"No . . . Momma and I are driving to Topeka this morning . . . to go shopping for school clothes."

"You working at the Arrowhead tonight?" I asked.

Most Saturday nights she does. She's a waitress. Truckers are starting to notice her.

"Yes."

"I'll see you there. Let's take our break at the same time, OK?"

She sighed again.

"OK."

"Hey, Andrea, it's all right. We'll talk. OK?"

And the last thing she said was, "Will you tell Adam?"

I said I would.

There was a lot I needed to tell Adam as well as a few things I needed to ask him.

"Andrea," I added, "I'm real sorry about Blackie."

She had trouble getting the receiver back in its holder.

Poor Andrea. Sometimes I believe she takes the deaths of animals harder than the deaths of people.

After Andrea's phone call, I fully intended to bike over to Adam's. I fixed myself some toast and orange juice, choked it down, and hunted for my sketchpad. Having jammed it into my backpack, I soon had the warm morning air sweeping around me and the hum of the motorbike in my ears. It would be another hot day in Warrior Stand. Dew covered the bluestem grass in all the pastures, converting the landscape to fields of tiny diamonds. The sun would harvest those diamonds in the span of a few hours. And the wind would pick up. It's your constant companion in this part of the state—the Flint Hills region—endlessly rolling hills, mostly treeless and magnificent, that touch something deep within me.

Just the sight of them makes me want to paint.

I wheeled through town. Nothing much shaking except a couple of folks waiting for the post office to open. The other early risers would be out at the Arrowhead, guzzling coffee and sopping up gravy and runny eggs with biscuits and triangles of toast.

This town wasn't ready for the events that loomed ahead.

No way.

The railroad tracks rattled my teeth; I downshifted, then wound out to high gear, destination: Adam's. But I didn't stop when I reached the Dodd turn-in. Never even slowed.

I couldn't. Or, maybe, I just wasn't ready to face Adam. The news about Blackie would upset him a lot. Besides that, I had to think about the incident in my bedroom the night before—what should I say to Adam?

Past the Snagovia place a ways, I parked my bike in a ditch and struck a path through John Snagovia's cornfield, a walking graveyard of dry, skeletal stalks nurturing ears of stunted, diseased corn. John must be the worst farmer in the whole county; every year he plants a quarter section of field corn and just about every year either the hot winds and drought kill it, or bugs and corn smut get to it. He won't use pesticides or any kind of chemicals.

So I brushed through the crackling stalks, gaining the pasture beyond. The Snagovias don't mind if me or Doc Newton comes out and sketches—long as we close gates and don't do anything destructive. Neither John nor Willa can understand why we would want to draw or paint their property. They have no eye for the stark and isolated beauty of the landscape and their dilapidated house and outbuildings.

Where the pasture rises to a gentle slope, I searched for a good vantage point. I'm always looking for some fresh angle, some frame of reference which, in turn, can create a good subject to be transferred to my sketchpad and from there to the canvas.

Well, that particular morning, I hit upon a dynamite possibility.

Boy, did I ever get excited.

You see, on the barbed-wire fence separating the pasture from the cornfield, John had hung three dead jackrabbits. He must have shot them the day before because the blood darkening their fur was still kind of fresh. He had probably planned to skin them, but had forgotten about them or lost track of them. John's like that. Doc Newton says he's a little retarded.

Anyway, they were big jacks, marked perfectly, black shading upon cream-colored sides and shoulders. John had strung them up by their hind legs and turned their heads the same way so that they resembled triplets.

I sketched like mad.

All the while, I thought about color quality and value: especially I wondered if I could capture the texture of the blood against the fur—a murky red. Doc Newton could. But maybe if I worked at it, I could, too.

I sketched for two solid hours.

Then I stopped. And I put aside the sketchpad.

This is going to sound silly maybe, but it's the truth. Those three jacks suddenly reminded me of another trio: myself and Andrea and Adam. I don't know why.

A weird sort of "twilight zone" feeling came over me.

I went home, curled up on the couch, and slept until nearly four that afternoon. All the excitement of sketching the jacks had drained away. And it was a good thing Leah was up and around or I'd have been late for work.

August traffic on the highway was light. That suited me fine. I was tired, mentally and physically.

"Howdy, pussy killer."

Don Slocumb greeted me in the usual fashion. He's Pudge's evening shift manager. Strange fellow. He's a bachelor who's in his forties, I'd guess. The vice-president of a bank in Kansas City for a number of years, one day he just walked out and came back to Warrior

43

Stand where he now lives with his mother. Never offered a word of explanation. There were rumors of an alcohol problem.

Far as I'm concerned, his main problem is women. Or sex. Or both. He tries to hit on every woman in the county—unsuccessfully, I might add. He has the hots for Andrea, and off and on, he renews his efforts to interest Leah in a date. She always politely declines. Slocumb has a stash of the most unbelievably filthy magazines in one of the tool drawers in the lube bay—pictures of naked women and animals and . . . well, you get the idea. I hate to seem like a prude, but that stuff is gross.

"Hasn't Adam come to work yet?" I asked him.

He rubbed his old-fashioned crewcut stubble of hair. "Nope. He's probably home laying his momma."

I always feel sort of slimey when I've been around Slocumb too long. How in the world did a guy like that get to be vice-president of a bank? Oh, well.

So it goes.

I ducked out of Slocumb's sight, busying myself cleaning oil and gas spots from the pump areas. And I wondered about Adam: Was he really sick? It wasn't like him at all to miss work. Had he fought with his dad about something?

Karl Dodd wouldn't hear of having a telephone in his home, so I couldn't call and check on my friend. Around seven that evening, I took my break; naturally, Slocumb joked about me going to see Andrea—or her mother—for a "quickie." The guy never turns it off, I swear.

"Hello, Robert. Ready for school to start?"

Once inside the Arrowhead Restaurant, I was greeted by Andrea's mother, Mrs. Helms. Molly Helms is easily the most attractive woman in Warrior Stand—she looks a lot like the actress, Lee Remick. I think sometimes it bothers Andrea that her mother is so pretty. Back when she was in high school, Mrs. Helms—she was Molly Newton then—was everybody's sweetheart, from what I hear: cheerleader, prom queen, the whole shebang. She married Joe Helms, a real good athlete, but when he came

44

home from Vietnam he developed paralysis—the after-effects of Agent Orange, they say—and he's now confined to a wheelchair. It doesn't slow him down in the kitchen, though. He can wheel around in there like crazy, flipping hamburgers, baking stuff . . . you name it. He hustles.

"No," I answered her, "I can't seem ever to get my mind ready for school."

"Oh, but you do so well. Such good grades. I wish you would influence our Andrea that way."

"Well," I stammered, "I guess I could try."

From behind the cash register, she smiled and looked me over head to toe. She does that to men and boys alike. Makes me uncomfortable.

"You appear to be in very good shape, Robert. Will we be seeing you on the football field this fall?"

I shook my head.

"No . . . no, I've never much liked football."

And I don't. Seems like a dumb game to me. Everybody trying to knock the other guy's head off.

"I suppose you came over to see Andrea."

"Yes, ma'am, I did. Is she 'bout ready to take her break?"

The woman just stared at me, holding my return gaze. She knew that I think she's pretty.

Finally she said, "I tell Andrea all the time that if you keep getting more handsome everyday I'm going to have to offer her some competition for you."

She winked.

I blushed. I thought she was just joking, of course, but there are rumors around town about Molly Helms and midnight truckers and the bread routeman and a salesman from Topeka and . . . well, she's Andrea's mother, so I try not to believe everything I hear.

I found Andrea in her grandfather's booth, her fingers curled around a tall glass of coke. She looked real nice in her pink waitress outfit—it even has her name stitched in script over a blouse pocket. But her face was covered by a thin mask of worry.

45

I plopped down across from her.

"You get a bunch of glitzy clothes in Topeka?"

She glanced out the big, plate-glass window and shrugged.

"Mostly Mom and I fought. Just like we always do. I wish I hadn't gone."

"Fighting with your mom . . . is that what you're upset about? Or is it Blackie?"

"I'm not really upset . . . I'm . . . concerned."

I touched her hand.

"Hey, can you look at me while we're talking? It feels like you're kind of distant from me."

She turned and halfway smiled.

"I'm sorry, Rob."

"No problem."

I hesitated. You see, I know Andrea well enough that when she's stewing about something, she'll tell you. She might take her own sweet time about it, but she'll tell you.

I went to the counter and ordered a burger, fries and coke. Joe Helms saluted me with his spatula from the kitchen.

I was chewing on a mouthful of fries when Andrea said, "What are we going to do about Adam?"

I gestured that I didn't follow her.

"Rob, you know what I mean. He did *something* to Blackie. I almost broke the promise we made with Adam. I almost told Grandpa about what happened in the cemetery. I've been thinking about everything, and it scares me."

"He didn't come to work," I said. "Adam didn't show up for work."

Andrea's eyes got big.

"Something real bad's going on, Rob. I can feel it. Woman's intuition. We have to *protect* Adam."

"*Protect* him? From what?"

She paused.

"Maybe . . . maybe from himself."

Andrea was directing the conversation into weird

territory, and like a fool, I slipped in a comment which steered her even further off the path of reason.

"I've seen something a lot stranger than anything we saw at the cemetery. Something involving Adam. Something I can't explain at all."

It drove Andrea nutso, but I refused to tell her. I did, however, promise to tell Adam about Blackie. There wasn't much else to say; we had to get back to work.

Andrea added one observation which hit closer to the truth than anything else that was said.

"We're the only friends Adam's got," she reminded me.

I realized something that evening: Whatever realm of darkness Adam had entered, we had pledged ourselves to enter it with him. For better or for worse.

"Adam's at the pond," Mrs. Dodd told me the next morning. "He's down." She shook her head and stared off into nothingness. "His spirits are so dark. And I couldn't persuade him to church this morning, but, of course, I prayed extra for him."

I stood there on the Dodd front porch, as always at a loss for words when confronted by Katherine Dodd's religious faith. So I plunged my hands in my pockets and calculated how to get away from her as quickly as possible.

Then she said, "It's his eyes, I believe. He hungers for the light. He needs a miracle. I continue to pray for a miracle to heal his blindness, just as I continue to pray for Mr. Dodd—that he'll hear the Lord Jesus Christ knocking at the door and open it and welcome Him into his heart."

"Yes, ma'am," I whispered. She apparently knew nothing of recent changes in Adam beyond his depressed mood.

I felt around in my pocket and located a quarter.

"Maybe you could add this to your collection," I said.

"Oh, Lord bless you! Bless you!" she exclaimed, her

tiny hands fluttering in front of her like caged birds.

You see, Katherine Dodd has been collecting money—mostly pennies, nickels and dimes—planning one day to take Adam to see one of those faith healer-type evangelists like Oral Roberts down in Tulsa, Oklahoma. She has money in jars and cans all over and around and maybe even *under* the house. She doesn't want Karl to know about it; she knows he wouldn't let her go off to see someone like that. The sad thing is that, according to Adam, she loses track of her various hiding places.

Every so often I give her what change I have. But not when Adam's around. And especially not when Karl's around. I don't believe much in Mrs. Dodd's kind of miracles, though. No miracle occurred the day that train crashed into my folks and Drew.

Well, Mrs. Dodd was getting teary-eyed, so I sneaked away. Passing the barn, I caught a glimpse of Karl hunched over a roto-tiller. Shirtless, his heavy rolls of fat spilled out of his overalls, and his curly black hair, peppered gray, glistened with sweat beneath a baseball cap. I was almost all the way by him when he straightened and glared—a chill wind cut through me as I met his black eyes, tanned face, and that silver-colored goatee-type beard.

To me, he was a perfect image of Satan; that is, if there really is a Satan and if you can imagine Satan as being heavyset and working for the Santa Fe Railroad. That was Karl Dodd. I had seen his temper; I knew his hands must be hard. The thought of being struck by them terrified me.

My walk accelerated into a trot.

Summer's Pond was low, two feet or so below where it would normally be that time of year. I have no idea how it got the name "Summer's Pond"—have never known it by any other name. It's only about an acre pond surrounded by bluestem grass and bunkered by a high ridge so that you can't see the water from the house or barn. At the far end of the pond is a lone weeping willow tree, and near that tree is a sunken duck blind with enough room for three people.

On that warm, windy Sunday morning, I headed for the duck blind.

About twenty yards from it, I announced myself.

"Adam . . . it's me, Rob."

After a moment his voice drifted out of the blind.

"Andy with you?"

"No. Just me."

Adam has always called Andrea "Andy." There was probably some gender confusion when they were both smaller. Who knows? It would really surprise me if he ever called her "Andrea."

"You sick or something?" I asked.

He was scrunched into a corner, wearing a white tee-shirt and jeans and no shoes. I noticed the black hair on the knuckles of his long toes.

"I didn't want to come to work last night," he said.

I climbed down into the blind. Out of the wind, it felt cozy and secretive there.

"Why not?"

"'Cause . . . 'cause I was afraid the Saturn Man would come back."

"Saturn Man?"

"The guy who gave me the night touch. I call him the 'Saturn Man.'"

I started to tell him all that was nonsense. Instead, I said, "I came out to let you know that Blackie's dead."

His expression never changed.

"I figured he would die. Andy pretty upset?"

I nodded.

"Thing is," I said, "she's like me . . . we're sort of puzzled. I mean . . ."

Adam pushed himself out of the corner and propped his elbows on the lip of the blind. I did, too. From that position we had a complete view of the pond.

"It's the night touch, Rob," he said. "I've got it, and sometimes maybe it's going to do good stuff . . . and sometimes maybe it's going to do bad stuff . . . to hurt, or . . . or kill."

49

"Bullshit, Adam!" I exclaimed. "That sounds like bullshit to me. A whole bucket full of it. You're talking like Andrea and her junk magazines."

The anger in me pulsed. The warm air in the blind was suddenly thick with tension.

Adam held up his hands. Like me, he was trembling.

"I know what I'm saying, Rob . . . I've seen . . . I've *felt* what these hands can do."

His eyes twitched and rolled. I couldn't deny that something very strange had been taking place the past few days. I just didn't want to have to admit it. Not about my friend.

What could I say?

Still angry, I turned away from him. The surface of the pond lay quiet—a dull brown, stagnant color. Here and there bubbles floated up from the muddy bottom to sparkle like a necklace of diamonds. But all else in sight seemed dead or dying to me. No lustre. No life. And my friend was hurting.

"You didn't *kill* Blackie," I said.

"How can you be sure of that?"

I heard a bitterness in his voice that I hadn't heard since those early months of his blindness when he believed the world was a cruel joke.

"Because they said . . . Andrea told me . . . the vet found some kind of nerve damage. You couldn't have done that just by *touching* Blackie. It must have been something he'd had for a long time. Or maybe . . . maybe the storm made it worse."

Adam leaned onto the edge of the blind and lowered his head upon his hands. For a long while, he said nothing. The Kansas wind shrieked, rustling over the rotting wood on the roof of the blind.

We had been friends for so many years that the silence threatened neither of us. When Adam eventually raised his head, I thought about what Mrs. Dodd had said— "His spirits are so dark"—and that seemed like a good description of him.

"You think Andy's gonna hate me from now on?"

50

he muttered.

"Are you serious?" I exclaimed. "Andrea? Hate *you*? You're more messed up than I thought if that's what's going on in your head. Andrea would never hate you. She wants to help you. That's what she told me. Honest."

That exchange appeared to boost his spirits some.

"You're probably right . . . it's just that I've been doing a lot of thinking."

He hesitated, seeming to gather courage to take the conversation in a different direction.

"Rob . . . you believe in curses? You know . . . like magic spells or evil spells?"

I laughed at first.

"Why? Did weird Willa put a curse on you? I asked you about that in the cemetery."

"I'm serious, Rob. My mother believes in them. Believes the devil or an evil spirit can put a curse on you. You remember Wheaties? That big collie we had?"

I nodded.

"It went crazy one day and my dad had to shoot it. I really loved that dog. Well, that same night when I went to bed, my mother explained that an evil spirit had gotten into Wheaties. That the dog had been cursed. She thought maybe Willa had called an evil spirit to get the dog because Dad and John Snagovia had argued about the boundary fence between our properties."

I shook my head slowly.

"Doc Newton told me and Andrea that Wheaties had probably been bitten by a rabid coon or skunk," I said. "There aren't curses and spells except in fairy tales."

Now I'm pretty sure Adam didn't believe in such things; he just wanted to make sure I didn't either.

"You think God gave this to me?" he followed.

"Why would He?"

He shrugged.

"My mother said he struck me blind as a test . . . a test of her faith and mine. I never have understood that."

He held up his hands again.

"Is this another test?" he asked me.

51

"You know I'm not too religious, Adam. God—if there is one—He doesn't go about things like that."

Another lapse in our conversation developed.

When it broke, it broke suddenly and painfully.

"Adam," I began, "I saw something by the cottonwood tree . . . and in my room the other night . . . I got to ask you about what I saw."

So I ran the whole story by him. Seeing the phantom figures. The electric fan going haywire. Everything.

It really upset him.

"Don't you be asking me about that, Rob . . . don't you be saying anything."

He was pale and shaking all over.

"What are you hiding from me, Adam? Tell me. I'm you friend."

He scrambled up out of the blind and I followed him.

"Get away from me!" he yelled.

I kept up with him because he couldn't move very fast.

"Adam . . . Adam, listen. Maybe you ought to see Doc Newton. Your dad wouldn't need—"

"No!" he shouted. "Leave me alone! You're not my goddamn friend anymore!"

I watched him stumble away. I regretted having mentioned Doc Newton. That was a bad mistake.

But I had no idea how to help him.

CHAPTER 4

I felt left out.

Riding the bus to school the next morning, I sat by myself. Adam and Andrea were sitting together, far enough from me that I couldn't hear what they were talking about. Conversation, laughter, a few shouts—the noise within the bus rose to a steady roar. I lost myself in my own thoughts.

It's a ten-mile trek to the consolidated high school east of Warrior Stand. One more year, and I wouldn't have to suffer the black and yellow noise machine. I would be able to ride my motorbike to school or maybe have a car. Pudge has some used ones at his salvage that he would sell cheap. I could hardly wait.

But on that first day of school, I couldn't help stealing glances over my shoulder at Adam and Andrea. In a way I was jealous. I imagined that Adam had told her about the episode at Summer's Pond—his side of it. All I had done was suggest that Doc Newton take a look at him. Being gullible, Andrea would probably accept Adam's version, making me appear the bad guy.

I hated to feel so paranoid.

Thing was, it seemed to me that what was happening to Adam should have brought the three of us closer together. Instead, it seemed to be splitting us apart. I wanted to help Adam—I really did. But he was hiding something from me. Something about those phantom shapes.

Before I turned back around, I noticed, with some

satisfaction, that Andrea was careful not to let Adam's hand touch her. She felt sorry for Adam—as always—and yet I could see a certain fear in her eyes.

And, damn, Andrea looked great that morning. New clothes. New hairstyle. In the last year she had changed so much physically. Becoming a woman. No doubt about it. I wondered if she realized how much she was beginning to resemble her mother.

Thoughts in a tangle, I waded into the stream of humanity which flowed through the freshly waxed halls of the school and forced myself to concentrate on the business at hand: A difficult schedule loomed ahead—I was taking advanced algebra, biology, English, American history, French, and a free elective. That elective served as the only course I was looking forward to, because the principal of the school, Mr. Turnow, and the art teacher, Miss Wilkins, had commissioned me to complete a mural at one end of the gymnasium. I say "commissioned"; they weren't going to pay me, of course, but they would give me an hour of credit for the work.

I had it all planned. In fact, Doc Newton had come over with me a couple of times during the summer to block it out and score it so the dimensions would be accurate. You see, our high school, Prairie Heights, has as its mascot or logo a tornado—Prairie Heights Tornadoes. I'd rather have painted them a lion or a wildcat, but I agreed to try a tornado—a nasty-looking one.

So I went about my day deliberately staying away from Adam and Andrea. Normally I would have helped Adam find his classes, his locker, etc., but he hadn't asked for my help so . . . well, it was the same with Andrea. I would wait for her to come to me.

Stubborn. I'm just plain ole stubborn sometimes. One of many negative traits. I can't help it. They had sat together apart from me and so I decided I could play that silly little game, too.

And I played it well until lunch.

Things came unraveled when I saw Andrea sitting with Brian Gunnellson and his two thugs. He had on his black and gold (our school colors) letter jacket with those disgusting brass football and basketball emblems.

Brian has always thought he was hot stuff. He barely stays eligible to play sports. Most of the jocks are that way—real airheads.

It really got to me to see Andrea there beside Brian.

I carried my tray to their table, hoping to think of something witty or aloof to say or do. Andrea hardly acknowledged me. So I said something neither witty nor aloof:

"I need to talk to you."

"I'm eating my lunch," she said.

Brian, whose eyes are always barely open—he thinks it makes him look sexy or macho, glared at me.

"Rembrandt—hey is finger-painting class over? Must be about nap time. Did you bring your napping blanket?"

His two parasites laughed; Andrea smiled, but mostly tried not to pay much attention. It was the kind of school confrontation you've seen in dozens of movies and television shows.

I reached for Andrea's arm and said, "I don't want you sitting with him."

Andrea pulled away.

"Listen, mister," she hissed, "I can sit wherever I please. You don't own me. You're not my guardian."

Brian and company hooted. Kids seated at nearby tables began to take notice. Smart thing, of course, would have been for me to retreat and lick my ego wounds. Well, how smart were you when you were fifteen?

"Are you saying you'd rather sit with him than with me?"

My tray of food was shaking in my hands even as I delivered those words. A saucer of chocolate pudding threatened to escape and my silverware chattered.

Andrea's anger wrinkle became more animated than I had ever seen it before.

At that point in those movie and television scenes, there's some name-calling followed by a fight which some benevolent teacher breaks up. I wish that had happened;

reality brought something much worse.

Brian stood up. Instantly I decided I would use my tray as a shield against his fists. But Brian, in a surprisingly intelligent move, did not resort to violence.

He merely called out, "Listen up, everybody. Listen up."

And the cafeteria obeyed.

I felt the tips of my ears burn.

What was Brian going to do?

"We're having a contest. Rembrandt Dalton has thrown down a challenge. Andrea Helms will decide the winner."

Out of the corner of my eye, the teacher on lunch hour duty stepped forward, but he seemed as curious as all the kids, and, since no fists were flying, made no move to stop Brian.

So the big meathook continued.

"Rembrandt says that Andrea would rather sit with him than with me. Okay, let's see."

He leaned down toward Andrea.

"Miss Helms, which will it be—me or Rembrandt?"

They say some moments stay in a person's memory forever. That one will for me.

The silence and tension sucked all the air out of the large room.

I couldn't breathe, and my tray had gained ten pounds or more. Somehow I managed to set it down and to scurry away from the humiliating scene. I looked at no one as I escaped into a hallway, trailing a swarm of murmurs and gradually rising laughter.

I felt sorry for myself.

But I felt worse for Andrea. How could I have done such a stupid-ass thing? It took a special talent, I guess.

The remainder of the day I tried to hide. From everyone. From all the razzing and giggles and knowing smiles and the jokes. Late in the day, I sought refuge back in the gymnasium at the wall of the planned mural.

I couldn't concentrate on it.

I felt sick to my stomach. Absolutely, totally

miserable. And all of it my own fault. Yet, despite accepting blame for the embarrassing incident, I wanted revenge. I wanted to smash in Brian's face or somehow make him feel as rotten and lousy as I did.

Last hour of the day the typing and computer room offered me a hideout. The only kids around were special education students—including a deaf girl, a paraplegic boy in a wheelchair, a slightly retarded boy, and Adam. Mrs. Eskey, who taught typing and computer skills, wasn't in the room.

Off in one corner, bunkered by a trio of electric typewriters, Adam sat listening to playbacks from his classes. The school provided a tape recorder for him, though sometimes he used it to record the voices of classmates or weird, scary noises.

"You doing homework?" I asked as I sat down next to him.

Adam brightened.

"Hey, you're the talk of the school. I heard what happened in the cafeteria. Boy, you really got some shit laid on you. Some real smelly stuff."

He cackled. And something about that curious laugh of his started me laughing, too. It felt good—even though I hurt like hell—it felt good to be sitting with my friend laughing.

"You aren't still mad at me?" I said.

He paused.

"Nope. Can't say the same for Andy."

I cringed.

"She'll never forgive me. Never, never, never."

"Maybe not," said Adam. "But you were right. I wouldn't want to see Andy sitting by Brian Gunnellson, either. The guy's scuzzy."

"I'd rather he'd punched me out than what he did. God almighty, I was embarrassed."

So we talked.

Wisely, I didn't mention anything about him seeing Doc Newton. We traded notes about school and a couple of new teachers and about how bad the cafeteria food

57

was—my empty stomach growled a few objections.

I watched the other special ed kids wrestle with their disabilities. Then Adam said, "I've been thinking 'bout what I should do . . . you know, 'bout this thing in my hands. 'Bout the night touch. What I've got to do, I think, is test it. Test the night touch."

I wasn't following him at all, and I disliked hearing him refer to his strange ability as the "night touch"—like something from a science fiction movie.

He tried to explain.

"It's like testing a piece of electrical equipment . . . you know, for capacity and output and stuff like that. That's what I'm going to do. I'm going to find out if my hands could do something that would . . . you know, hurt somebody. Or . . . or kill a dog."

"Hey, Adam, you didn't—"

"You can't say for sure," he exclaimed. "Can't say for sure what these hands can do."

He held them up and wiggled his fingers. There was a curious animation in his eyes that bothered me.

Then he brushed his fingertips over the keyboard of a typewriter near him.

"Maybe," he said, "all the time I've messed with electrical stuff . . . maybe it comes from that and not from the Saturn Man at all."

Adam was sounding very weird to me.

"What kind of tests?" I asked.

He thought a moment.

"Plug in this typewriter," he muttered.

"What for? You can't type and neither can I."

He grinned. Wiggled his fingers.

"This'll be a test. Put some paper in it for me."

So I plugged in the typewriter and inserted a sheet of paper. Mrs. Eskey still wasn't around, and the other kids were occupied elsewhere in the room.

"You been practicing typing or something?" I asked.

He shook his head. And concentrated.

His fingertips hovered less than an inch over the keys.

58

The scene reminded me of those moments in the cemetery when he identified the color of Andrea's blouse and when he wrote on the legal pad.

"My right hand feels funny," he said.

"What do you mean . . . *funny?*"

"Like it's not really mine."

He sucked in his breath and suddenly touched the keyboard. And I swear to God that typewriter jumped.

His fingers hammered those keys so hard and fast that I thought I was seeing things. The carriage return rang and slammed back and forth, shaking the whole table.

"Damn oh, damn," I whispered.

Adam appeared to be possessed. I mean his face twisted and contorted and his shoulders jerked. And his hands and fingers . . . well, the weirdest part was that at one point he seemed to be trying to pull *away* from the keyboard, but couldn't.

Donnie Hill, the kid in the wheelchair, rolled over to our table out of curiosity.

Suddenly Adam stood up.

"Get back!" he cried.

And that typewriter kept going . . . without Adam's fingers . . . until it beat itself off the edge of the table and crashed to the floor. Even then, it continued, jumping and bucking, carriage return chiming wildly. All I could think of was Blackie.

"Pull the plug on it!" Adam shouted.

And so I did.

Knees watery, I stood back and watched the typewriter flop around like a catfish out of water. Then it was silent.

Donnie wheeled up to the machine, reached down and cautiously removed the single sheet of paper. He read it, scratched his head, and then handed the paper to me.

I was pretty shaken up, I don't mind telling you.

Glancing at Adam, Donnie said, "I thought he was blind. How'd he do this? What's it say?"

I scanned it. It was filled with letters all run together. Gobbledygook. Or so I thought at first. A closer look, and

59

I saw what it was.

MarchwillsearchAprilwilltryAndMaywilltellifyouliveor-die.

The line repeated over and over again.

Luckily, the typewriter hadn't broken. I told Donnie the machine had locked up or something. I sat with Adam on the bus ride home. Naturally Andrea didn't want to get within several miles of me.

The typewriter incident had taken my mind off her. I asked Adam if he thought I should write her a note apologizing for my stupidity.

"Sure," he replied, but he really wasn't paying any attention to me. He rode all the way to Warrior Stand staring at the palms of his hands.

"What have I got here?" he muttered once.

I tried to make light of it.

"Beats me, but if you ever take typing, you've got an 'A'—no sweat."

But Adam had surrendered to some inner vision. He never even smiled.

"One of these days everybody will know, Rob. When I'm through testing . . . I'll show everybody. What do you think?"

I shrugged.

"Just be careful, man. We'll talk about it. Okay?"

"When? When can we talk about it?"

To be honest, I didn't want to deal with Adam right then. My thoughts had turned completely to Andrea and my own self-pity and self-disgust.

"Sometime. Sometime we will," I snapped.

"Promise me one thing, Rob. Promise me you won't tell me to go to Doc Newton or any other doctor. Promise me that."

"Okay, Okay. I promise."

When the bus hissed and rumbled to a halt at the Dodd driveway, I was thankful to see my friend grope his way off.

It had been one of the most miserable days of my life. At home, Leah greeted me, asking, of course, how my first day of school had been.

I started to tell her the truth, but when I glanced at her—she was at the kitchen table, papers and envelopes scattered in front of her—I saw something which stopped me.

I believe she had been crying.

"It was all right," I said. "School's school. I'll have to hit the books pretty hard."

She wasn't listening.

She punched absently at a pocket computer by her elbow.

I guessed what was going on.

"The bank after us again?"

Rocking back in her chair, she pinched at her forehead.

"We're running into a few . . . financial difficulties." She shook her head and faked a smile.

"Mr. Buckley called me this afternoon."

"Wait a minute," I said, "I thought he told us we were free and clear on things for another year. At least another year."

Mr. Buckley's our wimp of a bank president. His wife gives us garden vegetables and secondhand clothes; he gives us trouble.

"It's the movie building, Rob," said Leah.

My body tingled. And I thought of my dad and how proud he had been years ago when he had refurbished that old building downtown, turning it into the only picture show place in the area except for Emporia and Council Grove. It was more important to him than the farmstead.

"No," I whispered. "No . . . I'll quit school and work full-time. Whatever . . . whatever it takes for us to keep it."

"Rob . . . maybe it's for the best. We haven't rented the apartment there for over a year. We can't keep up repairs on it, and I'm not sure we can afford to keep

61

paying taxes on it regardless of where we stand on the loan. I think we ought to consider putting the property up for sale."

"No. No way, Leah," I muttered.

"Rob. Rob, I know . . . I know what that place meant to Dad, but . . .

I should have been a man about the situation. Should have helped my sister with that difficult decision. I wasn't feeling like a man—more like a six-year-old.

I went up to my room and flopped on the bed.

Perfectly lousy ending to a perfectly dreadful day.

Didn't come down until supper.

Leah and I talked, skirting, however, the issue of the movie building. I washed dishes and then wandered out to the barn while Leah watched television.

I just couldn't chase my black mood; it seemed to drape onto my shoulders like Dracula's cape.

Our farmstead has one of those old-style, long, low stone barns. It's collapsing upon itself—like everything else on the property. But I love that old barn. In the stanchion area, where we used to milk a couple of cows, I yanked on the only light in the building. It's a naked bulb, fly-specked and dust-covered; as a result, it throws off pretty meager illumination.

All the usual barn smells—manure, alfalfa, straw, sodden milo—were there. And the memories, too. I sat on one of the horses. No, not a real horse. We got rid of the three we had. The horses I'm referring to are actually fenceposts lying out flat with a wire looped around each end and then tied to a rafter. You can sit on the posts and they'll swing you back and forth. My older brother, Drew, built them, and he and I used to spend hours on those horses, racing away from Indians or from a sheriff's posse.

"Midnight"—that's what I named mine. Drew called his "Champion."

Good times.

So I rocked gently. Thought I heard Drew's laughter. In a way it made me feel better. In a way it didn't.

I got off Midnight and began looking for my secret rock.

You see, next to the stanchion and manger area is a stone wall—just a whole bunch of flint rocks piled together. Over the years, a rock or two works loose. My secret rock used to be Drew's. If he had something he wanted to hide from Mom and Dad, he'd wedge loose this one particular rock and there would be a neat little hiding place a bit smaller than a shoebox.

I always knew about Drew's rock. I knew what he hid there, including the time he stashed a marijuana cigarette in there. I never squealed on him. I'm sort of proud of that.

Anyway, I searched along the wall until I found it. I worked the rock loose and there it was, still wrapped in an oily cloth: a small red and gold carton rested beside the cloth.

When Mom and Dad and Drew were killed, Leah and I had a hard time deciding what to do with their stuff—you know, clothes, etc. We gave most of it away. Leah saved some of Mom's things, and when she asked me if there was anything of Dad's I wanted to keep, I could only think of one object.

I lifted the cloth from the chubby hole and unfolded it.

And, damn, the memories poured through me.

Dad's revolver. It's a .44 caliber, I believe. I don't know much about guns. He won it in a drawing at the hardware store years ago. He and I and Drew would go out to the pasture sometimes and shoot at tin cans we set up on fenceposts.

When I touch that gun, it seems like I touch Dad and Drew.

But the gun holds some dark memories, too. A couple of weeks after the train accident, I slipped out to the barn and loaded the gun and put it to my head.

I was so depressed then.

Well . . . I got over it . . . the suicide wish. Leah helped. So did Doc Newton. He talked to me. Made me get all the hurt feelings and anger off my chest. Andrea helped. And Adam, too. In fact, Adam seemed to understand loss better than anyone else.

I let the past slip away. But the gun felt so solid in my hand. That demon thought of suicide would always be somewhere in my mind, hidden there, waiting to be considered. Waiting for me to seek it out.

I twirled the gun on my finger à la Roy Rogers and found my thoughts bouncing wildly from suicide to Leah and the movie building and, finally, to Andrea. Had I screwed up our relationship so royally that she would never have anything to do with me?

I aimed the tip of the gun at the lone lightbulb.

A voice from the shadowy part of the barn behind me said, "Drop your gun, mister. This is Matt Dillon, United States Marshal."

Damn oh, damn, that scared me. I wheeled around, my bladder suddenly painfully tight.

"Who's there?"

Adam cackled.

"Hey," he said, "if someday you had to . . . if someday for some reason you had to shoot me . . . could you do it? Could you pull the trigger?"

I never even considered his question.

"Damn you!" I exclaimed, "You scared the hell outta me. That was a shitass trick."

And then I stopped.

"Wait a minute," I muttered to myself. "I know what this is."

I walked toward Adam cautiously.

He cackled again. And I said, "You're not real. It's like in my bedroom the other night."

I inched toward him and extended my hand, bracing myself for the feel of airy nothingness.

He grabbed me.

I almost screamed.

Trying to pull away, I shouted at him, "Shitass trick."

And he wrapped his arms around me and wrestled me to the straw floor. He has incredible strength for his size, and those long arms of his give him leverage. I struggled, but it was no use. He pinned my face down and locked my arms behind my back.

"Come on, damn it all. Let me up."

"Say the magic words," he said, applying even more pressure.

"Please," I groaned. "Pretty please. Abracadabra."

"Wrong."

He was laughing hysterically and I was tasting dust and straw.

"Okay, stop, you're breaking my arm. What are the goddamn magic words?"

My arms were on fire with pain.

"All right," he murmured, "I want you to say: 'Adam is a beautiful guy.'"

"Oh, shit," I whispered.

But he tightened his hold and laughed and I saw exploding balls of agony behind my eyes—green, red and bright orange ones.

"Okay. Okay. Adam is a beautiful guy. Now let me up."

"And . . . and say: 'Adam has magical powers.'"

I caught my breath and did as he demanded.

When I rolled to my feet, I said, "Truth is, you're an ugly little fucker and a big phoney."

I suppose only real good friends can call each other bad names and not start fighting.

He laughed again and made a move to throw me down a second time, but I dodged out of his way.

"Good thing about being blind," he said, "is I don't have to look at myself in the mirror."

We bantered back and forth some more, and I put my dad's gun away.

"Hey . . . just a second. How did you get here? I thought . . . geez, and how did you know I had that gun in my hand?"

He let me dangle a spell, pretending he had come the mile and a half or so between our homes in the darkness. Finally he explained.

"Mother wanted to visit Leah . . . on church business,

I think. So I rode along. But I saw . . . or *imagined* sort of . . . I knew you had a gun in your hand. The night touch—it helps me see if I concentrate."

I nodded. The memory of the typewriter incident flashed into my thoughts.

"Hey, you want to go for a ride?" I asked.

So I climbed on Midnight and he on Champion. And we rocked. And talked.

I told him about our possibly losing the movie building, and he told me about his dad slapping his mother at supper.

At one point he stopped rocking and said, "Someday I'll kill him."

His words charged the air.

"You don't mean that, Adam."

"Hell I don't. Mean ole fat bastard."

He held his hands out as if they were deadly weapons.

"I swear I will . . . if he keeps it up."

"Can't you tell somebody about him? County sheriff? Somebody?"

"I got a plan," he said. "The night touch—I'm gonna keep testing it, you know, and working on it. Then I'm gonna make money on it and take my mother away from him. She has a sister in Dallas. My Aunt Janie. We could go there. And I'll give some of my money to you and Andy."

I didn't say much for several minutes—just let him get some of the bitterness out of his system. It kinda shocked me to hear him talk about his dad that way though I had seen how abusive the man could be. And it made me sad to think that Adam might leave Warrior Stand, might leave me and Andrea.

"What if people just believe the night touch is a trick . . . and say you're crazy and put you in a nut-house?"

"I can show 'em. I can practice and show 'em the things I can do."

"Will you do something for me?" I asked. "Whatever you do, you know . . . to make it look like you're in another place. . . ."

I knew it was a touchy subject.

"I don't like to do that . . . it really scares me. First time I did it was an accident. I folded my hands together like I was praying . . . because I was . . . at home praying for Blackie. All of a sudden, I was by the King . . . by our tree. And that night I wanted to talk to you, but there was no way to . . . so I tried it again . . . and it worked."

He turned to meet my eyes.

"This is what scares me, Rob: That gun you keep in the wall . . . it's not loaded, is it?"

"No."

"But you wouldn't put it to your head and pull the trigger, would you? Even playing around, you wouldn't do it, would you?"

"No . . . no, of course not."

I couldn't see what he was driving at, but his whole body quivered anxiously.

"Why not?" he prodded. "Why wouldn't you?"

I stared at him.

"Because . . . you never know when a shell might be caught in a chamber . . . you never take for granted that it's not loaded."

Adam raised his hands in front of his face.

"That's right," he said, "and I never really know what the night touch is going to do."

CHAPTER 5

I love you, Andrea.

That's what I wrote at the end of my note to her. First time I'd ever spoken or written those exact words to her. My thoughts flashed neon jangles just realizing I had done the deed.

Did I really love her?

Well, if a fifteen-year-old boy is *capable* of loving someone of the opposite sex, then I support it's possible I did. I wanted to believe I did.

Thing is, when Andrea read that note—on the bus from school one day—she flipped out. Got seriously excited. Squealed. Made funny shapes with her mouth. Stayed blanket-close to me the rest of the way home, a look in her eyes so adoring it was comical.

We had made up.

And that look in Andrea's eyes promised something more interesting than holding hands. Maybe it goes without saying that I almost forgot entirely about Adam for a couple of weeks.

Gradually my role at school as the most embarrassed person who ever lived lost top billing to other concerns. My classmates became more interested in football games and rumors of drug usage and speculation about the sexual preferences of one of our new male teachers.

Andrea sat by me in the lunchroom. Every day.

Brian Gunnellson sneered disinterestedly, but I could tell he hadn't given up his pursuit of Andrea.

Life went on.

I saw Adam very little, though I knew that he was glad

to see Andrea and me back together. At least, I think he was. One day, in fact, he had said, "If I ever have a girlfriend like Andy, I'll never risk losing her. I'll never take her for granted."

He had said that almost in the tone of a warning. But, at the time, I thought nothing of it. I guess I was too busy.

There was schoolwork and weekend work at the Arrowhead. There was time spent with Andrea. Any remaining time I gave to my painting.

I'd join Doc Newton down at the hardware store—his studio—and we'd set up our canvases and paint. We never talked much. But I really liked being there with him, and he would, on occasion, offer me pointers.

I converted the sketch of the three dead jackrabbits to a freshly gessoed canvas. I planned to do it in oils, and the first week or so it went well—proportion, texture, the feel of it. But the color. Something was missing. I had the background color just right. And the fur on the jacks. But the piece wasn't coming alive as it should have.

So one Friday afternoon, I sat before the canvas stewing like an old setting hen that can't get comfortable on her nest. Doc Newton sensed my distress and stopped sweeping the studio—you see, before he starts a new painting, he spends several days "neatening up," unlit pipe in mouth, stirring up far too much dust. He reminds me of Norman Rockwell when he's sucking on that pipe. Anyway, Doc Newton sidled over to my canvas, studied it, took the pipe out of his mouth, studied some more, put the pipe back in his mouth and muttered, "Try this."

All he did was take a brush and dab some dark red on one of the jacks.

It about blew me across the room.

It was like that painting had been dead and he had brought it back to life.

Amazing.

I just sat and stared at it for several minutes.

From that moment, I had a title for that painting.

I called it "Summerblood."

*   *   *

The evening of that same day—a Friday—I had a date with Andrea. Not actually a date, of course. More like a meeting. Sometimes we would meet in the cemetery, but by the middle of September we had grown partial to Pudge's Auto Salvage, particularly the back section of a big ole '60 Chevrolet station wagon far to the rear of the salvage.

For several days before that Friday, Andrea had chirped about our upcoming "special night," careful not to be specific about what she meant. Usually all we did on our "dates" was talk and kiss some. Nothing to write home about. Certainly nothing to brag about in the boy's locker room.

Anyway, after supper that evening, I motored to Pudge's—it's maybe fifty yards behind the Arrowhead Truck Stop—and waited for Andrea. She was late. I had brought our "snuggle" blanket, which was actually a threadbare old quilt. Andrea was supposed to bring what she referred to as our "love candy"—strands of strawberry licorice—if you work at it, you can acquire a taste for it.

Pudge wasn't around, so I wandered through the jungle of wrecked cars until I reached the Chevy wagon. Andrea had dubbed it our "love boat." I spread our snuggle blanket in the rear section and started back to Pudge's little dilapidated shack he uses as an office. On the way, I took a detour to Adam's Winnebago. Not sure why I did it. Something just tugged at me.

"What do *you* want?"

Adam's voice halted me at the door of the junked vehicle.

"It's me . . . Rob."

"I know that."

"Can I come in?"

My foot rested on the step-up entrance to the Winnebago, the insides of which had been gutted by a fire. After hesitating a moment, Adam said, "Yeah, I guess you can."

Adam had created a neat little area, like a pocket, boundaried by seat cushions. He had taped slabs of

71

cardboard onto the windows and, somehow, had rigged up an overhead light.

He was shuffling some sheets of paper around when I entered the area. It was like a womb in there.

"You and Andy gettin' together tonight?" he asked. I nodded.

"Things are going pretty good between us."

The silence which followed kind of puzzled me.

So I said, "Seems like you're awful concerned about Andy these days."

"She's my friend," he answered. "She's . . ."

I'm real dense sometimes. Miss the point constantly. But right then, I saw something in Adam's face, heard something in his voice—he liked Andrea. More than friend liking a friend.

God almighty, why hadn't I realized that before?

Was he in love with her?

When surprising moments like that one occurred, my mother used to say, "You could have knocked me over with a feather." That old saying applied to me.

All I could do was awkwardly change the subject.

"Whatcha been doing in here?"

I thought I probably ought to leave. Adam wasn't himself. He seemed so quiet and depressed.

"Testing," he said.

I relaxed a notch. He was sitting on the floor, Indian-style. So I cautiously joined him.

"Is that what those papers are all about?"

I noticed that he tightened his hold on them.

"Yes."

"You've been testing your . . . your night touch on paper?"

He shook his head and frowned. Then, matter-of-factly, he said, "I can make myself have visions."

I chuckled nervously. I knew that his mother often talked of having had a religious vision or two when she was a teenager.

"Like, you mean, of Jesus or God?" I stammered.

"Hell, no," he murmured, cracking a smile.

I smiled, too.

"Then of what? And how do you *make* visions?"

"I put this right hand up here, just over my ear. Like this. And they come. Not every time. But they come. And then I . . . I draw what I've seen."

Well, I knew he was pulling my leg. Adam can generate a lot of bullshit when he wants to.

"You don't believe me, do you, Rob?"

"I didn't say that . . . it's just . . ."

He handed me one of the sheets of paper.

"Here. Here's one of the pictures I drew."

I took it and scanned it.

My chest got heavy.

"You drew *this?*"

"Three days to finish it."

It was good. Real good. Every bit as good as I could have done.

"Who is it?"

"The Saturn Man," he replied. "It's the guy who gave me the night touch."

I caught myself rocking back and forth slowly, nervously. The wizened face in the sketch, the deep sunken eyes, bald head, large nose, long jaw, high yet hollow cheeks . . . the man looked ghostly. Spectral. Especially those eyes. The sadness and misery there clawed at me.

Adam had strung a wire across his area maybe four feet off the floorboard. He tugged the drawing away from me and clipped it to the wire with a clothespin. He showed me two other drawings, offering an explanation of each.

"This is the palm of Saturn Man's hand. The double line running down from his middle finger—that means something, but I don't know what."

The drawing of the hand was remarkably detailed. With some difficulty, I swallowed a ball of saliva. How could he have drawn these pictures so well?

"And this one," he said, "of the bear—well, the Saturn Man, he stays around wherever this bear is. There's a big town nearby and mountains, I think."

Also remarkably detailed, the drawing of the bear captured the animal standing menacingly on his hind legs.

"Damn, Adam, these drawings are good. I mean real good."

"The night touch," he said. "It's something else the night touch can do. It's not me. You know I can't draw on my own . . . couldn't draw worth a shit without the night touch."

And he cackled at himself. I tried, without much success, to join him.

Then I said, "What is all this? What's it mean?"

I stared at the three drawings and Adam touched each one again.

"That's something I got to find out," he said. Then he added, "You better get goin'. Won't Andy be expecting you?"

She would.

So I got up to go, but something made me stop and ask him a question: "Adam, you and me, we're gonna keep being friends no matter what, aren't we?"

In the shadows, I saw him smile.

"Get your ass on outta here. You know we will."

Yet, I wondered.

Adam's curious drawings and the realization that he cared an awful lot for Andrea swirled lazily in my thoughts as I waited at Pudge's office. Where was all of this leading? Regardless of what Adam said about remaining friends, I really feared things would never be quite the same between us.

I blamed the night touch.

I saw it as a curse.

Pudge Wilson roared up in his old Ford pickup, raising dust and piercing the air with the shriek of brakes going bad.

"Can't never find good brake shoes for that mother," he exclaimed as he strode over to me, bow-legged, a slight gimp, slapping the dust from his jeans with his cowboy hat.

You can't help but like Pudge. He's a classic.

He's about fifty or maybe fifty-five. Doesn't look very old, despite the gray of his bushy moustache and sideburns. He's real skinny and his face is deeply tanned and wrinkled like the outside of a walnut shell. He wears thick glasses that make his eyes look bigger than shooter marbles. He drinks coffee by the gallon during the day, rot-gut wine at night. And he eats saltine crackers by the barrel.

Years ago he was a rodeo rider. Damn good one to hear him tell it. He has a couple of silver buckles in his office—says he won them from bronc riding, though a few folks in town think he stole them. He smashed up his leg steer wrestling; that forced him out of the rodeo circuit and he's been running the auto salvage and the service station at Arrowhead for quite a spell. He's still a cowboy at heart. Wears those colorful cowboy shirts, string ties or scarves, snakeskin boots, a belt buckle big as a car's headlight, and, of course, a cowboy hat—a real Stetson fancied up with quail feathers and a gold medallion stamped in the shape of a horseshoe.

He's always smeared with grease from working on cars and often insists that he'd much rather step in horseshit than an oil spot, but in his words, "a man's got to make a living." Pudge makes his scrounging auto parts and hoping east-west traffic keeps the Arrowhead alive.

Thing I like most about him is that he thinks the world of Adam.

He's pretty partial to me and Andrea, too.

Well, I told him I was waiting for her to meet me. He understood exactly. I sat down beside him on a bench he has outside his office. He strummed on his guitar, an ancient flat-top that he claims once belonged to Gene Autry. If Pudge has one major fault, it's lying. Boy, he can tell some whoppers.

We talked about the weather some, and I endured Pudge's pathetic attempt to make music come out of that guitar. I never mentioned Adam and his drawings. Thankfully, Andrea arrived a few minutes later.

God, she looked awesome.

Had on this blue, silky-looking blouse—nicely filled out—and white shorts and sandals. She had a small purse slung over her shoulder. I could almost smell the strands of strawberry licorice inside.

She came up and hugged me right there in front of Pudge. Her perfume was kind of strong.

"I'm all ready for tonight," she whispered.

She had on more makeup than usual. It made her look older.

Suddenly I felt younger and very unsure of myself.

Then, out of nowhere, Pudge stopped strumming and said, "You young ones bein' careful 'bout that AIDS shit?"

I blushed several layers of purple. I was speechless.

Andrea piped up and said, "Sure. They told us all about that in health class. Lovers today should be honest with each other and carry the proper protection if they plan to be sexually active."

Honestly, sometimes Andrea flabbergasts me.

"Gosh, damn, this is sort of embarrassing," I choked.

Pudge winked.

And Andrea grabbed my hand, destination, "love boat."

She had a certain eagerness about her I hadn't really seen before. We climbed into the back of that Chevy wagon as twilight shaded the world and the first stars made an appearance.

We sat down on top of our snuggle blanket and leaned against the back seat.

I started to say something about how nice she looked, but before any words came out Andrea threw her arms around me and kissed me so hard on the lips I thought I had chipped a tooth. She pressed her lips onto mine, maneuvering them up and down and back and forth, all the while forcing her breasts against me, rubbing, and moaning in a way that sounded pretty funny.

76

My temples throbbed. And down there in the groin area, gears were shifting faster than a souped-up car on a drag strip.

When she finally let me up for air, she looked at me, an intensely serious expression, and said, "Rob, I want to explore being a woman tonight. I want you to help me explore."

"Explore?" I stuttered.

It was as if suddenly I had no idea what that word meant. In fact, at that moment, my mouth still tingling from her marathon kiss, I couldn't have told you the meaning of about any word.

"Yes, explore . . . because you've admitted you love me. Now I'm going to show you that I love you in return. But I'm not a little girl anymore, Rob."

I quickly agreed.

She pushed my shoulders gently down to the blanket and leaned over me. I waited as she fumbled through her purse. Then I could smell the strawberry licorice. You see, Andrea has this kind of weird theory about strawberry licorice making kissing more exciting to her. So she stuffed a strand in my mouth and one in hers and started kissing me again.

The harder she kissed me the faster I chewed that licorice.

Then matters got more complicated as she did something we had never tried before. She worked the tip of her tongue between my teeth. A number of things happened at that point: One, my tongue touched hers and my whole body sort of waffled; two, a ball of half-chewed licorice bounced around at the back of my throat; and three, in a reflex action, I nearly bit my tongue off as the licorice threatened to choke me before I could somehow retrieve it and not lose the spectacular sensation of Andrea's eager tongue.

So it goes.

I had to push Andrea off me and cough and spit and discover a way to swallow that licorice. Andrea rocked back and laughed. When I had recovered, she pulled herself close and whispered, "I've hidden the last piece of licorice somewhere, but you have to find it."

Her voice had a cocky sultriness that should have driven me wild. But, for some reason, my thoughts shifted from her delightfully seductive act to Adam. Of all times for that to happen.

I could almost imagine Adam was watching us.

Weird.

"Maybe we ought to cool off a second," I muttered.

Well, Andrea wanted none of that.

Darkness began to grip the salvage in earnest.

"What'sa matter, Rob," she purred, caressing my face, her fingertips small points of fire, "don't you think I'm sexy?"

"Sexy? Andrea . . . sure, I mean . . . yeah, you are. It's just . . ."

I kept hearing Adam's voice, feeling his presence. My throat tightened.

"I suppose I'm going to have to work harder at this," she said. "Try to imagine that I'm Madonna or Tanya Tucker . . . and I'll do anything you ask."

Even in the shadows, I could see that she was unbuttoning her blouse. This odd little warm buzz sprang to life in my stomach and inched its way up my chest. Sweat beaded on my forehead; that ole Chevy wagon seemed to gather pockets of heat.

She took one of my hands—I swear to God I can't remember which one now—and placed it so that it cupped a breast. Before my hand went sort of numb, I could feel the satiny fabric of her bra.

She leaned forward and kissed my ear.

And I wondered if she had learned how to do all this from reading Silhouette Desires.

I heard the ocean roar.

She guided my other hand to the other breast. She reached around and unclasped herself, and I moved my fingers mechanically. She helped guide them.

I forgot all about Adam.

And I found where she had hidden the last strand

of licorice.

I rocked forward to kiss her, and something strange occurred. Real strange.

She screamed.

God almighty, it was a long, laced-with-fear scream. She grabbed her clothes and hugged them to her front, and I was so surprised that I jolted back, lost my balance, and slammed my shoulders down onto the snuggle blanket.

Then the old Chevy wagon appeared to come to life.

I'm not making this up—the overhead light flickered, the headlights and dashboard lights came on, and the engine cranked. There was a curious—and very frightening—strobe light effect for thirty seconds or more.

In the chaos and confusion, I happened to see that Andrea was staring at the back window.

I turned onto one shoulder to look behind me.

Just a glimpse.

That's all I got before I began to struggle.

There was Adam's face pressed against the window. And there was the outline of his hands, palms flat to the glass.

For a run of seconds, I thought I was going to die. Not from embarrassment or shock, but rather from having my throat crushed.

I squirmed, using my hands to tear at the pressure being applied to my whole neck. But by what or whom? It seemed to be some invisible force. Like a pair of shadow hands.

I grunted and moaned and thrashed about and tried to cry for help. The wagon lapsed otherwise into silence and darkness.

Then Andrea screamed again.

All I can recall after that is feeling myself slip into a huge funnel of blackness; I swallowed, tasting the sickly sweet remnants of strawberry licorice.

Don't know how long I was out.

When I came to again, a flashlight beamed into my eyes.

I heard Pudge's voice, but it sounded distant. Out in a field somewhere.

"I reckon he's gonna live."

I heard Andrea crying softly. Then I felt her head on my chest. She had dressed, and yet I could sense a certain naked fear in her touch.

Pudge and Andrea must have hovered there by me for several minutes.

Eventually they helped me out of the station wagon; my legs had all the strength of cooked spaghetti.

I coughed and hacked; Pudge slapped me on the back the way you do if you think somebody's choking on something. It felt like a knife was wedged in my throat. I could barely swallow.

"You gonna be all right, son," Pudge kept saying.

Andrea stayed close; she was quiet; her body trembled slightly from the aftermath shock.

"You got something in your craw?" Pudge asked.

When I finally cleared my throat, all I could respond was, "A piece of licorice, I think. It's okay, now."

Andrea kissed me warmly on the cheek, and I began to feel better.

Least until I got a little closer to Pudge's office.

"Listen to that," said Andrea.

The three of us stopped.

Over ·the background drone of night insects, we listened.

"Why . . . it's my ole guitar," said Pudge. "Somebody's playing my ole guitar."

"Whoever it is, they're good," Andrea added.

It sort of surprised me that they hadn't guessed.

"It's Adam," I murmured. "Adam's playing the guitar."

Pudge cocked his head and seemed to lapse deep into thought.

Then he chuckled.

"Naw, that can't be. That boy . . . he ain't never played a guitar. He can't do nothin' like that."

CHAPTER 6

But he could.

That and a whole lot more.

I had a sore neck the next day as proof.

Or could there have been some other explanation? Had I just imagined that Adam was somehow involved? Adam and his night touch? Had it been some kind of hallucination?

Do hallucinations almost strangle you?

And a much tougher question: Had Adam used the night touch deliberately to try to hurt me?

I woke up restless and confused. Often, when I'm in that state, it helps to sketch or paint, so I gathered up my sketchpad and rattled out to the Snagovias' pasture. There was a touch of fall in the air. The dead cornstalks looked like a whole battlefield of real thin zombies. But they did not inspire me to draw. Nothing at the Snagovias' that morning did.

So I wandered aimlessly toward the boundary of Karl Dodd's property, crossing a barbed-wire fence, then angling out around until I came to the far end of Summer's Pond. I thought to myself that it wouldn't be long before ducks and geese would be flocking in for a brief stopover on their way south.

The pond was clear. It normally got that way in the fall when some of the mossy, stagnant gunk died off. Looking at the surface of the water, I thought about something I had read in American literature—Thoreau's *Walden*—about this guy who went out and lived by himself by a pond for two years. Then he wrote about it. And he said something about being glad Walden Pond was a deep pond; it affected his thoughts more because it was.

Summer's Pond was pretty shallow, yet I think I understand what Thoreau was saying—and it's always been interesting to watch the old pond change season by season. When I read some of *Walden* to Adam, he got all excited and declared that we would live all one summer at Summer's Pond. We invited Andrea to try it, too, but her folks wouldn't let her. Adam and I lasted two nights. I wonder what Thoreau did about mosquitos?

As I sat by the willow, I wondered whether Adam had become my enemy? I just couldn't believe it. I just wouldn't believe it.

I let my eye skip over the water to the ridge separating the pond from the rest of the Dodd property. That's when I saw something which I knew I just had to sketch. Perched on that ridge, knees rucked up under his chin, Adam sat facing to one side, apparently having surrendered to some attack of thought. He hadn't sensed my presence.

It was a great scene because behind him, in the distance, loomed the Dodd house and barn. They made him look small—sort of like Karl Dodd himself was being represented by those buildings. Or maybe the big old barn was Karl and the house was Adam's mother.

I sketched. My fingers danced. Boy, do I ever get excited when a scene like that jumps out of nowhere. I never alerted Adam that I was there; he never looked my way. I knew that I would have to confront him about what had happened the night before. But not then.

I slipped away and raced back to town.

Doc Newton laughed at me as I hurried to transfer that sketch onto a gessoed canvas. I worked the rest of the morning and all afternoon. It was humming. Really clicking. Adam on the ridge, the house and barn beyond—and something more: A sort of shadowy element—like an aura—outlined Adam's body, flaring off in several directions, creating interesting, though abstract, designs.

You know how shadows are. They can resemble whatever you can imagine. Well, a couple of these shadows looked to me like hands. Like Adam's night touch. Geez, it kinda gave me a chill as I sketched it.

Doc Newton perused it.

"It has a good read to it," he said.

That's a compliment.

"I got a title for it," I said.

He grunted through his pipe.

"What is it?"

"I'm gonna call it 'Adam's World.'"

He grunted again, an approval of sorts.

"You've been good friends with Adam for a long time, haven't you?" he commented.

"Yeah, a long, long time."

"I recall the day Katherine Dodd gave birth to Adam. She believed an evil spirit had disfigured him."

I'd heard stories about Adam's birth as well, so I chimed in.

"Lotta people in town say she was frightened by a chimpanzee at that traveling circus that comes to Council Grove. And that's what caused Adam to look like he does."

Doc Newton shook his head and lit his pipe.

"Isn't it something what cock-and-bull things people will believe?"

I said it was, and then he got this funny off-in-space look in his eyes.

"Robert, I've been a physician for many years. I've seen more than a few things about human beings I couldn't possibly explain. I've come to believe there are people who . . . well, they seem to draw strangeness to them."

Those last several words ticked in my mind like a loud clock.

He hesitated then said, "Willa Snagovia's like that. And Adam—I believe he's one of those people, too."

He strolled over to a canvas he was working on, leaving

me to wonder.

What does he know?

What other strangeness will Adam draw to him?

The events which followed in the weeks ahead changed me. Changed Warrior Stand. I could not have imagined them. No one could have.

Strangers were drawn to our town. They touched our lives.

Darkness threatened my world and Andrea's world.

But especially, darkness threatened Adam's world.

PART TWO:

KANSAS GOTHIC

CHAPTER 7

"I don't like it in here."

Andrea glanced at the blackened interior of the Winnebago; she grimaced, and she stepped about cautiously as if she feared falling through a trapdoor.

"You wanted to see it," I reminded her. "This is where Adam spends an awful lot of time these days. Pudge lets him claim this place as his own."

"What's he do in here? He's not into drugs, is he, Rob?"

I could hear a motherly tone of concern in her voice. Adam would always be someone to be protected as she saw it. What would she think if I told her how Adam felt about her?

"No. Nothing like that," I said. "But there's something you ought to see."

I unclipped the drawings Adam had shown me.

"Look at these."

I gave her an explanation of each drawing—or, at least, Adam's explanation.

"He really believes this guy . . . this 'Saturn Man' . . . passed along the strange talents he has?"

"Yeah, he does. The night touch . . . that's what Adam keeps calling it. He's been testing it, you know, trying to determine what all he can do with it."

I felt uncomfortable doing it, but I went ahead and told Andrea what Adam had said about using the night touch to help get his mother away from his dad.

"Does he hate his dad that much?"

"I'd say he does. Told me he'd like to kill him."

Andrea cringed.

"You think he meant it?"

"Who knows for sure?" I replied. "But I'd lay money on it that he does."

I studied her as she looked around Adam's hideout. I tried to imagine her as she had been Friday night—warm and willing and eager. But Adam's intrusion had thrown cold water on her seductive mood.

It was Sunday afternoon.

I had spent most of Saturday painting and thinking. Saturday night at work I had planned to talk with Adam—did he remember trying to hurt me? I couldn't get the thought out of my mind. And my neck was still sore.

But we never really got a chance to talk because early in the evening Pudge responded to a wrecker call— eighteen-wheeler jack-knifed between Warrior Stand and Council Grove—and he asked me to help him. Took four or five hours to get that semi rolling again.

Andrea's main interest was in hearing Adam play the guitar. That's why we had come to Pudge's, hoping Adam would be there.

Well, I wanted to get out of the Winnebago as soon as possible. Didn't want Adam to find us in it. I felt like we were trespassing on sacred and personal territory. But there was something I needed to say to Andrea about Friday night.

So I let it all out: my theory that Adam had used his night touch to try to strangle me—not to hurt me bad, but at least to scare me.

Andrea reacted predictably.

"Have you gone all the way crazy, Rob? Mister, you forget pretty fast how long you guys have been friends. You and I both know Adam would never deliberately hurt anyone. The thing that happened to Blackie . . . I still can't believe Adam caused it. He wouldn't, Rob. He just wouldn't do it. There's no reason why he would."

Her defense of Adam pushed me to a line I hadn't

88

wanted to cross.

"Maybe he has a good reason," I said.

Hands on hips, eyes snapping, she glared at me. "Like what?"

"Andrea, you don't know this, but . . ."

"Know what?"

I couldn't tell her. Just flat out couldn't bring myself to do it.

Adam would have to tell her himself.

I felt foolish. Andrea stomped back to Pudge's office. I followed like a whipped puppy. When we got there, Pudge was working on his old truck, the upper part of his body swallowed under its hood.

"Pudge, you seen Adam today?" I asked him.

Emerging from the truck's maw, he looked like an Indian that didn't know how to apply war paint. Grease and oil smears covered his cheeks and chin. Because he was hatless, you could see a line separating the tan of his lower face from the paleness of his forehead.

He put down a wrench and wiped his hands on his jeans.

"Can't never understand why I waste my time on this mother," he snarled. Then, seeing Andrea, he added, "Excuse me, little miss."

"Adam," I repeated, "have you seen him?"

"He's been acting queerly," said Pudge. "I'd like for you young folks to explain to me what happened the other night. You and Adam not gettin' along no more?"

What could I say? Andrea and I had promised Adam we wouldn't tell anyone about the night touch. I wondered how much longer we could keep that promise.

"Most of the time we get along fine," I said.

Which was the truth.

I could tell by Pudge's expression that he was suspicious.

"Tell me this," he said. "How's it out of the clear blue that boy can play my guitar?"

He looked from me to Andrea, daring us to answer.

My brain stuttered.

89

Then Andrea said, "I taught him."

Pudge hesitated.

"Oh, you did, did ya? He's a mighty fast learner, ain't he?"

Andrea agreed that he was. Pudge didn't believe her story, but the lie slowed down his third-degree of us.

"There's nothing to worry about, Pudge. Adam's okay."

Pudge turned on me.

"Listen, son, I might be a broken-down, busted-up ole cowboy, but one thing I ain't . . . I ain't stupid. Like I said, that boy's been acting queerly. Goes back to that Winnebago and don't never come out and talk to me like he used to. He don't say much at work neither."

"Maybe it's school," said Andrea. "Maybe he's worried about school."

Scratching the back of his head, Pudge issued a doubtful-sounding grunt.

"You two hear me on this: Adam . . . I took a liking to him long time ago. Hell, his folks ain't hardly folks at all. Karl Dodd's the meanest son-of-a-bitch in the state. That wife of his drowned herself in the Bible. I'll probably burn for saying this, but she's so gone on God and churchy shit she can't be much help to a boy growing up."

He paused to gain some emphasis for his next words.

"What I'm telling you is this: That boy's kinda special to me. Donchoo be doin' him dirty . . . or if you do, don't let me find out about it."

His threat surprised me a little.

"Hey, Pudge . . . you know us. We're Adam's friends. About the only ones he has. We'd never do him dirty."

Andrea also put in her two bits to try and convince him.

When we left, he seemed satisfied.

On the way to the Dodd place, we stopped at Andrea's to get her guitar. She continued to insist on hearing Adam play, so we loaded onto the bike and tore off.

Mrs. Dodd met us at the front door still wearing her church clothes. She appeared genuinely glad to see us, quickly informing us that Adam had fallen into another one of his dark moods. She had been praying for him in the kitchen when we came to the door.

"He's at the pond," she explained. "I believe he goes there to be alone with his Savior."

Over her shoulder, I could see some of the massive outline of Karl Dodd slumped in an easy chair in front of the television. He was watching a football game on a screen which kept losing its vertical hold. Once or twice I heard him curse at the set.

Mrs. Dodd talked on undaunted, and before we could slip away from her, she gave each of us a pamphlet entitled, "Sex: Satan's Most Successful Temptation." It was subtitled, "A Guide for Teenagers on the Sin and Evil of Fleshly Desires." As I took hold of my copy, I recalled the delicious feel of Andrea's naked breast.

Boy, did my face flush.

I couldn't even look at Andrea, let alone at Mrs. Dodd.

Halfway to the pond Andrea started giggling.

"Mrs. Dodd's sure a holy roller, isn't she?"

"You can say that again," I said.

Andrea pressed a hand to her mouth for a moment, but couldn't stop herself.

"I'm laughing because I thought you were gonna faint right there on the front porch."

I tried to joke about it: "It was just a wave of fleshly desire came over me," I said.

"Not what it looked like to me," she shot back. "Looked more like your pants had fallen down around your knees."

She laughed some more and swung the guitar at me playfully, and I chased her all the way to the ridge. We thundered to the top of it, and suddenly Summer's Pond spread out below us.

And we saw a very strange sight.

I had to blink a couple of times to make sure I wasn't seeing things.

Well, there was Adam, standing smack in the middle of the pond, the water about waist deep. He appeared to be staring into the sky, arms extended to his sides, hands palms up.

We must have watched him stand that way for better than a minute. Andrea was about to holler at him when he slowly began to bring his hands together until they were clasped in front of him.

Here's the really weird part.

Summer's Pond is always still as glass; the water hardly ever moves. But it broke into a lazy swirl around Adam, continuing that motion for another minute or so.

"This is freaky," Andrea whispered. "I told you I thought an alien had come into contact with him. Now this is the proof."

"No damn proof at all," I hissed back at her.

But what was it? Another trick of the night touch?

"Does he know we're here?" Andrea murmured.

I shrugged.

Another thirty seconds passed, at which point Adam lapsed out of his trance-like position and waded toward the bank.

"Adam . . . it's us . . . me and Rob."

He smiled at the sound of Andrea's voice.

"Hello," he exclaimed, waving one of those long, curious hands in our direction.

We made our way over to him where he had sat next to a clump of pussy willows.

"Good day for wading," said Andrea.

And I was struck suddenly by how awkward it had become for all of us to talk. It never used to be that way. I longed for the old days—before the night touch.

"Yeah, I was cooling off my feet," Adam explained. "Real hot for September."

It was. Warm fall days in Kansas usually meant we were in for a cold, cold winter.

Adam smiled toward Andrea, but then said, "Why's Rob being so quiet? He afraid I'm gonna put the *touch* on him?"

With one hand he clawed in the air in a mocking, yet menacing gesture. He was poking fun at me, and I really didn't appreciate it.

"I can take care of myself," I said, maybe with more anger than I had intended.

"Hey, you guys . . . knock it off," Andrea interjected. "What's going on?"

There was a hollow silence, broken only by the ever-present wind rustling through the pasture grass.

"I'm sorry," said Adam. He spoke very softly. "I'm sorry about the other night. When you two were together . . . I thought it would be fun, you know, maybe to sneak up and scare you, but . . ."

He held his hands close to his face as I had seen him do in the past weeks.

Andrea placed her hand on his shoulder.

"No harm done," she said. "We probably needed to stop anyway."

She flashed a sly smile at me.

"There was harm," Adam followed. "I mean, there could have been. I felt something happen. Rob could have been hurt bad."

"No," I said. "I think I just got . . . too excited maybe. Also 'bout choked on some licorice."

I chuckled and so did Andrea as we tried to lighten things up.

Adam shook his head gravely.

"It's the night touch. Sometimes I can't control it. Sometimes it gets away from me."

"Is that what you were doing out in the pond when we came up?" Andrea asked. "You made the water swirl."

"Just testing it," Adam replied. "Sometimes it really scares me."

"But you can do good stuff with it, too. Like . . . like here. My guitar. Play it like you did at Pudge's the other night."

She shoved the guitar into his arms and he positioned it as if he had played the instrument all his life. He caressed the box; his fingers began to tremble.

Andrea sat there beside him, all anticipation and eagerness.

"Play something and I'll sing along."

His fingers froze an inch above the strings.

"Don't ask me to do this," he said. "Let me get away from it for awhile. I'm sorry. Let me get away from it."

He pushed the guitar aside, got up, and started walking to the other end of the pond.

Andrea looked at me helplessly, then shouted toward him, "Hey, wait. Adam . . . I thought you'd want to play. I didn't mean to make it seem like I was forcing you to."

We followed behind him at a distance.

I knew our little triangle of friendship was in for some rough times.

Yesterday. O, God, whatever happened to yesterday?

"Anybody remember our raft?"

Under the lone willow, Andrea and I gathered around Adam as he reamed the mud from between his toes.

I brought up the raft, even though the incident was personally embarrassing.

Andrea and Adam began laughing the moment I mentioned it.

It was a good memory in some ways—from the days when the three of us were thick as fleas.

"The 'Gloomy Roger,'" Andrea exclaimed. "Oh, that was some raft."

"The best raft ever made," Adam added. "No kids ever put together a better raft than that one. Man oh man."

Memory took over for each of us.

We must have been about eight or nine years old at the time. Suffering through a hot Kansas summer, we spent as much time as possible at—and especially *in*—the pond. But one day we heard the buzz of a chainsaw and went to investigate. We discovered that John Snagovia was clearing some small poplar trees between the Snagovia and Dodd properties. We watched, silently hoping he might slip and rip a part of his foot off so there would be some excitement. No such luck.

I think it was Adam's idea.

The raft, that is.

The three of us clomped around in the deadfall of poplars after John left the scene. Andrea remarked about how straight and clean the small trees were, and I suggested we take them and build a fort. I wish my suggestion had won out.

"No," said Adam. "I got a better idea."

Well, he ran his hands over the fallen poplars and smiled.

"Let's build a raft! Let's be pirates!"

And that met with loud and excited approval.

You know how little kids can get a wild hair up their asses and work like crazy on something—that's just what we did with that raft. Dragged the small trees to the pond, cut them about the same size, lashed them carefully together, rigged up a mast, and generally made it seaworthy. As ship's artist, I was commissioned to design a flag; Andrea and Adam wanted a skull and crossbones—you know the image. But in a creative burst of insight, I decided to try something different—I came up with a mean-looking, morose skull and dubbed our raft the "Gloomy Roger."

Our little flag flew proudly.

One Saturday morning, we christened the Gloomy Roger with bottles of Dr. Pepper and shoved off. We sailed forever, it seemed. We plundered, fought rival pirates—Andrea stole some of her mother's make-up and painted our faces—and we dominated the seven seas. We were the scourges of Summer's Pond.

"I remember the last day we sailed," said Andrea.

"Yeah, I do, too," said Adam, and both of them looked at me, laughter in their eyes.

I knew they would think of that incident.

Oh, well. I'll tell you about it: Late afternoon one day we had been sailing free as the wind. Then Andrea announced that she had to go home. When we had poled her to the shore, Adam and I returned to the middle of the pond, grappling as usual over who got to use the pushpole. A few minutes later, we heard Karl Dodd hollering for Adam to come to supper. At that point, Adam pulled a nasty trick on me. He dived into the pond, clinging to the pushpole, laughing as he escaped to land.

I hurled boyish profanities at him; he cackled.

And I was alone in the middle of the pond.

One thing I failed to mention: At that time in my life I was afraid of water—I mean heart-stopping, deathly afraid of water. I was okay on the raft . . . as long as someone was on there with me.

Geez, I was one scared kid.

I tried to get the raft to drift to the edge, but it foundered.

So I yelled. I screamed. Finally, I guess I cried.

"It was real, real dark when we saved you," said Andrea.

"All three families came looking," said Adam. "Everybody had a good laugh. And you wouldn't talk to us for a whole week. You were really pissed off."

That's right. I was.

Never set foot on the Gloomy Roger again.

I can laugh some about that incident now. It was typical of our good times. There was always some near-crisis it seemed—like the day Adam cut his foot bad, or the day Andrea and Adam dared me to drink a whole bottle of Pepto-Bismol. I beat that dare, but my insides were tied up for a week.

And there was the day just a few years ago when Andrea claimed that she had a secret. Something about becoming a woman. Adam maintained that whatever she had, he also had. No, she insisted. Only girls have it—it's a gift from Mother Nature and maybe God, she explained. Once a month she would receive the gift.

It sounded fishy to me, but I admit that we were a little jealous.

Boy, Adam and I were sure surprised when my sister, Leah, explained to us about Andrea's gift.

The memory of the raft transported us back to better days. Closer days. Days when we were endlessly children. So we laughed and pushed aside an ominous future.

"You as thirsty as I am?" Adam remarked. "I bet my mother has a cold drink in the icebox."

We scrambled back to the house.

Behind us, the ghosts of our former selves haunted Summer's Pond.

It was worth the sacrifice.

Bringing up the raft memory, enduring the embarrassment—it was worth it to feel that bond again that the three of us used to have.

Riding the crest of that good feeling, we filtered into the Dodd kitchen, greeted there by Mrs. Dodd and a pitcher of iced tea.

"How is school?" she asked, once Adam and I had sat down at the table. Andrea, meanwhile, wandered to the archway separating the kitchen and living room, pretending to be interested in the football game.

I offered some mindless little nothing of a response to Mrs. Dodd's question, and she said, "I understand you have a new business teacher. A Mr. Sears. Very young and—"

"Mother, don't," Adam snapped.

I suddenly knew what was coming. Andrea had made the right move by remaining apart from the table conversation.

"It troubles me," Mrs. Dodd continued. These . . . these people should not be allowed to teach in the public schools."

"Mother, nobody really knows if Mr. Sears is gay or not. Besides, what difference does it make if he is?"

"What *difference?*" Mrs. Dodd pressed her fingers lightly to her throat. Her voice got scratchy and strained. "It makes a *difference* to our Lord God. Such a young man is an abomination in His sight."

"Mother, the guy's lifestyle is his own business."

I agreed.

But Mrs. Dodd pursued the issue.

"I pray that it's safe for children to be around him.

What kind of effect could such a man have? Why, imagine . . . filling young minds with sinful thoughts and ideas, flaunting himself in front of them."

Adam snickered derisively.

And I heard Andrea saying something to Karl Dodd. He was responding in that sickly sweet, polite voice I'd heard him use around women. In a grotesque way, he could be a charmer.

"Robert, what do you think of these immoral people?"

Mrs. Dodd had pinned me down—words and concerned expression. But a phantom of righteous viciousness lurked below the surface of her moral stand.

I cleared my throat.

"You see," I said, "I really don't have Mr. Sears for a class."

Mrs. Dodd started quoting scriptures about the evil of a man cleaving unto another man. Through the fog of her rhetoric, I overheard something which set off alarms within me.

In the other room, Andrea said, "Did you know that Adam can fix that TV set?"

I glanced at Adam; he had heard it, too. His mouth set itself in a grim line. I figured he would bolt from the table. Mrs. Dodd was lost somewhere in Leviticus when Karl Dodd yelled, "Come on in here, Adam."

I turned and frowned at Andrea. When she saw that frown, she recognized her mistake, but it was an error she couldn't retract.

Everyone ambled into the living room.

Mrs. Dodd positioned herself between Karl and Adam.

"He's always had a knack for electrical things," she said. "A God-given talent. It's to compensate for—"

"Get out of the way, Katherine," said Karl.

Eyes riveted on Adam, he pointed at the television, its vertical hold slipping.

"Your friend says you can fix the goddamn set."

Mrs. Dodd gestured for him not to swear, but Karl crushed her with a glance.

"I don't know nothing about televisions," said Adam.

I noticed that his body had stiffened.

So had mine. I fumbled for Andrea's hand, part of me hoping we could find a moment to exit, another part of me wanting to stay and help my friend if he needed it.

There was one of those standing metal ashtrays, shaped like a column, near Karl's easy chair. His rough, fat fingers tapped at the edges of it.

"You defying your father, son? They say you can fix the goddamn set, so if you want to leave the room in one piece, that's what you better do."

"Karl!" Mrs. Dodd exclaimed.

But another glance from him wilted her into a corner.

Andrea had slid around behind me.

I heard her whisper, "Please," very softly.

The whole scene transfixed me.

Then Adam turned toward me and Andrea. He sort of smiled apologetically. He walked over to the set.

"Okay," he said, "I'll fix it. I'll fix it good."

And he laid those big hands of his on top of the plastic cabinet and pressed his eyes shut tightly.

Next thing I knew there was a loud bang. I jumped; Andrea screamed; sparks and smoke spewed from the back of the set, and the picture blinked to darkness with a nervous little pop.

Karl just stared at Adam for a second or two.

"Miserable damn fuckhead," he growled.

And then I saw the glint of metal and heard a whoosh and then a thud as Karl slammed that ashtray into his son's chest.

Andrea screamed again; I pushed her toward the door.

Adam stumbled and fell over a low coffee table; I dived to his side.

Karl Dodd loomed over us; Mrs. Dodd buried herself deeper in a corner. She was praying out loud.

"Kill you!" Adam cried. He got this weird look on his face and held his hands up in front of him. "I'm gonna kill you, you ole fat bastard!"

But I grabbed around his waist and tried to wrestle him away from his father.

Adam's strong. He threw me aside.

Father and son faced each other off. I knew that Adam could see, could *feel* his father . . . the ugly, destructive shape of him.

Karl knocked Adam down again with the back of his hand.

But Adam managed to press himself to his feet.

He would have gone at his father then. What stopped him? Maybe it was a glimpse, out of the corner of his eye, of his mother praying in the corner. All I know for certain is that Adam spat at the man and scurried out of the room. I followed.

Adam headed for the pond, stumbling, crying out in a kind of anguish which cut into me.

I wanted to help him, but Andrea and I needed to leave the scene.

The sight of Karl Dodd on the porch, suddenly brandishing a shotgun from somewhere, shouting threats at us clinched it. We climbed onto the motorbike. Like a defiant rancher in an Old West movie, Karl Dodd stood there, unaware that on that day, emotionally at least, he had finally succeeded in murdering his son.

CHAPTER 8

For a couple of days after that ugly Sunday, Adam lived with Pudge at the salvage. I guess he must have slept in the Winnebago; I know that he missed two days of school. Had Adam's mother not begged him to come home, he'd probably have moved in for good at Pudge's.

Naturally, Andrea and I got pretty upset about the Karl Dodd explosion—especially Andrea. She felt responsible, in part, for what happened to Adam. I tried to convince her that Karl Dodd was like a time-bomb ticking away. Sooner or later he was going to go off.

Well, we talked to Andrea's folks and to Doc Newton about what Karl had done. Doc Newton called the county sheriff, reporting the incident as child abuse, but you know what took place when the sheriff approached Mrs. Dodd about the matter?

She denied anything happened.

How could she have defended a monster like her husband?

It made me want to vomit. Andrea got super mad when she heard about it, and Pudge loaded his shotgun and threatened to remove Karl himself. Permanently.

Through it all, Adam said little.

By Wednesday, he was back in school. Things had blown over. Not deep inside him, of course.

Me, I sort of sympathized with Pudge's reaction. I thought about how easy it would be to shoot a man like Karl Dodd. Wouldn't Warrior Stand—wouldn't the world—be a better place without him? I even went out to

101

the barn one evening and put cartridges in Dad's revolver. I took them out before I got too worked up.

Basically, I'm a coward. Now Andrea—I believe if she'd had a gun during the week, she might have wasted him. She has a lot of grit.

I talked to Leah about Adam, and she said he was welcome to stay with us if he liked. I asked him, but he just shook his head and said, "Thanks anyway." He really kept to himself all week, acting like he didn't want anyone to get near him. It seemed to me that he was afraid all of his anger would set off the night touch—that he wouldn't be able to control it.

By Friday afternoon, Adam had shaken some of his misery; the three of us laughed and joked on the bus home from school. We planned to get together at the hardware store on Saturday morning. I managed to finish my painting, "Adam's World," and I wanted to show it to them.

I ended up showing that painting to someone else as well.

A stranger.

She came to town for just one day, but her visit changed Warrior Stand—and the three of us—forever.

"Is anyone here?"

We barely heard her voice at first. I was sitting before the canvas of "Adam's World" trying to figure out how much further to work it. You can kill a painting by fussing over little pieces of it, touching it up until it gets away from you. Andrea was hovering at my right shoulder, the not-so-delicate aroma of strawberry licorice drifting past me. She knew darn good and well what it reminded me of.

Adam was cracking his knuckles at my other shoulder. I think he liked the painting, though he didn't seem to understand the symbolism I had incorporated into it.

Doc Newton wasn't around; Mrs. Tenney had called to tell him Alma had wandered off to the post office somehow and wouldn't leave until her father came for her. Of course, poor Alma's father had been dead for years and years . . . well, that disease she has was pulling one of its cruel tricks on her.

Doc Newton would have to rescue her.

"Is anyone here?"

Someone was pounding on the hardware store's double screen doors.

"Come on in," Andrea called out.

We had no idea who it could be. At least, we didn't know anyone who would stop to knock first. Mr. Ryan still had a lot of hardware-type stuff stacked around. If folks needed a nut or bolt or an odd-sized nail, they just came down and helped themselves. Doc Newton never minded folks being around unless he was really into a painting. And sometimes Mr. Ryan repaired small motors and appliances in the shop area beneath the store.

So knocking meant a stranger.

We all turned at about the same time as a young woman—a very pretty young woman—strode confidently into our midst and said, "Hi, I'm Kristin Kelley."

We were so surprised we hardly said hello back to her.

She smiled at us and sort of laughed.

"I've driven down from Manhattan to study your town for my thesis."

"Study Warrior Stand?" Andrea muttered doubtfully.

"What in the world could you study about this town?" I added.

Her smile broadened, then she got bright and warm, and yet business-like.

"Well, you see, I'm training to be a sociologist. That's my course of study at Kansas State University."

"You're from K-State?" said Andrea. "I want to go there after high school if I don't become a country western singer."

Andrea was gushing; Kristin Kelley had impressed her.

"It's a good school," said Kelley. "I'm working on my master's degree. Have completed everything but my thesis and now I'm conducting some preliminary research on my topic, which is the economic and social dislocation of small towns. The title of my thesis will be 'Kansas Gothic: Dead and Dying Towns in the Sunflower State.'"

Adam chuckled.

"Warrior Stand fits that—the town's dead and *buried.*"

"Oh, now, please understand," said Kelley. "I'm not putting down your town. I think it has a certain charm, in fact. But I'm interested in small towns which, since the 1950s, have had difficulty remaining economically viable. I'm interested in the history of such towns, their buildings—and, particularly, their people, their sense of community in the face of decline."

I didn't know quite what to make of what she said. Seemed like a strange subject for someone to study, but . . . anyway, Kristin Kelley was obviously smart and we all took to her immediately. She had green eyes and a creamy complexion and long, shiny red hair that tumbled to her shoulders and rested there like a sleeping cat. She was dressed in nice clothes—dark slacks and blouse and a blazer. She wore gold jewelry and flashed a great smile. Smelled good, too. A camera case was slung over her shoulder, and she carried a tiny tape recorder in her left hand.

As an awkward silence began to surround us, Kelley said, "Hey, do you kids have names?"

"Gosh," said Andrea, "I'm sorry. Don't write in your thesis that we're not friendly people. My name is Andrea Helms, and this is Rob Dalton and this is Adam Dodd. We've been friends since we took our first breath."

Kelley reached out and shook Andrea's hand.

"Glad to meet you Andrea Helms and you, too, Rob Dalton."

It felt funny to shake a woman's hand; it was a soft and warm hand, but the grip was firm.

"And you, too, Adam Dodd."

By that time Adam had maneuvered around behind me

so that he merely nodded at her, carefully avoiding shaking hands with her. But I noticed that she didn't seem repulsed by him. Some folks who first meet Adam are pretty bothered, you know, by his appearance and the fact that he's blind. They even talk louder, as if they think he's deaf as well as blind.

Kristin Kelley was cool. A real neat lady.

"I love that necklace," said Andrea. "Look, you guys—it's a little gold wildcat."

Kelley lifted the figurine on the end of the necklace so that Andrea could see it better.

"Kansas State Wildcats—that's us," said Kelley. "Just don't ask how our football team's doing."

We all laughed about that. K-State's lousy in football, but they usually have a good basketball team.

"Did you always want to go to K-State?" Andrea asked.

"No. I'm not from Kansas. I was born in Independence, Missouri. My father went to the University of Missouri. Played football there. So he tried to influence me to go there. I just liked K-State better."

She was suddenly looking beyond Andrea. With a rush of nervous excitement, I realized she had noticed my painting.

"Oh-h-h, this is very good!"

She stepped closer to the canvas and appeared to study it intently. Then she turned to me and said, "Did you do this?"

"Yeah," I murmured. "It's not finished, though."

"Oh, it's excellent. You're very talented."

Even the soles of my feet felt a tingle of warmth.

"Can you figure out who the boy in the picture is?" said Andrea.

"Yes, of course," Kelley responded. "It's Adam, isn't it?"

Adam ducked his head around the canvas.

"I hope he made me handsome. He promised he would."

Adam was putting on an act.

105

A kind of tittery laughter erupted.

"Why, yes, he did," said Kelley.

I was real glad she was nice to Adam, even though . . . well, you'll hear the rest of the story eventually.

"He's got one over in the corner that's a picture of three dead jackrabbits," Andrea exclaimed.

"It's not a very good one," I followed quickly.

Kelley strolled around the studio area, and we told her about how Doc Newton had converted part of the hardware store for his own purposes, and I showed her some of his work. She liked it, too, and wanted to know all about Doc Newton . . . and everybody else in town for that matter.

At one point, she said, "Wait, I need to be getting some notes into this gadget."

The tiny tape recorder had an equally tiny microphone and cord. She switched a lot of buttons and then said, "This darn thing manages to quit working at just the wrong times."

That's when Andrea said, "I bet Adam could fix it."

Remembering the last time she'd said something like that, I got a queasy feeling in the pit of my stomach. I darted a glance at Andrea; she caught it and bit at her lip apprehensively.

"Could you?" said Kelley. "That would really help me out."

I knew Adam would be reluctant to do it. But he couldn't resist Kelley's smile—no guy our age could have.

She handed the recorder to him.

"The tape catches or jams or something."

"Yeah, it's probably jammed," said Adam.

His large hands dwarfed the small device. He took a deep breath, blinked his eyes rapidly, and then fiddled with a couple of buttons on the top of it. And suddenly we could hear a voice. A deep and garbled voice. Just a word or two.

Adam switched it off.

"It's fixed."

Clearly surprised, Kelley stared at the recorder as Adam returned it.

"That's remarkable," she cooed. "But it's odd . . . I don't recognize that part of the tape."

She must have pressed the rewind button. She tried to replay the curious segment.

It was blank.

She shrugged and smiled.

"Oh, well. As long as it works. Thanks, Adam. You're a real handyman."

I think I'd been holding my breath the whole time.

Then we listened as Kelley spoke into the device, giving the date, noting that she was in Warrior Stand— she even mentioned the three of us. We giggled like real little kids.

"Listen," she said, "would all of you be willing to do me another favor?"

Heck, we'd have done about anything for her. We told her to just name the favor.

"Would you take me on a tour of Warrior Stand? Answer some of my questions about it? If you will, I'll buy you lunch. Is there a good place to do lunch?"

Naturally, Andrea climbed into that one.

"The Arrowhead Truck Stop. My dad and mom run the restaurant there. It's not very fancy food, but a lot of truckers go off route to eat at our place."

"Sounds good," said Kelley.

"Avoid the chicken-fried steak," I quipped.

"Hey, mister," Andrea responded, shoving at me as she sometimes does.

We had another one of those good chuckles together.

We agreed to give her a grand tour, though, of course, the three of us felt kind of strange taking someone around our skeleton of a town.

When we bounced out of the hardware store, Kelley asked us why we didn't pull the inside doors shut and lock them.

"No reason to," I said. "Nothing worth stealing in

107

Warrior Stand. Nobody around to be afraid of."

I repressed a flickering image of Karl Dodd and a shadowy one of Adam's night touch. Nothing, I determined, was going to spoil this day.

We wandered up and down Main Street, Kelley firing questions at us about Mr. Ryan and the death of the hardware store and about the old grocery and barber shop and pool hall—all vacant and derelict. In fact, the only buildings with any life in them are the post office and the bank.

Kelley listened to all we said—Andrea and I fell over ourselves competing to see who could give her the most information. I admit to acting pretty foolish. Adam said little.

At the north end of Main, Kelley stopped and spoke again into the recorder, summarizing all that we had told her. I don't know how she remembered so much. Then she pointed at another vacant building and asked, "What's 'Sunset House'?"

Well, my chest ballooned proudly.

"It's the old movie house," Andrea exclaimed, before I could say anything. "Rob's daddy used to run it. But he got killed by a train and so did Rob's mom and brother."

Kelley turned to me and placed her hand on my shoulder.

"I'm so, so sorry, Rob."

I kinda ducked my head.

"I still miss 'em real bad sometimes," I murmured. Then I said, "You want to see what it looks like on the inside?"

She did, and so I pulled away one of the sheets of plywood boarding up the doors and we entered the darkness. I found the lobby light and switched it on. Kelley got very excited over the old posters we had kept in the glass wall displays: *Gone with the Wind, The Wizard of Oz,* and *Creature from the Black Lagoon.*

I apologized for everything being so dusty, but Kelley didn't seem to mind. She scurried around, appearing to be pleased by all that she saw. We took her into the main seating area; a few of the sidelights had burned out so that it seemed pretty gloomy in there.

Acting silly, Andrea tromped up on the stage and began singing an old Patsy Cline song.

"My dad wanted to have plays performed here, but the only one we ever had was the centennial pageant back about ten years ago," I explained.

"Oh, it's a marvelous place," Kelley insisted.

I wished my dad could have heard her say that.

Maybe he did.

If he has a ghost, I'd guess it haunts the Sunset House. He loved it so much.

Next, I took Kelley up into the projection room and we looked down at Andrea singing a medley of country western favorites. Adam was walking on his hands across the stage.

Kelley called down to them, "Andrea, you and Adam ought to take your show on the road."

All that did was encourage Andrea to sing louder; I just hoped Adam wouldn't fall off the stage.

"Back here behind the projection room is an apartment that my sister and I try to keep rented. It looks out onto Main Street. Not a great view, I guess."

But Kelley seemed fascinated by it all.

Then I told her about how Leah and I were having trouble holding onto the property.

"That must be very difficult for you and your sister . . . Sunset House must have a special meaning for you."

She was right.

Boy, I felt like crying just thinking about it all, but a guy can't break down and let the tears come in front of an attractive woman. What would she think?

She saved me by speaking again.

"There's a possibility," she began, "that during the final weeks of this fall semester I could be spending a lot of time in Warrior Stand . . . if the thesis topic is approved . . . and if I come back I'd need a place to stay."

I started smiling. Felt like that smile went all the way

over my scalp like a stocking cap.

"Would you really rent our apartment?" I blurted out.

"I think I'd like to very much," she said.

Damn, I believe I was falling in love with her. Sorry, Andrea.

"We'd fix it up, you know, clean it till it was spotless for you."

"It's settled then," she said. "If everything works out back at Manhattan, you'll have a new tenant."

I couldn't wait to tell Leah.

Well, we gathered up Adam and the singing cowgirl and continued the tour. When we had covered Main Street (it didn't take long), we got into Kelley's super neat car and drove all around the Warrior Stand area and halfway to Council Grove.

She had a Toyota or Nissan or something like that. It had plush seats and a stereo system that even impressed Adam. Andrea said the car was like a "little Cadillac." It also had this woman's voice that came on when your door wasn't quite shut. Lots of neat stuff like that.

Kelley kept her recorder next to her. Adam sat in the shotgun seat, and Andrea and I piled into the back. We drove to Pudge's and out past the Dodds' and the Snagovias'. Naturally, we told her all about John and Willa, and she dutifully summarized our stories into the recorder.

"Let's take her up to the cemetery," Andrea suggested while we were out that way. So that's where we stopped next. I wasn't sure Kelley would want to track through a pasture in her good clothes, but she seemed eager to do it.

As we neared the cemetery, she exclaimed, "That has to be the biggest cottonwood tree I've ever seen. I've got to have a picture of it . . . oh, I know. You kids get in front of it and I'll snap a souvenir picture of you, too."

And so a moment from that innocent October day was captured.

I couldn't help thinking about Blackie as we walked from one headstone to another. Were Andrea and Adam reminded of Blackie, too?

Kelley asked about various names, drawing connections among a few of the residents of our town. Then she asked, "Where's the name come from? 'Warrior Stand' . . . how'd the town get to be called that?"

Andrea and Adam sort of deflected that one to me.

"Everybody has a slightly different story," I said. "But what I've always heard is that a group of settlers were coming through this way in covered wagons. The Santa Fe Trail is just a little north of town, and, well, they had been warned about a band of renegade Indians—Pawnee, I think. The renegades were led by this one real weird Indian. He was crazy, I guess. Even the other Pawnee were scared of him."

I paused, noticing that Kelley had moved the tape recorder's microphone closer to me.

"Well, and then one day some of the friendlier Pawnee were trading things with the settlers when this one crazy Pawnee and some other braves attacked them. There was a big fight and the settlers and the friendly Pawnee made a stand against the renegade warriors. That's the story I've heard."

Kelley applauded and Andrea whistled that awful whistle she does by putting two fingers in her mouth. Adam cackled.

"It's a good story," said Kelley. "Shows that the people of Warrior Stand have fought against threatening forces since the town itself originated."

She made it sound like some grand, ongoing drama. Like a movie.

Next, we drove toward Council Grove and Kelley pulled the car over at one or two spots and we all gazed out over the rolling, treeless Flint Hills. She spoke into her recorder again, describing the area and how it made her feel. I wish I could remember some of the words she used. They were like poetry. Like a James Michener novel.

It was early afternoon by the time we herded into the Arrowhead for lunch.

The weather had been good. Indian summer warmth.

111

But October in Kansas is always just a north-wind shift to colder temperatures. Frosts come before anyone is ready for them. Warm fall days are thus rather precious.

Once inside the Arrowhead, Andrea's mom, typically eager to meet any stranger, introduced herself, and Andrea asked her dad to wheel out from the kitchen to say hello. When Kelley explained why she was in town, Andrea's mom suggested that she talk with Vesta Tillman before driving back to Manhattan.

Miss Tillman—she's 80, never married—knows probably more about Warrior Stand than anybody else around, including Doc Newton. Believing herself to be a journalist, Miss Tillman writes a weekly "news" report or gossip column for the Emporia paper. She calls it, "Down Warrior Stand Way" and mainly has old ladyish little entries in it like the following:

> Sunday dinner guests of Mr. and Mrs. Harold Burnley were Harold's brother, Glenn, and his wife, Vera, from Topeka. After dinner, the two couples strolled down memory lane as they spent several hours looking at old family photo albums.

Stuff like that. Leah gets after me if I make fun of it.

Well, as bad luck would have it, Don Slocumb slithered his way into the Arrowhead while we were talking with Andrea's folks. True to his character, Slocumb ogled Kelley, staring at every inch of her anatomy with that disgusting leer on his face.

Doc Newton refers to Slocumb as an "idiot boy." Don't know what that means, but I like the ring of it. Seems to fit Slocumb like a glove. And, speaking of Doc Newton, he was in his booth drinking coffee when we came in. Seeing us, he invited us to join him. I pulled up a chair to the booth so that all five of us could sit together. I sat in the chair; Andrea and Doc Newton took one side of the booth and Adam and Kelley the other side. I believe Adam really enjoyed sitting beside Kelley. Who wouldn't?

Introductions out of the way, Kelley leaned toward Andrea and said, "Your mother is beautiful. I see where you get your attractiveness."

Andrea blushed and gushed and the rest of us ordered lunch. I wanted to punch Andrea and tell her not to act so squirrelly, but I suppose all of us were guilty of it some. It's just that nobody like Kristin Kelley had ever come to town before.

Plates of hamburger steak (the Saturday special) in front of us minutes later, Kelley asked, "Dr. Newton, what kind of town was Warrior Stand when you first set up your practice here?"

Her tape recorder was running.

Doc Newton smiled wistfully and let his gaze drift out the window; memory drifted, too.

"I put out my shingle in 1947. The following year I married Alma Hocking, a local girl. Living in this town was comfortable—like slipping on a pair of old shoes you don't want to get rid of. The town felt right. And it was alive. Ryan's Hardware was going strong. Bill Fletcher had the grocery. Saturday nights everybody would come to town. All the farmers. It was a social occasion. Fletcher's wife, Ruth, popped popcorn. Everybody visited with one another; the women swapped gossip; the men talked farming and politics; and the kids farted around as kids have farted around since Adam and Eve had Cain and Abel."

I was sort of embarrassed that he said a word like "farted" in front of Kelley, but she honestly didn't seem to mind. She really appeared to be interested in what he was saying.

Doc Newton's smile broadened as another wave of memory splashed through his thoughts.

"Oh, it was a real good place then. Folks dreamed of having a piece of farmland, raising some livestock, planting a garden, raising a family, having a few nice things. They feared God, but they never feared their neighbor. They supported the local school. On basketball game nights, they rolled up the sidewalks so to speak—

113

everybody went to those games. And in the summer, there was a traveling picture show company that would sweep into town and set up a big white projection screen down by the American Legion building and pay kids to help put out folding chairs. Whole community enjoyed that."

It was hard for me to imagine Warrior Stand that way—healthy, thriving.

"In your opinion," said Kelley, "what happened? What killed towns like Warrior Stand?"

Doc Newton mused a moment. Shook his head.

"The world passed us by. Some new century dawned and we weren't to be part of it. Economically, the co-ops hurt local business. And people began to shop in Emporia or Council Grove or to buy through the Montgomery Ward catalog. That wiped out places like Ryan's Hardware. Then finally the farm economy started to slide. The small farmer's dreams faded; people had to move to towns like Topeka or Wichita to find jobs. To survive. Not many stayed in Warrior Stand."

"It's a shame," said Kelley. "Part of this country dies if a town like Warrior Stand can't stay alive."

"One point on the bright side," Doc Newton added, "is that this town has been through about everything horrible imaginable. Nothing else can threaten us."

Doc Newton was wrong.

No one seated at that booth realized it. But he was wrong.

Warrior Stand was headed for the worst moments in its history.

After eating lunch and talking some more, Kelley gave Adam and me a ride back to the hardware. She planned to visit with Vesta Tillman, promising to stop by the Arrowhead to say goodbye before leaving. Adam and

114

Andrea and I would be working our usual Saturday night shifts.

Traffic moved sporadically that evening. Don Slocumb busied himself in the lube area putting a new water pump on Delbert Duncan's '64 Mustang; of course, Slocumb couldn't resist sharing a few vulgar observations about Kristin Kelley and how he'd like to accompany her to Manhattan—describing various positions in which they would occupy the front seat.

Adam and I decided that if a dirty mind could drive a man insane, then they had better strap a straitjacket on Slocumb soon.

We also talked about Kelley.

"She's real nice, isn't she?" I observed.

"Yeah, I wish she'd be coming back to see us."

"Well, she said she would. Hey, and she told me she might rent the apartment. Leah and I could hang onto Sunset House if she did."

Adam sorta moped around after we talked. Something was bothering him, but I didn't pursue it.

It must have been eight o'clock before Kelley pulled into the Arrowhead to gas up and to say goodbye. I hustled to the restaurant and got Andrea. Funny, but in just one day we felt we had all become close friends.

Kelley said that she and Miss Tillman had covered the entire history of Warrior Stand, had perused dozens of old photos and news clippings, and had downed several cups of Miss Tillman's strong herbal tea.

We gathered around the cash register and talked as if we never wanted to stop. Kelley promised she'd bring Andrea a wildcat necklace on her next visit, and she encouraged me to keep painting and she thanked Adam again for fixing her tape recorder.

She went to the restroom and then told us she had to be getting on the road.

"I like your Warrior Stand. I'll be back," she exclaimed.

I thought Andrea was going to cry.

Kelley had started up her car when I noticed that she had left her camera case on the cash register counter. Adam volunteered to take it to her. He used his walking cane to maneuver out to the service island. Andrea and I watched as Kelley thanked him and said a final goodbye.

We couldn't wait until she returned to Warrior Stand.

CHAPTER 9

When Kelley pulled away from the Arrowhead, I pretended I was sailing high above Highway 56 following her small car as it carried her toward Council Grove where she would turn north for Manhattan. A partial moon glazed the countryside, and I imagined her pretty face, and I wondered what she was thinking as she drove along. . . .

Rob's like Kurt.

Kristin Kelley switched on her brights. The image of the young man she had almost married—had wanted so desperately to marry—ghosted through her thoughts. Kurt Sannerfield. Artist. Kurt. She recalled how he had rented a barn from a farmer south of Manhattan and had lived there . . . no furniture, no television . . . nothing . . . except his canvases and brushes and oils. One night she had slept with him there in the heavy sweetness of the alfalfa hay, a blanket beneath them to protect against the sharp straw points.

And she had fallen hopelessly in love with him.

The foolishness of it all. Trying to tie down such a free spirit. Talking to him of marriage, of being his partner, his inspiration. How, she mused, could I have been so naive? And yet, something beautiful had been destroyed when he could not share her vision. Never again would she commit herself to that depth of love.

"You're strangling me."

117

That's what he had said one night.

And one morning the loft of the barn was empty.

"I'm going away. I can't be the me you believe I am," he scrawled in a note left for her. After all the tears, she had recognized what a mistake it would have been. At that point, some aggressive animus figure within her had taken over.

I became a career woman, she reflected. A professional. Men became competitors. She had murdered the Angel of the House—that meek, passive, submissive woman who desires only marriage, a home, and subjection.

Part of her still longed for a pioneer love story.

Warrior Stand and Rob and Andrea and Adam had transported her back to that innocent Kansas projection of how simple, and, possibly, how good life could be.

"Kristin Kelley, you are a terminal romantic," she chided herself.

But Kurt Sannerfield could touch her and make her forget the world.

"What is wrong with you, Kristin?" she asked herself.

On impulse, she turned off the highway onto a dirt road and stopped, an expansive night view of the Flint Hills and thousands of stars spreading before her. She got out of the car and walked around as if literally attempting to walk away from the past.

Her hands tingled. Or was it just her left hand? Or did she only imagine it?

Exhaustion. Too big a day. But a good day. A transcendental day.

Back in her car, she buckled her seatbelt and clicked on the recorder.

She spoke into the microphone.

"Just now I'm reminded of a line from Ralph Waldo Emerson. He wrote, 'Even the corpse hath its own beauty.' That applies to Warrior Stand—a corpse of a town, but there is beauty in its resignation, the struggle of its businesses, the hope reflected in its young people."

She vowed to write a good thesis. Make Warrior Stand the centerpiece. She wanted to understand how such towns had mustered the wherewithal to battle forces they could not fully comprehend. Vengeful demons. Dark destinies.

She drove on. Thought she felt something touch her hair.

Images of Kurt. He liked to touch her hair.

She played the radio. Hummed along with it. Glanced once over her shoulder.

"Woman, you're imagining things."

Things like someone in the back seat. Someone crouched right behind the driver's seat.

She switched the radio off. Let the recorder reel forward.

She hovered on the edge of a revelation about Warrior Stand. What she needed was a single line, an impact sentence. Nothing came to her.

From the mid-seat console, she retrieved a tape of Whitney Houston's latest album and pressed it into her stereo.

Couldn't shake the feeling that someone had somehow slipped into the back seat.

Waiting for the tape to begin, she pulled onto the shoulder and stopped the car. She leaned into the back seat area. And whispered to herself.

"Satisfied now? No bogeyman."

She laughed at herself. Steered onto the highway again.

Whitney Houston never sang.

Kelley braked and swerved. Her small car skidded on the loose chat at the edge of the road. The car banked sideways and stopped dead in its tracks. She managed to keep the engine running.

Her heart raced.

And the male voice on the tape repeated its curious lines:

March will search, April will try,
And May will tell if you live or die.

Not scream, she told herself. I will not scream. Someone has played a trick on me. One of the guys back

119

at the apartment complex. She released the tape. And, again, she laughed at herself, at the ridiculousness of the situation. Her car beaming its lights out across the Flint Hills, her hands trembling on the steering wheel.

She shook her head and reached down to switch off her recorder.

When everything shut down.

Headlights. Dashboard lights. The car's engine.

This time Kristin Kelley screamed.

Hands she could sense but not quite feel jerked the necklace chain against her throat, choking off her scream. She struggled. The chain snapped free. She pressed her door open.

The hands pursued her. More seconds of fighting to survive. Her seatbelt held her firmly in place.

No chance for escape. Only a frenzied surrender to blackness.

Her head slumped onto the steering wheel.

A woman's voice, cool and calm and mechanical, broke the gathering silence of the scene.

"Left door is open," said the voice. "Left door is open."

Cold thoughts flowed in cruel directions.

I tried to concentrate on the movie.

All of the old images paraded before me. Images I had loved as a child: dwarfs singing as they marched off to work, a wicked queen interrogating her mirror, an old crone draped in black offering the reddest apple I had ever seen, and Snow White, her porcelain-white beauty and delicate movements—life almost lost.

The colors washed across the screen at Sunset House. All the joyful music was there; the animation captured the spirit of the rejected girl and her seven soulmates,

120

and yet . . .

"God, why?" I whispered into the darkness. "Just tell me why."

I had hoped the movie would cheer me up. No, that's not true. Nothing would cheer me up, but Disney films had always given me an escape. They were usually the most popular films we had shown at Sunset House. So I had come to town late Sunday morning. Hadn't bothered to wake Leah; she needed her rest; and didn't need to hear the news.

In the projection room, we had stored perhaps a dozen reels of film—distributor's copies, or a few copies my dad had bought to have on hand permanently. *Snow White* was one of those films.

I watched as the dwarfs gathered around the body of Snow White. All of Nature wept for her—a real tear-jerker of a scene. But, of course, the story did not end there. The prince arrived, offered his love, and amid the throb of syrupy, yet soul-inspiring music, Snow White, almost a victim of the wicked queen's evil, rose from the glass-domed coffin.

Moments later, credits rolled.

I could not escape the reality of Mr. Helms's phone call that morning.

"Rob, I have very bad news. Tragic news. How can I . . . they, you see . . . they found Kristin Kelley west of town . . . she's been murdered."

I don't remember what I said to him. I believe he asked me to come into town and be with his family. Maybe I told him I would be all right.

I floated around in a bubble of shock.

I knew it couldn't be true. Just couldn't be.

I rode up and down the roads on my motorbike. West of town, I came upon a rectangular plot boundaried by yellow strips of paper: "County Sheriff's Investigation. Do Not Disturb," a sign read.

I cried a little. Not much. Mainly I got mad. I ran out onto one of those rolling green hills and I yelled at the top of my lungs. Rage filled me. I tried to empty it all out by

121

shouting, roaring at all the hurt I was feeling.

That's when something was triggered within. I heard Snow White singing that song, "I'm wishing . . ." it begins. Curiosity seekers were slowing at the scene of the crime. I raced past them into town. To Sunset House. To hear Snow White finish that song.

I felt absolutely numb. Wasted.

The reel clicked off.

Sunset House was dark.

"Rob? Rob . . . are you in here?"

It was Andrea.

I wished to God she hadn't come. I just wanted to be alone in the darkness.

She found a lobby light and switched it on. Must have seen my outline in the shadows. I heard her running toward me.

"Oh, Rob."

I held her in my lap and she cried the hollow cry of someone who has been crying and has few tears left. She trembled all over. I rocked her, but I said nothing. Couldn't feel the words that might comfort her. Maybe there weren't any.

We sat like that for a long time.

Finally I said, "I wonder if anybody's told Adam."

"I think Pudge did," Andrea murmured.

A strange sort of dizziness tugged at me.

Andrea was talking, but I couldn't make out all of her words.

"Don Slocumb . . . out that way . . . drinking . . . asleep in his car."

I felt like I was suffocating, so I pushed to my feet and Andrea held on around my neck tightly. I staggered. Andrea buried her head against my shoulder.

"She was our friend, Rob. We liked her and she liked us."

We managed to get to the lobby, supporting each other like wounded soldiers.

Wounded. That was it. That's what I felt. Andrea, too, I think.

Some awful wound had been inflicted upon us.
God, it was going to take a long time to heal.

Doc Newton met us at the front door.
"You kids all right?"
A young-looking man got in a car beyond him.
"Who's that?" I asked.
Andrea melted into Doc Newton's arms. He whispered
something to her, and then, to me, he said, "Reporter.
From the Topeka paper, I believe. Said he wants the
town's reaction to all this."
Shuffling us into his old Ford, Newton drove to the
Arrowhead and deposited Andrea there. I hugged her and
told her I'd see her later. I should have stayed with her, I
guess, but I was feeling an odd selfishness, a kind of
better-help-yourself-before-you-can-help-someone-else
attitude.
I rode with Doc Newton back to the hardware. Gray,
winter-threatening clouds had rolled in from the west—a
hard, cold, depressing sky. The temperature was dropping.
Inside the hardware, I said, "Will those reporters be
talking to me and Andrea and Adam? I mean, we'd been
with her you know . . . with Kristin Kelley about all day
yesterday."
Doc Newton didn't answer me immediately.
"I've got fresh coffee. You want sugar and cream?"
I nodded.
Cold winter nights working at the Arrowhead, I had
picked up a taste for coffee. Dump enough cream and
sugar in it and it wasn't so dang bitter. Doc Newton had
his own little table, equipped with coffeemaker and
containers of sugar and packets of some kind of instant
cream.
He had his pipe in one hand and cup of coffee in the
other.
As he started to say something, I thought about how
we had met Kelley in the hardware, how she had admired

my painting, and how Adam had fixed her tape recorder.

"Reporters and the sheriff, too," said Newton.

The last part of his comment jabbed at me.

"Why the sheriff? Oh . . . wait a minute . . . yeah, I get it. We had to be one of the last to . . . God almighty."

"Right now, though, I expect the sheriff's boys are grilling Don Slocumb."

"Is he their main suspect?"

Doc Newton explained what I had heard in bits and pieces from Andrea. Slocumb had been found asleep in his car on a dirt road less than a mile from where they discovered the body. Suddenly I wondered who had actually come upon Kelley's car, who had found her there. I asked Doc Newton.

"Karl Dodd," he replied. "Driving back from Council Grove. He thought it was a car accident."

"Karl Dodd and Don Slocumb," I exclaimed. "It had to be one of them. Two most likely candidates around Warrior Stand."

In that moment, I was blindly certain one or the other had committed the murder.

Doc Newton shrugged, but didn't reject the possibility.

I started thinking out loud.

"Karl Dodd's crazy enough to do it. A psychotic if you ask me. I've seen him go over the edge around Adam. Just last Sunday. He would kill. He would do it. So would Slocumb. He thinks so much about, you know, about sex. It's messed up his mind. He reads all those magazines about men torturing women. About kidnapping them and making sex slaves or something like that out of them."

The more I talked, the louder and more certain of my theory I got—Karl Dodd or Don Slocumb. It was obvious. Then, I got this icy cold feeling. There was something I had to ask Newton.

"Did they . . . when they found the body, had anybody done anything to her . . . like . . . done anything more to her?"

"You mean had she been raped?"

Again, I nodded.

He hesitated.

"Of course, you realize that I'm not supposed to breathe a breath about this matter. So this has to be between you, me, and the cold north wind. I was called in to attend to the body, and based on my preliminary examination, I'd say no, no physical violation of that kind."

I found myself staring at him.

"You . . . you *saw* her dead body?"

Worse yet, I thought to myself, he had had to *touch* it.

"You forget that I'm not only a physician, but also the local undertaker and coroner and dead body expert."

My mind was reeling. Suddenly I couldn't see Doc Newton as the sensitive, talented artist, but as something like a ghoul. I had only one other question.

"How was it done? How was she murdered?"

"Strangulation, it appears. Apparently she had been wearing a necklace—I seem to remember vaguely that she had been—that necklace and some very strong hands did the deed. They searched in and around the car all night but couldn't find the necklace."

"Oh, God," I murmured. "It had a wildcat on it. Andrea, she admired . . ."

I felt a little faint. Couldn't finish my sentence or my coffee.

"You probably ought to mention anything like that to the sheriff. Any details that could help them in the investigation," said Newton.

I don't recall saying much after he offered that advice.

Doc Newton paced back and forth. He said something about having a strange feeling. Something about feeling kind of like he did when they couldn't really figure out what had led to Blackie's death.

At the time, I made no connection. Not a conscious one anyway.

But I knew that suddenly I wanted to see Adam. Thought he could help me deal with the whole business. So I told Newton that's where I was headed.

"Yes," he said, "you ought to go talk to Adam."

Funny how a person's mind gets locked onto something and won't let go of it. In Doc Newton's words I heard that old familiar dislike or perhaps distrust of Adam.

But I was too caught up in my own depressed thoughts to think much about it then. I rode to Pudge's, figuring that Adam would seek out the Winnebago to be alone. Pudge himself met me, shouldering his shotgun. His face had a weirdly florid cast to it.

I parked my bike and approached him.

"You seen Adam today?"

The scarecrow-thin man stood his ground like a sentry at an army base. It struck me as being kind of comical.

"Possible I have. Why would you be wantin' to find him?"

His harsh and defensive tone threw me a little.

"I'd like to see him, talk with him, you know . . . about what happened. You've heard about Kristin Kelley, haven't you?"

"I have," said Pudge, and he hacked up a mouthful of spit and watered down a rusting truck rim. "That's why I've got some firepower handy. We got us a killer loose around these parts. Folks better be ready to protect themselves."

"The county sheriff's investigating . . . been questioning Don Slocumb."

He tightened his jaw and wiggled his fingers on the stock of his shotgun.

"Sorry fucker for sure. Slocumb's a sorry-ass fucker, and if I ever catch him in this junkyard or the truck stop I'll put the end of this here shotgun up his ass and pull the trigger and then he'll have buckshot for brains. Which'ud be more than he's got now."

"You fired him?"

"I have. He don't know it yet. But I have."

For a moment, I forgot about Adam.

"Doc Newton says Karl Dodd's the one who found her. He coulda done it. Karl Dodd, he's maybe crazier than Slocumb."

"Maybe," said Pudge. "That don't help Slocumb none.

126

His ass is fired one way or the tother. Caught him whacking off in the restroom night 'fore last. Tired of a man whose prick's more important to him than taking his work seriously. So that's done. Maybe he's a killer, maybe he ain't. I'm done with him."

"Can't say I'll miss him," I said.

Pudge seemed to relax a notch.

"Come on in the office," he said.

I followed him into the tiny shack. It had two chairs, a small table, a pot-bellied wood stove, black as night, a shelf of rodeo trophies, and a bunch of calendars—everywhere calendars. Pudge sort of collected them. Most had a picture scene of the old West. Frederic Remington art. He also had one of my real early paintings of a horse. I kind of cringed to see how lousy it was. Someday I promised myself I'd paint him a better one.

He offered me coffee and, of course, some saltine crackers. He puts away a box or two a week. Doc Newton claims those crackers will clog up Pudge's bowels one of these days and they'll have to use Liquid Plumber to unclog him.

"No thanks," I said.

"You know," he began, "there's one other bullgoose looney around coulda killed that young lady."

I frowned.

"Who's that?"

He munched noisily on a cracker. Pieces flew when he answered me.

"John. Ole John Snagovia. Tell me he's not a looney bastard. Betcha a hundred dollar bill if that witch of a sister of his told him to snuff somebody out, he's looney enough to do it."

I couldn't argue with him.

Three suspects. Maybe Warrior Stand wasn't as idyllic as we had pictured it for Kristin Kelley. No, I guess it wasn't.

Pudge and I talked a few minutes more about murder suspects and about how the whole tragedy would shake up our little town. But then I was eager to see Adam.

127

"Hold on a spell," said Pudge. "Now, I ain't so sure Adam wants to see anybody. When I drove out to tell him what happened, he got mighty, mighty quiet. Rode in here with me and went straight to the Winnebago. All's I'm sayin' is, donchoo be upsettin' him more'n he is already."

In a way, hearing his words made me feel good. He cared for Adam. That was pretty obvious. A voice inside me kept whispering: *Adam will need people who care.*

So I told Pudge I understood.

Not sure what to say to Adam, I made my way to his hideout. I hollered to let him know I was coming in, but he seemed kind of surprised when I came into his area. He scrambled around as if trying to put some things out of my sight.

"How ya doin'?" I asked.

He was squatting on the floor, Indian-style. It appeared that he'd been working on a large drawing of a bear—that same one I'd seen before—rearing up on its hind legs.

"I'm feeling super damn shitty," he said.

"Yeah, me, too. But did you hear about Don Slocumb?"

He hadn't, so I told him about Slocumb being questioned and about what Pudge and I talked about regarding suspects. Adam didn't really respond until I mentioned that the sheriff would probably want to question the three of us.

"Why?"

"'Cause we'd been around her all day. Might be we were the last to see her, you know . . . alive."

"What do you think of my drawing?" he said.

The abrupt way he changed the subject caught me off guard. He held the pencil drawing of the bear up so that I could see it more clearly.

"It's good. Better than I could do probably."

It was. It never stopped amazing me to see his artwork.

A smile flickered across his face, then quickly disappeared.

"Not me. Not me doing it. It's the night touch. It's the goddamn night touch."

Suddenly he got real upset and tore the drawing into a half dozen or more strips.

"Hey, what's wrong with you?" I exclaimed.

He pushed his hands toward me.

"These!" he shouted. "Can you understand that!"

I was afraid the loudness of his voice would bring Pudge.

"Okay, okay," I muttered. "Calm down, man."

"My mother says it's the last days," he whispered. Then he glanced up at me and smiled in a way that made me cold all over. "Last days. Darkness in the minds of men. She says the apocalypse is coming. You believe that, Rob?"

I kind of shrugged off his question.

"I guess probably I don't."

He grew quiet.

"I told you she wouldn't be coming back. Kristin Kelley."

He stared at his hands.

"I had a feeling," he continued. "A strong feeling."

"Hey, let's don't talk about it anymore. The sheriff, he'll find who did it. Slocumb, or maybe a total stranger. They'll catch him. You'll see."

Adam's weird smile broadened.

"Rob, you know what I think?"

I wasn't sure I wanted to hear.

"Rob, there's a bear in the book of Revelations. Apocalypse. I keep seeing that bear. You know what I think it means?"

I could feel the ragged pull of my breathing.

I shook my head.

"I think it means the bear did it. I think the bear killed Kristin Kelley."

"Jesus, Adam, . . . don't talk like this. You're sounding . . . looney."

Pudge's word came back to me.

Adam stood up and brushed off his jeans.

129

"You're right," he said. "Don't pay any attention to all that. There's something more important I got to tell you."

He had me so confused I wasn't sure how to react.

We were standing face to face, and I had the curious sensation that he could see right into my eyes . . . past my eyes, right into some secret part of myself I wouldn't want anyone to see.

"What do you have to tell me?"

"Promise you'll help me. You and Andrea. Pudge, too. Help me because somebody's gonna be coming after me."

"Who? Why? What do you mean?"

"Because of the night touch. They'll be coming."

I swallowed back any other questions.

"I'll have to protect myself," he added. "That's what it'll come down to. Are you gonna be on my side?"

Baffled. That's what I felt.

Like I was hanging upside down from a rope tied to the cemetery cottonwood.

CHAPTER 10

I must have said yes.

Not knowing what on earth he was talking about, I still said yes. Because he was still my friend. If I had been able to see into the future . . . well, if I had been able to see events of the next month and a half, I believe I might have packed a few things, climbed on my bike, and headed west. Away from Warrior Stand. Far away.

Instead, I got into a big fight with Andrea. You see, we learned that on Wednesday Kristin Kelley was to be buried in Independence, Missouri. Andrea wanted to go to the funeral; I didn't. I tried to explain to her that after being forced to attend the funeral of my parents and brother, I swore to myself I'd never suffer through the experience again. She said we needed to pay our last respects. I said I'd pay my last respects in my own way. She cried. Called me insensitive. She tried to get Adam to go with her, but he refused, too.

She went. Doc Newton drove her over there.

To make matters worse, the day after Andrea returned from the funeral, she started messing around with Brian Gunnellson again. Damn, that made me mad. Upset Adam, too.

Well, the following weekend—Halloween—Adam's prediction came true.

Another stranger arrived in Warrior Stand. Oh, there had been some outsiders all week: the sheriff and his men, newspaper people, curiosity seekers, and the like. And the sheriff had asked Adam and Andrea and me some

131

questions, and Warrior Stand had made the news report on the Topeka television channel, but the stranger, he was different somehow from all that.

I studied him some at first—and a whole lot sometime later—and tried to figure out what exactly he was up to. I wanted to know what he was thinking. . . .

"Find him and kill him."

Clay Lawrence hunkered down by the side of the highway and examined what remained of tire tracks in the loose chat. A chilly wind whipped at his face; there were no trees on the mantle of the hills to break the raw, numbing effect of the sudden gusts. But Lawrence barely noticed the cold or the wind.

The words of his friend, a man whom he had admired all his life, cut through him more sharply, more harshly than the Kansas elements.

"Find him, Clay . . . find the bastard who did it and kill him."

Hugh Kelley had been Lawrence's high school coach long ago, had dogged him and pushed him to do well in academics and athletics. Through Kelley's help, he had gotten a football scholarship to the University of Missouri. And the two men had stayed in touch as Lawrence entered police work.

They had talked far into the night the day Kelley and his wife, Marianne, had decided to end twenty-plus years of marriage. And Lawrence had known Kristin from the time she was a day old. "K.K." he had called her. Kristin Kelley. Beautiful. Smart as a whip. An angel of a girl who always sent Lawrence a birthday card. Never failed.

Loving. Filled with life. Energy. Kristin Kelley.

Dead.

Lawrence rubbed the scruff of his beard.

Emotion welled into his throat. With one finger, he traced the grooves of the tire tracks.

The face of a girl, flaming red pigtails, a front tooth missing, mirrored forth in his thoughts. Snuggled into his lap, she smiled up at him and wigwagged her hand as if keeping time to a lyric she had shared with him over the years.

"Tell me you like me/And I'll do you no wrong. Tell me you love me/And I'll sing you a song."

And she would sing every song she could think of.

The memory ghosted away.

Lawrence stood up, clenched his fists, and walked the rectangular outline of where Kristin Kelley's car had come to a halt one week ago. He called these reviews of a murder scene, "retrieval exercises," and there was a time, not many years ago, when he possessed an uncanny ability to pick up some overlooked clue during these reviews.

But he was drawing a blank on this one.

Nothing added up. No sign of another car having pulled her over. No sign of another human being having been in the car with her—no sign except a throat cut by a necklace, then crushed by strong hands.

But no fingerprints. No fiber traces. No pieces of hair from her attacker.

Suddenly he was reminded of the homicide case which had changed his life. How long ago had it been? Three years? Four? As a police specialist on child murders, he had been called to the sleepy southern hamlet of Goldsmith, Alabama. Two young girls had been savagely murdered.

The Granite Heights Killer—that's the label they gave the child murderer. Lawrence had tracked him down, and with the help of a young boy who had appeared to have almost supernatural powers, he had shot the killer—a loner named Maris McCready.

But the killer had haunted him for months afterward.

McCready's ghost? Lawrence was never able to determine what it was. Something. Something had come after him, stealing his peace of mind, threatening to steal his sanity.

Until Lawrence quit. Much to the displeasure of his Uncle Nelson Cromartie, the man who had coaxed him

133

into law enforcement, he had retired from police work, washed up in his mid-thirties. For the past two years he had tried his hand at being a private investigator homebasing from Atlanta.

It had brought him decent work. Easy assignments mostly. Men hiring him to follow their wives; women hiring him to follow their husbands; parents hiring him to follow their son or daughter. A few "insider" corporate assignments. Nothing that really challenged him.

Then, last Sunday, he heard the news about Kristin Kelley.

After the funeral, he had sat in Hugh Kelley's car and talked briefly.

"I want you to take the case, Clay. I won't be able to live with myself till this is resolved."

"Local authorities should crack this one," Lawrence had responded. "Kansas homicide people are some of the best in the country from what I hear."

Kelley had shaken his head and gritted his teeth.

"Don't want him arrested, Clay."

"Not arrested? Then what do you want me to—"

Kelley nodded.

"That's right. I'll pay you, Clay. As much cash as I can get my hands on. Twenty, twenty-five thousand. Or whatever figure you name."

"Hugh, it's not money . . . it's . . . vigilante justice. You don't want a private investigator. You want a bounty hunter."

Kelley had smiled, a hard, tight smile. The smile of a man whose life was filled with hours of quiet desperation.

"I want a friend. But call it bounty hunting or whatever the hell you need to, Clay. Me, I call it blood revenge. It's the only justice left to a man these days. The only justice."

Every ounce of civilized reason in Lawrence had resisted agreement.

"Do you hear what you're asking me to do?"

Shifting in his seat, Kelley had pulled out his billfold.

"Loud and clear and deep in my soul . . . yeah, I hear myself, Clay."

Lawrence had stared at the billfold, assuming Kelley was about to dangle money in front of him. Instead, the man flipped through a stack of plastic photo holders.

"Got a little present for you," Kelley had muttered. He handed a wallet-sized photo to him.

"Kristin's college graduation picture," Kelley said. "She wanted for you to have one. Marianne sent me a half dozen of them a few weeks ago. That one's yours. Kristin had started graduate work, you know. That's what had taken her to that small town. Warrior Stand. She had gone to do research. So will you."

The beauty of the young woman in the photo had drilled into Lawrence like some precision tool.

Tell me you love me/And I'll sing you a song.

"God, she did grow up to be a pretty lady," he murmured. "She is really something, Hugh."

"No," the other man had replied. "Not *is* . . . she *was.*"

The wind swirled around him, mocking him as did the murder scene.

But Lawrence had resigned himself on two points: one, he believed—term it "intuition," term it "sixth sense" or whatever—he believed the murderer remained in the Warrior Stand area; and, two, he knew that if he tracked down the murderer, he could do it. He could kill him. For Hugh Kelley. For the memory of "K.K." For all those instances in which blood revenge would have balanced the scales of justice.

In his rented car, he drove back to Warrior Stand.

Needed a place to stay.

At the Arrowhead Truck Stop, he crawled into a booth next to the front windows and ordered a cup of hot tea. An attractive woman with "Molly" threaded on her blouse pocket eyed him flirtatiously.

Wasting your time, lady, he thought to himself.

All his drives—even sex—had been dulled. All except one.

Everything had been sublimated to one task: *Find him and kill him*.

Yet, Lawrence knew that he had to keep a low profile. Not give himself or his intentions away. That would be difficult—very difficult—in a small town. First order of business: look for a place to stay. No motels around, but surely someone would rent him out a room in one of the large frame houses off Main Street.

He glanced around, taking in a sweep of the Arrowhead clientele. At the counter, beefy truckers guzzled coffee and bantered with Molly. In the booth next to his sat an elderly gentleman lost in his thoughts.

Probably a local, Lawrence guessed.

And so he got up and introduced himself.

The older man shook his hand and gestured for him to be seated.

"Good to meet you, Mr. Lawrence. I'm Jake Newton."

"Didn't mean to interrupt your reverie, but I'm in the market for a roof over my head while I finish some business here. Anyone around who has a room to rent?"

Newton paused a moment.

"Now, let me see. Too bad the old hotel, down across from the grocery, is closed. Years ago, it had some surprisingly fine accommodations. A room? Let me see. Sure, yes, I believe I can direct you to one."

"Good. I'd appreciate that."

"Above the old movie house . . . it's closed, too, but Leah Dalton and her brother, Rob, have tried to keep a room available to rent there. Even a view of Main Street."

"Sounds like just what I'm looking for. Did you say Dalton?"

"Yes, Leah Dalton. She's a nurse. Her brother works here at the truck stop on Saturday nights. In fact, he normally comes in around four o'clock. Should be in soon. I believe they'd be grateful to have someone rent from them. They've struggled to keep it occupied. Last

136

weekend's tragedy has been the only thing to draw people to Warrior Stand in years."

Lawrence reached inside his coat, retrieved a notepad and pen, and scratched out a few words.

"I'll be in touch with them. Thanks. I really do appreciate this."

He looked into Newton's eyes, flashed an obligatory smile, and started to excuse himself.

"Welcome to sit a spell," said Newton. "Like I said, Leah's brother ought to be around soon. He can show you the room or call Leah in to show it to you."

Lawrence relaxed a notch.

"Thanks. I'll join you, if you'll let me buy your coffee."

"You got a deal, Mr. Lawrence."

"Clay."

Newton smiled.

"Jake, here."

A few moments of awkward silence passed before Newton said, "You're a cop of some kind, aren't you, Clay?"

Lawrence ritched back, feeling a surge of tension.

"Is it that obvious?"

"Well, not many strangers come to town carrying a .44 revolver—unless they're meaning to use it on one of the bad guys. But I'd also figure you aren't with the county or state boys. Private investigator maybe?"

"Right again. Wouldn't want that to become common knowledge just yet."

"No problem."

"Thanks, Dr. Newton. I mean, . . . Jake."

Newton registered surprise.

"Touché. I'm semi-retired, though. How'd you guess I was a sawbones?"

"That caduceus pin. Gives you away same as my revolver does me."

Newton took a sip of coffee.

"You're observant."

"Got to be. And I remember your name now as the

physician who attended Kristin's body."

"Horrible incident," the older man murmured. Then, after a moment or two of pause, he said, "Occurs to me that if you're planning to take a room in town you must think the killer's not gone far."

"That's my hunch."

The two men talked about the case, Lawrence providing background material—his association with Hugh and Kristin Kelley and his former work as a homicide specialist, and Newton reviewed what he had noticed at the murder scene as well as what he knew about Warrior Stand which might fill in some blanks for Lawrence.

"What can you tell me about Don Slocumb and Karl Dodd? Sheriff's office doesn't seem to be finding much. No case there near as I can tell."

"Slocumb . . . he's a bum," said Newton. "A drunk. A pervert. And I'm being kind."

Both men laughed.

"But . . . I'd swear to this: Don Slocumb's no murderer."

"You're probably right. Besides that, testimony would show that he was still around the truck stop about the time Kristin was slain."

"Don Slocumb lacks the cold, mean, calculated wherewithal to kill someone. Now, Karl Dodd, on the other hand . . . a cruel and, by turns, vicious man."

"From what I gather," said Lawrence, "his alibi is weak."

"I've know the man for years, and I realize that as this town's physician I ought to maintain a more confidential stance regarding its citizens . . . but, to me, Karl Dodd is fully capable of any manner of violence. Just ask his son, Adam."

And Lawrence thought to himself: *I'm sure I will.*

"Jake, is there anyone else? Any other local suspects? You know the people of Warrior Stand and this area. Anyone else who would be capable of committing this kind of crime?"

Newton rubbed his jaw.

"Hell of a note, isn't it? Here I am . . . I should be talking of what's positive about this town. Instead, I'm pointing out potential killers."

Lawrence laughed softly.

"Sorry. This isn't the most pleasant topic of conversation, but . . . it's a grim necessity for me. I've reviewed the evidence gathered, and it's skimpy. Any lead, any bit or piece of something I could follow up on . . . well, it would sure ease the mind of Hugh Kelley if I could make sure whoever did this faces cold justice."

"I understand where you're coming from," said Newton. "I don't envy you your job, believe me. Back to your question: the only other individual I'd mention is John Snagovia. He lives outside of town with his sister, Willa. Basically, he's harmless, but he does have a history . . . it's been years ago . . . a history of aberrant behavior. Most of it a product, I suspect, of childhood brain damage. Psychotic acts, under the right set of circumstances, are a possibility. I would have to doubt, however, that he was even aware the young lady was in town last Saturday. The Snagovias keep to themselves."

Lawrence sighed heavily.

"Hard for *me* to accept that she was here," he said. "That a person with so much life could have that life taken away."

Newton glanced at his watch.

"A week ago at this time, Kristin Kelley was sitting exactly where you are, asking me about this town, excited about her research."

Lawrence met Newton's eyes and solemnly shook his head.

"Hard to accept," he muttered.

"The bathroom is tiny," Leah Dalton explained. "We put in this shower area last year. Barely enough space to turn around in, I'm afraid."

Lawrence perused the bathroom, though most of his

139

attention was drawn to the young woman, her modest beauty, the honesty in her voice.

"This will be just right for my purposes. Just right. I'd like to rent it from you."

Leah brightened.

"Oh, good, That's wonderful. And if you'll give me an hour or so I can make it more presentable. It could use a dusting."

"No, it's fine. Really. I'd like to go ahead and bring my suitcase in. No need to fuss anymore with it. I'll write you a check for a month's rent in advance, but I can't guarantee that I'll be staying longer than that."

"No matter, Mr. Lawrence. Rob and I are so pleased to have a paying customer, we won't be concerned about how long you'll need it. We just hope you'll be comfortable."

She smiled at him, and the eye exchange lingered until she looked away nervously, self-consciously.

"I met your brother at the truck stop," he continued. "He certainly did seem excited about possibly having the room rented."

"Yes, Rob loves this place. My father lavished some care on Sunset House, and when he and my mother and my other brother, Drew, were killed in a train accident, Rob made it a special aim of his for us to keep hold of the property. It's been difficult, staying one step ahead of the bank and taxes."

"So you and your brother have had to go it alone? That's . . . that's admirable. Shows a lot of character. Kansas pioneer toughness."

Leah raised her eyebrows; her eyes sparkled.

"No, we just did what we had to do. The people of Warrior Stand have been so kind to us. It's a good town . . . despite what happened last weekend, or the obvious fact that the town's a ghost of its former self."

Lawrence said nothing, surprised as he was at the immediacy of attraction to her. He wrote the check and when she took it, she said, "If there's anything you need, give us a call. Rob or I, one, should be available.

140

The hot water heater takes awhile to build up full steam . . . I almost forgot to mention that."

"Thanks for telling me."

A few awkward moments passed as he accompanied her to her car, and as she drove off, he wondered whether the attraction was mutual.

This all seems so wrong, he thought to himself. Coming here with the intention of killing someone.

The setting was all wrong, too. People like Leah Dalton don't belong around such violent intentions.

But then, he reminded himself, neither did Kristin Kelley.

Having settled in, showered, and relaxed, Lawrence returned to the Arrowhead a couple of hours later to eat. Molly, still on duty, introduced him to her daughter, Andrea, and then kiddingly inquired as to what costume he would be wearing that evening—Halloween.

It felt good to banter with her, a woman whose beauty most men would favor over that of Leah Dalton, but to Lawrence, there was a counterbalancing attraction in the young woman who had rented him the apartment. Something about her he couldn't define. But it was there.

Thoughts of her accompanied him back to the apartment after dinner. That is, until cold practicality intruded.

Didn't come here for romance.

A brown paper bag on the bed suddenly claimed his attention.

The county sheriff's office had released Kristin Kelley's personal effects—items found in her car at the time of her death. Lawrence knew that the objects would have been inspected carefully, but, with authorization from Hugh Kelley, he requested to see them, holding himself responsible for them.

Most of all, the objects—a camera, a tape recorder, and a half dozen tapes—possessed a certain magic, bringing him nearer to good memories of "K.K." At the bottom of the bag were several prints, photos taken on Kelley's fateful visit to Warrior Stand and developed by the sheriff's office—photos of the decaying downtown area and one of three kids posing in front of a massive cottonwood tree.

Lawrence recognized them: Leah Dalton's brother, Rob; Molly's daughter, Andrea; and their blind friend, Adam. Seemed like real nice kids. The photo captured innocent, fun-loving smiles on their faces. They were apparently close friends. Kristin Kelley had obviously taken to them immediately.

Putting aside the photos, he toyed absently with the camera, then picked up the tape recorder. He played it through Kelley's opening entry, stopping once to replay it just to listen to the young woman's voice.

"Jesus God," he whispered, emotions threatening to overwhelm him.

He let the tape reel forward.

A young man's voice—Rob's, he believed, haltingly told the story of how Warrior Stand got its name. Then Lawrence recognized the voice of Jake Newton talking of earlier days in the town.

The tape glitched, reached blankness.

He was about to switch it off, assuming Kelley had recorded no more, when her voice emerged again.

"Just now I'm reminded of a line from Ralph Waldo Emerson. He wrote, 'Even the corpse hath its own beauty.' That applies to Warrior Stand—a corpse of a town, but there is beauty in its resignation, the struggle of its businesses, the hope reflected in its young people."

He mused at Kelley's statement, impressed with her perception.

The tape picked up music, apparently from the car radio, and even snatches of Kelley humming. Then one thing more.

Lawrence bolted out of his reflective mood.

One brief stretch of tape. Kelley had said something. He had to replay the tape four times and to listen very carefully. Radio music almost blotted it out.

But there. Yes. He heard it. Softly. Not very distinctly. He heard it.

"Woman, you're imagining things."

Then more blank tape.

Lawrence felt a tightening in his chest.

Then Kelley's voice again. It sounded distant.

"Satisfied now? No bogeyman."

He replayed the line several times, listening always for something more.

What in God's name was going on?

He let the tape continue. But it rolled silently to its end.

Into the stillness of the apartment, Lawrence spoke aloud.

"No bogeyman."

He stared at the opposite wall, straining every muscle of his imagination to recreate a scene that would fit Kelley's curious remarks.

"Jesus God," he whispered, "what was going on there?"

He walked around the threadbare room, the tightness in his chest relenting by degrees. He sat on the bed and examined the record tapes: Bon Jovi, U2, Whitney Houston, and a few others. Unfamiliar with contemporary music, he slipped the Bon Jovi tape into the recorder. But the music was fast, throbbing, a certain eager meaninglessness about it.

He picked up the Whitney Houston tape, thinking that it might be more relaxing. He hesitated.

Satisfied now? No bogeyman.

Kelley's words—her last words?—would not release their hold.

It was time to jog, his favorite method of clearing his head. He tossed aside the Houston tape, donned his running outfit, and trotted into the virtual emptiness of downtown Warrior Stand.

There was a crisp chill in the air, but no wind.

A block away he heard children laughing, a sound at odds with the deserted downtown. Then, as he directed his route toward the Arrowhead, he focused his attention within.

The old anger returned.

It possessed two levels: one, a more superficial anger aimed at himself for not more seriously challenging Hugh Kelley's "blood revenge" theory; and, two, a deeper anger reserved for Kristin's slayer—the latter, a more primitive instinct which dismissed notions of civilized behavior and justice.

He jogged to the edge of the truck stop, blotting out the protest of a stiffening knee, a football legacy brought to life by cold weather.

Don't let Leah Dalton or anyone else sidetrack you.

The intensity of that inner voice surprised him, but the words rang true.

He had come to town to kill.

Or perhaps be killed.

If the killer remained in the area—as he believed he did—then wasn't he making himself an open target jogging alone as he was?

On the way back, he began to notice figures. To hear laughter and muted conversations. Bodies lurched through the semi-darkness.

Vampires. Ghosts. Witches. A boy with a skeleton mask.

Just kids. No killer.

No bogeyman.

Lawrence felt a nervous rush of heat in his throat.

He clambered into Sunset House certain that someone was following him. Climbing the set of stairs, he thought he heard someone shuffling in the shadows of the lobby. Perhaps the harsh sound of heavy breathing.

Someone waiting?

And what if they were waiting *inside* the apartment?

He wasn't carrying his gun.

Goddamn it. I never even locked the door.

Once inside the apartment he switched on a light and sought out his revolver.

Face pressed against the door, he listened.

144

Silence.

But he could imagine, he could *feel* hands on the other side of the door.

And coming *through* the door.

"Jesus God," he muttered.

He spun away from the door and held both hands on the revolver, bracing himself to fire.

The lights flickered off.

"Who's there? Goddamn it, if there's someone out there, you'd better be identifying yourself."

Any move, he told himself, *any move and I open up.*

Nerve-rivening seconds passed.

He thought he heard someone. Laughter. A cackle.

"Jesus," he murmured. "Trick or treaters. That's all."

He felt foolish.

The lights flickered on.

What would it be? Beyond the door, he knew he would find a timeless reminder of Halloween tricksters. A bag of cow shit? Out on the street the windows of his rented car would be soaped.

Cautiously he opened the door.

To find absolutely nothing.

That night he slept with his revolver next to his pillow.

CHAPTER 11

Another week passed.

I saw very little of the stranger, Clay Lawrence; my ongoing tiff with Andrea occupied my thoughts—that and the lingering sadness surrounding Kristin Kelley's death. Too often, I guess, I found myself biking out to the cemetery, to the cottonwood where she had taken a picture of Andrea and Adam and me.

At that time I had no deep or profound thoughts about death. But, to me, death wasn't black—it was a mottled gray, sort of swirling and maybe flecked with darker shades and specks of white. One evening I tried to capture it on a canvas. No use. I didn't feel much like painting during those first days in November.

The mural at school stayed in a rough state. People asked how it was coming, but I always put them off by saying that I was contemplating the overall effect of it. I've learned that a painter can get away with that kind of bullshit talk. Throw around words like "inspiration" and "ambience" and everybody thinks you're a real artist. And they leave you alone.

Truth is, the mural left me cold. School left me cold.

First nine weeks report card came out: one A, the rest B's—and two of those B's were gifts—I'm not lying. Worse yet, I was headed for C's—C's, like death, are the color gray. To be perfectly honest, I had to consider the possibility of that black realm below C's.

So one evening I showed my report card to Leah. And we talked.

147

She got quiet. I could feel her disappointment.

"Look," I said, "it's been a tough nine weeks. I started out okay. Then, well, you know . . . Kristin Kelley . . . and I just haven't been able to concentrate."

That wasn't the whole truth.

"Rob, you know I've never pushed you about grades. But you're capable, so capable of exceptional work. I was willing to give up some of my plans because I could see so much potential in you. Mom and Dad—"

"Okay, there's more to it," I stammered.

Leah rarely put me on a guilt trip; she wasn't that way. At the kitchen table, she folded her hands and listened.

I was scrambling for something to say.

"There's one other problem that's bugging me. Real hard thing to resolve. It's . . . you see . . . it's me and . . . and Andrea."

Her name came to mind, and it was partially the truth. She and I weren't exactly hitting on all cylinders.

"Anything you want to talk about?"

"Leah, sometimes I can't figure her out. She's still mad at me for not going to Kristin Kelley's funeral with her. You know how I feel about funerals. Why doesn't she understand?"

"Relationships—if they're to have any substance—have to have some give and take, some compromise. Are you sure you're meeting her halfway on most things?"

"There's *no* halfway with Andrea," I exclaimed.

"Sounds like there's no halfway with you, either."

Well, my sister had me. I hate to feel that I'm being selfish or self-centered. But how do you avoid it?

"What really messes up my mind," I said, "is whenever we aren't getting along, she starts flirting with other guys . . . like with that scumbucket, Brian Gunnellson."

"Like mother, like daughter," said Leah. "I mean, she sees how Molly acts around men."

"Yeah, you're right. Like now. You ought to have a video camera on her while she flirts with that guy, Clay Lawrence. Pudge says she only has one thing on her mind."

Leah fell into another silence for a moment.

"How does Mr. Lawrence react to her?"

I shrugged, and then something about the tone of her question got its claws into me.

I sat down at the table and looked into my sister's eyes.

"You hot for Lawrence?"

She almost slapped me.

"Robert Dalton, *that* is none of your business."

"Why isn't it? I talk about Andrea with you. You like him, don't you? Sure, I can tell."

She recaptured her composure.

"Seems like a pleasant man. Polite. Mature. A little older, but a professional man."

"He's a cop . . . or a private detective. That's what Joe Helms told me. He checked into the guy . . . like you and me should have. The guy's here investigating the murder of Kristin Kelley."

"I've heard it's something like that, but I'm not going to pry into the private lives of our boarders."

"Yeah, but you'd like to, I bet."

"I wouldn't mind having some decent male company every once in awhile. In case you haven't noticed, your dear sister may wind up an old maid."

"You saying I'm not decent male company?" I teased.

"You know what I mean."

I leaned forward.

"You going to bed with him?"

Next thing I knew she had chased me out of the house. Goodnaturedly.

We had joked about the matter, but down deep I sure as hell didn't want anybody to hurt my sister. From what I'd seen of private detectives on television, it seemed like they went through a lot of women.

Funny thing, I hardly knew Lawrence, and I was already building up a dislike for him. Frankly, I couldn't see what woman saw in him—scruffy beard and moustache, a certain seediness about him, though he appeared to be in pretty good shape. Pudge said he noticed him out jogging one night, and Joe Helms reported that the guy had been a real good football player

149

in college.

By the end of the next day I had put aside all thoughts of Leah and our resident private detective. I wanted to mend some fences with Andrea. I'll have to admit that I kept thinking about our night in the back of the Chevy station wagon—the night Adam, jealous, I guess, interrupted us at the worst possible moment.

I don't want to sound like Don Slocumb, but I've awakened any number of times dreaming about Andrea's breasts and the way she acted that night. But since then, I hadn't been able to get her in the mood.

Was it really Andrea that night?

Anyway, after school the next day I talked her into going up to the cemetery with me. We didn't do anything. Just talked. My goal was to maneuver her into another session Friday night in the Chevy wagon.

I'll tell you, I even coughed up nine bucks for Reba McEntire's latest tape; I thought she'd be thrilled. We were leaning against the old cottonwood when I gave her the tape. She thanked me for it and then said, "Have you noticed how weird Adam's been acting lately?"

There are times when Andrea frustrates me so much I'm tempted to drown myself in Summer's Pond.

"Don't see Adam 'cept on the bus," I said. "He camps out down in the typing room most of the day. That tape has all the songs you like."

"Did you know his mother wants to get him a seeing-eye dog?"

"He wouldn't go along with that. 'Sides, what happened to her plan to take him to Oral Roberts or some faith healer like that?"

"How should I know?"

"Andrea, you're the one who brought up Adam. You think I brought you up here to talk about him?"

"He's our friend, Rob. I feel like he's in trouble. He's been acting so weird."

When I start getting exasperated, my wrists go limp.

"So what in the damn hell has he been doing?"

"No call to swear, mister," she shot back.

"Okay, okay. Please, dearest lady, tell me what Adam's been doing that's so weird."

She hesitated and sort of looked away so that the unusually warm November breeze tossed the longer strands of her hair. And for just an instant I could imagine how beautiful she would become in the years ahead.

Made my whole body feel weak.

"It's not so much what he's been doing—more what he's been saying."

Like what?"

"Like . . . the other day he said, 'Andy, would you like to have one of those wildcat necklaces like Kristin Kelley had?'"

I wondered why Andrea couldn't see how Adam felt about her.

"What's so weird about that?"

"Then he told me he had seen the ghost of Kristin Kelley out at Pudge's. She was wearing that necklace, but she hid it somewhere in the junked cars. He said he's been having visions of the Saturn Man and the bear— that's what he said—Saturn Man and the bear—and something about the night touch, too."

The back of my mouth got real dry.

I told her it was just his imagination.

"He's starting to scare me, Rob. And he talks about how much he hates his dad."

"I'd be saying that, too, if Karl Dodd was my dad."

"Yeah, but that's not all. He said that Mr. Lawrence . . . you know, who's renting from you and Leah . . . he said he's gonna bring a lot of trouble to Warrior Stand."

I shook my head.

"Listen, Andrea, sometimes Adam talks kinda crazy. You know that. All this night touch crap and what's going on in his family . . . it all messes up his mind sometimes. Don't let it scare you."

"But it does. I'm afraid . . . I'm afraid he might hurt someone."

Well, we talked a few minutes more, and I pretty much

151

succeeded in assuring her Adam would never hurt anybody, probably not even his dad. Then I got around to mentioning our night in the Chevy wagon and how I wanted us to resume our exploration of her womanhood that coming Friday.

That's when she dropped the bomb.

"I can't Friday night. I've got a date."

"Who with?"

Man, I wish I hadn't asked.

"Brian Gunnellson."

I don't remember exactly what I did. Yelled a lot. Swore. And generally went nutso. Andrea got pretty hot, too, and stormed off to town on foot.

Even though I was steamed, I did offer her a ride on my bike.

She threw rocks at me as her way of saying no; I kept after her for about a quarter of a mile. I was losing my patience.

Then, the crowning blow: she gave me the finger.

Damn oh damn, that made me mad.

Crazy woman.

When Friday evening rolled around I was about as miserable as I could be. For a couple of days school had been an absolute disaster. I'll spare you the details. At home, Leah could sense my dark, dark mood and just sort of stayed out of my way.

I biked out to Pudge's, determined not to be anywhere near Andrea's place at the beginning or end of her date with Gunnellson. If she wanted to date a scumbucket, then so be it.

Wasn't going to bother me.

Not much.

Pudge was working on two vehicles at once when I pulled in—one, his old truck, the other, a '53 Dodge; it appeared that he was swapping out parts, unable to get either of the wrecks to run.

I poured out my whole story to him. Andrea. The fight.

152

Her date.

At one point he emerged from the throat of the Dodge, wiped his nose on a greasy sleeve, and said, "You sure enough gone on that gal, ain't you?"

I maintained that I wasn't.

Then he said, "Hellfire, son, I ain't uh likely person to talk to 'bout women. Go see your buddy out in his Winnebago. He's done dug a hole in himself and crawled in it."

Of course, he was referring to Adam. A good way to put it—Adam had done just that: buried himself within. I look back at that Friday night now and wonder how I could have been so selfishly wrapped up in my own small problems. There was a storm raging in Adam, a storm which had already wrought some horrifying damage, and there was a friend crying out for help.

All I could think about was Andrea and my bruised ego.

"What's with the hang-dog look?"

Adam greeted me with those words. He was tucked away in his pocket, a tiny lantern by one foot giving off only enough light to flood the area with eerie shadows.

"Can you really see my face, or are you just guessing?"

"Hell yes, I can see it," he exclaimed. "I can see what I want to see."

And he held up his hands and cackled in that weird way I'd become accustomed to.

"Don't be strange, Adam. I'm feeling pretty shitty."

"Sit down and we can feel shitty together. You tell me what you're feeling shitty about, and I'll tell you what I'm feeling shitty about. That's what friends are for."

Sounded like he was making fun of me.

"Go to hell," I said.

"Hey, I'm serious."

Then I could see that he was. He rocked back and forth very slowly. Seemed nervous. Well, I started telling him about Andrea, though he interrupted me once to push a bag of stale fig newtons under my nose. I nibbled on one; Adam stuffed about four in those chimpanzee cheeks of his.

"Can you believe she'd go out with that sleazeball?" I said.

Through his mouthful of fig newtons, he muttered, "Whatcha gonna do 'bout it?"

"Do about it?"

Adam swallowed.

He got real excited all of a sudden.

"Yeah, you know, maybe beat the shit out of him or slash his tires or something. Can't let him get away with dating our girl."

"*Our* girl?" I whispered.

It was a curious thing for him to say.

I wanted to get up and leave my friend right that second. I wished I hadn't said anything about Andrea's date.

"Are you afflicted, man?" I exclaimed. "Brian Gunnellson plays football. He went to the Junior Olympics in wrestling. He lifts weights. He'd tear me into confetti. Get real."

Adam rocked back and cackled.

When he had finished, he leaned close to me and said, "Not with me helping you."

There was a look on his face I'd never seen before. I would see it again in the weeks to come, though. As I stared at him, only one thought flashed into my mind.

You're not Adam.

But, of course, it was.

"Forget it," I said. "I'm not fighting Gunnellson. I'm dumb sometimes—not silly-ass crazy."

"I told you I'd help. Listen, let's go over to Andrea's and wait around for him to bring her home. Tell him this is the last time he takes out our girl."

There was that phrase again. God almighty, it gave me a funny feeling.

Then an idea hit me—not Adam's exactly—but something in his suggestion.

"I'm gonna go apologize to her," I exclaimed.

"What? Why would you do that? She's dating that guy

154

to make us jealous. Don't apologize to her."

"No, . . . I've been acting like a big-time jerk. I'm gonna go apologize to her."

"Let me ride over there with you."

"Adam . . . damn, this is private and personal."

"Think about it, Rob. I oughtta be there in case Gunnellson gets mad and kicks a lung out of you. Come on . . . please. I won't be in your way."

I reached a new level of stupidity when I allowed Adam to climb on my bike behind me. For some insane reason I was bound and determined to talk to Andrea that night. Nothing could change my mind.

We waited by the big elm in front of Andrea's house from about ten o'clock until close to midnight. A streetlamp bathed the scene. Bored, Adam scurried up the tree—he's a fantastic tree climber—and I stood around feeling sorry for myself and envisioning that my girl parked somewhere making out with a scuzzy guy. I also rehearsed my apology.

Twice I almost decided to abandon my idiotic plan.

Stubbornness won out.

"He's coming. I hear his car," Adam called out from somewhere up in the elm.

My tongue got real thick.

As the *varoom* of Gunnellson's Camaro drew closer, I tried to firm up my resolve. Somewhere in the elm, Adam cackled.

"Remember, you promised to stay out of this?" I yelled up at him.

He didn't respond.

Car lights flooded the scene; I pressed myself against the trunk of the tree. Then I realized that my bike was in plain sight. When Gunnellson switched off his engine and lights, I stepped forward, looping toward Andrea's side.

From that point on, things moved at weird speeds—sometimes incredibly slow, but with a crystal sharpness—sometimes fast with speech slurred and actions blurred.

155

"What on earth are you doing here?" Andrea snapped at me.

She looked terrific. I felt like my heart must have been enlarged to the size of a football.

She had rolled down her window halfway; she seemed embarrassed and puzzled and angry—and maybe even scared—all at the same time.

"I want to apologize to you."

I bet I sounded about like a third grader.

"Rob, please go home. We can talk tomorrow."

There was an odd pleading in her voice that gave me hope.

Then Gunnellson leaned over and ducked his head so that he could see me.

"What can we do for you, Rembrandt? It's awful late for little boys to be up, isn't it?"

"Brian, this is none of your business. It's between me and Andrea."

That's when things really got fuzzy.

I heard Andrea say, "Please, Rob. This is humiliating."

Her words seemed to float up into the elm like bubbles.

Then I heard Gunnellson's door slam.

"I'm gonna ask you just once to get your ass outta here, Rembrandt. If you leave, fine . . . if you don't, I'm gonna shove your face into that tree. Right through the bark."

And I thought to myself: *Rob, how could you have done this?*

Is there some law of adolescence that says every fifteen-year-old boy has to make an absolute and total fool of himself at least once a month? I believe there must be.

I sorta froze.

Something dropped heavily out of the night.

I hoped I was dreaming . . . you know, that this was all just a bad dream.

I heard Gunnellson swear. Andrea screamed.

Adam hit the pavement and rolled to his feet. He

156

pounded his fists on the hood of the Camaro, and I seemed to lose all feeling in my body from about the neck down.

"Rob and I got some business with you, Mr. Scumbucket," Adam exclaimed.

There was a lot of craziness in his eyes; the streetlamp captured glints of it.

"Adam, Jesus, no," I whispered hopelessly.

Gunnellson was dumbfounded.

Adam continued. "You go ahead and say goodnight to our girl. Then, sleazenuts, you haul your ass downtown and we'll teach you a lesson 'bout stepping into somebody else's territory. Come on, Rob. We'll be waiting for you, Gunnellbutt."

I've never fainted in my life, though once when the school nurse was drawing up blood tests, I got woozy. I believe if I hadn't been scared out of my mind, I might have fainted right there on the spot.

I ran—more like leaped—to my bike.

I don't remember what Gunnellson yelled at us.

I don't even remember Adam jumping on behind me.

Survival.

That was my only thought.

God almighty, I realized that certain death or at least dismemberment was at hand.

I made that bike of mine hop. Adam held on for dear life.

Blindly I roared a couple of blocks away before skidding into the small gravel parking lot of the Warrior Stand Christian Church.

"Have you lost your goddamn mind!" I screamed at Adam over the rough idle of the bike.

He cackled.

"Stop it!" I shouted. "If we get out of this without Gunnellson killing us, we'll be damn, damn lucky. What's wrong with you?"

Adam dismounted, reached past my arm, and turned off the key.

I couldn't believe how fast my heart was beating.

157

"Calm down, ole buddy. Everything's cool."

My friend—my *demented* friend—leaned onto the handlebars and smiled through the darkness.

And I said, "Gunnellson won't let us get away with this. We won't be able to hide from him forever. He'll get us, Adam. I'm real damn sure of that. Oh, man, we're dead meat. Dead meat. Do you understand that?"

I must have sounded kinda hysterical.

"Hey," he replied, "Gunnellbutt's harmless. He wouldn't stoop so low as to beat the hell out of a blind kid. Would blow his reputation."

"Yeah, well remember . . . *I'm* not blind. So it won't hurt his reputation a dime to beat the hell out of me."

Adam laughed and did a funny little dance and chattered like, well . . . like a chimpanzee.

"I can handle the guy," he exclaimed. "Ole Gunnellbutt."

I winced.

"Oh, Jesus . . . we are dead."

Then I gestured for him to get back on the bike.

"I'm taking you home," I said.

I took the long way from the church, angling to the west of Main Street, hoping to reach the railroad tracks and speed out of town sight unseen. The plan worked until we turned south.

Then I heard it.

The thrum-thrum of a turbocharger.

Gunnellson apparently had been waiting by the old hotel. I never saw his car. He spun out and laid rubber on the deserted main street.

A small cry escaped my throat. I squeezed off second and third gears. Adam laughed wildly, maniacally.

It was futile. No way we could outrun an angry Camaro.

The suction blast when he passed us nearly toppled the bike. His taillights flashed a hot neonlike jangle; tires squealed and smoked as he jerked the powerful automobile around about fifty yards ahead of us.

Then he came right at us. I hugged the shoulder of the

158

road, but at the last second, I chickened out and swerved for the ditch. I felt Adam release his hold and fly free of the bike, crashing onto his shoulder. The bike recoiled at the bottom of the ditch and pinned me down like a wrestler would. I managed to squirm free, my leg on fire from the stab of a broken spoke.

Gunnellson loomed at the top of the ditch.

And it torched a fury in me.

"Goddamn you," I cried.

Out of control, flailing, cursing, I launched myself at him.

I'm afraid the rest of the scene was rather predictable. My part of it, at least. Somehow my forehead, with Gunnellson's help I believe, rammed into the side of the Camaro. I remember a fist striking the side of my head and one driving into my stomach. I remember being shoved down, scraping across some loose chat.

Mostly, I remember sorta lifting free of my body. I viewed the remainder of the scene from about ten or fifteen feet above it. Here's what I saw, or perhaps imagined:

Rubbing his shoulder, Adam staggered up from the ditch.

"Go on home," Gunnellson yelled at him. "I don't want to have to hurt you. Look at your friend."

Adam made this weird chattering sound. I could hear it even over the growl of the Camaro. And I could see my body crumpled there by the side of the road.

"Go on home," Gunnellson repeated, but as Adam continued to approach him, he raised his fists defensively.

Then another sound came from Adam.

Man, it was awful. Like the howl of some wounded animal.

Gunnellson firmed up his stance. And swung at Adam's head.

I seemed to hear the snap before I saw what happened. With lightning reflexes, Adam caught Gunnellson's fist and wrenched it around—as if Gunnellson's fist were a doorknob and Adam was turning it to open a door.

Snap.

The wristbone.

Gunnellson screamed.

From town, a car appeared.

I felt myself being pulled back into my body. I heard the Camaro tear away.

And Adam laugh.

Maybe nobody can ever know what really occurred then. Brian Gunnellson and his broken wrist and his journey out of town toward Council Grove. But now I think I can speculate, can imagine the scene as he accelerated just before reaching the Rock Creek bridge. . . .

He steered with his left hand; the right wrist flamed.

He felt chilled; his teeth chattered. The events of only minutes ago were excerpts, vague splices from some movie he thought he might have seen on television.

He kept his eyes on the road.

Blackness rushed by on both sides of the car.

Seventy miles an hour, cresting the hills, an amusement ride gathering momentum.

Eyes fastened to the road. Concentration intense.

A growing, crawling, searching fear.

He shivered.

But could not look at the presence in the other seat.

It was simply a shadow; perhaps a phantom of nothing at all lodged in his peripheral vision.

"Stay away from me," he whispered, still not looking at the presence.

Chilled, but sweating. Mouth and throat dry.

He sensed the hand reaching toward him.

Couldn't avoid it.

Fingers touched his neck, pressed and spread onto his jaw.

"Get back," he roared, angry, frightened.

160

Down the hill onto Rock Creek bridge.

Accelerator to the floor.

A struggle against the pressure crushing his throat.

His hands left the steering wheel.

The Camaro drifted right.

Brian Gunnellson managed one final, strangled scream and then hurtled into the darkness waiting below.

Impact. Fireball.

And the night flared.

PART THREE:

THE CROSS OF
DARK FORTUNE

CHAPTER 12

I woke to Leah's smile.

"How you feel?" she whispered.

Truth is, I couldn't feel a thing. I was in my own bed, but I couldn't remember how I got there. I shifted, and tried to speak; my mouth and lips were so dry that no words dribbled out.

The movement awakened pain—a throb on one side of my head, a scream of protest from my stomach muscles.

"Just relax, Rob," said Leah.

I finally managed a word as she studied my face.

"Water."

"Sure. I'll get you some."

While she was gone, pieces of the night before pressed into place as if an invisible hand were completing a jigsaw puzzle of events in my head.

I leaned forward and drank the water.

My throat opened. I coughed. My head and stomach reminded me not to move too quickly.

Suddenly I wondered what Leah knew. I guessed that someone had told her about the fight. And beyond the fight, I knew nothing. Not then.

"You probably think I'm real stupid," I mumbled.

She smiled weakly and shook her head.

"Rob," she said, "about last night. . . ."

"Dumb, I know. Real dumb." I hesitated, then asked, "How's Adam?"

"Oh, he's fine. I'm sure he's been told."

Her last words there didn't fit. Like odd-shaped pieces

of that puzzle in my head, they wouldn't fit no matter which way that invisible hand turned them.

"Been told? Adam's been told?"

She reached forward and smoothed my cheek. Her hand smelled of some kind of lotion. Usually she smelled a lot like a hospital.

"There was a bad accident last night," she began.

More words that didn't fit.

"Something happen to Adam?"

"No . . . Adam's fine, I believe. It's Brian Gunnellson."

Once again I heard that snap. Snap. The ugly sound of his wrist breaking. A doorknob turning.

"He had it coming," I said. "Wasn't Adam's fault. Brian had it coming. Just his wrist. Keep him out of basketball a few weeks, maybe."

Talking so much at one time sorta dizzied me.

Saliva went dry.

Leah had an almost comically serious look on her face. I glanced away, then up at the ceiling. Before she could speak, I said, "Andrea's real upset. I'll talk to her. I will."

My sister grasped my hand and squeezed it. I looked at her, and she took a deep breath and gathered herself.

"Rob, Brian Gunnellson was killed last night. His car ran off Rock Creek bridge. More than likely, he was killed instantly."

That invisible hand inside my head scattered the puzzle pieces as a mischievous child might.

"Why would you say that about Brian?"

"Because it happened, Rob. I'm very, very sorry. But it happened. It's tragic."

"Brian Gunnellson?"

She talked on for several minutes. The words failed to register.

A funny cold spot in the pit of my stomach began sending out chilly vibrations.

Adam? My God, Adam. What's going on?

Muttering something about leaving me alone, Leah slipped out of my room.

She insisted that I stay in bed; I didn't argue. In fact, I slept until mid-afternoon, putting Brian Gunnellson's death out of my thoughts, it seemed. Maybe I hadn't accepted it as the truth yet.

Around two-thirty or three, a parade of visitors began. First, there was a deputy from the sheriff's office—just some routine questions about the Gunnellson incident. I told him exactly what I remembered, and he said not to worry because there appeared to be no criminal intent, or something to that effect. He was nice. Apparently not suspicious.

Doc Newton followed him. He joked with me, telling me I'd probably live. Then turned a notch more serious.

"Trouble seems to follow you and Adam like a shadow," he said.

He was driving at something. Hard to tell what.

"All my fault," I admitted. "And Adam, you see, he was just being . . . being protective."

"I think your friend needs help."

"Help. What do you mean? What kind of help?"

"Professional. Psychiatric help. That's what I'd suggest."

"For Adam? You saying he's going crazy or losing his mind?"

I felt a hot rush of emotions—anger, fear, confusion—all at once.

"I've seen enough, heard enough to believe Adam could profit from counseling. He could become dangerous to himself. Perhaps become suicidal. Could become dangerous to others as well."

I shook my head.

"Suicide?" It had a bitter taste to it. "No, he would never do that. He would never hurt . . . I mean somebody would have to provoke something, you know. You're wrong about him."

"I hope so. I truly do."

When Doc Newton left, my head was spinning.

He was a man who always said much less than he knew.

I got scared, real scared without even understanding

167

the source of the fear. But it seemed an odd coincidence that not thirty minutes later Pudge and Adam showed up at my door.

"Howdy, son," Pudge greeted me. "You gonna be all right?"

I nodded.

Adam came to the bed and laid a hand on my shoulder.

"How'd it feel to have the hell beat outta ya?"

I laughed.

"Pretty damn shitty."

It felt good to have him there. Strange, but my head and stomach suddenly didn't hurt as much.

Pudge hooked his thumbs in his belt; I could tell he was nervous.

"Say, they uh . . . they towed that Gunnellson boy's hotrod car to the salvage. I'll guaran-damn-tee ya it's a sight. Frame twisted liked barbed wire. Yeah, it's a blessed sight."

There was a brief silence.

Then Adam said, "We don't much feel sorry for him, do we, Rob?"

"Don't hardly be no call to talk like that, son," Pudge responded.

"Can't decide what I feel," I said. I searched Adam's face. His eyes wandered. "I just don't understand what happened."

"Nobody does," he said. "A sheriff's deputy, he told me it looked like an accident plain and simple."

"It was the boy's time," Pudge added. "Old bronc rider's saying—when your number is up, it's up. The Man upstairs has got it planned. It was that boy's time."

Minutes later, they left. I forgot to ask Adam about his shoulder; he didn't appear to favor it. I had to miss my Saturday evening shift at the Arrowhead.

I thought about calling Andrea. Decided against it. Took some of the pills Doc Newton gave me. Next thing I knew it was Sunday morning.

Leah had stayed home from her midnight shift, declaring that the "zoo" would have to operate without her. I wished that she hadn't stuck around just because of me. I was feeling much better. Got up and dressed and started to call Andrea probably five or six times. Couldn't imagine what I'd say to her. Sorta hoped she would call me.

There was one thing I definitely hadn't hoped for.

Detective Lawrence came for our Sunday meal.

That took me by surprise, though once the three of us sat down at the table I could tell how much Leah liked him. And I guess maybe he liked her, too.

"Finding any clues about who killed Kristin Kelley?" I asked him.

"Rob," Leah exclaimed, "that's not Sunday dinner conversation."

I sorta shrugged and mumbled an apology.

"A few," he replied.

So I took that as an indication he didn't mind the topic. "You think it was Don Slocumb or maybe Karl Dodd?"

Following a swallow of green beans, he said, "I've found nothing that suggests any specific person."

Leah managed to shift the conversation to something more pleasant until after dinner. Over a piece of rhubarb pie, Lawrence said, "It's curious to me how you and your friend, Adam, have had the misfortune of being so close to two separate tragedies."

The comment hit me wrong.

Lawrence was sounding a little like Doc Newton.

"What's that supposed to mean?" I snapped.

Leah glared at me. Lawrence cautiously surveyed my face before responding.

"In my line of work, a person trains himself to notice such things. It's not meant to *mean* anything."

Thankfully, he chose to leave soon after dinner, explaining that his friend, Hugh Kelley, was having terrific difficulties coping with the death of his daughter and that he had asked Lawrence to come to Independence, Missouri and spend a few days.

Leah said it was probably a good idea for him to lend

169

some emotional support to his friend.

Evening rolled around. All I could think about was calling Andrea. I didn't. Chickened out.

During the next week, I occasionally thought about Lawrence, too. And I wondered why I was starting to dislike him so much. . . .

Clay Lawrence had intended to stay in Independence for no more than a few days, but those days stretched to nearly a week. By Friday, Hugh Kelley agreed that his grief required professional attention.

The two of them had tried all week—talking, crying some, venting anger—yet the grief remained, hard and solid and stubborn. Local contacts put Lawrence in touch with a victims of violent crimes support group. Hugh Kelley reluctantly joined.

But as Lawrence readied to return to Warrior Stand, his long-time friend spoke to him from the bottom of his sorrow.

"Clay, I won't ask you to stay on the case. I have no right to ask you to chase after a phantom. Can't bring her back. Nothing can bring Kristin back."

"You trying to fire me, Hugh?"

"No . . . no, but I don't want you out there wasting your time. He's gonna get away. Her killer. I feel it in my guts. Just the way it is."

"Look, you're paying me to do a job, and I've started it and I damn well plan to finish it. My job won't be over until I'm standing by the dead body of her murderer. I'm more determined than ever to get that job done."

Kelley, locked in his quiet misery, sought out his younger friend's eyes.

"Is he there? Could the bastard still be around that town somewhere? Is that your hunch?"

"More than a hunch. I *know* it just as certainly as I'm here in the flesh. It's gonna come down to which of us survives—him or me. He's trying to scare me off—you know me, Hugh. I won't scare easily. Besides, this one's for Kristin. Couldn't live with myself if I didn't finish what I've started."

Kelley shook his hand and said goodbye and one more thing: "Be careful."

It was a long drive from Independence to Warrior Stand, meandering through two Kansas Citys, then a mostly straight route of interstate. Such a road affords a man plenty of time to think.

Hugh Kelley hadn't asked how he knew the killer continued to haunt Warrior Stand. Lawrence had prepared his story; it was bizarre, every bit as strange as what he had encountered in the case of the Granite Heights child murderer.

Kristin Kelley's murderer was slick.

He had announced his presence on several occasions to Lawrence. Notes. A drawing. Stalking him while he jogged the vacant, dusty streets of Warrior Stand. Whoever it was, he had easy access to the apartment, and he was a master at not being noticed, at not raising suspicion.

Twice Lawrence had discovered slips of paper on his pillow—"I'm here," one exclaimed in a sweeping, rather beautiful hand—"I'm watching you!" said another. One note included a drawing, a skilled drawing of a bear standing on its hind legs.

And on the Sunday he had left to visit Hugh Kelley, he found a large sheet of sketchpad paper tacked above his bed. Again, a flowing hand had styled a peculiar message:

"March will search, April will try,
And May will tell if you live or die."

A prank? Mischievous boys? Leah's kid brother?

His intuition told him *no*—a dangerous cat-and-mouse game was under way.

It could have only one conclusion.

Lawrence concentrated on the road.

Time swallowed up the miles.

At a rest stop he called Leah, catching her before she

171

left for her Friday night shift. Her voice warmed his cold thoughts; he told her he would be in Warrior Stand within the hour.

She sounded glad. He hoped to see her tomorrow.

When he reached his destination, he cautiously parked behind the Sunset House; it had become a habit to hide the rental car and enter as secretly as possible.

Around front, he found the door open. Accordingly, he drew his revolver and kept himself alert as he stepped into the dark lobby and proceeded upstairs. His apartment door was ajar; light spilled through it.

He braced himself, revolver ready.

Before he nudged open the door with his foot, he heard someone humming. Puzzled, he watched the door swing to one side.

"Who's here?" he exclaimed.

Leah Dalton wheeled to face him, dustrag in hand.

"Clay! Oh, I didn't hear you come up the stairs."

Relieved, he lowered the gun.

Her smile flickered away, but then he went to her, feeling a need to hold her, to hold some part of the world capable of warmth and love. They talked, and when she left for work, she promised to return early Saturday morning.

She arrived before dawn. And she stayed, realizing the risk. People would see her car even though she parked a block away. People would talk.

"I need you here with me," he told her.

"No," she said, "I'm the one who needs you. The loneliness . . . this town—it's a good town, but not if you're alone. I love Rob, and I don't regret holding onto the farmstead so he would have a place. It's just that life seems always out of reach. Women I know my age are married—some not happily—but their lives have some kind of . . . of texture or substance. Sometimes when I get home from work I feel totally empty."

"I know the feeling," he murmured.

"I'm not asking much of you, Clay. I understand, or I think I do, the kind of life you've chosen. There's no

172

room for a wife in it. Just please take away some of the emptiness."

In the warmth and closeness of their naked bodies, some of that emptiness dissolved. And they made love, and outside a cold and windy, yet sunny day emerged.

Before she left, Leah asked him one question: "If you catch the one . . . Kristin Kelley's murderer, what will happen to him? A death sentence? Life in prison? I want to know what you would see as justice."

He touched her cheek, studied her face.

He paused as if searching for the right words. Then he shook his head.

"If and when I catch him, there'll be no trial. I've promised Hugh Kelley. I've promised myself. The only justice is to ensure that her murderer is dead. A blood revenge. It's not morally right, I suppose. But in my own mind, it's just."

She said nothing.

They parted, and the emptiness returned.

You wouldn't believe the rumors going around school all week. Kids were saying that Adam had put some kind of "spell" on Brian Gunnellson, causing his car to go out of control. Others hinted that he and Andrea and I had linked up in a satanic power pact to kill Brian. Incredible stuff.

But it got to me. My grades suffered. And I gave up on completing the tornado mural. Friendly teachers tried to help. Tough as things were for me, I could see they were even tougher for Adam and Andrea—especially for Andrea. Many of her girlfriends began sorta shunning her. In fact, one consequence of the whole matter was that the three of us had been driven closer together.

We had each other.

The rest of the world seemed to be rejecting us.

We survived the nightmare at school, quietly jubilant to see the Thanksgiving break arrive. As usual, Joe and Molly Helms prepared a big dinner at their home, closing

173

the restaurant for the day. They invited me and Leah and Pudge, Doc Newton and his wife, and the Dodds, though Karl, thank goodness, didn't come. They also invited Clay Lawrence.

I thought it would be a pretty dreary dinner, but as it turned out, it wasn't so bad. Adam kept his distance from Lawrence, but otherwise everybody seemed to enjoy themselves. Lots of good food.

Before we all went our separate ways, Adam asked Andrea and me to meet him up at the cemetery the next day. Said it was real important. We had a light snow Thanksgiving evening; most of it had melted off by the following afternoon.

"What's going to happen, Rob? The school year . . . I feel like it's been ruined already. I wish I didn't have to go back. I hate it. I hate what everybody's thinking about us."

We huddled between a couple of the older, taller headstones, our backs turned against the north wind. The sun was deceptively bright; all its warmth seemed to be deflected by the wind.

I put my arm around Andrea; I felt insecure.

"I'd like . . . you know, I'd like for my folks to be alive," I said. "I'd like to have my dad to talk to. He could always make it sound like no problem was so bad, you know. Damn, I miss him."

I just about cried.

Andrea hugged me and kissed my face right by my eye.

"Sorry we've been fighting," she said. "If I hadn't gotten mad at you, I wouldn't have gone out with . . . with Brian and none of this would have happened."

"More my fault than yours. And I shouldn't have let Adam get involved."

We kept talking like that for awhile as if we were trying to siphon off our guilt. Pretty childish maybe. It was hard to feel adult. Hard to take a rational, mature look at things.

174

Reason didn't fit all that we were experiencing.

We held each other for I don't know how long before I saw a dark speck moving up the slope below us. Suddenly, inexplicably, I hated the sight of our friend probing his way toward the cemetery.

"Adam's coming," I whispered to Andrea.

She turned so that she could see him approach.

"He's been our friend for a long time," she murmured.

It was a strange comment, I thought. Thinking back on it now, I guess it set the scene. That meeting at the cemetery—it was based upon friendship and a shared understanding that we would help each other.

Something else: Andrea's comment softened my hatred.

"Yeah," I said, "like forever."

Stumbling and fumbling along, Adam called out, "Hey, you guys, this is just like old times, ain't it?"

Old times.

The old times were gone as far I was concerned; the times we had played for hours in the cottonwood or roamed the surrounding pastures, innocent, unaware that the future might bring darkness.

"Come get out of the wind," said Andrea.

As Adam hunkered down beside us, he slipped something into his pocket.

"What was that?" Andrea prodded.

"Oh, nothin' much. I'll show you later."

He rubbed those big hands of his together, and I could have sworn the air in our little triangle heated up ten degrees. Probably my imagination.

"What took you so long to get here?" I asked him.

His jaw stiffened, and I could hear him grind his back teeth.

"Lawrence," he hissed. "Son-of-a-bitch. Sorry for swearing, Andy, but the guy's after me. He was out to Pudge's snoopin' around. I saw him and I told him to stay away from my place . . . you know, the Winnebago."

Andrea frowned.

"What do you mean, 'the guy's after me'?"

"He is. Has been ever since he got to town."

I had to chuckle at Adam's paranoia.

"Geez, man, you're talking off the wall. You hear what you're saying?"

His expression darkened; those heavy eyebrows touched as his forehead wrinkled.

"Never mind," he said. "Never mind about Lawrence."

He held his hands up to us, palms out.

"Never mind about anything but this," he added. "You guys gotta help me. Promise you'll help me get rid of this. Help me find a way or I'll have to kill myself."

Andrea glanced at me.

Disgusted at his overly serious display, I said, "God almighty, do you *have* to act so damn weird?"

"Wait, Rob. Let's hear him out. What do you mean, Adam? How can we help?"

"The night touch—it won't go away. It's gettin' worse. Most of the time I can't control it. Help me find somebody who can make it go away. I'm serious. I mean it. I can't stand it much longer."

"We will," said Andrea. "We want to help. We just don't know how."

"I think he ought to see a psychiatrist," I said.

Adam lowered his head and toyed nervously with his hands.

"No," he muttered, "not that."

"Maybe Rob's right in part," said Andrea. "Maybe a lot of this is in your mind."

I was glad she didn't offer some theory hatched out of *National Enquirer*.

Then Adam said something which changed the conversation dramatically.

"Brian Gunnellson being dead's not just in my mind. That's real. That happened."

He paused to survey our faces.

"And *I* caused it. *I* made him wreck his car."

"Stop that!" Andrea shrieked.

She scrambled to her feet.

176

"I mean it, Adam. Don't say things like that," she exclaimed.

Snap.

Suddenly I heard that familiar sound. Brian Gunnellson's wrist.

I felt as if I were in the center of a tiny but furious stormwind, a howling blizzard which encased me.

I believed him.

I recalled also the night with Andrea at Pudge's—the strangling shadow—it was the most incredible realization I'd ever had, but in that moment I believed that Adam just might—somehow, some way—have caused the death of Brian Gunnellson.

Adam followed the sound of Andrea; he was agitated, very upset.

"Andy? . . . Andy, I'm not lying. Don't walk away from me. Rob? Where's she going? Rob, say something to her. There's more I got to tell. Bring her back."

She had wandered down to the cottonwood. I went after her.

"I think we better listen to him, Andrea. I got a feeling he's handing us the truth."

"Maybe I don't want to hear the truth," she whispered.

But she took my hand, and I led her to Adam.

We sat down, our bodies leaning forward to seal off some of the wind.

"I'm sorry, Andy, to have to tell you these things, but you guys are all I've got. If I told my mother all this, she'd claim the devil had possessed me. And Pudge, he can't help none. Not really."

Andrea was quiet.

So I said, "We'll help. Problem is . . . we're not sure how to."

Adam fidgeted with something in his pocket.

"I got one more thing to confess," he said.

That imaginary blizzard returned, and I was suddenly lost in its icy swirl and the awful howl of its wind. I sensed what was coming.

Adam took a deep breath.

"I think I'm responsible," he began. "I mean . . . I believe the night touch . . . killed the Kelley woman. Kristin Kelley."

Andrea's reaction scared me because it was no reaction at all. She said nothing. Her face never changed.

I turned my attention to Adam.

"How could it have happened? You were mad at Brian . . . but Kristin Kelley . . . what set off the night touch?"

Hearing my own words, I realized that I was believing the unbelievable—that Adam had a supernatural power which could kill another human being.

"Right before she drove away that night," said Adam, "she thanked me for bringing her camera to her. She grabbed my hand . . . and somehow that triggered it. The part of the night touch I can't always control. She triggered it by grabbing my hand. That's all I can figure."

The wind whistled mournfully around us.

Andrea stared at the ground.

I heard myself say, "Can you be sure, Adam? Beyond a shadow of a doubt . . . can you be sure?"

"Hold out your hand," he said.

I glanced at Andrea. Tears were rolling down her cheeks.

My hand shook.

My eyes met Adam's.

And into the palm of my hand he placed a gold necklace with the Kansas State wildcat figurine at one end of it.

CHAPTER 13

I rocked on Midnight, the back and forth motion calming to me.

Adam's revelation that afternoon buzzed around in my head; there was no escape from it. I sought out the barn so that I could think.

I was worried about Andrea. You see, Leah and Detective Lawrence invited her and me to go on a double date with them to Emporia—go out to eat and then take in a movie. Now I wasn't wild about the idea of being around Lawrence—didn't much like him getting so close to Leah—but a night away from Warrior Stand could have done us some good. Andrea said she'd rather not go.

Below her surface vulnerability, I had to admit that Andrea can be tough. If she's backed into a corner, she'll fight. Adam's news had shocked her; she would be determined, though, to help him. But how?

As I rode Midnight's strong, hedgepost body, I gripped my dad's revolver and let my thoughts shift to Adam. Was our friend really a murderer? And if we helped him, wasn't that a crime, too? Did Andrea and I realize what we were getting into?

Well, to me, Adam would never fit in the same category with psychopathic killers. No way. . . . And yet I couldn't dismiss my intuitions about the deaths of Kristin Kelley and Brian Gunnellson. Something very strange had occurred. Strange and deadly.

I stared down at the revolver and Adam's voice echoed through my memory.

. . . if someday for some reason you had to shoot me . . . could you do it?

. . . could you do it?

. . . could you do it?

"Stop!" I yelled. Then I tossed the revolver into the straw.

When I got hold of myself again, I pursued the same old question:

Why Adam?

What kind of a universe allowed a kid who had already suffered blindness to be given such a weird and horrifying thing?

Another voice. Another echo of memory. It was as if some deeper layer of my mind was answering the questions I was asking. This time it was Doc Newton's voice.

I've come to believe there are people who . . . well, they seem to draw strangeness to them.

He had lumped Adam together with Willa Snagovia, Weird Willa.

Who could tell? Maybe his theory was correct—Adam had drawn the strangeness.

The next morning, a Saturday, I went to talk to my friend; I found him at Pudge's in his Winnebago. He had sorta barricaded himself behind a stack of seats he had ripped out of junked cars.

As I approached the area, I smelled smoke.

"Adam, what in the hell are you burning?"

I heard his familiar cackle; that meant he wasn't in one of his dark, dark moods.

"Got me a new trick," he called out. "Come see it, man. It's neater than shit."

I had to laugh at that.

"Shit's not neat," I exclaimed as I climbed over the barricade.

Adam had his hands spread over a small flame rising up from a pile of seat stuffings. I hunkered down beside him;

180

the smoke burned my eyes. Didn't seem to bother Adam.

"I don't need matches to start a fire," he said. "Watch this."

He snuffed out the flame and fanned away the excess smoke. Next, he tore out a couple handfuls of seat stuffing—some cottony-looking material—and heaped it in a pile. Then he glanced at me and grinned.

"I'd like to see a Boy Scout do this," he said.

He lapsed into what appeared to be some intense moments of concentration, ending when he rubbed his hands in a quick, circular motion over the heap.

Fire suddenly mushroomed like a tiny, tiny atomic bomb.

"Whoa! Damn, that's something!" I exclaimed.

"And you never know when bein' able to do that could come in handy."

"Yeah, I guess you're right."

I watched the heap burn down, mesmerized by it, dreamingly considering the implication of still another night touch talent.

I suppose it was curiosity. Like they say, curiosity killed the cat, but there was one particular night touch talent I just had to ask about. I had seen most of what it could do: I knew, for example, that when Adam concentrated, it could help him see—it gave him sight— not exactly a physical sight, but a sight nevertheless; and I had seen its effect upon electricity and upon Adam's ability to play a musical instrument. It allowed him, as well, to have visions and to draw as if he had practiced for years.

Yet, it was the darkest, most violent talent of his night touch which intrigued me most.

As Adam fanned away the remaining wisps of smoke, I said, "Will you show me how you do it? The thing that kills. You know, the shadow hand that tried to strangle me once and that, well . . ."

My voice trailed off into almost a whisper.

At first, Adam pretended that he hadn't heard me.

"You see my latest drawing?" he asked.

181

I shook my head, inwardly determined I wouldn't back away from my request.

"This woman, she's important somehow. She and the Saturn Man and the bear. I've dreamed about her for a week or so."

He handed me a finely detailed sketch of a woman's face, a very fat Indian woman, high-mounded cheekbones, wise yet warm dark eyes.

"What do you make of her?"

I just shrugged.

"Maybe it was somebody who came into the Arrowhead."

I knew it wasn't.

He studied the drawing for several seconds, then set it aside.

"Why, Rob? Why do you want to see it? It destroys."

I had no answer for him. Not a good one anyway.

"To help me understand, you know, what is is . . . how it works."

"How it kills?"

I guess he had me there. Morbid curiosity.

Then he said, "Move back this way from the seats."

We crawled to the rear of the gutted Winnebago, some thirty or forty feet from the barricade of car seats.

"I can't promise what this'll do, Rob," he added. "You still want me to do it?"

A claw of fear raked down my backbone, but I nodded.

He motioned for me to give him some room. He squatted in a duckwalk stance, closed his eyes, and clasped his hands together—the hands rested on his knees.

It took maybe twenty seconds for something to happen.

When the shadow thing broke free of him, he crashed to the floor. I tensed up and scooted on my bottom a few feet farther away.

I felt something like anger in the air; that sounds crazy, I know. It's the only way I can describe it—anger like smoke or a fog drifting out from my friend.

Hands still clasped, he raised them kind of like you might aim a revolver. His teeth clicked, and his lips curled back in a rictus smile.

And those seats forming the barricade appeared to explode.

It was like those film clips you see of hungry sharks feeding on chunks of meat; the car seats were being ripped and tossed by some invisible force—an invisible shark swimming in a sea of anger. To me it was an absolutely terrifying scene.

The worst part came at the end after the seats had been destroyed—not just torn, but crushed and bent as well. At that point, something shadowy and formless drove into Adam's body like a piece of elastic snapping back from pressure exerted upon it.

Adam jerked and cried out. He toppled over; not a muscle moved.

Heart pounding, I stayed away from him for a few seconds. Then I swallowed my fear and leaned down close by his shoulder.

"You okay, man?"

Slowly, very slowly, he revived, and I kept repeating my question.

Finally, he sorta smiled.

"No, you silly son-of-a bitch . . . I'm not."

I had to chuckle nervously about the stupidity of my question.

And Adam managed to laugh pretty hard; he rolled on the floor, in fact. Laughed until I could see tears in his eyes. He inched his way toward me.

Suddenly his voice was scratchy and tear-lined.

"I'm a murderer, Rob. A cold-blooded murderer."

The rapid shift of his emotional state threw me off balance. I looked into his pathetic face, scrambling to regain myself.

"No. No, you're not."

"I'll go to prison," he whispered. "Or else they'll lock me away in a nuthouse forever. Criminally insane, you know. That's what they call it."

183

"You're not a murderer," I insisted. "You never planned to kill anyone. It wasn't you . . . you weren't responsible for what happened."

He stared at his hands.

"Lawrence . . . he's gonna get me."

"No. He can't know. Nobody but you, me and Andrea could know. Not even Pudge. And they couldn't prove you did it. Nobody could prove it, Adam. Nobody would believe the whole thing. They can't get you—Lawrence, the county sheriff—nobody."

As I spoke those words, I think I believed them. I sure wanted to.

More than that, I wanted Adam to believe them.

The Saturday evening shift at the Arrowhead moved at breakneck speed; Thanksgiving weekend traffic—lots of it. Adam and I didn't get a chance to eat supper till close to ten o'clock. Andrea wasn't working; her mother said she had asked to take the night off to visit a girlfriend. That sounded curious to me. What could she be up to?

I was dead tired by the time midnight rolled around. The temperature was dropping, and there was a spitting of snow—not flakes, but those tiny ice pellets about the size of a BB. They stung your face when the wind gusted.

Visions of a warm bed dancing in my head, I offered, as usual, to give Adam a ride home.

"Rob, I've got something I want to show you—something I had a dream about the other night. Out west of town. Something I've got to do."

"Is it really important? Man, if we stay out in this weather very long we'll freeze our asses off."

"Please. Yeah, it's important. Like I said—something I've got to do."

So we rode.

Somehow Adam knew the spot. I got a funny kind of tight feeling in my throat when we stopped alongside the highway.

"This is where they found Kristin Kelley," I exclaimed over the whine of the wind. But, of course, Adam knew that.

"She's still here," he said.

Damn, that gave me a weird feeling.

"You mean, like her ghost?"

He sorta shrugged, then said, "Watch."

So there in the darkness and the cold and the wind at the edge of the Flint Hills, my friend raised his hands, palms up, out to the sides of his body—and concentrated.

I can't honestly say that I saw much: A few minuscule lights—or were they pellets of ice?—gathered, swirled, shaped themselves into almost a human form, though it could have been my imagination.

Yet, I *felt* she was there. Near. Kristin Kelley. Her presence.

It was as weird as could be.

Then Adam started talking, a nonstop babble, rising to a shout at times. He was pleading for her forgiveness, I think. But he talked so fast, it sounded mostly as if he were speaking in tongues.

The whole episode couldn't have lasted more than a couple of minutes. When it was over, Adam seemed relieved. We got back on my motorbike and he directed me to the Rock Creek bridge. Truth is, I expected that.

The county had repaired the bridge railing through which Brian Gunnellson had crashed, but if you climbed down the slippery bank toward the muddy creek you could see the point of impact and other traces of the accident: scattered pieces of glass and metal and signs of an explosion and a burning.

A thin coating of ice slowed the meander of the creek. Having no light, we had to be careful not to slide into the water.

"I have to do this, Rob. It eases my mind some."

As Adam began his ritualistic concentration, I noticed a car slow near the bridge, but I gave it no further thought when the air around us took on a change. This time it was kind of like the smell close to where someone has shot off a bunch of fireworks.

185

Adam shifted into his babble.

It came from the depths of his soul—I could tell that.

And just as with the spot where Kristin Kelley was murdered, I felt something there by the soft, cold purl of that creek.

Brian Gunnellson.

He was there.

It was more than I could take. Before Adam finished, I started climbing my way back up toward the bridge. And I saw someone standing there by a car. And when the door opened, I was certain Detective Lawrence got in behind the wheel.

"You're up and about bright and early, aren't you? You have the curse, too?"

Clay Lawrence turned in the direction of the man's voice.

"Good morning, Jake," he muttered, then groped his way to the older man's booth. "What curse is that?"

Newton smiled.

"The one that won't let certain people sleep. I've had it for years. Never found a way to remove it."

"Physician heal thyself—isn't that how it works?"

"'Fraid not. Sit down here and join me. I'll buy you breakfast."

"Oh, thanks. Mighty generous of you. Maybe some hot tea and toast."

And so they settled into an easy conversation about weather, the economy, football, and everything else except what was occupying Lawrence's thoughts. The Arrowhead "regulars"—other lonely men who couldn't sleep—filed in to eat breakfast and wonder at the small miracle that another day had been granted to them.

"Say, how did those sound tests on that tape come out?" Newton asked eventually. "Or would you rather not talk about the case this morning?"

Lawrence gestured that it didn't matter.

"Nothing. I just can't figure it. Something was going

on in that car that night, but it's beyond me. Kristin was aware of something. *Something*."

"So there's nothing new?"

Lawrence hesitated.

"Just hunches."

Newton waited for the follow-up comment he knew was coming.

"I did some tracking last night," said Lawrence. "The boys—Rob and Adam—just a hunch, a suspicion from way out in left field."

He told Newton what he had witnessed below the Rock Creek bridge.

The older man let out a deep breath.

"Well, . . . I could say they were simply curious. But you're assuming it was more like a return to the scene of a crime."

"That's right," Lawrence replied softly. "Absolutely nothing of substance to go on. Not a speck of proof. Nothing but a nagging intuition that haunts me day and night."

"And what you really want to ask me is whether I think there's any way in hell you could be right?"

"Yeah. Any way in hell."

"You can rule out Rob Dalton. I'd stake my soul on that. But there's a certain strangeness which surrounds his friend. I couldn't begin to explain it in medical terms . . . an inexplicable darkness that bears watching. There's darkness in Adam Dodd."

"Adam!"

I beat on the sheet of plywood he had nailed across the only entrance to the Winnebago.

"Hurry, Rob. It's freezing."

Trying to generate some warmth, Andrea hopped up and down behind me, punching at me impatiently. Snowflakes dusted her hair and the top of her scarf.

"Looks like he's winterized his place," I said. "He's done this since yesterday."

187

I continued beating and yelling until I heard the plywood being pulled back.

"Whatchoo guys want?"

Adam's face appeared through the few inches of opening.

Pushing in front of me, Andrea said, "Let us in. We've got something we have to talk about. I've found somebody to help you get rid of the night touch."

He looked past her to me.

"That true, Rob?"

"She says it is. I don't know. She won't tell me who it is. Might as well let us in."

So he did.

It was an otherwise quiet Sunday afternoon. The snow, gaining intensity by late morning, had discouraged traffic; people were inside their homes taking naps or watching pro football games.

Gushing with excitement, Andrea had called and ordered me to pick her up and find Adam. She claimed she had good news for him. I was skeptical.

Inside the Winnebago it was surprisingly warm and cozy, though Adam had nothing even so much as a portable heater going. He had reconstructed his barricade of car seats; now it was a veritable fortress behind which we sat on the floor around a small lantern.

"Before you guys say anything," said Adam, "I've made up my mind to go away. Leave Warrior Stand and find the Saturn Man. And make him take back the night touch. But I can't go yet. My mother has her Christmas party in a couple of weeks. Another week after that and it'll be Christmas. Because of her I won't leave until maybe Christmas day or the day after."

He looked at us, wanting, I believe, for us to understand.

"You won't have to go," Andrea exclaimed. "That's what my good news is. You won't have to go. You can get rid of the night touch. I've found a way. I've found somebody who'll help you."

"This better hadn't be a dumb idea," I said.

Andrea turned on me. I suppose I had it coming.

"Listen, mister, it wasn't easy talking to her and arranging this. I'm trying to help Adam because he's my friend."

Adam stared toward her face; I couldn't be sure that he saw her distinctly, but there was no mistaking the love for her in his expression.

"Talking to *her?* Who's her?" Adam asked.

Glaring at me a final time, Andrea rocked forward, holding us in suspense.

"I didn't tell her your name," she began. "I made it like a hypothetical situation . . . of a friend being cursed or bewitched. And I asked her if she could remove the curse or whatever it is because it's making him do evil things. She said she thought possibly she could."

"Damn it, Andrea, who is it?" I growled.

"Yeah, Andy, I want to know," Adam agreed.

"Okay. Okay, I'll tell you, but . . . you have to kind of prepare yourself."

I was tempted to strangle her.

Adam's face was a mask of puzzlement.

She glanced from Adam to me and then back to Adam. My heart pounded high in my chest.

"Willa Snagovia," she said.

I was pretty certain I hadn't heard her right.

"No," said Adam. "No way."

"Who?" I whispered. "You didn't say 'Willa Snagovia,' did you?"

"Yes. Now wait a minute, both of you, wait."

But we howled our protests. Andrea calmly bore up under them.

"Grandpa Newton went with me," she said. "I talked to Willa; maybe she can help."

Then it hit me. It took a lot of courage to do what Andrea had done, even if Doc Newton had gone along. Made me feel like a real ass for knocking her plan. But I knew it was up to Adam.

"No way I can go in that house," he said. "That old woman's creepier than hell. I won't go. I won't do it."

I held back and let them have at one another.

Andrea persisted. Eventually she delivered the break-through line.

"For me, Adam. Won't you just please do it for me?"

His face melted like butter.

I could tell he wouldn't be able to turn her down, and, damn it all, I felt sorry for him, and yet I also sort of admired Andrea's grit.

"She won't do something real weird, will she?" said Adam.

Andrea set her jaw firmly.

"No. I promise she won't. Nothing weird."

And so that was that. Adam agreed to see Willa Snagovia.

"When?" I asked. "Did she say when she'd see him?"

"Well . . . all she said was that she'd let me know when it was all right to come. She said she'd send word."

Andrea looked at me, a pleading in her eyes for me to help assure Adam we were doing the right thing. I did my best.

Adam wanted to be hopeful. He really did. But the night touch wasn't like a sore throat or the flu—it wouldn't go away that easily.

Did Willa Snagovia possess a cure?

We would have to wait and see.

We waited another week, pestering Andrea each day to see whether Willa had contacted her. The passing days gave us time to build up our fears and anxieties—and hopes. At school, kids and teachers alike continued to treat us like lepers, and there was a rumor that Brian Gunnellson's father was going to seek revenge against us. But, as with all of the other rumors, nothing came of it.

The more I thought about what Andrea had done, the more impressed I was. Sure, Doc Newton maybe had helped her go see Willa. Still, it had taken more guts than I had—showed she really cared for Adam.

As for Adam, well, he was pretty quiet all week; I guess

190

you'd have called him cautiously optimistic. Anyway, on the following Saturday's evening shift, Andrea gave us the word: "Two o'clock tomorrow. And she said don't bring any adults with us."

I couldn't understand the stipulation about adults—not that we had planned to bring any—and yet, I didn't much like having to play entirely by Willa's rules. I'm certain Adam didn't either.

Did we have a choice?

Not much of one.

And, on top of that, Detective Lawrence kept trying to spy on us.

So it was that on a clear, cold December Sunday, we met at the end of the Snagovias' long driveway and I said, "He knows something."

"Who?" Andrea asked.

"Lawrence."

I looked at Adam, his lips chomping nervously like a horse with a cube of sugar in its mouth.

"Not gonna worry 'bout it now," he muttered.

"What do you think he knows?" said Andrea.

I took her hand.

"Could be he knows about Adam."

She sucked in her breath defiantly.

"Nobody nowhere can prove anything."

"That's right," I said. "We're going to beat this. Going to stick together and beat it."

When I glanced at Adam again, his eyes were locked on the imposing graying white structure at the top of the hill.

"Let's get this over with, you guys," he said.

I can't speak for the others, but I felt about seven years old as we trudged up the rutted driveway, and that house still reminded me of my images of the Usher House in Poe's story. I even surveyed the outside of the front facing to see if I could see a big crack in it somewhere.

"'Member the last time we went in there?"

It was Adam's question. And, suddenly, I did remem-

191

ber. Andrea probably did, too, though she never said anything.

We were maybe nine years old that summer. Thing is, one day we saw a car pull into the Snagovias', saw John and Willa get in, saw the car drive off. Well, it was just too much of a temptation to resist; the three of us sneaked into the house before twilight came on.

Never stayed long.

What I remember is that we poked around in the Snagovias' big, empty front room and their big, empty kitchen, all the while mustering courage to trek up their steep, narrow, spooky-looking staircase to the second floor. Never made it upstairs. You see, there was this dark, windowless room off the kitchen that drew us off course—a strange room filled with shadows cast out by a single kerosene lamp which had been left burning for some reason.

The room was also filled with skeletons. No, not human skeletons—at least, I didn't *see* a human skeleton—these were all animal skeletons mounted on little wooden shingles with all the bones glued together just the way they should be: small animals probably— you know, rabbits, raccoons, maybe a possum or a skunk. Andrea wouldn't go into that room. So I took Adam by the elbow and steered him into it. Well, he felt the tail of one of those varmints, and a tip bone came off in his hand and we couldn't stick it back on and so he put it in his pocket and we panicked and ran.

Not much of a story except that the next day when we were wading around in Summer's Pond, John Snagovia came over and told us we'd better never ever sneak into their house again. Scared the shit out of us. How could he have known? we wondered—unless he found that tail bone missing.

"Yeah," I said. "I remember the last time."

We buckled in our fear, and Andrea knocked on the door.

After nearly a minute, John Snagovia poked his head out. I suddenly had the feeling he remembered that missing tail bone and would demand that we return it or else. . . .

Well, Andrea reminded him why we had come. Mainly, John just listened and stared at Adam. Eventually he invited us in and told us to wait a spell. He sort of slinked up the stairs, and when he came down again he said, "She comes up first."

Andrea immediately turned to us and indicated it was okay. I almost said something, but I could tell she really wanted the whole thing to work out; I noticed that Adam watched her go up behind John, then he stared at his hands.

"You think weird Willa can help?" I asked him.

He shrugged.

"Can't hurt, can she?"

I had to agree with that. We had reached near desperation as far as what to do about the night touch.

Well, maybe a minute passed before John came down by himself.

"Where's Andrea?" I demanded, a little frightened.

He jerked his thumb over his shoulder and said, "Go on up."

For the remainder of what happened I have a spotty recall—some things intensely clear and some things clear as mud. All the rooms and walls we walked by were bare and dusty and smelled kind of sour.

Then Andrea met us and directed us into a room at the far end of the second floor. I remember it had no windows; I remember that Andrea put a finger to her lips, warning us to be as quiet as possible.

I put my hand on Adam's shoulder; I remember that his body seemed to throw off a lot of heat. Next thing I remember distinctly is seeing Willa; she was sitting in the shadows created by a kerosene lamp, a real antique one, and she was sitting at this old desk, a schoolteacher's desk—another antique. And behind her were shelves which semicircled the desk, and they spilled over with junk: I saw horseshoes, beans, rocks, all kinds of necklaces, bones, acorns, cards and dried roots—gypsy-looking stuff, but she had no crystal ball.

In fact, she really didn't even resemble a gypsy.

But I stared at her; and, as John had, she stared at Adam.

Andrea talked. Willa asked a few questions. Funny thing is, I don't remember anything they said. It was all like a bad phone connection. Besides that, I was too busy gawking at Willa, I suppose.

She was a sight—gray hair taking flight in all directions, out of control despite a pink bandana; her skin had dark splotches and her eyes were milky; most of all, she smelled bad—like a dead animal rotting at the side of the highway.

At one point she asked Adam a couple of questions. Again, the nervous roar in my ears blocked out words. That is, until he stepped forward and put his hands, palms up, on Willa's desk.

Time split off into photographic stills.

Willa must have studied Adam's hands for several minutes; she never touched them, but she never took her eyes off them either. And Adam never took his eyes off Willa.

The tension was awesome.

In my peripheral vision, I could see Andrea's face— her bottom lip was quivering as if she were about to cry.

All at once Willa spoke and her voice seemed to be amplified as if she were speaking into a microphone.

"You have the Cross of Dark Fortune."

It sounded like she was naming some incurable disease; and then we watched her point to an area near the middle finger on Adam's left hand and to another near his thumb. She was careful not to make contact with his hand.

"What does that mean . . . 'Cross of Dark Fortune'?" Andrea suddenly whispered.

Willa paused.

When she spoke again, it was in a distant tone.

"God has placed signs in the hands of all the sons of men, that all the sons of men may know His work." She hesitated a moment, then continued. "The cross of Dark Fortune banishes life. It means he will be a wanderer."

I heard Andrea whisper the word "wanderer" as if she had no familiarity with it.

"Can you help me?" Adam asked.

Willa pulled open a desk drawer.

"Yes," she replied. "I can help you."

Relief coursed through me; I glanced over at Andrea and her smile fought through the shadows. God, it was a great feeling.

Then something flashed.

Willa stood up. She lunged forward.

I heard a dull thump on the desk top. Just a dull thump. Saw another flash.

A flash of light reflecting off a steel blade.

CHAPTER 14

I saw the blood spurt from Adam's left hand even before he delivered a howl of pain that I'll remember as long as I live.

I absolutely couldn't move.

Adam writhed as Willa leaned her weight upon the knife handle, pinning his hand to the desk. I heard the sickening sound of bones crunching.

Andrea. It was Andrea who acted. She screamed, but quickly she jumped at Willa, pushed at her, finally wrestled with her and shoved her back.

Before we all ran, before the terror of the moment lost some of its shock value and allowed me to move, I watched, stunned, as Adam used his strength to pry the blade free.

Then he pressed his right hand over the gushing wound.

And the blood, in a matter of seconds, stopped flowing.

"Does Pudge know you're gonna stay here?" I asked.

Adam tossed his bundle of clothing aside and climbed onto the four-high stack of alfalfa hay. A bandage on his left hand was the only apparent evidence that anything violent had occurred three days ago at the Snagovias'.

"Yeah, he told me I could use it as long as I needed it. Said he wouldn't tell my folks or nobody else where I was—I trust him."

"You not going to school the rest of this week?"

197

Adam snorted.

"School? School? Shit, Rob, . . . what good's school gonna do me?"

I had to admit he was probably right.

"So what happens now? I mean, you can't live out here forever."

As Adam considered my question, I found myself thinking back to the episode at the Snagovias' . . . to the awful thump of that knife penetrating Adam's hand . . . to Willa, to our escape, the terror, the shock . . . and to that blood ceasing to flow.

And to poor Andrea.

She blamed herself, of course. I tried and tried to assure her there was no way she could have known what Willa was going to do—that the woman would go berserk.

The three of us—we told no one else what happened. We agreed we wouldn't.

Andrea wanted Adam to see Doc Newton, to show him the hand wound, but he refused. Truth is, the night touch seemed to miraculously heal it. I don't know how because there had been blood everywhere. Some had sprayed onto my pants leg and some on Andrea's shoes.

Somehow we managed to hide the incident pretty well, though people around us must have known that we were upset about something. And I had a sneaking suspicion that if anyone were ever to catch wind of the whole matter, it would be Detective Lawrence.

Anyway, by the time mid-week had rolled around, Adam told me he had to get out of his house. The uneasy peace between him and his dad threatened to break out into full-scale war, so I agreed to bike him several miles west of town to an abandoned farmhouse—property owned by Pudge—some land he farmed occasionally. He stored hay and sometimes milo in the house.

It was a perfect place for Adam, more concealed and isolated than the Winnebago; I just wondered how he would keep from freezing to death. Maybe the night touch could generate some warmth.

And maybe Detective Lawrence wouldn't find him.

"I told you before that I'd stay till Christmas, then I'm gone. Got to find the Saturn Man. Got to get rid of the night touch."

I surprised myself by what I said in return.

"Don't wait, Adam. Go today. Tomorrow. Sometime soon. Seems like things around Warrior Stand are just going to get worse."

Adam jumped down from the stack. We leaned against the bales, shoulder to shoulder; outside it was clear and sunny, and yet the temperature hovered at the freezing mark.

"I got two problems," said Adam, "or I'd go. Well, maybe I've got three problems. First problem is—I can't leave my mother before Christmas—I've told you that. I'm serious. All that religious stuff's made her crazy in the head, but . . . but she . . . she deserves some happiness. I'm going to her Christmas party this weekend— I'll make her happy."

A lump formed in my throat as I listened.

"Second problem—hell, I have no idea where the Saturn Man is. I thought, you know, that maybe I'd get a vision of where he is. I haven't yet. 'Nother problem— how would I go anywhere? Walk? Take a bus?"

That hadn't occurred to me.

"I could loan you some money for a bus ticket. Andrea would pitch in some, too."

He shook his head.

"I've been thinking on it. Could be the night touch would help. Could be it would let me be able to drive a car, and I could borrow one from Pudge and just hit the road and keep driving until I found the Saturn Man."

I reeled back, flabbergasted.

"You serious? God almighty, Adam, you can't drive a car!"

He smiled. Wiggled his fingers.

"You know that for sure?"

I just sort of sighed helplessly and changed the subject.

"I can bring you out some food tonight. Anything in particular you want?"

"Fruit. And get me one of those cans of mixed nuts and a six-pack of cherry Coke."

"Hey, you gonna pay me back for all that stuff? Mixed nuts are expensive."

"Put it on my bill, cheapskate."

He wrestled me down and tried playfully to smother me in loose hay. He almost forgot his own strength.

Having skipped school, I spent most of the day with him wasting time mostly, talking some. We rearranged a bunch of the bales to make it a little warmer, and before I left I watched my friend draw—always the same pictures—sketches of the Saturn Man, the bear, and the fat Indian woman.

"Pudge'll probably come out to see you," I said as I got ready to go late that afternoon. Your mom's gonna be looking for you this evening."

"If she gets in touch with you, tell her I'm stayin' with Pudge."

I told him I would.

"Anything else you want?"

He thought a moment.

"Well, . . . yeah. Would you . . . see if Andy will come out. I'd like, you know, to have her come out next time you do."

A wave of something like pity washed over me at that moment. I've always tried not to feel sorry for Adam—I knew it would do him no good. But, damn, the way he cared about Andrea—I felt all torn up inside. What could I do? What could I say?

"Sure. I'll pick her up."

"Thanks, Rob. Thanks . . . and remember, things probably gonna get hairy in the next couple of weeks. I'll understand if you want to stop being an accomplice to a murderer."

"Damn it all, you're not a murderer!" I shouted. "You're not!"

Adam was sitting down, leaning back against a bale; he clasped those long hands of his around his knees and gently rocked.

"I hope everybody else will believe that when they find out."

"Don't worry about everybody else. Andrea and I—we're gonna help you get through all this. We will."

The dark winter afternoon claimed the dilapidated house and I pushed off on my bike, leaving him there to haunt the place . . . and to haunt himself.

Through the cold air I sped, struck by the unfairness of the world as I often was. Why Adam? Why had the night touch been visited upon him and not me or somebody else? Why? I barely concentrated upon the road, losing myself in those thoughts; but reality slapped me in the face when I got home and found Detective Lawrence's car in the driveway.

My heart beat faster.

Did they know I had skipped school?

Then another thought: Was this an indication that things were getting hotter between him and my sister? Or was there, increasingly, another pursuit which kept him hanging around our place? How much did he suspect? I wondered. How much did he know?

I didn't go inside right away, choosing instead to fiddle around with my bike in the barn, hoping Lawrence would leave soon.

"It's on one of those tapes you gave me," said Leah.

Clay Lawrence studied the serious cast of her expression and the way she nervously hovered near the stereo's tape deck.

"You mean, one of Kristin's?"

"Yes. A voice comes on instead of music . . . it's very strange. I thought that since you took the tape from Kristin's car, perhaps you should listen to it."

Puzzled, Lawrence asked, "Which one is it?"

She handed him the Whitney Houston tape.

"It's probably nothing that important, but . . . I'd feel better if you'd listen to it and see what you think."

He smiled at her and took the tape, and then he put his

hand to the back of her neck and pulled her gently to him.

"Wish we could have met and got to know one another under different circumstances," he said. "You don't get a look at my best side when I'm on a case."

She moved away from him.

"It's better for people to see each other, warts and all, isn't it?"

"Sure. It's just that a case like this one—I have to be cold. I know what I have to do. I know what I've promised I'd do."

In one continuous, yet mechanical gesture, she retrieved the tape from him and slid it into the tape deck.

Lawrence rubbed a hand across his beard and listened.

There was a brief series of glitches and pops.

And then a voice. A male voice, curiously familiar.

> *March will search, April will try,*
> *And May will tell if you live or die.*

A solid buzz enveloped the rest of the tape. Lawrence switched it off, hunkered down beside the deck, hesitated, and then replayed through the odd lines several more times.

Leah, arms folded against her breasts, looked down at him.

"What is it? Who is it? Does it have something to do with Kristin?"

Outwardly, he forced himself to remain calm; inside his nervous system was rattling and racing like toy trains out of control.

"To your first two questions, I can honestly answer that I'm not sure. But I believe it does relate to Kristin. Just a hunch. But I believe it does."

"How? That saying—'March will search'—I used to hear that as a child. It was a rhyme we said when we were cloosing up sides, or sometimes we even recited it when we jumped rope."

Lawrence fidgeted with his beard.

"Leah," he said. "I'm going to play the tape again.

202

Listen very carefully. Doesn't the voice sound vaguely familiar?"

She began shaking her head.

"No, please don't play it again."

She cupped her hands over her ears and started to run from the room, but he caught her and jerked her around.

"You're going to listen, Leah. Because it's important. Because you can help me identify that voice."

"No, please. I don't want to be involved in this."

He leaned his face close to hers.

"But you are involved. Don't you see that? All of Warrior Stand's involved."

"Clay, please."

He held her. She didn't cry. And from that he judged that she was tough enough to follow the bizarre line of reasoning which his mind was pursuing.

They listened again.

When he switched off the tape for a final time, he said, "I've been in Warrior Stand for over a month; I've heard nearly everyone in this town speak at one time or another—many of them dozens of times. I've heard that voice. So have you."

"It's too deep," she said, her lips tight, her face blanched. "Too deep . . . it's no one—"

"Yes, it is. It is someone you know, Leah."

She shook her head.

"But it can't be him. It can't be Adam Dodd. Unless it's some kind of trick. He's always doing something with gadgets. That's all it is."

She looked at him for assurance that he shared her thinking.

He allowed his body to relax, then strolled about the room, sifting through the rush of possibilities occurring to him.

"You could be right," he said.

Seconds passed in which neither spoke. Leah eventually broke the silence, her tone strained.

"Clay," she said, "there's something I have to ask you. Something I have to know. Adam Dodd is Rob's friend, his best friend. If you found that he . . . that he somehow played a part in the death of Kristin Kelley, would you stand by what you told me? Would you resolve the case like you said you would?"

He stood before her, and out of the living room window he could see the dark form of Rob approaching from the barn.

"Yes," he said. "If he's the killer. But we don't know that. And it seems highly unlikely that a young man, blind, probably without transportation, could have intercepted Kristin on the highway that night. And there's no apparent motive besides."

She searched his eyes and composed herself.

"I think you'd better go now. There's a part of you I can't accept . . . a part of you I don't want to be close to."

She looked away, and he lifted a hand to touch her, but then stopped.

"Do me one favor: Don't call things off between us until I've had a chance to follow this lead as far as it goes. Too much is unexplained. The answers are still out there somewhere."

He wanted to say more, but at that moment Rob entered; hastily, Leah removed the Houston tape and returned it to Lawrence, thanking him for letting her borrow it.

Mrs. Dodd beamed at the centerpiece.

"I saved all year for it," she explained, "a dime here and a nickel there, and the Lord saw fit to let me save the whole nine dollars, and I sent away for it 'specially for my Christmas party. Saw it in a gift catalog and could just picture it on my table—and there it is. I am blessed. Truly blessed."

"It's neat," said Andrea. "So delicate. I'd be afraid I'd break it."

Adam ran his fingers over the centerpiece, and I thought maybe I saw him smile, or maybe it was simply that his mother was happy.

204

It was the Saturday before Christmas, the traditional day for Mrs. Dodd's holiday gathering. Mercifully school had closed for the usual two-week vacation. Adam, temporarily, had moved back home, and Mrs. Dodd had asked me and Andrea to come help her son decorate the Christmas tree that morning before guests arrived early afternoon. All morning she had been buzzing over the centerpiece: a blown-glass display of Santa and his reindeer—the dang thing must have been four feet long and she had it set on a green tablecloth and had tied little red ribbons all over the sleigh. Then elsewhere on the table she had candy—peanut brittle, divinity fudge (two kinds), cookies, and a pound cake and a mincemeat pie and tiny cups of M & M's and a big punch bowl filled with pink lemonade and a 20-cup coffeemaker percolating away—yeah, it was a sight. And, like I said, Mrs. Dodd beamed.

As Andrea, Adam and I hooked colored balls and strung lights (many of which didn't work) on the sickly cedar tree, I thought about Leah and Detective Lawrence. I believe I'd broken in on an argument a few days ago; I hoped it signaled an end to their relationship, and so I wondered whether they'd come to the party together. No amount of pumping and prodding would get Leah to tell.

At one point in our decorating duty Adam dropped a colored ball and it shattered.

"Jesus Christ," he hissed. Then he looked in my direction. "Why does mother try to do this? This house—everything that's happened lately—how can there be any spirit of Christmas?"

We gathered up the pieces, and I said, "It seems to make her happy, Adam. Don't you wanna see her happy?"

"Just be thankful your dad won't be here," Andrea added.

I had to second that. Karl Dodd always put on a disappearing act the day of his wife's get-together—went off to Council Grove, probably to drink himself into a

205

royal state of meanness.

Well, we finished decorating the tree; it was kind of pathetic, and yet what would a Christmas party be without a Christmas tree in the living room, or a roaring fire in the fireplace? Adam and I started the fire—actually, Adam started it—without matches.

"God almighty, that's a good trick," I whispered to him.

He grinned, and I hoped it was a sign he wouldn't be in a dark mood all afternoon.

People began arriving about one o'clock: Mr. and Mrs. Buckley, Mrs. Tenney, Joe and Molly Helms, Doc Newton and Alma—I noticed that Detective Lawrence came with the Newtons—Leah came by herself. Don Slocumb and his mother showed up, too. Among the invited guests absent were John and Willa Snagovia and Pudge. But they had never come, a fact which did not, however, keep Mrs. Dodd from extending them an invitation each year.

The gathering warmed to a nice glow despite Mrs. Dodd's long prayer thanking God for delivering us through the dark tragedies of recent months. There was lots of conversation and eating and sprinklings of laughter. Mrs. Dodd asked Andrea to get out her guitar and lead everybody in some carols, and so, with a country western twang, we took on all the old favorites from "Jingle Bells" to "Hark the Herald Angels Sing."

I kept an eye on Leah and Detective Lawrence as much as possible, and I'll have to admit that it gladdened my heart to see Leah spending her time with the other women; Lawrence mainly huddled near Doc Newton or helped escort Alma to and from the food table. Poor Alma couldn't recognize anyone, and I know I shouldn't laugh at her, but after we had all stopped singing carols she continued belting out little snatches of "Noel." Everyone smiled at her tolerantly.

About mid-afternoon Adam and Andrea and I bundled up and headed down to Summer's Pond—the grownups would get along fine without us, we reasoned.

"Is the pond frozen over?" Andrea asked as we passed

the barn.

I knew it would be after two nights in a row of fifteen-degree temperatures.

"Hey, I'll get it," said Adam.

Just like old times.

Our friend dug the old red yet rusting sled out of the barn, and for a score of minutes we forgot about the night touch and all the darkness it had brought. We forgot about the disastrous school semester and Kristin Kelley and Brian Gunnellson and Detective Lawrence and Willa Snagovia and Karl Dodd—we became real kids again, tiptoeing, slipping, running, falling, laughing, sliding across the frozen surface, Andrea's screams of delight echoing over the Kansas prairie.

God, it was good.

We needed it.

Well, while Andrea and I horsed around on the sled, Adam scurried along the edge of the pond picking up kindling which he heaped into a pyramid.

"Watch this, you guys," he exclaimed. "This is how the gods gave fire to man."

He rubbed his hands over the pile and I kid you not, it burst into flames; Andrea squealed, and I applauded. We slid over to where he was and gathered some more wood for the fire, adding to it until we had a pretty good-sized flame.

We sat around it and warmed ourselves.

"I had this dream," said Adam. "The other night I dreamed that I was somewhere—in a park, I think—and I was talking to the Saturn Man and you guys were with me. And he told me there was somebody who could help me. He said her name, but I couldn't hear him. I just couldn't make out what he said. But I woke up and I felt okay because I thought that maybe I really would find somebody to help me."

"Sure you will," said Andrea. "We'll make certain you do."

She turned toward me, expecting some positive comment.

"If you can just find him—the Saturn Man—if you can get where he is—that's the deal."

"I've got that figured out. You see, Pudge has that old '53 Dodge he's been working on—the one that has the ram's head hood ornament . . . well, you see, I'm gonna drive it."

Andrea did a doubletake.

"Adam, how would you *do* that?"

"The night touch and . . . and Rob's gonna be my teacher next week. You know, help me practice driving."

My stomach rolled into a series of backflips and other gymnastic stunts.

When Andrea glanced at me again, I sort of shrugged helplessly. Then, lo and behold, she hugged me and kissed my cheek.

"That's why I love this man," she said, "because he's kind and considerate and loyal to his friends."

I was wishing she wouldn't get lovey on me in front of Adam. I didn't know how much of her display he could *see*, but for sure he could *hear* it. Finally, she let go of me and stood up.

"I feel great," she exclaimed. "Happier than I've felt in a long time. Everything's going to be fine. I know it will be."

With that, she raced out onto the ice, fell once, got up, smiled, skated and slipped her way to the sloping embankment and climbed to the top. She swung around and around, singing à la Julie Andrews in the opening of that movie, *The Sound of Music.*

I had to chuckle at that.

Then she suddenly stopped.

"What's she doing?" Adam asked.

"Looking toward the house," I said.

I could feel Adam's body tense.

Down the embankment she scrambled as if terrified, and when she was within thirty feet or so of us, her warning came forth as a hysterical whimper.

"Adam, your dad came home!"

I looked at him; his face appeared to crumple.

"Damn it, why?" he whispered.

We left the fire burning and ran to the house.

As we approached I could see people leaving: the Buckleys and some others, including Leah. I jogged up to my sister.

"What's going on inside?"

"Nothing yet," she responded, worry lines tricking out her forehead. "You ought to take Andrea home before there's trouble."

"Karl drunk?"

She indicated he was, then said, "Everyone's going quietly. No one wants a scene. It would break Katherine's heart."

"Yeah, I know."

Andrea hooked an arm through my elbow and tugged at me.

"Adam's gone in."

I waved at Leah and followed Andrea to the porch just in time to help Doc Newton nudge Joe Helms carefully down the steps in his wheelchair. Molly whispered something to Andrea, probably a warning not to go in the house.

Once Joe had been safely maneuvered off the porch, Doc Newton took Alma by the shoulders and guided her toward their car; Detective Lawrence stood in the front doorway. To no one in particular, he said, "Maybe I should stay a moment. He seems about ready to explode."

Of course, I knew he was referring to Karl Dodd.

From below, Doc Newton exclaimed, "Best for all of us to just get out of his way. Katherine's party's over."

He glanced at me as if to say: "If you're smart you won't mess with that man."

I pushed on past Lawrence, Andrea trailing at my shoulder. In the kitchen things were surprisingly calm. Mrs. Dodd, busy stacking dishes and plates, hummed some Christmasy tune; Adam sat at the table, directing his attention toward his dad who slouched in a corner, a coffee cup in one hand and a large slab of mincemeat pie

209

in the other—no saucer or plate. Coffee sloshed onto the floor, and he made disgusting sounds as he ate the pie.

I looked at Andrea, unsure what to do—I felt we were intruding upon something. So I told Adam I thought we'd be heading off, and I was about to thank Mrs. Dodd for the nice party when Adam grabbed my arm.

"Don't go, Rob. Stick around."

He spoke with such a guarded intensity that I felt a chill skate down my spine. I eased over to one side and took Andrea's hand—more for my own sense of security than hers.

Karl Dodd finished his pie and gulped some coffee. I couldn't help staring at him; a mean scowl held his expression.

"Say, boy," he said, beady black eyes locked on Adam, "help your mother clean all this Christmas shit off the table."

My body braced about the same time Andrea's did.

There was an angry feel in the room.

"Mother wants it here. It's her Christmas table," Adam responded.

His hands were trembling even as they rested on the tablecloth.

"Oh, Adam, my lands," said Mrs. Dodd, "your father's right. Our holiday party's ended for another year, but, oh my, wasn't it pleasant?"

She smiled toward me and Andrea, and I knew that we should have excused ourselves right then, but, I swear to God, I couldn't move.

"Hear your mother, boy? She said the shit needs to go. And then you better go, too. You don't live here no more anyway. Ungrateful fuckhead of a son."

Adam stood up suddenly and pounded a fist on the table.

"Shut up, goddamn you! You fat ugly bastard! Just shut your mouth!"

"Here, now here . . . please . . . please, Adam."

Mrs. Dodd rushed to him and embraced him around

the chest and talked to him, her voice treading on the thin ice of tears.

"Please, Adam. Let's not spoil our day with harsh words. It's the season of our Lord. Hope and peace. Birth of the Christ child. And, oh, I've had such a fine day. Everyone liked our party . . . didn't they?" She turned to me and Andrea, and we sort of nodded through our shock.

Karl Dodd strolled to the table and tapped a finger on the green cloth.

"Get all this shit outta my sight."

Mrs. Dodd released her hold on Adam and started gathering up more dishes and silverware.

"Leave it, Mother. Leave it all where it is," said Adam.

"Please, now, please . . . I've had my joy. Everyone . . . I can honestly say this—everyone thought my Santa centerpiece was beautiful. Just beautiful. It was worth saving for all year just so I could offer it to my guests, my friends. Now, as your father says, it's time to put it away until next year."

She smiled into Adam's face and kissed his forehead.

"He's not gonna spoil your day, Mother. He's drunk. I'm not gonna let him ruin the one day of the year you look forward to."

"Oh, I *have* enjoyed it, Adam. I *have.*"

Karl Dodd smiled. Then he laughed. The way I imagine Satan would laugh.

I yanked at Andrea, and we stumbled toward the kitchen entryway.

"Hold it right there!" Dodd roared.

I was so scared that my knees locked up.

Again, the huge man smiled.

"You can't go till you've seen my Christmas trick." Spittle dripped from either side of his mouth.

Adam pushed away from his chair, his body rigid.

A pathetic helplessness shone in Mrs. Dodd's eyes.

I saw Karl Dodd grasp the tablecloth and pull hard— and time slowed to a splash of green and to an inch-by-

211

inch slide of plates and cups and silverware and the Santa centerpiece toward the end of the table—then speeded up dramatically.

Mrs. Dodd screamed.

And the sound of glass breaking pursued me and Andrea all the way into Warrior Stand.

CHAPTER 15

A cold, raw wind whipped through Pudge's collection of dead cars. Pudge, his thick glasses fogging, kicked at the fender of the old blue Dodge.

"I sunk a hunder dollars into this sorry-ass wreck, and I'll be damned if I can make her run. You boys is wastin' your time; this ole whore ain't gonna put out for nobody."

I didn't argue with his assessment, for what I knew about cars you could write out on a notecard in big letters; Adam, though . . . I could tell he had taken a liking to this particular derelict.

"It has a good feel to it," he murmured as he traced his way around the body, hesitating at the driver's door; then he opened it and climbed in and my heart beat a rhythm I'd never heard before. My friend wrapped those big hands of his onto the steering wheel and peered through the windshield—and smiled. It was the smile of a very determined young man.

He had found his wheels.

"What the hell's he doin'?" Pudge asked me.

"Just pretending. That's all."

I thought it was better not to let Pudge in on what Adam had planned. Not yet, anyway.

"Why don't you boys save up your money and get your asses to Council Grove or Emporia and hunt you up a decent used car? Or, be patient, and like as not I'll get a wreck in here I can put in running condition."

"Thing is, Pudge, we really wanted something to drive

213

around in over the Christmas break. So we're sorta in a hurry. We both have learner's permits."

I didn't mention that we were required to have an adult with us whenever we drove.

Adam continued to clutch the wheel, bouncing up and down the way a real little kid would; and we could hear him making *vroom, vroom* noises out of the side of his mouth.

Pudge shook his head. Then he squinted at me.

"Tell me the God's truth—you want a car 'cause you've got a mind to chase skirts. Sweet young pussy. That's about the size of it, ain't it?"

I almost laughed at how far off Pudge was.

I paused and decided to go along.

"Well . . . yeah, I guess you got us figured out. I mean, how can we take girls out on the back of a motorbike?"

He slapped me warmly on the shoulder and chuckled.

"Hell, son, I'm not so old I can't remember the feeling. Shit, yes. Times they was I couldn't keep my mind off women—not like that sorry fucker, Slocumb, you know, but a *clean* wantin' . . . that's what it was, a *clean* wantin'."

I stuffed my hands deeper in my pockets.

"Adam's got his heart set on this one."

Pudge chuckled some more and gestured toward the figure behind the wheel.

"What the hell's he care? He ain't gonna be drivin'. Can't even see the blame road. What's it matter to him?"

I shrugged.

"It just does."

Pudge thought a moment.

"Let's get our balls inside before they turn to ice cubes. I got to have some coffee."

I just about had to drag Adam out of the car; in fact, the only way I could get him to come was to tell him Pudge wouldn't let loose of the car unless we talked some more.

Inside his shack of an office, Pudge poured coffee and

began chomping on his ever-present stack of saltines, slowing only to nail a couple of new calendars to the already cluttered wall. Well, we sat there and drank coffee and listened to the howl of the wind, and, for the umpteenth time, Pudge told us the story of how a rodeo bull named "Maniac" threw him in Cheyenne and broke three of his ribs—the ribs ached when it turned cold weather.

Then, out of nowhere, he changed the subject.

"You boys is actin' mighty strange. Why you so fuckin' quiet?"

"Just thinking about that car," I offered.

He looked from me to Adam; he was suspicious.

"You like that there Dodge, do you?"

"I like it," said Adam. "I need it."

My pulse throbbed in my forehead.

"What he means is . . . it'd be a nice Christmas present if you'd at least let us borrow it."

Munching his crackers thoughtfully, Pudge studied us.

"All right then," he said. "Tell you what. I got to be goin' back in to the Arrowhead. You can have that old Dodge, lock, stock and barrel . . . if you can get her started."

After Pudge left, Adam and I sat a minute, basking in our victory. My friend was happy; that homely face wore a smile which a few days before would have seemed impossible: He had wanted to kill his father. No one could have blamed him; and I believe only one person had the power to stop him—his mother.

Later, I wondered what she had said and done to control him. Andrea and I had fled, a cowardly but sensible act. And what about next time? Would Mrs. Dodd be there to whisper whatever cautionary, motherly words it took to calm the raging anger of her son? And just when would Karl Dodd, in all his abusive fury, choose to turn upon his family again? I hoped it wouldn't happen before Adam could get away, before he could launch his quest for the Saturn Man.

215

My thoughts returned soberly to the business at hand.
"How we gonna make it run?" I asked.

That smile on Adam's face widened.

He raised his hands and wiggled his fingers.

"You'll see, good buddy. You'll see."

So we braced ourselves for the cold air. I have to admit
that I didn't have much confidence. That old Dodge
might not even have all the necessary parts—maybe we
were wasting our time.

"I'm gonna look under the hood," Adam announced.

He felt for the release and swung up the heavy hood as
if it didn't weigh a thing. I leaned into the inner workings
of the greasy, dusty engine compartment and shook my
head.

"God almighty, Adam. This damn car probably hasn't
run for years."

"It hasn't had the proper coaxing. That's the only
problem."

"The battery cables are corroded," I countered.

His fingers walked along the top of the radiator and the
sidewall before pausing at the battery. Then he touched
the air cleaner and both sides of the engine and the
distributor cap.

"I think it has some life in it, Rob. Get in and try to
start it."

So I did. But when I turned the key, all we heard was an
unpromising click.

"Dead," I muttered. "Deader than a doornail."

With the hood raised, I could see through the opening
if I ducked my head a little. I watched Adam pull himself
up and onto the engine.

"Son-of-a-bitch," I whispered. "What is he up to?"

Methodically Adam pressed his hands onto about
every working part of that engine and electrical system.
When he finally scrambled out from under the hood, I
heard him yell, "Crank her up again."

So I did.

And the engine coughed a couple of times, and to my
amazement, it almost started.

"I'll be damned," I exclaimed to myself. "I'll be damned."

Then I heard Adam chattering. Nonsense stuff. He was excited. And I saw him get up onto the engine again and press his hands onto the gasket covers. He mumbled something as he concentrated. Again I heard him yell. This time very energetically.

"Crank this old motherfucker. It's gonna run."

I cranked.

And it did.

Man, oh, man. The night touch had struck again.

Adam slammed the hood shut and cackled like he'd gone off his rocker. He climbed in on the shotgun side.

"Let's ride, good buddy. Let's ride."

"Listen," I said, "I got to tell you. I don't have a good feeling about you driving this thing."

His eyes rolled wildly; I couldn't determine what he could and what he couldn't see.

"Drive outta town," he exclaimed. "Get me on a country road, and let me have the wheel."

I took a deep breath and guided the big tank of a car a couple of miles west of town.

"Far enough," he said. "Trade me places."

Reluctantly I did. We were on a flat, open stretch of sand and gravel road; no other cars; just a big ditch on either side.

"Now, Adam, listen—"

"Quiet!" he shrieked. "Jesus . . . I got to concentrate."

Which is what he did for better than a minute, one hand on the steering wheel, one hand pressed over his eyes. The old Dodge idled like a volcano about to erupt.

When he eventually removed that hand from his eyes, I realized that I'd been holding my breath.

Adam blinked.

"I can see the road," he said. "Most of it."

That wasn't entirely reassuring. For the next several minutes, I explained about the gears and the clutch—believe me, I gave special attention to the brake pedal.

"Got it all?" I asked.

He smiled a mischievous smile.

"Shi-i-i-it, yes!"

The rear tires spun and threw gravel, and we were off.

Adam howled and bounced up and down behind the wheel, and I had to laugh myself, but beneath the surface I was so scared I was about to wet my pants.

"Slow down!" I screamed as we snaked from one side of the road to the other.

That next half hour or so is kinda hard for me to describe.

Adam had an unusual sense of speed and timing; his coordination, or lack of, led him to do strange things: For example, instead of backing off the accelerator on turns, he would actually press down further.

"Hang on, Rob. Hang on, buddy," he would shout as we fishtailed, often skidding inches from a deep culvert.

"Goddamn it!" I would yell. "Slow down!"

No use.

And he would try to hit every bump he saw—if—I say *if* he saw them. My head slammed against the roof a half dozen times, but it never knocked any sense into me because if I'd had any sense, I'd have jumped out of that car—regardless of how fast it was moving.

"You know what I wish, Rob?"

I shook my head, hands welded to the inside door latch.

"I wish this sucker could fly."

"If you don't slow down, it will. I swear to God, it will."

He cackled.

I'd never seen Adam happier.

Then, inevitably, one of the corners tripped us up. The old Dodge, far from being a sophisticated race car, slewed and bounced and stalled; and as Adam celebrated the excitement of it all, the big tank rolled backward, the rear tires clunking over a rocky ledge of the ditch.

"Who-o-o-we-e-e! Damn, that was fun!" my friend shouted.

Scared, mad, and yet relieved that we were still alive, I reached over and plucked the keys from the ignition.

"Driving lesson's done. You're dangerous. The highways of the state of Kansas are not ready for someone like you."

Well, we got out to survey the damage; it didn't bother Adam. Using his considerable strength, he simply put his shoulder to the rear of the car and eased it out of the ditch.

"No problem," he exclaimed.

And I suppose there wasn't, yet I cringed at the thought of my friend on a real highway meeting and passing other real cars—made me sick to my stomach.

But I knew I wouldn't be able to talk him out of driving to find the Saturn Man. So I drove us back to Pudge's; he hadn't returned. We sat around and warmed ourselves— the Dodge had no heater—and I noticed that Adam was pressing his fingertips into the palm of his left hand.

"Your hand pretty much healed these days?"

I edged my chair closer to his and he showed me the palm; there was virtually no sign that Willa Snagovia had wounded him.

"It's okay," he murmured. "That old witch-bitch Willa tried to cut off my hand. She was scared."

"I wonder why. You remember what she said? Something about the 'Cross of Dark Fortune' and how it meant you'd be a wanderer."

He nodded.

"Maybe she's right," he said. "If I can't get rid of the night touch, maybe that's what'll happen."

For awhile, neither one of us said anything. My nerves had calmed down some from the wild driving lesson. I glanced up at the walls, taking note of the new calendars Pudge had tacked up.

Just to break the lull in the conversation, I said, "You think someday I'll be a real artist, maybe a commercial artist, and paint scenes like those on Pudge's calendars? Lot of the new ones have photographs instead of drawings and paint—"

Right there I stopped dead.

Adam looked toward me.

"What is it?"

"God almighty," I whispered.

I stood up and walked over to one of the new calendars. I put my nose right up close to it.

"What is it, Rob? Come on, damnit, tell me."

I couldn't believe my eyes.

"Adam . . . you better come over here to this calendar."

He did.

Man, my whole body tensed with excitement. Tiny bright lights were flashing behind my eyes. My throat went dry. I coughed once and took Adam's hand and placed it onto the calendar's January photo.

"Concentrate on this. Use the night touch to see this. You won't believe—"

"God! God, I see it!" he immediately exclaimed. "God, this is it!"

He tore the photo from the calendar.

"God, Rob! God, this is it!"

I swallowed.

"Yeah, it sure seems like it."

I read the calendar ad.

"It's from the Denver Chamber of Commerce. Denver, Colorado. But it doesn't say what the building is behind the statue. It doesn't say where this is."

"But it's Denver, right? Someplace in Denver?"

"Yeah, I'd say so."

Adam concentrated on the photo—a statue of a huge bear standing on its hind legs.

"It's my bear, Rob. Son-of-a-gun and damn my hide— it's *my* bear, isn't it?"

He stroked his fingers lovingly over the photo. Apparently he could see enough of it to be certain.

"Yeah," I said. "Yeah, I'd bet money it's your bear."

My friend got super quiet. His hands trembled as he continued touching the photo.

"The Saturn Man," he whispered. "The Saturn Man's

there. Near the bear. I'm gonna go to Denver and
him back the night touch."

He tossed the photo into the air and whooped and
hugged me and danced and laughed.

"Don't lose that picture," I exclaimed.

And I was so happy for him, I just about cried.

The next day was the day before Christmas Eve, clear
and not very cold. That morning Leah took Adam and me
Christmas shopping in Emporia; I bought a perfume set
for Andrea and a nice pair of leather gloves for Leah—
I'm not a very imaginative shopper. Adam bought his
mother a new bible, a white one with her name embossed
(free of charge) in gold letters.

It seemed to me that Leah was kinda down, a condition
somehow related, I guessed, to her breaking up with
Detective Lawrence. On the way back to Warrior Stand,
Adam and I sang and acted silly and tried to make her
laugh and sorta succeeded.

That afternoon, Adam wanted another driving lesson,
and so we cranked up the old Dodge—Pudge was
flabbergasted that we had gotten it started—and headed
out. This time I drove by the Arrowhead and picked up
Andrea . . . for moral support, I suppose.

She about flipped out when we stopped on a country
road and Adam got behind the wheel.

"Is this for real?" she exclaimed.

"Yeah," I said. "*Real* danger. You better hang on."

For a chaotic hour, Adam turned the sparsely traveled
roads on the edge of Warrior Stand into his private
speedway.

Andrea squeezed my elbow so hard it lost all feeling.
She squealed and screamed—all of which provoked our
friend into accelerating. Out at Pudge's abandoned
farmhouse, we parked and Adam proudly showed Andrea
the photo of the bear.

"Denver, Andy. That's where I'm goin'. I'll spend
Christmas with Mother. Then I'm gone. Denver. Denver,

221

Colorado. That's where the Saturn Man is."

Examining the photo, Andrea said, "It's just like your drawings."

She looked at me.

"Rob, he's found it."

"Yeah, I know. We don't know exactly *where* in Denver this is. But if Adam can get there, then probably he can find that statue and the big building behind it."

"Don't say *if*, Rob," Adam interjected. "We'll find it. We will."

Well, it hit me. It hit me hard: Did Adam expect that Andrea and I would go with him?

"Adam . . . hey, you're not really counting on us riding along to Denver, are you?"

Surprised, he stared through the windshield.

"Sure . . . I thought you probably would. You know, the three of us. You . . . you guys promised you'd help me."

We didn't close the door completely on the idea; we simply tried to make him see that it was his personal quest—no point in all three of us taking off. Adam's disappointment hung in the air all the way back to the Arrowhead where we let out Andrea.

I tried to think of something that would cheer him up.

"Let's go out and show your mom that you can drive."

It was kind of a desperate suggestion on my part.

He brightened.

"Good idea. Damn good idea."

As Adam pulled the Dodge up to the house, I could see Karl Dodd's pickup down in the pasture beyond Summer's Pond; he appeared to be dumping a big load of trash in a ravine he used for that purpose. I guessed he would be occupied for awhile.

I kept my fingers crossed.

"Listen," I said. "I'll go in and get your mom and have her come out here. When she's out on the porch, I'll holler, and you loop around the driveway."

Adam smiled.

"Oh, yeah," he exclaimed. "She'll freak."

222

I hoped it wouldn't shock her too much.

Inside the Dodd place I couldn't help thinking about the ugly scene of Karl yanking that Christmas center-piece to the floor. I even half expected to see pieces of glass around. But there were none.

I hesitantly called out for Mrs. Dodd a couple of times. Got no response. I walked from room to room, almost feeling like a trespasser. Could she be taking a nap? Or maybe praying? She prayed a lot.

I went upstairs, called out again. Still no response. Not home?

I started back through the living room and got the weirdest feeling.

Mrs. Dodd's here. Somewhere.

Geez, I scrambled out onto the porch and hollered Adam's name. Well, just as big as you please, Adam looped around the driveway several times before I could catch him and tell him to stop.

He looked toward my mouth.

"She won't answer?" he muttered. "What do you mean, she won't answer?"

Jesus God, I felt funny. Funny scared, I mean.

"You better come on inside," I said.

CHAPTER 16

They buried Hugh Kelley next to his daughter. "Died of grief."

As Clay Lawrence walked from the green tent, graveside services concluded, he heard someone offer that remark. And he considered whether it could be true. Cause of death: severe and prolonged grief?

Avoiding lingering associates of Kelley, Lawrence sought out his car to be alone with his thoughts and to escape the cold. A rekindling of resolve was flaming up within him, and he felt a deep need to understand it. And to understand Hugh Kelley's death.

"Wasn't grief," he muttered to himself in the safe confines of his car. "Wasn't grief. It was a bullet to the head. Self-inflicted."

From his coat pocket, Lawrence retrieved a crumpled and much-read note. A suicide note addressed to him:

Clay,
    I thought I had all this licked. I thought I could handle it and get on with my life. I've never been a quitter. You know that. Kristin was all I looked forward to. Her life. Her career. Her marriage someday. Grandkids, maybe. It's all lost.
    So I've got to go through with this. I also thought I could forgive her killer. Write it off somehow. I can't. You know what I'm going to ask: Stay on the case.

Find the bastard and kill him. Kill him and I'll
rest in peace.

Coach Hugh

Lawrence stared at the words "Coach Hugh" and the
flood of memories momentarily overwhelmed him.
Nothing specific. Just a collage of good images, tough and
demanding times. Hugh Kelley's gravel-rough voice
demanding more effort.

Then another voice intruded.

Clear, soft, framed in innocence.

> Tell me you like me
> And I'll do you no wrong.
> Tell me you love me
> And I'll sing you a song.

Somewhere, swirling in the darkness of his thoughts, a
notion of justice materialized. Kristin's little-girl song
served as its anthem.

Back to Warrior Stand.

He had withstood endlessly boring days there; had
consumed endless cups of hot tea at the Arrowhead; had
shared his thinking with Doc Newton; had nearly fallen
in love with Leah Dalton; had listened to voices for any
clue. . . .

On the long drive from Independence to Warrior
Stand he heard one other voice. Like a magnet, it drew
him toward a final act of blood justice:

> March will search, April will try,
> And May will tell if you live or die.

And he asked himself: What would Coach Hugh say if
it turned out that his daughter's killer was the same age as
those boys he used to drive toward gridiron excellence?

CHAPTER 17

"Mother?"

I sorta stood back out of the way as Adam followed pretty much the same route through the house as I had.

"Mother, where are you?"

His voice trailed away upstairs.

Below, standing in the living room, I could trace his steps from room to room. Then I heard him quicken his pace, taking several steps at a time back downstairs.

"Mother!"

The sudden intensity in his call hit my heart, drumming it like a boxer fisting a punching bag.

He looked in my direction.

"She wouldn't leave."

I kinda shrugged.

We went into the kitchen.

"Mother?"

"Adam, what's that smell?"

Then I heard a curious ticking.

"It's the oven," he said. "She's baking something. She wouldn't go off and let something go untended in the oven."

"Jesus, it's burning."

Smoke began seeping out the corners of the old-fashioned oven even before I yanked open the door. The kitchen rapidly filled and we coughed and I hot-padded two breadloaf tins off the wire platform.

"Banana nutbread," said Adam. "I know that smell—burned or not, I know it. God! God! Where is she, Rob?"

I went to the back porch and propped open the screen despite the cold air. Smoke filtered its way out. I coughed some more and lowered my head through the drifts of smoke and my eye caught something in the corner.

A storage closet stood ajar a few inches.

I could see Mrs. Dodd's shoe and part of her ankle.

I grabbed Adam as he entered the back porch.

"Listen, man, I've found her. But just stay calm. Okay? Stay calm and come over here in the corner."

"What the fuck, Rob?" he exclaimed. "Why the hell you holding me? What is it, goddamn it?"

He wrestled away, too strong for me to hold. But I could tell that he wasn't able to concentrate well enough to use the night touch. He stumbled around the porch until I took his elbow and guided him to the storage closet.

"Mother?"

God as my witness, I didn't want to look.

Adam threw open the closet door and his foot bumped into his mother's.

I heard her groan.

I felt relieved in a way.

At least she was alive.

"Mother?"

Adam hunkered down, but Katherine Dodd wasn't able to reach out toward him. So he reached for her.

"Mother?"

And he touched her face and hugged her to him so that her chin rested on his shoulder. I could suddenly see her more clearly.

Her eyes had been blacked; her lip had swollen; drying blood trickled away from it. She groaned again, then tried to mouth a couple of words. At first, only a raspy whistle escaped through a space left by a missing tooth.

"Don't let it burn," she eventually mumbled.

I put a hand on Adam's shoulder.

"What happened to her?" I asked, and before he even turned to face me, I knew the answer. It was obvious.

"Doc Newton," he said. "I'll stay here. Go get Doc Newton."

228

I made it into town in record time, finding Newton at the hardware store.

"Come to the Dodds' quick," I exclaimed, sputtering, surprising him at a canvas. "Karl's beat up Mrs. Dodd real bad."

Doc Newton dropped his brush immediately.

"I'll run by the house and get my bag," he said.

Minutes later, we burst into the Dodds' house, and I led the way to the back porch. Mrs. Dodd was sitting up—it was sadly comical to see her try to smooth her unruly hair into place when she saw Doc Newton.

"What is this fuss?" she whispered.

"Don't move," said Newton. "You may have something broken."

And that's when Adam brushed past me, a look in his eyes—well, I've always heard the expression "murder in his eyes," but I'd never seen such a look until that moment.

Like a damn fool, I said, "What are you going to do?"

He headed for Summer's Pond.

I felt like a scared little boy as I followed along. At one point I said, "Maybe you ought to let the sheriff handle this."

Adam marched to the top of the embankment; he pressed at the sides of his head, and as I joined him, I realized that he could see his dad's pickup slowly wend its way from the trash dump area.

I wanted to stop him. No—*part* of me wanted to; *part* called out for revenge.

Adam scrambled down to the frozen-over pond; I stayed on his heels. Our combined weight caused the hissing echo of cracks to develop. We waited on the opposite bank for the pickup to pass by.

I was excited and terrified at the same time.

Adam remained calm, but there was anger; it radiated from his body. Standing next to him was like standing next to a furnace.

Soon enough, Karl Dodd pulled up within forty feet of us, rolled down his window, and said, "Get off my property, boys. You're trespassing."

The body of simmering rage—my friend—let out a howl like the one I heard the night Brian Gunnellson was killed.

"Fuckhead boy," Dodd yelled. "Get out of here, or I'll give you some of what I gave your mother."

Well, things happened fast. I watched, but I'm still not sure I believe what I saw—it was incredible.

It started when Adam raised his hand and sorta pointed it at the truck—and the door on the driver's side exploded, peeling away until it rested flat against the left fenderwall, hinges buckled, metal popping and screaming.

Karl Dodd sat behind the wheel; he looked naked and scared. Very, very scared. He didn't move.

But something moved him.

Watching the whole thing unfold, all I can say is that it was like invisible hands grabbed Dodd by the shoulders and yanked him out of that truck. He thudded to the ground, swearing, determined suddenly to get at Adam.

He never got close.

That same invisible presence—the force of the night touch, I guess—dragged him to the pond and out onto the ice. His screams of anger turned to screams of fear. And finally to pathetic pleading.

Karl Dodd is a huge man. But that invisible force rolled and sledded him over that ice as if he were an empty barrel.

Then it released him in the middle of the pond.

Sprawled on his back, Dodd twisted over and got to his hands and knees.

A roaring silence gripped the scene.

I felt a curious relief because I thought Adam had gotten his revenge—his dad had been terrified nearly out of his mind—I saw it as retribution.

Whimpering, the man pushed himself to his feet. And getting to his feet, he appeared to calm his fears and steady himself.

"You're dead, boy," he shouted. "For this, you're dead!"

230

The ice growled.

Echoes of the cracking fingered toward the bank.

Karl Dodd stared at his feet.

When he broke through, it was as if he were falling into a trapdoor.

He bellowed and thrashed and splashed.

The icy water surrounded him up to his armpits.

He struggled like some massive animal caught in quicksand.

He cried out again and again for help.

Not being able to take it any longer, I ran.

I reached the house in time to help Doc Newton get Mrs. Dodd into his car. She protested that she was fine. Newton whispered to her reassuringly, and they drove away.

I must have sat on the Dodd front porch for ten or fifteen minutes before I went back to Summer's Pond. Adam had climbed onto the embankment and was sitting there.

Out in the center of the pond stood the frozen statue of his father.

CHAPTER 18

"I'm not sorry about it, Rob. I'm not. I don't care what they do to me. He didn't deserve to live."

I had brought my friend a bag of cookies for breakfast and gestured for him to eat as I glanced around Pudge's abandoned farmhouse. Once again, it had become Adam's hideout, his refuge.

It was the morning of Christmas Eve.

I couldn't shake the image of Karl Dodd, his frozen corpse sprouting from Summer's Pond like some leafless tree.

"We gotta decide what to do," I said.

Through a mouthful of cookie, he replied, "Never mind that—how's Mother? Does she . . . does she *know?*"

I let out a deep breath.

"Yeah, . . . I didn't have to tell them. Everybody . . . Doc Newton . . . everybody else . . . they figured right off it was you who . . . killed your dad. But, your mom, I think maybe she's not too bad. Crying a lot, you know. I heard that your aunt's coming in from Dallas. And, Leah, she volunteered to stay out at your place for a couple of days just so your mom would have company."

"That's good. Good. I'm glad. Your sister, she's real nice. It's real nice she's doing that for Mother."

"Burial's gonna be the day after Christmas."

Adam tossed a half-eaten cookie into the hay.

"Waste of a good coffin. That's what it is. I hope he

233

roasts in hell, the ugly bastard."

"I'm scared, Adam. About all this. I mean . . . I've already lied to the sheriff when he asked me where you were. You can't stay around Warrior Stand. They'll find you."

"Sorry you had to lie," he said softly. "Sorry. But tomorrow's Christmas. I'm gonna sneak in and see Mother and say goodbye to her. Then it's on the road to Denver. I'm through hurting people with this night touch. When I've gotten rid of it . . . well, probably I'll face up to what I've done."

I couldn't find any words. Confusion. It was all I felt. I knew it was wrong to be aiding a murderer—but he really wasn't a murderer—couldn't make myself accept that he was.

"Say, Rob . . . how's Andy takin' all this?"

At first, I wouldn't answer; I didn't want to think about Andrea. I didn't want her involved any further.

"Shocked, I guess . . . upset and . . . scared . . . wondering what's gonna happen to you. She's been with Doc Newton. Thing is, the whole town's shocked, but they kinda understand, too. They know how cruel your dad was."

I fidgeted nervously with a roll of bills I had stuffed into the front pocket of my jeans.

"Nobody could really know," said Adam, "unless they'd lived around him."

I nodded soberly and then pulled out the wad of bills.

"I saw Pudge right before I came out. He's worried, you know, concerned about you. I told him you might be running . . . and he seemed like he understood . . . and he gave me this money and said to give it to you . . . gas money, that kind of thing. There's two hundred dollars here."

My friend took the money; his fingers caressed it.

"Good ole Pudge . . . He's always liked me."

"Yeah. He's a strange dude sometimes. But he likes you."

"You and Andy . . . you've been friends to me, too. All along."

"God almighty," I said, "let's not get mushy, okay?"

He smiled and punched at me.

"Mushy, my ass," he exclaimed.

Then that cackle of his.

Gradually a silence surrounded us.

"The ole Dodge working?" I asked him.

"Yeah. I smell some oil blow-by. It'll get me where I need to go."

"That car's better than a snowplow in rough winter weather."

He laughed again.

"I had a dream about the Dodge, Rob. I did. A weird one. I was driving in snow—the hardest snow I'd ever seen. Couldn't see the road. Couldn't see nothing except the headlights and this thick curtain of snow. But I just kept my hands on the steering wheel and the Dodge found the way. It found the way."

I studied his face for a moment.

God, I hoped that somehow, some way, things would work out.

"A regular snowmobile," I said. "That's the Dodge." Then I added, "I've got to get going, man. But I'll be back late tonight. You need anything?"

He hesitated a second.

"Peace of mind," he murmured:

The words kinda tore at me.

"Wish I could bring it to you."

"Well, if you can't come up with that, then hustle me a big, juicy steak and one of those twice-baked potatoes 'bout the size of a football and throw in a whole pumpkin pie—whipped cream on top."

"Go to hell," I chuckled.

"Goin' to Denver first," he shot back.

I left with a lump in my throat.

It was still there as Andrea and I talked to Doc Newton that afternoon at the hardware store. Although against it at first, I gave in to Andrea's desire to share Adam's problem—our problem—with somebody. Somebody who could give us sound advice.

We told Doc Newton everything.

Adam and the night touch.

The Saturn Man.

Kristin Kelley.

Brian Gunnellson.

Karl Dodd.

The bear. The calendar. The Denver plan.

It took us the better part of an hour. Did he believe us? Mostly.

In tears, Andrea sought out her grandfather's arms. "What should we do?" she murmured.

He motioned for us to sit down as he flared a match to his pipe, then thoughtfully puffed on it.

"He can't get away," he replied softly, matter-of-factly. "You kids must see that, don't you? He can't come away clean."

"But he's innocent," said Andrea. "Don't you believe that?"

"Honey, I suppose I do. Honestly. Somebody else will have to decide guilt or innocence, though. It's not for me to say."

I sat there, feeling miserable, convinced we had betrayed our friend, broken our promises to him.

"What do you think Adam should do?" I asked.

After a long pause, Newton said, "Give himself up."

"No," Andrea protested. "They'll just put him in prison forever . . . or in some weird asylum. They'll say he's crazy."

I agreed.

It took him another hour or so, but he won us over to his thinking. He kept insisting that what he advised would be in Adam's best interest.

"It could make it easier if he would surrender to Detective Lawrence—surrender quietly—no problems. Lawrence and I could help him find a lawyer, too."

I objected.

"I don't trust Lawrence. Neither does Adam."

"You kids are going to have to trust someone," said Newton. "Convince your friend to trust Lawrence."

"Could we talk to Lawrence first?" Andrea asked.

I had a hard time believing she considered accepting the detective as a go-between.

"I'll go ask him to come over," Newton offered. "Size him up for yourselves."

When he left to find Lawrence, Andrea and I got into a pretty heated exchange. Finally I backed off. From confusion, if nothing else. Maybe Doc Newton was right—something inside me, however, said *no*.

Detective Lawrence greeted us, managing to defuse some of our explosive wariness and distrust. He charmed Andrea and somewhat placated me.

"He'll be treated as he should be treated," Lawrence explained. "When the full context of his father's abusive nature is aired, no judge and jury would come down hard on the boy."

As Lawrence continued, I realized that Doc Newton apparently hadn't told him of Adam's connection with the deaths of Kristin Kelley and Brian Gunnellson. Or had he?

Something felt wrong.

But Andrea grasped my arm; teary-eyed, she seemed very relieved.

"Let's talk to Adam," she said. "This is the right thing, Rob. I feel like it is."

A small voice within nearly prompted me to remind her that she had felt the same way about taking Adam to see Willa Snagovia, and yet, I sensed that this was different.

Adam would have to face the consequences of his actions.

He couldn't run forever.

So I turned to Lawrence.

"Okay. We'll see if he'll agree to surrender, but you have to promise us—give him all the help he deserves."

Lawrence smiled reassuringly.

"I promise I'll do exactly what I feel is best for him."

We left the hardware feeling that a great burden had

237

been lifted from our shoulders. We had come clean, as they say. I managed to shout down all my inner doubts, buoyed by Andrea's contagious enthusiasm.

"Adam's finally going to get help," she declared.

"Now all we have to do is make *him* see that," I said.

"He will," she bubbled. "I just know he will."

"God, I hope so," was my response.

Andrea and I worked that evening till midnight at the Arrowhead; Christmas Eve always strikes me as kind of a depressing shift: people on the road when they should be safely in the bosom of their loved ones. People should be home for the holidays.

Adam wasn't.

That stung me.

Usually Christmas music puts me in the spirit. Not this time. And Pudge gave me a little Christmas bonus—the money didn't mean much, though. In better times I would have been excited about buying some painting supplies. Truth is, I hadn't picked up a brush for weeks.

Well, after the shift, Andrea sneaked off with me. Don't know what she told her folks. It was cold, but a sky filled with stars loomed over us on our ride into the outer darkness of the country roads. I made certain no one followed us.

Andrea packaged up some hot food for Adam: a chicken-fried steak smothered in gravy, some mashed potatoes, green beans, buttered rolls, and a piece of pumpkin pie—an extra large one. By the time we reached Pudge's abandoned farmhouse, the container Andrea was carrying the goodies in got bounced around—green beans coated the potatoes and the gravy covered the pie as much as the steak.

No matter.

Adam wolfed it all down.

He had one of Pudge's flashlights standing on end in the center of one room; bales of hay, stacked four or five high, semicircled him.

"It's like a cozy nest," said Andrea.

Adam kind of smiled.

"My interior decorator has big plans for it."

I laughed, genuinely impressed that my friend could joke, considering the circumstances.

"Are you keepin' from freezing your ass off?" I asked.

He pointed at his bottom.

"Still, there, ain't it?"

After he finished eating, he unfolded a map in the half shadows cast by the flashlight.

"Got my route all planned," he exclaimed.

Andrea and I exchanged glances; she bit nervously at the corner of her lip.

"Following highway 70?" I muttered.

"Yeah, . . . the whole way smack out to Colorado."

I noticed that he was blinking his eyes a lot more than usual and so I said, "You havin' problems with your eyes?"

"Some," he admitted. "The night touch sometimes won't hold. Gives me a headache."

Jesus, damn, I thought to myself.

"You think maybe . . . well, that maybe you shouldn't try the Colorado trip . . . I mean if you won't be able to see good, how can you—"

"Got to, Rob! Damnit, I got no choice."

That's when Andrea said, "Yes, you do. We came out to talk to you about a choice. The best choice."

He sorta shrank back into himself.

"What are you guys talkin' about? Rob, what's Andy saying?"

Oh, God, I was so tense that a noise roared in my ears as if a jumbo jet had taken off in the cold, hard field beyond the house.

"Please, Adam, . . . listen to us," I said. "We've been talking to Doc Newton."

"You guys promised me . . . goddamn it—I'm sorry, Andy—you guys rat on me?"

"No," said Andrea. "Please hear us out."

He did. Though his face contorted and he sputtered

239

and spewed.

Then he really surprised me: tears came to his eyes, and for the longest time he just stared at his hands. Andrea spelled out the whole plan. I guess I thought he would reject it—hoped he wouldn't—but expected him to.

When he eventually raised his head, he directed his comment toward Andrea.

"Is this what you'd really like for me to do?"

Well, she was in tears, too.

"Yes," she said, and hugged him.

God, it was an unforgettable moment.

A minute or so later Adam folded up his map.

"Whatever happens, you guys, I want to say goodbye to my mother."

We told him that, sure, he'd be able to do that.

I wasn't entirely comfortable with his reaction: he had agreed too quickly, too easily. I suppose a lot related to Andrea—he would have done about anything for her—even trust Lawrence.

On Christmas morning, a gray, fog-ridden sky rolled over Warrior Stand, but my spirits were high, all sunshine and clear sailing. I woke convinced that Andrea and I had done the right thing for our friend.

I biked into the hardware to wait.

Adam said he would meet me there, and after surrendering to Lawrence, we would slip out to the Dodd place and have a small Christmas. I had explained some of the plan to Leah—my sister's pretty tough—she handled the shock of all of it in stride. Nurse's training must have steeled her for most kinds of tragic and near-tragic news.

I had promised to see Andrea later that afternoon, though I kind of wanted her around for moral support when Adam turned himself in.

"I just couldn't bear watching him do that, Rob," she had exclaimed. "It's what Adam should do, but it would break me down to see it."

I knew how she felt.

Our little pissant town had on its Christmas mask of solemnity as I wheeled onto Main Street—not a creature stirring. Most folks would be gathered around the tree exchanging gifts, boys frowning when they unwrapped a shirt or socks instead of a glitzy toy.

There was a light on in the Sunset House apartment; Detective Lawrence would be waiting, his job nearing its end. He had caught his man. Or boy. Not really "caught" him, but I had felt all along that he was determined enough to stay on the track of Kristin Kelley's slayer for however much time was necessary.

At the hardware, I had expected to find Doc Newton, but the place sat empty and dark, and so I eagerly switched on a light and strolled among the canvases in the studio area, stopping to study my piece on the three dead jacks—yeah, it still sorta reminded me of Andrea, Adam and me.

I surveyed "Adam's World," a damn good painting even if I did say so myself. Right then is when I started wondering seriously what would happen to Adam next. Would anyone believe him about the night touch? If he gave them a demonstration, they would have to believe it, wouldn't they?

Would he be ruled insane?

I had no idea what fate awaited my friend. What I did know was that the horrible weight of past weeks no longer bore down upon me. My dad used to say: "It'll all work out somehow." I kept repeating that line to myself.

Thing is, I had no real control. That was frustrating. I had to trust and trust and trust. And so did Adam.

Bracing my arms against my chest, I tried to hug away the chill of the studio; I thought about firing up Doc Newton's space heater, then decided I wouldn't be around there long enough to make good use of the heat.

I lost myself in a gray funnel of thought which reached toward a bright light, and I couldn't tell you how much time passed before the clatter and shudder of Adam's old Dodge slapped me back to reality.

241

I met him at the door.

He seemed grim, and it appeared that he had one of his headaches.

"Good-looking set of wheels you got there," I joked.

Slamming his fist playfully onto the fender, he exclaimed, "Only went in the ditch twice on the way to town. Yeah, this ole buggy's sweet. Real sweet. I'm gonna miss the hell out of her."

"Pudge and I'll take care of her. She'll be just like you left her, when you . . ."

God, my words seemed to slip into another dimension.

Adam held his arms out full length, fists clenched and pointed downward.

"Slap on the cuffs," he teased.

I chuckled at that, but the seriousness of the scene returned with a vengeance.

"You really sure?" I asked him, fixing my attention on his wandering eyes; his hair was longer—eyebrows, too. He suddenly appeared smaller and darker to me. "This is really your decision, isn't it? Not just something Andrea and I talked you into?"

"My decision. Yeah . . . it'd be hell to keep running and hiding out. Wish I coulda got rid of the night touch—wish I'd never had it."

I turned his hands over, palms open. I noticed that his right hand felt cold, but his left was very warm.

"You'll need the nght touch to prove it wasn't your fault, you know . . . the deaths."

He glanced off to one side and half smiled.

"People of Warrior Stand, when they hear the truth, well, they'll think of me like that crazy Indian they had to fight off back a long time ago."

I didn't respond at first because I was staring at his hands. The right one seemed to have gotten smaller—to have shriveled. I blinked my eyes. And then I concentrated on the left hand.

"Jesus, Adam," I exclaimed in a harsh whisper.

In the middle of the left palm, what appeared to be a candle flame of yellow light flickered beneath the skin,

242

and where the Cross of Dark Fortune was, some purple gunk oozed from a small opening, reminding me of those grotesque photos you see of nuns and holy men who bleed from the nail points of Christ's crucifixion—stigmata, I think they call it.

"God almighty, what is this?" I murmured.

He took his hands away, shrugging as if genuinely puzzled or perhaps totally indifferent.

"Some weird-like transformation's been happening. My right hand—it has no power now. None." He flexed it and shook his head. "But this left one, it's gotten stronger, or stranger, at least. Here, I'll show you."

We stepped inside the hardware out of the cold.

"Electricity and fire . . . shit, I almost burned Pudge's farmhouse down during the night."

After a moment or two, his gaze rested on the doorknob of the front door about ten feet away.

"Watch."

He tensed his face, then extended his hand, and blue-white threads jumped from his fingertips to the knob, coating it, buzzing it—sounded like static electricity—then it exploded from the door and I had to dodge the flying metal. It was like a miniature thunderstorm resided in his hand—and had struck the knob with lightning.

I swallowed.

"And here's my blowtorch," he added.

God, I about popped out of my shoes. He wheeled around and pushed his palm out as if demanding that someone stop approaching and a four- or five-foot spear of flame cut and hissed and gushed from the center of his hand. It lasted maybe two seconds, then sucked itself into silence.

Afterwards, the air smelled coppery and sooty at the same time.

"Jesus, that's super weird," I said.

I was shaking.

"Yeah, maybe I ought to wear an asbestos glove."

He was kinda joking, but I couldn't catch my balance

firmly enough to kid around about the phenomenon I'd just witnessed.

"I'm a goddamn freak, Rob!" he suddenly shrieked. And then he cackled until I thought he might break into tears.

My curiosity was hyper.

"The invisible thing . . . you know, that strangles. You still got that?"

He nodded.

"Won't never use it again. Won't never use the night touch to kill. Ever again."

I relaxed a bit.

"You're not a freak or a murderer, Adam. I've told you that before. Just some incredible stuff has happened to you. Like to nobody else in history maybe."

He wasn't listening.

"There's another new power," he muttered. "Last night, when I put my hand to my ear, I could hear my mother praying about me . . . and she was talking to me. I could hear every word but couldn't talk back to her."

No words would have conveyed my sense of wonder at what he had done and said. We were quiet for awhile. Then I said, "You wanna get this over with?"

"Yeah, I sure as hell do."

The fog smudged close to the street as we walked to the Sunset House.

"Why don't you wait here in the lobby and I'll go get Lawrence."

I watched him stroll out into the darkened theater area where he climbed onto the stage. As if giving me one last performance, he let a blue-white single stroke of lightning crackle from his middle finger; the lightning danced and writhed, illuminating the stage briefly.

It's over, I thought to myself. Thank God, it's finally over.

I could even smile at my friend's wild talent.

Leaving him there among the shadows on stage, I walked up to Lawrence's room, feeling mature and proud of myself. I knocked two or three times, heard shuffling,

244

then the door creaking open a couple of inches.

The barrel of a revolver slipped through the gap.

"It's me. Rob Dalton. You can put away the gun. It's Rob Dalton."

I wasn't prepared for the sight of Lawrence—he looked terrible: eyes bloodshot, hair uncombed, beard heavy and flecked with lint. He smelled strongly of body odor like our locker room at school. He wore a wrinkled trenchcoat and an equally wrinkled white shirt.

The hunt for Kristin Kelley had transformed him.

"You bring your friend," he muttered.

"Yeah, he's downstairs waiting."

That news seemed to perk him up considerably.

"Good. Good. I'll take care of matters from here on."

"Just a second," I said, still staring at the revolver. "Why you need that? Adam's giving himself up."

Lawrence paused.

"Sure. You're right. Of course."

He stuffed the revolver into his slacks.

"You all right?"

"I'm fine," he said. "Don't interfere. I've got a job to do."

I stepped aside.

"Where will you take him? Emporia? Topeka?"

"Take him? Oh . . . sure. Sure. Emporia first."

I followed him downstairs.

"He's in the theater area. Up on the stage."

Lawrence turned and put a hand on my shoulder.

"Son, why don't you wait outside. I have a few routine questions to ask him. Routine. For legal purposes. There are so many technicalities these days. I have to handle this carefully."

I nodded and edged away, though something made me hesitate there in the lobby. I decided to eavesdrop on his questions.

"Adam Dodd?"

From the stage, my friend's voice answered, "Yeah, it's me."

"Did you cause the death of your father, Karl Dodd?"

"What?"

"Did you kill your father?"

"Yes."

"Consider very carefully your response to my next question: Did you cause the death of Kristin Kelley? Did you kill her?"

The mistake of the surrender suddenly closed around me like a huge fist.

I heard Adam quietly reply, "I-I never meant to. It was the night touch."

As I stepped into the theater, I saw Lawrence raise his revolver in a two-handed grip, saw the tip of it quiver and jerk.

God, I couldn't believe it.

"Adam!" I shouted. "Watch out!"

"This is for Hugh Kelley! Found you and gonna kill you!"

Adam must not have been able to see him clearly—wasn't concentrating on the night touch.

Lawrence squeezed off two shots, the explosions deafening. And I saw a puff of smoke at Adam's left ear, saw what could have been bits of hair and flesh tear and burn away. Heard Adam scream before I dived at Lawrence.

"Goddamn you! Goddamn coward!" I yelled, tackling him around the waist.

Then, incredible heat and blue-white light and a storm of flame.

Lawrence lurched forward and slammed his head against the edge of one of the seats. I looked toward the stage where Adam, on his knees, had one hand extended, a fireball gushing from it.

"Run!" I cried.

Flames engulfed the stage curtains and ridged along the carpet. Holding his ear, Adam scrambled out the back.

Sunset House was burning like matchsticks.

But suddenly all I could feel was rage; I beat at Lawrence's shoulder and head with my fists—I beat at him until the heat surrounded us. Then, with all my strength, I tugged on him, staying barely ahead of the spreading fire.

"I ought to let you burn!" I screamed at the unmoving body. "You bastard! I ought to let you burn up!"

One thought echoed in my mind: it happened again.

Like it did at Willa Snagovia's. We had led Adam into a trap. Andrea and I . . . our stupidity . . . so damn gullible . . . goddamn.

Lawrence groaned as I dragged him just beyond the front door. He would come to any second, I judged. The heat from the burning building would bring him around. I wasn't proud of saving his life.

I pushed away from Lawrence. The Dodge was gone, and I knew where.

Then I glanced back at Sunset House. Smoke curled away from the roof in massive columns, adding thickness to the morning fog.

"Oh, Jesus, Dad . . . I'm sorry," I whispered.

And the fire began spreading to the hardware.

"Oh, Jesus."

I thought momentarily about my paintings, but it was Adam who commanded my attention. I had to see him one last time. He would run now. Head for Denver. The world had turned against him—I had to see him, tell him I was sorry . . . help him to get as far away from Warrior Stand as possible. And as quickly as possible.

Amid a backdrop of shouting voices and the sting of billowing smoke, I kicked my starter. My lungs ached, and I was angry, so angry I had to fight to control my bike as I roared out of town to the Dodd place.

CHAPTER 19

I parked my bike beside Adam's Dodge, and there pooled at the driver's door, glouts of blood shimmered and glistened. God, how bad is he hurt? I wondered. I glanced in at the steering wheel and the driver's seat—more blood. And in the seat toward the other door, he had laid a road map and some of his drawings. And from the rearview mirror dangled Kristin Kelley's necklace and wildcat figurine; it felt weird seeing it there where guys a little older than me would hang a token from their girlfriends.

I slipped inside the house, greeted by Mrs. Dodd's mournful wailing and crying. In the living room, Leah was tending to Adam's head and ear as Mrs. Dodd, wrapped in blankets, sat on the couch, and, through her tears, seemed to be praying very earnestly.

"Lord God, save my baby! Save my baby!"

I pressed close to Leah, and she wheeled, blinking at me unbelievingly.

"I've never seen anything like this," she exclaimed, turning back to Adam's wound.

"Is it bad?"

At the sound of my voice, Adam, who was sitting on the edge of the coffee table, squirmed around and gave me a thumbs-up. On his knees rested a brightly wrapped Christmas gift.

Leah studied Adam's ear and the scalp above it. I could see that neither was bleeding, that the blood had dried, though the skin had been torn and the tip of his

249

ear was missing.

Leah fluttered her hands; I've never seen her quite so freaked.

"He was bleeding and he stopped it. He put his hand to his ear and the bleeding just . . . stopped."

Again, she blinked at me as if I might offer an explanation for the virtual miracle.

"I know," I said. "It's the night touch."

"God's touch," Mrs. Dodd exclaimed. "Call it the truth. Call it what it is. God saved my baby because He has plans for my baby's life."

It was a confusing scene, and I felt that Adam had no time—he needed to be gone. So I pulled Leah into the kitchen.

"What did Adam tell you?"

Leah stiffened and began to compose herself.

"That Clay Lawrence shot him. Is it . . . is that true?"

"Yeah, it is. Adam's got to leave right away. His wound, is it healed enough for him to travel?"

She seemed baffled.

"Somehow it is. But where can he go? And the fire in town—he claims he started it."

"Let's just let him say goodbye to his mother. There are things he has to do."

"I should have warned you," she suddenly admitted. "I should have warned you about Lawrence. He had told me what he would do if he caught who he was looking for. He suspected Adam. He told me he did."

"Never mind all that now," I said, and I embraced my sister and could tell she was scared and very upset. Hell, so was I.

We held onto each other as we entered the living room; Mrs. Dodd was tearing the wrapping off her present. She fingered the box open and you would have thought she just received a mink stole or a new car, a diamond necklace, or a check for thousands of dollars.

"Oh, for joy! For joy! A new bible—the Lord's book."

She clutched it to her bosom.

"Has your name, Mother," said Adam. "There, in gold letters . . . your own name."

Mrs. Dodd cried in great wracking sobs. Leah cried silently. And, yeah, well, I got pretty misty myself.

"I'm going away, Mother. Something I have to do. There's a kind of . . . of evil got into my hands. I'm going to get rid of it so I can live the rest of my life free. I want to be free of it."

She bracketed his face with her hands.

"The Lord has already forgiven you for your father . . . for the taking of a life, because it wasn't your father, Adam. You must see that. Demon drink changed him. Made him the way he was. You took the life of a demon—not your father."

Adam gestured that he understood.

"When I come back, I'll face what has to be faced. While I'm gone, Mother, if you'll think of me, I'll be able to hear you. You can talk to me in your mind. I can't talk back, but in a sense you can be with me."

She hugged him tightly.

"Goodbye, Mother. I love you."

He started to pull away, but she suddenly became animated and held him like winter vines.

"Oh, wait . . . your present. Wait. Leah, over there under the tree."

It was the only package beneath that pathetic cedar we had decorated.

Mrs. Dodd took the package from Leah and handed it to Adam.

"You'll need these . . . on your trip. I'll understand. If you feel in your heart that you must go. The Lord will watch over you."

Those long fingers deftly unwrapped the package: It was a bright orange woolen scarf and a matching bright orange stocking cap.

"Here," she said, "let me put them on you."

I had to chuckle when she had finished. The scarf throttled his neck and the cap rested all the way down

251

over his eyebrows.

"I'd like to place a dressing on that ear," Leah interrupted cautiously.

A minute or so later she had found some gauze and white tape and Adam was pronounced ready to go.

"Let's leave them alone one last time," I suggested.

Leah and I drifted to the front porch. We didn't notice the cold.

"Won't the sheriff be looking for him? Roadblocks? And how can he manage to drive as he is? No driver's license either. He doesn't have a chance, Rob."

My sister was right.

"But he's a survivor," I followed.

"You going with him?"

"No, he doesn't really need me. As long as the night touch is working, he can handle the car. He'll be okay. And he knows where he has to go."

Just about at that moment, Adam came out onto the porch.

"Thanks, Leah," he said. "For tending to Mother. I'd like to pay you something for your time."

She shook him off.

"No. No, no, . . . I was happy to be able to help."

"Aunt Janie should be here tomorrow. She can go to the funeral with mother . . . and decide what's next."

I looked toward town, saw the smoke, and could hear the fire truck sirens—Warrior Stand's own workpatch vounteer crew. Maybe Council Grove had been given a call, too.

"You better get moving," I said to Adam.

"Thanks again," he whispered to Leah.

She had to bite back some tears.

Out at the Dodge my heart was beating so fast it sorta staggered me.

Adam, clad in his bright orange scarf and stocking cap, slid behind the wheel.

"Mother sure liked my present."

"Yeah, I figured she would."

252

Then I started to recommend the best route to highway 56 so he could avoid going through Warrior Stand. Adam hit me with a sledgehammer comment before I could say another word: "I might not ever see you again, Rob."

As he said that, a mournful little grin formed at the edges of his mouth.

Oh, God.

My tongue seemed to fill the back of my throat.

Lucky thing the Dodge was there for me to hold on to because right then I was awful damn shaky.

"God almighty . . . don't," I somehow managed to exclaim.

"It's true. You and Andy both."

"Shitfire, Adam, you don't have time for this. They'll be coming after you."

Out of the corner of my eye I saw the smoke feeding into the fog, creating a black dome over our hometown.

Hometown—Jesus, that struck me as a strange word.

"Would you tell her something for me, Rob? Andy. Would you tell Andy something I never got around to telling her?"

I fell into his trap; maybe I wasn't listening close because I wanted him to get away.

"Sure. I will. I'll tell her."

"Tell her I love her. I love her as my friend, and I love her, you know . . . more."

That word "more" hung in the cold air, radiating warmth and a wave of embarrassment.

"You'll tell her, won't you, Rob? I know she's really your girl, but . . . I can't help it."

"Jesus Christ, Adam! I said I would!"

I wish I hadn't yelled at him; that ugly, chimpanzee face of his was so hapless I had to look off to one side.

"I'm ready," he said.

"Go south," I told him, "and turn up here at the Harper place and stay on it to 56. Then turn on 177 in Council Grove and take it to highway 70. Get out on 70 and haul ass as fast as you can to Denver."

He bounced excitedly in the seat, hands clamped onto the wheel.

"Haul ass—gotcha, friend."

It was all I could stand. I pushed myself away from the Dodge and jumped on my bike and sped toward town—I wasn't about to watch him drive off. God's truth . . . it would have broken my heart.

PART FOUR:

WINTER ODYSSEY

CHAPTER 20

The sadness burned away fast.

Adam was on his way, on the road, speeding toward the Saturn Man. Well, not exactly speeding, for the ole Dodge probably couldn't hit double nickels unless it was heading downhill.

Would the car make it that far? I tried to recall the distance from Warrior Stand to Denver—500 miles stuck in my thoughts. Jesus, it sounded like a trip to Mars. Would he be stopped by the highway patrol along the way? Would the night touch hold so that he could see to drive?

I should have been scared out of my wits for Adam. But I wasn't. In fact, I was hyper happy as I bounced over the railroad tracks into the smoke and commotion of town. Nothing mattered except that Adam had escaped. That's what it was—an escape from circumstances he couldn't control.

The fire appeared to be mostly out, though smoke continued to billow from the Sunset House and the hardware. Parking across from the hardware, I hollered at Ned Wathan, the chief of our volunteer fire outfit, "Anything left inside the Sunset House?"

I had a flickering hope there might be.

Wathan, a big man with protruding teeth and a pitted complexion, brushed at his cheek, spreading soot like warpaint. He squinted at me, unsure who I was at first.

"Smoke," he said. "'Bout it. Fire gutted the whole thing. Glad your daddy isn't around to see it."

Then he turned and shouted toward one of the other firemen, directing them to the vacant building beyond the hardware. I watched him, my thoughts given over the last part of his comment.

I was trembling.

Sunset House gutted. Dad not around to see it. Thank God.

I thought about going into the charred remains, but decided against it—no point. My gaze drifted to the hardware as Doc Newton emerged carrying two canvases which appeared water-soaked.

Suddenly even my paintings didn't matter to me. My emotions went completely blank.

"Rob, Rob, what's happened?"

Andrea, breathless, bundled up to fight off the cold air, hovered at my shoulder, her cheeks red and shiny.

"They're gone," I said, gesturing across the street. "Sunset House. My paintings. And I really don't care."

She grabbed me and pulled me out of earshot of anyone else.

"Where's Adam? Detective Lawrence is here, but I haven't seen Adam. They're saying he started the fire. They're saying he ran."

I guess it was the absurdity of everything, and especially the absurdity of Adam being blamed for the fire, that sparked my emotions back to life.

"Well, goddamn it, they're wrong. I'll tell you what happened."

And so I did.

As quickly as I could, touching all the appropriate details, recalling the incredible moment when Lawrence raised his gun to try to shoot our friend.

Andrea listened and shook with a gathering rage.

"Let's find him," she cried.

She yanked my arm and I had to follow or lose it. She stomped past a scattering of onlookers and over a couple of firehoses until she came upon Doc Newton hunkered down near a canvas—my "Summerblood" still-life. Behind Newton stood Detective Lawrence, rubbing the

258

side of his head, obviously groggy from having fallen against a seat in Sunset House.

"He's a coward," Andrea shouted, finger pointed at Lawrence. "A chickenshit coward."

A few of the onlookers turned our way at the angry sound of her voice.

Newton stood up, a hand out in front of him as if to calm her down or maybe protect himself.

"It's his job, honey. The boy's dangerous."

I felt something snap inside. Snap. Like the sound of Brian Gunnellson's wrist that night weeks ago.

"No!" I yelled. "No, I saw it all! Adam never did a thing except in self-defense! That son-of-a-bitch was going to shoot him down!"

Lawrence stepped forward.

"Your friend's a murderer and I'm going after him. This time you won't be in the way."

"Andrea's right," I exclaimed to him. "You're a damn coward."

Doc Newton glanced around nervously; then he herded the four of us to the other side of Lawrence's rental car, a blue sedan.

"Rob, this is a matter for the authorities to deal with. Don't stay involved or you could get yourself into big trouble."

I looked beyond Newton to Lawrence, aiming as much hate at him as I could muster. Yet, curiously, a wave of reassurance poured over me.

"You'll never catch him now," I said. "He's gone, and you won't be able to follow him. You don't know where he's going."

"You're wrong about that," he replied smugly.

I glanced at Andrea. There was something in the air I couldn't figure.

"No way you could know where he's headed," I followed. "You're bluffing."

Lawrence opened the door to the rental car and nodded toward Newton.

"Some folks in Warrior Stand are willing to do what's

right. I'm going to Denver to finish what I came here to do."

Dumbfounded, I watched him drive off.

"Grandpa?" Andrea whispered.

The hurt, the disappointment cut through me, tearing, ripping—not a clean cut. Someone I admired had turned on us.

Doc Newton wouldn't meet my eyes. Or Andrea's.

"You bastard!" I exclaimed. "You told him! Why? My God, why?"

"Your friend has to be stopped," he returned, and then walked away.

Andrea ran after him.

"Why, Grandpa? Why? Why would you do that?"

The man turned and took her by the shoulders.

"I did what was best. You'll see that eventually."

He sorta stared her down; I watched, helpless, puzzled. Right before my eyes, Doc Newton transformed into someone I didn't know. Someone different. No, of course, there was no physical transformation, but I would never be able to relate to him in the same positive manner I had. In a twinkling all that had changed.

Stumbling into my arms, Andrea whimpered,

"Why did Grandpa do that? Why does he hate Adam?"

I held her. I had no answer. Instead, an awareness of what I had to do flared in me—I saw events unfolding—God, it was obvious: I had to help my friend.

"I'm headin' out," I told her.

She pulled back.

"What do you mean?"

I had to pause to listen to the thought-echo of my own words.

"I'm going out there to help Adam. He won't know Lawrence is on his heels. He'll be a sittin' duck."

She fell silent, and it gave me a moment to calculate some things, to throw together a ragged plan.

"I've got to go home and get some stuff," I said. "Tell Leah not to worry. And don't you worry either."

I thought she'd be crying. But, no, . . . her jaw

260

tightened, and she said, "I won't worry about you, Rob . . . because I'm going with you."

"What? Oh, Jesus, no, Andrea . . . don't make this any harder than it already is."

Well, she spun me around and pushed me toward my bike.

"Go get what you need and then pick me up at home."

"What are you going to tell your folks?" I exclaimed over my shoulder.

"I'll think of something. Now get."

I started to renew my protest, but there was something in Andrea's defiance which warmed me from head to toe.

"Give me fifteen minutes," I said.

Sure, it was crazy.

The cold, the danger, the fact that it was Christmas—and would we be able to do anything to help our friend? Those were good, rational points, and yet reason mattered little in the scheme of things.

This was something I had to do.

We had to do.

At home, I tried to consider what we would need. More warm clothing—a stocking cap, a woolen scarf, another pair of gloves—and I hurriedly slipped on some long thermal underwear. Money? I had Pudge's Christmas bonus—over a hundred bucks. Andrea always had some cash, too.

Food? No, we had to travel light.

What else?

Something in the back of my mind, some small voice, must have led me out there to the barn. I straddled Midnight and wished I could be a little kid again racing against Drew. The wire supporting the fencepost horse screeched out its metallic song—I was wasting time, hoping the private movie of my life would roll back its reel of film and erase the moment. Lots of moments.

I went to my secret rock.

That voice inside me became more insistent. And I gave in.

For a few seconds I held the revolver, studying its clean, hard smoothness. It seemed that the very act of taking it along guaranteed violence of some kind—violence would follow the weapon the way rain follows a river.

So it goes.

We might need it, that inner voice cautioned.

I wrapped the revolver and container of shells in the woolen scarf and hit the road into town, and I gotta admit that I had my fingers crossed—mentally, at least. I was afraid Andrea had changed her mind, that she would back out.

I wanted her beside me.

But as I wheeled under that big leafless elm in front of her place, something rumbled in my thoughts—God almighty—an avalanche of reality threatened to bury me—and my ridiculous plan.

I sat on my bike wondering how I could have been so stupid; in fact, I was so lost in thought that I didn't hear Andrea slam out of the house and scramble down the front steps.

"I left a note for my folks," she explained, "but I never mentioned where we'd be going. I couldn't leave them with no word at all. Maybe I'll call them tonight."

I looked at her and smiled a totally futile smile.

"We can't do this," I murmured.

Andrea stopped buzzing. Her whole face became a question mark.

Then, anger rose from her momentary confusion.

"You better have a good explanation, mister, because I just made a real hard decision and my head's all scrambled up inside, and if you're playing some kind of game, you better knock it off right now. I'm serious, Rob."

She was.

The beginning of a sob gurgled in her throat—the sound of something getting caught in the drain of a sink.

I gestured helplessly.

God, the air seemed to be getting colder.

"We can't . . . *do this!*"

My voice gained sharpness, and I pounded my fist against the handlebars.

Andrea hitched a large purse onto her shoulder, a massive tote bag that had big letters reading, "The Bag."

"We can," she replied calmly. "We *can*. We have to. We promised Adam we'd help him. So far all we've done is screw him up. Now stop acting like a baby, Rob. Let's go."

"We can't go on the bike," I exclaimed. "Think about it . . . Jesus, we'd freeze in no time. We can't do it."

"Then we'll get a car."

She responded so quickly it threw me off.

"A car?"

"Yes, Rob, . . . a *car*," she echoed sarcastically.

I sorta sputtered and spewed, speechless and feeling like the biggest fool of all time.

"For Christ's sake, Andrea, where we gonna get a car—steal one?"

"If we have to."

The calm, hard, intense lining in her tone surprised me, though it shouldn't have. It was part of that inner steel she possessed, and, oh, God, that steel was about to be tested.

I slammed my thoughts into gear.

A car? Where the hell can we . . . ?

Of course, one place in town had lots of cars, if you could get any of them to run.

"Okay, maybe . . . jump on. I've got an idea."

So she did. And hugged my neck tightly and kissed my ear—a full-lipped, sloppy, slurpy kiss that would turn to ice in the wind.

I smelled something familiar.

"Andrea . . . you been eatin' strawberry licorice?"

She kind of giggled and goosed me in the ribs. And we took off.

A minute or two later I slowed the bike and helped her climb down.

"Pudge?" she exclaimed.

I carried the woolen scarf with me out into the graveyard of cars.

"Yeah, it might be our best shot."

"These are junkers, Rob. They can't take us to Denver."

We angled around until we reached Pudge's office. His old black Ford pickup was parked next to it. I slapped the pickup's tailgate, feeling a sudden surge of hope.

"I think I found an answer. Let's go inside."

Pudge was jamming little blocks of starter wood into his stove, swearing at the cold. He lost his frown when he saw us.

"Come in out of that friggin' North Pole air. Soon as I get this thing hummin' I'll offer you some coffee."

"Don't have time for coffee, Pudge."

He glanced up at me.

"I been to town," he said. "Sorry 'bout the fire burnin' out your place. You two hidin' the boy again?"

"No. No, not exactly. That's what we need to talk about. We need your help. Adam needs your help. We need a car. Fact is, we need your truck. Could we borrow it?"

He took off his cowboy hat and screwed up his face as he scratched the back of his head.

"Better sit a spell and run this by me kinda slow-like."

I didn't sit and I probably didn't explain the whole thing very slowly, but I felt Pudge would understand. I couldn't believe my ears when, after I had finished recounting everything, including our plan, he said, "No, I ain't gonna let ya."

"You've got to!" Andrea cried.

"Pudge—goddamn it, we're trying to help Adam."

"Help him get hisself killed. That'd be 'bout the size of it if you go chasin' out there. If anybody's goin', it'd be me. Me and my shotgun."

Something came over me right then. It was a real strange, clawing kind of desperation. I unrolled the woolen scarf and said, "Give us the keys to your truck. I

264

mean it."

He stared at the revolver.

Andrea whispered, "Rob, where did you get that?"

"Never mind," I told her, keeping my attention on Pudge.

"You ain't bein' sensible, son. You ain't a gun person. Like as not, you'll get somebody hurt."

"The keys, Pudge. Goddamn it, we don't have time. Lawrence is after him. We got to try to stop him—it's our way. Our way!"

I was shouting those final words.

Pudge put his hands on his hips; he looked from me to Andrea and then back to me. I had no idea what he was going to do. I wondered whether his shotgun was close by.

Then he did something I wasn't expecting.

He smiled. Smiled and shook his head.

"You're a wild-haired son-of-a-bitch of a kid, aren't you? Both of you. Well, I reckon I can see you're doin' this 'cause of how you feel about the boy."

He took the keys out of his pocket and tossed them to me.

I lowered the revolver.

"Jesus, Pudge, . . . I'm sorry I pulled this on you . . . I really am."

Andrea had ahold of my arm, and we sorta leaned against each other.

"One more thing," said Pudge.

"What's that?"

He nibbled at the corner of his moustache and gave us another version of his classic shit-eating grin.

"Good luck."

Once Andrea and I had bundled into the truck, Pudge offered a final piece of advice.

"Keep an eye on the radiator, son. I suspect it's sprung a pin-hole leak somewheres. She might run hot on you, so pour her a big drink of water often as you can."

I nodded and gave the ignition a crank. Took four cranks to catch.

Fingers of nausea squeezed my stomach.

Jesus, can this junk heap even get us to Council Grove?

Pudge flashed us a brave wink, and we half-heartedly waved. I took back roads west until we could hook up with highway 56 again. It was about one o'clock in the afternoon—Adam had a half an hour headstart on us, and Lawrence . . . well, that bastard was somewhere between Adam and us.

Funny thing, but Andrea and I never spoke a word to each other before we swung down the long slope into Council Grove.

"Damn, I hated to pull a gun on Pudge," I muttered.

"It seemed like you had to," said Andrea. "He wasn't going to let us have the truck."

Those were the words I wanted to hear, but as I glanced at her out of the corner of my eye I could see how tense she was. Her back wasn't touching the seat; it looked as if she couldn't bend her upper body.

That struck me in a curious way.

I had to laugh; I just couldn't help it. And it felt good.

Andrea turned, pinned me with a stare that told me she thought I'd gone whole-hog looney.

As we rolled past the Madonna of the Trail statue, she had to laugh, too. I guess my laughter was infectious.

"Damn you," she exclaimed, laughing harder, punching at my shoulder. "What are you laughing about?"

"What are *you* laughing about?"

We took a right onto highway 177.

"I'm *not* laughing. There's *nothing* to laugh about," she sputtered.

"You really want to know why I'm laughing? It's because this is so crazy. That's why," I said, lapsing into a more serious tone. "I guess that's the reason. And seeing you sitting there like you got a ramrod down your back— you look like that poor ole Madonna statue."

I shook my head and continued. "You know, we really got to be out of our minds to be doing this. I don't have a real driver's license. This truck might stop running any second. And we could get ourselves all shot up . . . or, if nothing else, we'll likely freeze to death between here and Denver."

"You're very comforting, mister," she growled, all the laughter having disappeared.

Gray, Christmas afternoon clouds and a stiff north breeze greeted us at the top of each hill; 177 is a roller coaster of a road cutting through an endless spectrum of treeless landscape.

From our vantage point, the scene held no promise; it was forbidding. It seemed to taunt us, daring us to continue. And I wondered how in the world the early settlers had bested this land, gaining some edge over it as they traveled west.

Traveling west.

That was us. And oxen probably would have been more dependable than Pudge's truck.

At the entrance to highway 70, the interstate which would direct us to Denver, the heater went out.

"I'm cold," Andrea whispered.

I fiddled with the heater controls.

"Shit!"

Andrea stuffed her hands deeper into the sleeves of her heavy coat.

"Sorry, babe," I murmured. "Think warm thoughts."

She stuck out her tongue at me.

"Sing a hot song," I suggested. "Rock and roll—not country western."

Instead she switched on the radio; it winced some static as if she had poked it with a sharp stick.

"Radio doesn't work either? Rob, this is a total junker. And I'm free-e-e-e-zing."

"Beats ridin' on my bike. If you think you're cold now . . . geez, you'd be a block of ice before Junction City."

"Do you really believe we made a mistake doin' this?"

She shivered and looked forlorn, expecting me to say something upbeat, I guess.

I disregarded her question, my eyes straying to the temperature gauge which was creeping to the "H." I sucked in my breath.

"Keep a watch for highway patrolmen."

"This truck couldn't break the speed limit," she sneered. "We've got no worries there."

"Not what I mean. Somebody may have alerted them that Adam's likely to be taking this road. Watch along the exits."

"Maybe Adam will get off the interstate somewhere, you know, on county roads."

She had a point. Maybe he would.

"Let's watch for Lawrence, too."

Andrea grew quiet, as if she hadn't wanted to be reminded of that name.

Christmas traffic on the interstate was surprisingly light; folks must have reached their holiday destinations. Not much Christmas cheer out on the rolling landscape past Junction City.

I began to calculate a stop for the radiator. No use pressing our luck, I told myself.

Well, about then, I said something pretty dumb.

"Hey, Andrea, there's one thing I haven't told you."

Her head whirled and a strange sheen of anxiety covered her face.

"Is it about this truck? Because if it is, I don't want to hear it, Rob. I'm serious."

I reached over to touch her arm.

"No, it's not the truck."

She wrinkled her brow.

I smiled innocently and said, "Merry Christmas, babe. That's what I hadn't told you—Merry Christmas."

Some things about women I'll never understand. The way they can shift emotions without using a clutch, for example. You see, when I wished Andrea a "Merry Christmas," she started crying.

Bawled like a baby.

I almost had to stop the truck.

God almighty.

The signs for the Abilene exit began looking more and more inviting. As Andrea sobbed, the temperature gauge wiggled a tiny bit closer to trouble.

"Please don't cry," I said. "We'll turn into Abilene and get water and gas. We'll go inside somewhere and warm up. I need to use the restroom. Do you?"

She mumbled something under her breath.

"What, babe?"

She mumbled it again through a wrack of subsiding tears.

I leaned her way as I angled onto the Abilene exit.

"What'd you say?"

She took a big, deep breath, cleared her throat, and forced a smile.

"Merry Christmas, Rob."

And turned on the waterworks again.

"Damn," I whispered to myself. "This is gonna be one hell of a long drive."

We pulled into a truck stop, easing up to one of the pump islands behind a station wagon, the rear section of which threatened to burst it had so many Christmas presents jammed into it.

"Here," I said, handing Andrea a dollar, "go into the restaurant and get you some hot chocolate. I'll take care of the truck."

She blew her nose, then checked her face in the rearview mirror.

"Lord, I'll have to work on this before I can let people see me."

So as she pored through that massive totebag of hers, gathering a handful of cosmetics. I inched up to the self-service pump, the Christmas-laden station wagon having driven off to its appointed rounds.

I raised the hood and the heat from the radiator steamed against my face. It actually felt good as long as I could put aside the grim image of the thing heating up on us and stranding us out west somewhere. The radiator cap was too hot to remove by hand; I decided to let the cooling system lose some heat, using the time to examine the radiator hoses.

Andrea popped around the front of the truck, forcing a smile.

"Prettier than Tanya Tucker?" she chirped.

"Yeah . . . well, maybe."

I dodged her punch and she headed for the restaurant. She did look pretty—I had to admit that.

But the radiator did not. Damnit.

I swung my boot up and kicked at the cap and the next thing I knew a miniature Old Faithful geyser spewed hot water and antifreeze everywhere. I burned my hand and drew the attention of several motorists.

"Shit! Shit! Shit!" I muttered.

The upshot of the experience proved costly: a new radiator cap and a fresh batch of antifreeze. Finished creating a watery mess, I parked the truck on the restaurant side of the area, figuring I better let the sucker cool down a while longer. At the service station cash register, I paid the bill in cash and tried to act older than fifteen—a tough trick for me.

On a Kansas map above the register, I checked mileage. It was kinda disheartening; Abilene to Hays, 117 miles, Abilene to Goodland, 258.

We'll never make it that far, something within me cried.

I found Andrea in a booth in the restaurant, her spirits considerably enlivened. I glanced around for highway patrolmen, saw none, felt a notch or two more relaxed. I ordered some coffee, and Andrea, sorta offhandedly, said, "Abilene used to have lots of gunfighters and outlaws, didn't it?"

Suddenly I thought about Dad's revolver wrapped in the scarf lying right out on the front seat. Possession of a handgun without a permit—oh, Jesus, why hadn't I stuck it *under* the seat?

"Eisenhower," I exclaimed. "That's what Abilene's known for now. President Eisenhower's hometown. Don't you remember that fourth-grade field trip we took? We rode up here on the bus and saw the Eisenhower Museum."

270

She remembered. And laughed.

"Adam ate four hot dogs and threw up all over Wendy Perry on the way home."

I had forgotten about that.

Then Andrea's pretty face darkened. She'd said the magic word—"Adam"—and I knew I'd better drink my coffee as quickly as possible. In fact, I burned the roof of my mouth gulping the hot, black stuff down when it came. Burned mouth to go with a burned hand.

"We'll find him," I told her. "This will all work out somehow."

I wanted to believe that.

"We better go," I added.

Just as we got into the truck, a couple of guys in a beat-up old gray van were leaving, too. The driver, a round, smooth, fat face, diamond-studded earring in his left ear, stared at us. His partner, a ratty-looking, very thin character in a black stocking cap and shoulder-length hair, gave Andrea the onceover and drummed his palm on our fender.

"Ranger Man," he called to his shiny, pink-faced friend, "look at that sugar cunt."

And the fat-faced one grinned and slurred out some words very slowly.

"You got you a good eye there, Doyle. Sure do."

Doyle, the skinny one, in full view of me and Andrea, put his hand to his crotch and obscenely lifted himself up on his tiptoes.

"Honeypot, my stars! My stars!" he called out.

Well, I started for them, but Andrea grabbed me.

"Don't do it, Rob."

I had to bite back my anger.

They drove off, laughing and leering, with me smoldering and helpless and humiliated.

CHAPTER 21

I felt like running them down.

As we hit highway 70 again, and followed that gray-black ribbon west, I watched for them, certain they had also turned west. Sure, I had no business thinking about getting revenge, but damn, oh, damn, they made me mad.

"Where you suppose Adam is?"

Andrea brought me back to reality. I took a peek at the temperature gauge, saw the needle had stationed itself halfway between the "C" and the "H," and breathed a sigh of relief. My inner temperature gauge adjusted accordingly.

"Up ahead," I replied. "Probably not far."

"Rob, please forget about them."

"Them?"

"You know . . . those jerks in the van."

Well, of course, I knew all along who she was talking about; I assumed my dumb act.

"I'm more concerned about Lawrence."

That was an outright lie at that moment.

But suddenly I did experience a case of gut-wrenching anxiety: Lawrence was out there, the man who apparently had come to Warrior Stand for one reason and one reason only—to kill. And Adam had no inkling of the danger he was in. Or did he? Could he use the night touch to sense that he was being pursued, being hunted down?

Where was the hunter? How close to his prey?

Could he be stopped in time?

Was I capable of stopping him?

Lawrence, you bastard, leave our friend alone. . . .

At the first roadside rest area between Salina and Russell, Clay Lawrence craned his neck for a glimpse of the old Dodge.

Show your face, kid.

Let's get this over with.

His jaw ached from tensing it, from working his back teeth together, grinding, determined to catch up with his prey.

He drove past the rest area and relaxed his grip on the revolver in the seat beside him.

In his mind, he saw blue-white threads of electricity; he saw fire spearing toward him; he saw his revolver discharge; he felt Rob Dalton's body slam into his. When his head had crashed into the theater seat, he had dropped into a whirlwind, and within that maelstrom of sound and fury, he had heard the voice of Hugh Kelley. He had seen Hugh Kelley's face in the wall of the whirlwind—had seen the man's lips moving:

Find the bastard and kill him.

Kill him and I'll rest in peace.

The wall had closed upon his friend, Coach Hugh, and, wafting over the dull roar of the spinning storm, Lawrence had heard a young girl's song:

> *Tell me you like me*
> *And I'll do you no wrong.*
> *Tell me you love me*
> *And I'll sing you a song.*

Kristin's face had ghosted through a dark curtain of wind and clouds, and Lawrence had seen her hand and had reached for it . . . but for an eternity she had remained out of reach.

Drifting onto the shoulder of the highway, Lawrence

274

caught himself, shook himself out of the deep reverie.

"Can't hide forever," he whispered into the silence of the car. "You can't hide from me forever. You can't run away from me."

One clear shot, he cautioned himself. One clear shot, and my job's done.

CHAPTER 22

"I wish you hadn't brought that."

Andrea was pointing down at the scarf and the revolver nestled within it.

"We might need it," I argued, but, rather sheepishly, I slipped the scarf and revolver under my seat. "A gun evens the odds against Lawrence."

She hugged herself, irritated at me and the fingers of cold air which had found numerous openings in the old floorboard of the truck. There was misery in her eyes, and I had no idea at the moment how to make things better.

I stared out at the stark, undulating prairie.

It was late afternoon, and a gathering darkness, a "gloam," I think the word is, was spreading across the very center of Kansas in that long stretch of highway between Salina and Russell. Shades of gray and faded purple touched the landscape, but it failed to inspire. I wondered, in fact, whether I would ever be inspired to paint again.

Andrea crawled within herself and didn't speak.

I thought it best not to poke at her. If we could only catch up with Adam, the trip would get better for her. She would see that we had done the right thing.

Green-clad exit signs for places like Ellsworth, Wilson, and Dorrance whizzed by; people in those towns would be recovering from a morning of gift-giving. Some of the kids would have already broken some of their toys.

"It's about forty miles to Hays. Probably a good place

to stop and eat and give the radiator a drink."

Andrea remained silent. I caught myself thinking of Pudge—I had borrowed his phrase about putting water in the radiator. God, had I really pulled a gun on him?

Forgive me, Pudge.

And I wished right then that Adam and Andrea and I were sitting in Pudge's pissant little office, drinking coffee, watching the old guy put away a box of saltines and listening to his artful lies about rodeo days.

Mostly, I wished we could be with Adam.

Damn, I missed him.

I thought about the night touch and about that final scene of him saying goodbye to his mother, and I guess that triggered something. Adam had claimed that through the night touch he could hear his mother talking to him, praying about him even though they were miles apart.

I glanced at Andrea. She had leaned into the far corner, head tilted against the glass. I couldn't tell whether she was asleep; I doubted she was.

My thoughts shifted again to Adam.

I felt kinda silly trying it, but, what the hell, I reasoned—it could work. I concentrated, imagining Adam's chimpanzee-like face:

Adam, there's trouble. Lawrence is after you.
Me and Andrea, we're on the road. We want to
help you. I want you to be with us. Be careful,
friend. Be careful.

I had no sense of having made contact. Figured I hadn't.

Suddenly I felt terrifically lonesome, and so I started singing the first song that came into my head—Willie Nelson's "On the Road Again."

I began kinda low and twangy, then gained some momentum and was belting it out in no time at all. Frowning, Andrea jolted awake. And I sang even louder.

She held her ears.

"That's awful, Rob. Your singing is awful."

Well, it was. But it changed the atmosphere within the

truck. Boosted our spirits.

You see, Andrea took over the song, and with a little coaxing, she sang others, including every one of Reba McEntire's she knew, and a medley of Dolly Parton, Barbara Mandrell, Loretta Lynn, and Patsy Cline.

She must have sung thirty or forty songs between Russell and Hays.

"Time for a commercial, babe," I hollered over one of her tunes.

She lunged over and kissed my cheek.

"Guess you're feeling better," I said.

She nodded and winked at me.

As I flipped on the turn signal for the Hays exit, I pushed aside the dark thought of possibly driving all night to catch Adam. With Andrea in a good mood once again, I wasn't about to dwell on negatives.

We found another truckstop; I pumped some gas into our transportation and checked the radiator. It was hot. Much too hot. Damn—it was still losing water. I knew it might hold on all the way to Denver, or it might . . . well, I slammed the hood on that thought.

While Andrea scrambled into the restaurant—it had turned colder, a north wind gusted—I parked the truck in an isolated corner of the truckstop area, a corner dark enough that maybe no highway patrolman or a local policeman would notice. I suppose I had no reason to be so paranoid, but I was.

"I'm starved," Andrea announced as I sat down in a booth next to her.

"Yeah, me, too."

We ordered hamburgers and french fries and hot chocolate and coffee; both of us planned on dessert.

"I feel like an outlaw," Andrea exclaimed. "Don't you? Sorta like Bonnie and Clyde—you know, the bank robbers in that movie."

"Remember what happened to them?"

"Oh, Rob . . . we're not *really* like them. Just sorta."

I can't say why exactly, but, minutes later, there in that restaurant, warm food and hot drink in our stomachs, we felt good, a crazy kind of good.

"How far have we come?" my companion asked through a mouthful of french fries.

I started to figure it exactly, then gave up.

"A long ways."

"What's the radiator look like?"

"Trouble. Keep your fingers crossed."

She shrugged it off. I watched her eat, and out of the clear blue I found myself thinking: I love her. I love Andrea Helms. I almost told her so. Almost.

"Hey, I've got to call my folks," she said. "Don't worry—all I'm gonna say is that I'm okay and we're trying to help Adam."

Part of me didn't want her to call; part of me knew she should.

"Tell them to tell Leah I'm okay, too."

I gave her some change for the pay phone located near the restrooms. I went to the men's room, thinking I'd empty my bladder and then have one more cup of coffee before we left. I decided we'd try to make it to Oakley before stopping again—about 90 miles.

When I stepped out of the restroom, my heart froze.

"Oh, Jesus, no," I muttered beneath my breath.

It was the one called Doyle. Standing at the cash register, he pored his weasel-like eyes over a display of candy with the same kind of hunger and sleazy fascination in his expression as when he had looked at Andrea.

Not wanting him to see us, I grabbed Andrea and dragged her back to the booth.

"What in the world's gotten into you, Rob?"

"It's that creep."

I gestured over her shoulder toward the cash register. I saw her tighten up.

"Do you think he and the other one followed us?"

"Wouldn't be surprised . . . wait, okay, he's going into the restroom. Let's pay up and hit the road."

The woman at the register took her time, pecking at the keys like a befuddled chicken deciding which kernel

280

of corn to eat.

"Geez, we're in a hurry," I complained.

She glanced at me over the rims of her glasses, and, if anything, grew more deliberate.

"Keep the change," I exclaimed finally.

Andrea and I hustled back to the truck, thankful that the darkness hid us.

I opened my door and heard kind of a gasp from the other side of the truck; Andrea couldn't work the door because the handle didn't always catch.

"Hold on a second," I shouted as I reached across the seat and pushed at the inside of the door.

Knife at her throat, she slid in.

I just stared.

I couldn't move.

"We've been lookin' for you," said the one called Ranger Man.

His fat face glistened with sweat visible even in the shadows and despite the cold air.

The blade of his knife appeared to be more than a foot long.

"What do you want? Let us alone."

"Donchoo be makin' too many demands, pecker boy . . . or I'll use your gal friend to change the color of your seat covers. I like red, if you catch what I mean."

He smiled, wrinkling that round, disgusting face; his diamond earring glinted.

"Please," I said, "don't hurt her. What do you want? Money?"

Andrea had closed her eyes. Appeared to be praying.

God, it hurt to see her being held like that. I thought about the gun just under the seat. Could I risk going for it?

Then, behind me, a voice.

"You've found my honeypot, Ranger Man. How 'bout that?"

The blade of Doyle's switchblade pressed into the skin below my ear.

"Should we take 'em back to Shooter's?" Ranger Man

281

asked his partner.

"Naw . . . naw, we can find a nice country road off the interstate where we gonna need to get . . ." and he paused as if searching for the right word ". . . *intimate* with honeypot."

"Intimate . . . yeah, intimate."

Ranger Man repeated the word with a panting glee which sickened me.

Andrea began to cry softly.

"You can't get away with this," I suddenly, stupidly exclaimed.

I wheeled around.

Pain jolted me. I doubled over at the impact of Doyle's knee in my crotch.

Andrea tried to scream, but Ranger Man closed his hand over her mouth.

I swallowed huge bites of cold air before Doyle lifted my head, the point of the switchblade under my chin.

"Looks like you won't be gettin' in on the fun, son. Too bad. Too bad."

Things got fuzzy for me, though the terror of the situation never let up. They directed me to drive the truck, following Doyle in the gray van as Ranger Man kept a hold on Andrea.

We drove west of Hays. I don't recall how far; I could barely stand to operate the pedals.

"Don't cry, Andrea," I managed to say. "They won't really do anything. They just want to scare us real bad."

I would have given my right arm to be certain of that.

"We ain't so terrible," said Ranger Man. "I mean . . . we ain't gonna kill you or nothin' like that."

He said it matter-of-factly, which seemed to intensify the sinking horror I felt. I couldn't imagine what Andrea must have been thinking. I wanted to vomit. In fact, I thought I was going to pass out.

"He's turning off," said Ranger Man. "Stay on his ass. He's thought of a spot for us. These is his stomping grounds."

He squeezed Andrea and she squirmed, gritting her teeth.

"No!" she shrieked, and I thought about the revolver. I dropped by left arm between the door and seat.

"Both hands on the wheel, pecker boy."

Ranger Man controlled Andrea and was able to keep an eye on me at the same time.

Oh, God, Adam, we need your help.

Somewhere between Hays and WaKeeney we angled north onto a county line road, the winter darkness revealing only a scattered farmhouse or two. It was a place in which you could have yelled for help at the top of your lungs and nobody on God's earth could have heard you besides coyotes and jackrabbits.

The van eased onto the shoulder of a narrow, dirt road. I braked the truck maybe forty feet behind the van.

Ranger Man waited for Doyle to approach, and when the smaller, much thinner man opened the truck door on the shotgun side, he grinned at Andrea, holding out something toward her between his thumb and forefinger.

"Care for a Life Saver?"

He snickered and tossed candy into his mouth.

To Ranger Man, he said, "Flip a coin to see who goes first."

"Go ahead, Doyle, be my guest."

And the comment struck Doyle with amazement.

"Ain't Ranger Man a gentleman? Fuckin' world don't have many gentlemen these days . . . but Ranger Man, he's one. He is one."

I tried to think, to concentrate, to watch for an opening. I could imagine the revolver wrapped in the scarf; I could feel it in my hand; I could see myself pointing it at these bastards—could see the sudden reflection of fear in their eyes—could hear the discharge as bullets blew them away.

But it was all in my mind.

As they shoved Andrea out of the truck, I tensed every muscle. She made a quick move to spin away, scratching and kicking at Doyle, but he pinned her arms behind her and cursed at her.

And I heard him say: "Gonna make it hurt. Gonna make it hurt bad for that."

I couldn't wait any longer. I slammed my shoulder against the door.

"Keep your hands off her!" I shouted.

And my right elbow caught fire.

Ranger Man's grip was a steel vise. I groaned, maybe half-screamed—I can't even remember.

"You'll get a turn, pecker boy. But you have to act like a gentleman. Hear me? Like a gentleman."

He pressed his lips against my ear, hissing the words, his breath hot and stinking.

Through the windshield I could see Doyle throw open the back of the van, and I watched helplessly as Andrea tore at his hold. I heard her scream as he repositioned his lock on her arm.

Then it happened, happened so unexpectantly that for a split-second or two I thought I was imagining it: she broke free. She ran, and Doyle scrambled after her, cursing.

Ranger Man loosened his grip on my elbow just a notch. The fire there flamed down.

Into a ditch and up onto the edge of a pasture Andrea frantically stumbled, Doyle close behind. She was eluding him, but not by much.

God, my chest nearly exploded.

"Come help me, goddamn it," Doyle yelled.

"Stay right where you are, pecker boy."

And with that, Ranger Man pushed himself out of the truck.

I immediately jammed my hand under the seat and jerked the scarf up into my lap; I opened the box of shells, scattering them everywhere. Fingers trembling, I flipped out the chamber of the revolver so I could stuff a few shells into it.

"Damn! Goddamn!" I muttered as the first two shells skittered away.

I glanced up into the pasture where Andrea, terrified out of her mind, continued to stay beyond the grasp of Doyle and Ranger Man.

Click.

The sound was solid. Two shells in place.

I jumped out of the truck and raced toward the pasture.

"Hold it right there, you bastards!"

But they never stopped.

I fired. And it seemed like an incredibly loud roman candle going off—sparks and flame, and the explosion echoed and echoed across that vast, dark, empty landscape.

"Hold it, or I'll blow your goddamn heads off!"

Andrea circled, crying hard, avoiding them until she could angle to my side.

The two men stood like statues.

Clutching at me, her entire body quivering, Andrea nearly toppled me.

"Get in the truck," I told her. "Right now."

Then, to our attackers, I said, "Don't try to follow us, or you're dead."

Ranger Man stepped forward.

"Doyle . . . I don't hardly believe this pecker boy has the balls to shoot us. Let's try him."

I squeezed off the last shot just over his head—and prayed they wouldn't force the issue further.

"Christ alive!" he exclaimed.

They didn't move as I felt my way to the truck, started it up and spun dirt and sand. Somehow—I guess it's her basic toughness—Andrea had calmed down; she hung on my neck and quietly sobbed.

For the better part of a minute, I couldn't think; I watched the rearview mirror so intensely I almost put the truck in the ditch. They weren't following us.

"We lost them, babe. We've lost them. It's okay. We're safe."

But I had no idea how to return to Highway 70.

Minutes later, I stopped at a farmhouse bearing a sign in the front yard which read "Member of Palco, Kansas 4-H Club." A red-faced, Irish-looking farmer gave me directions, eyeing me rather suspiciously. Couldn't blame him. I must have appeared to have been on drugs or something.

"Home, Rob," Andrea whispered. "I can't do this. I want to go home."

"But, babe, we have to—"

"Please, Rob."

She had drawn her lips together so tightly she could barely speak. And I realized she was right. After what she had gone through . . . well, I had no right to ask her to continue.

I'm sorry, Adam. We tried. We just can't go on.

"Okay, babe. I'm turning back."

She hugged me, burying her head on my shoulder.

"I'm sorry, Rob."

"No," I said. "Nobody has to be sorry. We just had some . . . bad luck."

We bore ahead due east on the interstate, passing Russell; I was determined not to stop again until we got at last past Salina.

"We should tell the police about those men, shouldn't we?" said Andrea.

I knew we should. But I didn't want to get involved, to raise questions about what we had been doing.

"I don't feel like we can."

I sensed that Andrea was pondering something more.

"Will Adam be all right?" she followed. "Tell me he will, Rob. Tell me he will."

"He's got the night touch," I replied. "That's something we don't have."

Then we lapsed into silence for miles and miles.

It was cold, a cold worsened by a north wind which occasionally gusted, plunging the wind chill factor.

In a way I felt sad giving up and returning to Warrior Stand.

Good luck, Adam. God knows, you'll need it.

"Are we low on gas?"

Andrea's quetion drew my attention to the gauges.

"No, we could make it almost all the way home before we had to get some."

I happened to notice the temperature gauge.

Oh, Jesus. Look at that.

I said nothing, not wanting to frighten Andrea.

The needle had dropped clear against the "H."

I searched approaching signs for an exit. The next one—five miles.

A mile later Pudge's old truck shut down.

"What is it, Rob?"

As I drifted onto the shoulder, I could hear the radiator give way through a rupture somewhere. Water gurgled and spattered; steam rose eagerly from under the hood.

"Oh, this can't be!" Andrea exclaimed.

"I'm afraid it is."

I let the truck roll to a stop and laid my head on the steering wheel.

"Maybe it's not as bad as it seems," said Andrea. "Maybe you could fix it."

I had to chuckle at that. A miserable chuckle.

We got out and lifted the hood. Andrea leaned near the hot radiator for warmth while I tried to flag down a car or semi. A half a dozen passed us before a pair of lights slowed.

I ducked over to the radiator and warmed my hands on the steam; I forced a smile at Andrea.

"Somebody finally stopped. We'll get to a service station and call your dad or Pudge or someone and have them come get us."

I held her and kissed her forehead.

"I've been a bad luck charm," she whispered. "You should have gone without me."

"No. No, babe. You haven't been bad luck."

A voice careened around from behind the truck.

"You folks havin' trouble?"

I stepped to the side and looked into the darkness to greet our good samaritan.

"Ranger Man, these two young folks look kinda familiar to you? They sure do to me. Didn't they threaten to shoot us?"

My insides turned to water.

287

"Rob!"

Andrea held me hard.

"The pecker boy's no gentleman," said Ranger Man. I watched as he dug around in the front seat until he found the revolver. In the meantime, Doyle strolled up to us.

"Honey pot, Mr. Ranger Man and me got a lim-o-zine waitin' for you. Your boyfriend can come along. To watch. We'll teach him how to do a thing or two."

Doyle drove.

They stashed us in the back of the van up close to the front seats where Ranger Man sat, bracing the revolver an inch from my ear. Andrea scrunched up next to me.

Doyle and Ranger Man talked non-stop. Angry talk. Filthy talk. I couldn't believe it, but they even sang Christmas carols. Psychotics. We were in the company of two psychotics, and despite their earlier claim that they wouldn't kill us, I was convinced they would.

We rode for maybe ten minutes before the van left the interstate, rolled past a series of service stations and restaurants until it chugged into a small, dimly lighted station.

I felt a surge of hope.

Maybe we could shout for help.

A car had followed us into the station, but then it pulled on behind the building on a dirt road and I lost sight of its taillights.

A young attendant—couldn't have been any older than me or Andrea—came out to the van.

"Merry Christmas, Shooter," said Doyle, lowering the window. "We got you a live one. Warm and willing. Need to borrow your tire shed."

Shooter had long black hair and a grotesque case of facial acne. He peered in at Andrea. His cold, mean expression never changed.

"Don't wear her out before I get a jump at her." Then he added, "Traffic's slow. Come relieve me in about a half hour."

Half hour.

I figured that was all the minutes of life we had left.

"I've got over a hundred dollars," I pleaded. "You can have it if you let us go."

Doyle smiled.

"You see, son, a hundred dollars is our fee for this here lim-o-zine and the party we's gonna have in the tire shed. I right about that, Ranger Man?"

The fat one nodded.

They took us back to a metal shed behind the station. It was probably forty feet by forty feet and filled with stacks of tires and rafter racks also lined with tires.

One single light bulb pushed away shadows.

In the center of the shed was an Army cot.

The carbon stench of the tires burned at my nose.

I tried to reassure Andrea, but I had run out of things to say.

Doyle yanked her away from me, tore off her coat and shoved her toward the cot. She screamed and fought at him like a wildcat, scratching, clawing; I moved to help her, shouting, flailing my arms. Quickly both of us were silenced: Doyle caught Andrea with a cupped hand at the side of her head; the impact spun her onto the cot.

I was choking. Several inches of the barrel of the revolver had been thrust into my mouth; my tongue ridged pain and two large chips from my bottom row of teeth dribbled out onto my lip.

"Quiet, pecker boy. You won't be able to hear Doyle work."

Ranger Man forced me to watch.

I couldn't tell how hurt Andrea was. The blow apparently knocked her out.

Doyle stood over her, unfastened his belt, and removed his jeans.

The revolver was nearly strangling me, but it did no good to struggle—Ranger Man had me in a defenseless position.

God, oh, God, Andrea, I'm sorry.

Before he began to take off Andrea's clothes, Doyle turned toward us, rubbing his arms, grinning broadly.

"Need some heat in here. I know just the way to bring some."

Ranger Man snickered a little boy's snicker, and I thought maybe I heard another sound, an odd chatter, before realizing it was probably my teeth clicking against the revolver.

"Honeypot, I got something hot for you."

Doyle half-turned again to make sure Ranger Man and I had a good view.

"Something hot," he murmured, winking at us.

But suddenly his grin disappeared.

I *felt* the blast of heat before I saw it.

A ball of red-orange fire the size of a basketball hit Doyle in the stomach; he doubled over with it as if catching one of those weighted medicine balls. And screamed. Then he stumbled back and back, losing his balance as the flame stitched from his chest toward his face and from his crotch toward his feet.

He cried out like a crazed animal.

Ranger Man pulled away from me and raised the revolver and squeezed the trigger; the hammer clicked several times and he stared at it in disbelief; he kept the unloaded weapon pointed at the door as Adam stepped farther into the shed.

And I prayed to God it wasn't some spectacular hallucination.

Extending his left hand, Adam drew a mask of concentration over his face. The blue-white threads of electricity spun away from his fingers, coiling around the barrel of the revolver and up and around Ranger Man's arm, and he, too, began to scream—a frightened pig's squeal. He jerked back and forth, trying to tear his hand from the gun. He bit off the tip of his tongue and the diamond stud in his ear popped out like a kernel of popcorn popping. His bloody tongue lolled onto his chin and blisters beaded on his forehead and cheeks.

Then he crashed to the floor.

Andrea had come to and I ran to her and lifted her from the cot as Doyle rolled over and over, extinguishing the

290

flames, but not his agony. Some of the tires had caught fire and the shed began to fill with smoke.

"The Dodge is out behind," said Adam.

I wanted to grab him and kiss him. God's truth, I did. The three of us scrambled out of the shed.

And found the one called Shooter blocking our path, tire iron in hand.

He rushed at us.

Adam threw a ball of fire at his feet, and he retreated a few steps.

"Stay back or I'll fry you to a crisp," Adam called out at him.

Two more balls of fire proved convincing, though I heard my friend grimace in pain as he delivered them.

We hustled into the Dodge; Adam, taking the wheel and obviously in a lot of pain, roared away from the smoke and fire and the nightmare.

CHAPTER 23

"The end of the goddamn world."

As Clay Lawrence relieved himself, he whispered into the empty walls of the restroom. He had made it just beyond Oakley—seventy miles or so from the Colorado line—and the vast and vacant territory through which he had journeyed mesmerized him. And the highway promised no final destination.

He shivered involuntarily.

"What the hell am I doing?"

He splashed his face with cold water. If it were possible for a road to hypnotize a driver, then Highway 70 west of Hays could do it, for you could not help but look into the face of a desolate darkness which invited you to slip into oblivion.

Stepping outside the restroom area, he stretched and yawned.

The last few sleepless nights were catching up with him.

"Where are you, kid? Let's finish this before I go batty."

Have I lost him? he considered.

The crawling suspicion that he had glimpsed the old Dodge on the other side of the interstate would not release him. But Newton had insisted that the kid was going to Denver—why would he turn back?

A semi, air brakes hissing, pulled into the rest area, parking beyond Lawrence's rental car. A large man, bulging belly, cowboy boots, got out; Lawrence watched him stroll along the trailer and kick at two of the rear tires. The trucker kept the semi running, and it gave off an eager, thrumming noise. Lawrence imagined it to be the breathing of some prehistoric creature.

"Evening, fellow traveler," the trucker called out in a surprisingly gentle voice when he was still some thirty yards away. Though he did not feel like talking, Lawrence waited until the man drew closer.

"Hello," Lawrence muttered. "How you doing?"

"Just fine. Praise God," the trucker exclaimed. "I'm Perkins Coffman—folks call me 'Perky'—I don't mind, I tell them, long as the Lord calls me on Judgment Day and has a spot for me in Heaven."

Groaning inwardly, Lawrence made a move to return to his car. But the trucker extended his hand and so he felt obliged to linger.

"My name's Clay Lawrence."

The huge man placed a heavy hand on Lawrence's shoulder.

"Glad to meet you, Mr. Lawrence. Are you making your way home? Or does your business take you away from your family on this beautiful Christmas night?"

Temperature in the upper twenties, wind gusting from the north—Lawrence fought the impression of the night as beautiful.

"Business," he replied.

Coffman jerked a thumb toward himself.

"Me, too. Me, too. I got millwork in that trailer. Window walls, doors. That kind of thing. Running out of Wichita. Finishing a week's route. Supposed to finish up two days ago, but had trouble with the blower. God didn't plan for me to be home on Christmas. He has his reasons. I ain't complaining."

The trucker took a short breath, then added, "You a . . . a salesman, Mr. Lawrence?"

There was something in the hesitation that set off a tiny alarm in Lawrence.

"No. No, I could never sell anything. I'm sort of a representative for a client of mine. Some business in

Denver. Say, uh . . . about how far is it to Denver?"

A twinkle in his eye which unnerved Lawrence, Coffman said, "I believe you'll find it's right at 250 miles."

"Another four or five hours," Lawrence murmured as much to himself as to the trucker.

"You have family, Mr. Lawrence?"

"Well, I'm . . . I'm not married. I have parents and a sister in Missouri."

Coffman issued a long whistle of regret.

"The road must be a special kind of lonesome for you. Me, I'm the luckiest soul on earth. Here, look at what I've been blessed with." He removed a giant wallet from his back pocket and pressed a photo under Lawrence's nose. In the dim light of the rest area, he could make out a heavyset woman, two equally heavyset girls, and a pathetically crippled young boy.

"These are mine," Coffman continued. "For me, every single day is Christmas 'cause I know these people love me and they're waitin' for me to come home. My wife, Judy—kids, Becky, 14, Sandra, 12, and my lucky star there—that's Perry—he's 10—he won't never walk, doctors say—I pray every hour of the day he will. Someday he will. I believe that. I love that boy with all my heart. He's my lucky star. He makes me the strongest man in the world. You know how he does that, Mr. Lawrence?"

Lawrence swallowed and shook his head.

"With love. He tells me I'm the greatest daddy in the country, and when he says that, Mr. Lawrence, it makes me feel so good, so strong, well . . . I believe I could walk right over there to that rig and lift it clean off the ground."

There was silence except for the wind.

"You are fortunate," said Lawrence, gazing out into the darkness.

"I expect you're in a hurry to get to your business," said Coffman. Then he reached out and, to Lawrence's surprise, patted at the outline of the shoulder holster and revolver beneath Lawrence's coat. "I hope whatever your business is you don't have to use that. But if you do . . . may God forgive you."

Lawrence smiled wearily.

"Mr. Coffman . . . I just hope I can forgive myself."

Back at his car, Lawrence ran the heater. And waved as Perkins Coffman pulled on his blowhorn and eased onto the interstate.

And then Lawrence waited , staring out at the millions of stars shining down on the Kansas prairie, wondering if any one of them might be lucky.

CHAPTER 24

"How is she?"

Adam had the Dodge at top end, speeding west. There was fear and concern in his voice.

"I can't really tell. She got smacked pretty hard on the side of the head by one of those bastards. She's groggy."

I was in the back seat, Andrea's head in my lap; she appeared to be awake or conscious, at least, and yet she didn't open her eyes and her face felt cool and clammy. Is she in shock? I wondered, trying to remember our health class unit on first aid.

"Maybe there's a hospital in Hays," said Adam. "We oughtta let a doctor take a look at her."

"Adam . . . I think the best thing would be for me to get her back home. I can call someone from the next town and have them come get us . . . and that way you can keep going. And there's something you need to know."

But at that moment Andrea raised her head and pushed herself upright.

"Not going home," she muttered.

Adam and I just listened.

"I'll be okay," she continued. She reached forward and touched Adam's shoulder. "Now that we're all together, I don't want to go home . . . I want us to help Adam."

She sounded kinda zoned to me; her fight and spunk had partially returned, though, and that was a good sign.

Adam twisted his neck around.

"What do you think, Rob?"

I went blank for a second or two. My mind replayed, in rapid sequence, the whole episode at the tire shed.

"Police or highway patrol will be on the lookout for us for certain once they investigate what happened back there."

"I hope they're dead," said Andrea in a hollow tone. "They deserve to die. To suffer the way they made . . ."

She stopped and lunged into my arms.

"I won't do something like that again," said Adam. It sounded like an apology. "I did it to save you guys, but . . . I won't use the night touch to do that again."

Over the top of Andrea's head, I saw Adam wince and noticed that he was having trouble keeping the Dodge on the road.

"Pull off, man," I exclaimed. "What's wrong?"

He said nothing, but he did as I asked.

Andrea leaned out of my arms as the car rolled to a stop. I got out and went to the driver's side.

"Move over and let me drive."

Adam was holding his left arm, obviously in pain.

"It's turning on me," he murmured.

Pushing herself forward, Andrea hovered near him, her elbows propped on the seat.

"Can we do something, Adam?" she asked.

He had scrunched himself up in the seat, his left arm pressed against his chest.

"Keep driving, Rob. There ain't much time."

Neither Andrea nor I had the courage to pursue the direction of that last comment. I simply drove and Andrea stayed where she was, quietly watching him the way a concerned mother watches a sick child.

Out of the corner of my eye I glimpsed something peculiar about Adam. Noticing it, too, Andrea slid over to me and whispered, "Is he in a trance or something?"

"I guess so. Let's leave him alone."

"Rob, are the police really gonna be after us?"

I sighed. Everything was so crazy, so incredible, I had no judgment and no clear sense of what was taking place.

"I would think so. I don't know. But . . . Lawrence is

still out there somewhere. I'd bet on that."

"Are they dead? Those two guys?"

"I'd say they probably are—badly burned, at least."

"They deserved it."

"Are you feeling okay?"

She rubbed at her head.

"Not super. Better, though. I'm worried about Adam."

"Yeah. Me, too."

"He saved us, Rob. He saved me from . . . how? . . . how did he find us? How did he know where we were?"

I explained about how the night touch allowed him to be aware of people who were thinking of him. I told her how I had mentally called for his help. Then Andrea said something remarkable.

"That would let him know Lawrence is after him, wouldn't it?"

I felt a surge of something like a hopeful energy.

"Yeah. Yeah, I guess you're right.

I glanced over at our friend, who remained in his trance.

"As long as Lawrence is thinking about him," Andrea added, "Adam will know . . . he'll be able to keep away from him."

Damn, I suddenly felt a helluva lot better.

But I never completely relaxed, one eye always vigilant for the highway patrol and for Lawrence, and for any other psychotics like Doyle and Ranger Man. Somewhere between Hays and WaKeeney, Adam sat up, claimed his arm didn't hurt anymore. And I thought of the stab wound to his hand and the gunshot wound to his ear.

"You're healing yourself again, aren't you?" I said.

"Sorta. Yeah. The night touch—can't tell what it's doing exactly. I feel like it's draining the life away from me."

"We're getting closer to Denver," Andrea observed hopefully. "We'll find that Saturn Man and make him take back the night touch."

"Not sure he can," said Adam. "Fact is . . . he's maybe not the one who can do something with the night touch. I

299

think it's the Indian woman. And that's why I don't have much time."

"What do you mean, Adam? Tell us."

Andrea was practically in the front seat, her eyes flashing concern.

"Back down the road this afternoon I had a . . . a vision, I guess . . . of the Indian woman. Don't know her name. She was thinking about me. She knows I'm coming. I tried to see where she is, but it was a dark cave and . . . something else. She's dying."

I felt crystals of ice forming in my throat.

"Is she that important?" I asked foolishly.

"She has powers. The Saturn Man . . . he'll know where she is, I think. I think she's the only one."

"The 'only one'?" Andrea stammered. "Don't talk in riddles, Adam. Please."

"The only one who can save me."

Unconsciously, I suppose, I pressed a little bit harder on the accelerator, though the old Dodge was running about full tilt—fifty-five edging toward sixty miles an hour.

After a long silence, Adam said, "You guys, I'm hungry. Feeling weak. I need to eat something."

"Okay," I mumbled. "WaKeeney's the next exit."

I hated to risk stopping, knowing the law might be hot on our trail—knowing, as well, that Lawrence could be waiting.

Curiously enough, Andrea must have been thinking the same thing.

"Adam . . . can you see where he is . . . you know, Detective Lawrence?"

He stiffened. And it was like a dark cloud came over his face. He put his left hand to his head and appeared to concentrate hard. He made a funny kind of smacking sound with his lips.

"No. No, he must not be thinking about me. But the kid back at the tire shed is. I don't believe he's told the cops. Afraid to, maybe."

I wheeled onto the exit ramp, and Adam tried to reassure me.

"I think it's safe here. You guys, don't worry so much. Okay?"

We got gas, and I decided not to park again in such an isolated area. We shuttled into another restaurant.

"Hey, we could write a guidebook to truckstop restaurants on Highway 70," Andrea said, her spirits seemingly more upbeat than they had been.

"They all look the same to me," I answered.

And they did.

Country western music playing in the background. Bored waitresses, some surviving by flirting with truckers. The truckers—road-wise, tough—hands permanently curled into a steering wheel grip, left arms sunburned, right arms pale. Strong coffee. Hot and reasonably edible food. Worn and splitting plastic in the booths and on the stools at the counter.

Andrea and I weren't that hungry; I had coffee, she a cup of hot chocolate. Adam ate a "Trucker's Special" sirloin and finished things off with apple pie à la mode. Wolfed it down.

"How do you keep from getting fat?" Andrea asked him.

He smiled that dopey smile of his and said, "Food turns to sawdust instead of fat when it gets in my stomach. There's a buzzsaw down there."

She wasn't real sure he was kidding.

I kept glancing around nervously—any minute I expected to hear sirens and the voice of some law enforcement official demanding that we give ourselves up. Funny, but I hadn't thought that much about how Andrea and I had become accomplices to Adam's actions—I couldn't call them "crimes" because I didn't believe they were.

Andrea and Adam joked around with each other as I drank a second cup of coffee; I was glad to see them like that; both had been through a lot, and there was more of the same ahead, I reasoned.

But suddenly Adam's mood shifted.

"She's bad off," he exclaimed.

301

Andrea and I, puzzled, looked at each other, then at our friend.

"The Indian woman . . . I got to get going . . . while there's time."

So we paid up, took a restroom break, and shuffled out to the Dodge.

"Hey, it's snowing," said Andrea, "or more like sleeting."

She pressed close to me as the ice pellets, thankfully intermittent, pinged against the hoods of cars and trucks like grains of sand.

"Good thing the Dodge has snow tires," I said, directing my comment behind me to where I assumed Adam was following. But he wasn't. And I felt a stab of panic.

"Adam!"

He bobbed up from near the front tire of a car.

"You guys, look what I found."

When she saw what he was holding, Andrea laughed. "It's so *skinny!*"

Boy, it was. I mean it was the worst-looking stray cat I'd ever seen—a faded orange with what appeared to be patches of mange on its flank, a torn ear, and a fierce and wild cast to its eyes. The thing didn't even meow right— more of a high-pitched cry as if its tail had been caught under a rocker, or maybe it was about to lose its voice entirely.

"Hold him, Rob. I'm going back in to buy some meat."

Adam pushed the pathetic creature into my arms; frightened, it clawed its way up under my chin.

"Adam, what the hell . . . ?"

He disappeared into the restaurant.

"Wow, this is a seriously sorry cat," Andrea murmured, petting it but careful to avoid the patches of mange.

Minutes later, the three of us and the stray cat were in the Dodge.

"Here's some hamburger, fella."

Adam put a greasy, steamy pattie of meat right there on

the front seat and the cat nearly broke something digging into it, chewing, swallowing, growling so fast I thought it was going to choke itself to death.

"Poor thing must not have eaten in days," said Andrea.

Adam watched it and cackled.

When the cat had polished off the meat, it licked the greasy residue for a minute or so, then climbed into Adam's lap, nosing at him as if certain he was concealing another pattie somewhere.

"I'm gonna take him with me to Denver, you guys . . . you know, as a good luck charm."

I sorta cringed.

"He's in bad shape," I cautioned. "Look at that stuff on his sides. You're liable to catch something from him. We all are."

Staring at the cat, Adam stroked its fur, and almost immediately it began to settle down and purr contentedly.

"Maybe I can make him well."

"You're not gonna touch those sores on him, are you?"

Andrea screwed up her face at the thought.

Well, he did touch them.

Damnedest thing, too.

Right there as we sat outside that restaurant, Adam concentrated, placing his left hand over the patches of mange and the scabby sores. And the cat appeared to fall asleep.

"Go ahead and drive, Rob. WaKeeney's gonna rest while he heals."

"'WaKeeney'?" I exclaimed.

"Is that his name?" Andrea added.

"Sure . . . yeah, . . . he found me—or I found him— in WaKeeney. So I'll name him 'WaKeeney.' Sounds like an Indian name. He'll be a good cat. You'll see."

The sleet was beginning to fall harder as we hit Highway 70 again—three stray cats having picked up another stray on Christmas night, heading west.

"The road's gettin' slick," I muttered after several miles.

It was, and that cold north wind was bashing against the shotgun side where Adam had curled up with WaKeeney, causing me to hold more firmly to the steering wheel. The Dodge's heater worked fine, kept us warm—maybe too warm. Truth is, I had developed a real buzz, the kind that comes on right before I get seriously sleepy. Andrea was lying down in the back seat, humming some country western lyric.

"God almighty," I exclaimed, "talk to me or I'm liable to doze off and end up in Nebraska."

My two companions started to chatter at the same time.

That's when I saw something in the rearview mirror that shocked me wide awake.

"Oh, Jesus! This is it!"

"Rob?"

Andrea rocked forward; I could feel her breath on my ear.

"Let's be cool," said Adam. He saw what I saw. "Maybe I can get us out of this."

The red and blue flashing lights had closed to within a hundred yards; the faint shriek of the highway patrol siren echoed within earshot.

"Damn it, I can't outrun him!"

"Don't try," said Adam. "I don't want you guys getting into trouble over me."

"Jesus, we're already *in* trouble," I shouted. "I bet they found those creeps in the tire shed."

"We could let Adam out and he could run for it," Andrea suggested.

I glanced again into the rearview mirror.

"Too late for that now."

"WaKeeney says not to worry."

The cat had stirred and was rubbing its head into Adam's throat.

Reflexively, I slowed the Dodge.

Then, swear to God, my heart skipped a beat.

304

The speeding patrol car swung around us.

Andrea cheered and applauded.

Adam cackled.

My stomach felt as if I'd swallowed a pack of razor blades.

"God almighty."

"I bet there's been an accident," said Andrea.

I realized immediately that she was probably right. Sure enough, two miles beyond, a semi had jack-knifed. Two patrol cars, lights beaming out into the emptiness in eerie pulsations, had blocked the right lane.

"You think they'll stop us, Rob?" Adam asked.

I drummed my fingers on the steering wheel.

"God, I hope not. They'll probably just direct us on through."

"Everybody needs to try to look older," said Andrea.

Adam made some funny, squeaky noises with his lips, and the cat batted a paw at him.

"WaKeeney says not to worry."

I couldn't join in Adam's silliness; I slowed the Dodge way down as we neared a patrolman standing in the middle of the road, motioning us forward with one of those cone-shaped flashlights.

"Wonder if the trucker's hurt?" Andrea murmured.

But I couldn't think about that; I was dead certain the patrolman would notice how young we were and stop us—or maybe recognize us from the description on an APB.

"Don't anybody call extra attention to us," I warned.

Well, I guess that was too much for Adam to resist. For, you see, as we rolled past the patrolman, Adam held WaKeeney up to the window, took the cat's paw, and worked it in a waving gesture.

Oh, Jesus.

The patrolman simply smiled.

And returned WaKeeney's wave.

You had to wonder when our luck would run out.

I drove for another hour, mostly listening as Adam and Andrea talked on and on about nothing very important—school, weird stories in *The National Enquirer*—and they playfully argued back and forth for half an hour about which music was better: rock and roll or country western, Adam supporting rock and roll, Andrea defending her twang and whine stuff.

I remained neutral even though they pressed me to be the final judge.

Once, I interrupted them to ask Adam about Lawrence.

"Nothing," he replied, touching fingers to his head. "Maybe he's quit chasing me, or maybe my connector's stopped working."

Well, that worried me.

Something else had me worried, too. I could tell that Adam was trying to let Andrea know his real feelings for her. Oh, he was being subtle. But the way he looked at her, the way he smiled when she petted WaKeeney—of course, it could have been that he just wanted to take his mind off the night touch and the dark journey we were on. Yet, I wondered. Would Adam do something foolish? Truth is, I had no idea what I meant by "foolish."

So it goes.

The weather was changing dramatically; one minute we could see clusters of stars, the next minute, low clouds scudded over us. The sleet and spitting snow fizzled out until we got to the Oakley exit. Then the road turned kinda icy, and besides that I needed to stretch my legs and let Adam drive for awhile. It must have been around midnight when we pulled into the first rest area beyond Oakley.

I parked at one end; another car was camouflaged by shadows at the far end. So we had the area almost entirely to ourselves.

"Hey, you guys . . . take a look at WaKeeney now."

Andrea and I were in the midst of climbing out when Adam directed our attention to the cat . . . to the patches of mange. Which were gone.

306

"Adam . . . you made him well," Andrea squealed, reaching forward to plant a kiss on his forehead. I thought she was going to kiss the cat, too.

Me, I just stared. Damn, it was strange. I mean, I had *seen* those patches with my own two eyes. Within an hour or so, the fur had grown over them. Adam smiled proudly. Still basking in the glow of Andrea's kiss, I guessed.

"WaKeeney, you're one goddamned lucky cat," I muttered.

And that's when Adam said, "Rob . . . would you mind if Andrea and me had, you know . . . a private talk?"

"Uh, yeah . . . sure. No, I don't mind. I need to go to the uh . . . the restroom," I stammered.

Back of my knees went limp. And the pavement, ice-glazed, made the trip to the rest area's main building hazardous. I could feel my pulse in my throat.

What in the hell exactly would he say to her?

What would she say?

I loitered around in the restroom for as long as I could stand it, took a deep breath, and wandered back to the Dodge. Opening the driver's side door, I tried not to glance at Andrea. Both of them seemed kind of somber.

"You wanna take the wheel?" I asked Adam.

He nodded. Mumbled something I couldn't quite catch.

"Pavement here's real slick," I added as we met each other in front of the car.

"I can handle it," he said.

Things were tense. In the back seat, Andrea was gazing blankly out the window at the snow flurries. Snatches of what their conversation must have been like reeled through my thoughts.

Adam guided the Dodge toward the opposite end of the rest area; WaKeeney tried to curl up in his lap, but he pushed the cat away and I reached for it.

Suddenly Adam slammed the accelerator to the floor.

"Damn it, get down!" he yelled.

I thought the car was exploding.

307

Two shots were fired.

Adam's window shattered, showering the front seat with glass. I heard Andrea's strangled scream, and I cried out because I thought she'd been hit. Adam's body pinned me to the seat, and the cat was clawing frantically to free itself from both of us.

"It's Lawrence," Adam exclaimed as somehow he kept one hand on the steering wheel.

The Dodge fishtailed.

Two more shots rang out.

And the night roared.

CHAPTER 25

Apparently our luck had a way further to go before it ran out.

Or maybe it wasn't luck. Maybe it was the night touch. All I know is that Adam kept the Dodge on the pavement through the shooting and screaming and general chaos. Man, it was wild—no, it was terrifying.

When we reached the rest area turnout, I stole a glance behind us, and for a moment my fear dissolved. I cheered at what I saw.

"He went in the ditch!" I shouted.

Adam whooped. Andrea had folded herself down into a corner. Wasn't saying anything. But my attention was glued to Lawrence's car, the rear tires of which had slipped into a ditch right by a steep culvert. He was gunning the engine, but that little car wasn't going anywhere.

"He'll have to call a tow truck," I exclaimed. "Holy shit! What a piece of luck! A-w-w-w-w right!"

Adam and I slapped palms; WaKeeney, freaked out of his mind, had sought shelter far under the seat.

We raced onto the interstate.

"Andrea? Hey, Rob, see if she's okay."

"Babe, did you get cut?"

She had. A nick on her cheek. I had a small cut on my forehead and one below my ear. The ricocheting bullets had just missed my knee. Having ducked in time, Adam had no marks upon him from the attack.

Shaking pretty badly, Andrea leaned forward.

309

"I'll be fine. Just concentrate on getting as far away from Lawrence as possible."

I looked at her face. In the shadows, she appeared older—thirty or forty—she seemed no longer a girl or even a young woman.

"I'm sorry, Andrea," I murmured.

"No," said Adam. "I'm the one who should be saying I'm sorry. I got everybody into this. I should have been aware that Lawrence was waiting for us . . . but he must have been sleeping or something. I'm sorry."

Andrea got real ticked.

"Will you two stop this! Stop telling me you're sorry, because if you keep doing it, I really am gonna think you're *sorry*. Sorry pathetic. Just stop it!"

She sank back into the seat and didn't say another word for quite a spell.

Thing is, we had another, even more pressing problem—there was now no window on Adam's side; cold air flooded in.

"Rob, you think there'd be any cardboard in the trunk?"

"Pull over and let's see."

Well, there wasn't, but Pudge had thrown an old poncho in there and so we tied it up over the opening— not much help—and turned the heater up full blast. After awhile, it wasn't too bad.

We drove on another fifty miles before exiting at Goodland; the wind had torn away the poncho, forcing us to find an all-night truckstop for repair. Coffee and hot chocolate, too. A small carton of milk for WaKeeney.

With the window securely taped, we were off again.

Andrea fell asleep.

Adam and I talked, mostly just to keep each other awake; we didn't touch upon what he had told Andrea back at the rest area. I pretty much knew. I sorta felt sorry for him; Andrea, too. I hoped the threeway friendship wouldn't be destroyed. Considering the bad situation, that was probably a stupid thought to have.

At one point the conversation naturally shifted to Lawrence.

"He's one determined son-of-a-bitch, ain't he?" said Adam.

"Yeah . . . he's like an old west bounty hunter," I replied.

Adam smiled weakly and whispered,

"I'm his man. He's thinking about me right this second."

"You won't get away . . . I won't miss next time. Damnit. Goddamnit."

Clay Lawrence shoved his hands in his coat and bounced up and down on his toes. But the cold barely affected him; anger, like a hot bead of molten metal, warmed his body.

"Losing too much goddamned time," he muttered.

He hated to wait, but had no choice. A tow truck was on the way from Oakley; he had called from the rest area's pay phone, finding only one available wrecker service.

The longer he waited, the more futile, the more frustrated he began to feel.

"Coach Hugh . . . Kristin . . . I'm trying."

Helplessly he surveyed the rear tires of his rental car.

"Damnit!" he shouted, kicking at the back fender, slamming his fist against the roof.

And the cold air seeped through his anger.

The tow truck's yellow flashing light revived his spirits somewhat. He flagged down the driver, a roly-poly young man, maybe seventeen or eighteen, who huffed and puffed his way down from the truck, bundled in a parka as if he were on an expedition to Antarctica.

Lawrence led him to the culvert.

"Stomped on it too hard and those back tires just wouldn't bite. Sorry to have to call you out on a night like this."

Under the hood of the parka, the young man had on a baseball cap with the name "Hubie" stitched over the bill; he had on thick, black-rimmed glasses partially fogged over.

"Not as fucking sorry as I am, friend. Son-of-a-bitchin' Curry told me I could have Christmas and the day after Christmas off to work on my car—got a vintage '58 'Vette—and that son-of-a-bitch calls me out of a warm bed, says get your ass down to the station, Hubie, I need help. I tell him, 'Forget it, Curry. We got a deal.'"

Hubie glared at Lawrence, who, in turn, shrugged and said, "Like I said, I'm sorry. Won't take long to pull me out of this."

Bustling around behind the car, Hubie studied the situation, then returned to Lawrence's side.

"Know what I'm gonna do, by God?" the young man exclaimed, jabbing a finger toward Lawrence. "I'm gonna fix Curry . . . I mean, fix the son-of-a-bitch but good. *But good!*"

Hubie's fury was building; Lawrence stood back and watched as the young man methodically maneuvered the tow truck and attached two cables beneath the rear of the car. Breathing heavily, he shoved himself into Lawrence's face.

"He's not gettin' away with this, the son-of-a-bitch. You know why he thinks he can get away with this?"

Lawrence shook his head, deciding to let Hubie empty out his frustration.

"Because he's my stepfather and he thinks he's some fuckin' general can order me around just because he's humpin' my mother . . . and about every other woman in Logan County hard up enough to want him around. But I'm gonna *fix* him."

It took no more than thirty seconds to free Lawrence's car.

Joining Hubie in the front seat of the tow truck, Lawrence reached for his wallet.

"Listen, I really do appreciate this. What do I owe you?"

The young man was searching beneath the seat. Then something metallic threw off glints of light.

"You ever see what this can do to a man's chest? It's a .357. Got it from a guy across the Colorado line. Looks like a simple gun, don't it?"

Lawrence reeled back as Hubie stuck the tip of the barrel a few inches from his chin.

"It's not a plaything, son."

Hubie grunted.

"I'm gonna tell you a secret, friend. This ain't a gun . . . or a plaything . . . it's *freedom*. You hear that word?"

"Yes, I hear you," said Lawrence. "Just let me settle up with you, so you can get back. Wouldn't want you to lose your job."

"Lose my job?" Hubie whispered. He fondled the gun a moment. "I'm talkin' about freedom. I ain't gonna lose nothin'. Nothin'. You know why? 'Cause I've got it planned. I know Curry's ways. See, 'bout every weekend Curry drives down to Russell Springs. East of there is a place on the Smoky Hill River where he hunts. Next time he goes, I'm following him. Tomorrow. I figure he'll go again tomorrow."

"Here . . . here's forty bucks," said Lawrence. "That ought to cover it."

"Hold up, friend!" Hubie exclaimed.

The gun was aimed at Lawrence's nose.

"You haven't heard my plan. See, what I'm gonna do is stalk ole Curry. Scare that son-of-a-bitch out of his mind 'cause one time he hit me. Slapped me in the face. So I'm gonna hunt him down. He's gonna be like a scared rabbit. Then I'm gonna shoot him. Waste him. Dump his body in the Smoky Hill River. And I'm only gonna have one regret."

Lawrence stared into the young man's hate-filled black dots behind the thick glasses. Black holes. Not eyes.

"One regret," Hubie continued. "Curry's body's gonna pollute that whole river. But I'll be free. Slapping me was a mistake. Calling me out tonight—mistake number two. I shoulda had days off. Yeah . . . *this* is freedom."

He smiled at the gun.

Lawrence put the money on the seat and slipped out the door.

Shaken, thoughts whirling in a dark funnel, he drove away from the rest area, trying to blank out the image of the young man's eyes, his voice, his anger.

He felt empty. Alone. Desolate.

Exhausted, needing some sleep badly, we exited from the interstate at Burlington, Colorado just beyond the state line. We found a little picnic area. It looked inviting. No one else around.

"This should be okay unless a local cop runs us off," I said. "Lawrence won't know we're here, so it'll be a safe place for a quick nap—we need it, Adam. You know we do."

He agreed, closing his eyes, leaning back, wiggling his shoulders to relieve the tension from driving.

"Our window's holding pretty tight. Andrea's not cold, is she?"

I glanced into the back seat.

"She's sleeping like a baby."

"Good."

It was an awkward moment. I guess I wanted to say something about him and Andrea—something.

"We're gonna lick this thing, Adam . . . you know, the night touch."

"Yeah," he grinned. "Stomp its ass."

"I wish I hadn't lost dad's gun. Might have come in handy against Lawrence."

Adam shook his head.

"Rob, if he's bound to get me, he's bound to get me. It's what he feels like he has to do. I killed someone he loved. I understand how he feels."

"That's not what happened," I countered.

He closed his eyes again, and WaKeeney sought out

his lap. He petted the cat's head; loud purring filled the car.

"WaKeeney says not to worry."

I had to chuckle at that. Maybe I was so tired I was becoming delirious.

We both dozed off without another word.

I dreamed.

And in the dream, I was painting on this massive canvas. Man, it was as big as one of those old drive-in movie screens. I struggled with huge brushes—it was like painting with a broom. I included everything that had happened; I mean, I covered the canvas with a bunch of scenes—like me and Andrea and Adam up at the cemetery. Blackie was there. In one corner of the canvas Leah stood in her nurse's uniform; in another, Mrs. Dodd beamed over her Christmas centerpiece; in another, Karl Dodd, a frozen mannikin in the middle of Summer's Pond. There was Kristin Kelley talking into her tape recorder. Doc Newton. Brian Gunnellson. Willa Snagovia. Joe and Molly Helms. Pudge. Several scenes involving Lawrence. One of Doyle and Ranger Man.

Dead center of the canvas I painted a large, dark hand.

The final scene.

You see, that was it—the final scene sort of painted itself in the palm of the dark hand, but I couldn't make out what happened. Couldn't see details.

I jolted awake.

That's not the way it's supposed to end, I thought to myself. But what had I seen? A flash of something. The touch of someone's very cold hand.

Adam was already awake, staring through the windshield.

"I just had the weirdest dream," I said.

"She's dying, Rob," he mumbled, paying no attention to me. "If we hurry . . . if we hurry. . . ."

The way he said it, well, it scared me as much as anything else that had happened.

"Let's go. We'll find her," I exclaimed. "We can hit Denver city limits by dawn if we put a foot into it."

315

"You're a good friend, Rob. Best I can imagine."

Jesus, I felt like crying. Felt like hugging him.

Guys don't do things like that, you know. Never understood why.

We just don't.

So it goes.

"We ought to make Limon 'fore we need gas again."

Adam nodded. And set WaKeeney off his lap.

"Buckle your seat belt, kitty. Time for some serious driving."

"Tell me when you need a break," I told him, noticing he was squinting over the steering wheel. As an afterthought, I asked, "Your eyes bothering you? Seeing okay?"

He hesitated.

"Pretty well." Then he grinned. "I ain't exactly blind no more, Rob. The night touch keeps me from being flat-out blind."

"Just checking."

Andrea slept from Burlington to Limon, a moonscape stretch of road—seventy-three miles—but it seemed like 200 to me. Lots of time to have to pass.

It's funny how we talked some about the future as if everything would eventually get back to normal and how we'd get on with our lives, forgetting about the night touch and the death and sorrow it had caused.

At one point, though, Adam shifted the conversation.

"You probably think I'm seriously messed up to kill my father. It's like one of the worst sins, they say . . . and I wish I could make my mother understand why I had to do it. I had to, Rob. And if they put me in the electric chair or gas chamber or whatever and they ask me if I'm sorry I did it . . . you know, give me a chance to confess my sin . . . I won't do it. I killed him. And I'm glad I killed him because my mother, she . . ."

Something gurgled in his throat.

I fought off a rush of sadness.

"He was a godawful mean man," I said. "If I'd been you, well, maybe I'd done the same thing. Probably.

316

Probably would. I saw how he was, Adam. All of the people in Warrior Stand knew it, too. Nobody blames you."

"I'll never kill somebody ever again, Rob. It's the worst thing . . . feeling what I've felt."

I sat there. Numb. Couldn't think of anything else to say.

Thankfully the miles clicked by.

We got gas in Limon. Andrea shook loose from sleep long enough to use the restroom.

"Please don't look at me," she whispered. "I'm a sight . . . look like a whore after a long night."

Adam and I laughed at that.

And, boy, we needed a laugh.

I picked up a map of Colorado and a city guide to Denver.

"Only seventy-three miles left," I called out to Adam as we started to leave Limon.

He held his hands out and studied the dark sky.

"Snowing. Hope it doesn't get heavy."

I guess you'd have to term that an ironic prophecy—at least from what I remember about "irony" from my English class. Anyway, we took off, Andrea and WaKeeney curled up in the back seat as if they were hibernating.

Thirty miles later Adam said, "Lawrence is ahead of us. Not sure how far."

"Damn," I muttered.

Adam glanced over at me.

"Maybe we can lose him in Denver."

"Yeah," I said, fear tickling my spine as the snow thickened over the spray of the headlights.

The wind was gusting, shoving at my door.

I recall an exit sign for some place called Deer Trail—it was the last sign we saw for miles—it was also the last time for miles that we could see the road.

"Jesus Christ, Adam!"

"It's . . . gonna be . . . okay," he stammered.

A solid curtain of white closed in front of us. That's the

317

only way I can describe it. White. Solid white. Snow too thick for the headlights to penetrate.

"Pull over," I exclaimed.

Andrea stirred, and a moment later she propped her elbows on the seat and opened her eyes.

"Rob!"

"Goddamnit, Adam, you can't see the goddamn road. Pull over."

I grabbed at his arm and he pushed me away.

"I can handle it. Leave me alone. I need to concentrate."

Unbelievable. The snow. The solid whiteness.

We were speeding along at fifty, fifty-five miles an hour. No sign of the highway in front of us.

"Rob, make him stop!"

Andrea had dug her fingernails into my shoulder.

Then Adam did something totally insane.

He took his hands from the wheel.

He put his left palm flat against the side of his head. It was unreal.

I held my breath.

Andrea sort of whimpered and sank down, not wanting to watch.

"Oh, God," I murmured. "God, oh, God."

Adam closed his eyes.

And the Dodge rolled through that blizzard as if it were a clear and sunny day, visibility unlimited. Passing through all that whiteness, it reminded me of the time my family flew to Washington D.C. We flew through clouds, and they surrounded us—like a huge patch of cotton.

For I don't know how many miles, I just stared at Adam. His hands. The steering wheel. What was guiding us?

Letting go.

Those two words ghosted into my thoughts.

Adam had surrendered to the night touch—it was our passage through the storm.

We rode that way to the edge of Denver, at which point Adam snapped awake and grasped the wheel. And once

318

again I could breathe.

But the snow drifted across the roads despite the city snowplows. Being early Sunday morning, there weren't many cars out. Just enough to keep the road open. Behind us, patrolmen were closing Highway 70.

We stopped near Stapleton International Airport, and Adam said, "Everybody all right?"

Andrea revived.

"Freaky. Freakiest thing I've ever been through."

I had to agree with her.

"Any feeling 'bout where the Saturn Man is? Or the Indian woman?" I asked Adam.

He looked real sad.

"Nothing. I'm drained."

I unfolded the Denver map and studied the streets and scanned the advertisements of big hotels and fancy ski resorts and places of interest and something about the Denver Broncos football team.

"It's gonna be like looking for a needle in—"

I froze.

"Adam! God almighty! See this?"

I shoved that map into his face.

"What is it?" Andrea questioned.

"Son . . . of . . . a . . . bitch—there it is!" Adam exclaimed.

Andrea about crawled over the seat.

"What? What?"

"The bear. See it? It's Adam's bear."

The map rattled in my trembling hands.

"Does it say where it is?" Andrea asked.

So I read below the picture of the statue of the bear.

"Museum . . . of . . . Natural . . . History. It's by the City Park. Not far from the airport."

"He's there," Adam muttered. "The Saturn Man . . . he's there. In the park."

"I'll drive," I said.

Well, we got kind of lost a couple of times. Side streets were slippery. Ten inches or more of snow had fallen, clutching the city like a giant white fist. Eventually we

319

angled around, saw a sign or two.

And found it. The park. The sprawling museum building.

Snow-silenced and open to the sky, the park was absolutely beautiful that morning. A few kids were out skating on a lake in the middle of the park.

"I'm gonna find him," said Adam, putting on his orange stocking cap and scarf.

I parked the Dodge and Adam jumped out; Andrea and I watched as he ran, excited, like a kid who was intent on scattering a flock of birds in his path.

It was a great sight.

I glanced at Andrea.

Tears streamed down her cheeks.

"He made it," she sputtered.

By damn, he had.

"Let's go after him," I said. "Be careful WaKeeney doesn't get out."

In the distance, we could see Adam standing in the middle of the frozen lake, turning slowly in a circle as if sending out radar waves.

In fact, that must have been what he was doing—using the night touch as radar to seek out the Saturn Man—for soon he was running again, toward a picnic table under a pair of tall trees.

We followed.

"Rob, he's found someone. Is that him? Is that the Saturn Man?"

It was too far away to tell much of anything.

As we made our way across the lake, kids squealed and laughed, chasing one another, farting around on the ice as kids will.

We approached the picnic table; I could see a hatless man in an old navy peacoat hunched there. Adam was talking to him.

"Should we leave them alone?" Andrea asked.

"No . . . no, I think it'd be all right to show him we're with Adam."

The man, his bald head leathery, his eyes large, his

chin long, jutting sharply, glanced up at us.

"These are my friends," said Adam. "They came to help me get rid of the night touch."

The Saturn Man's eyes were ghostly; a milky residue covered one, but at the same time they were penetrating eyes, eyes that had seen life's mysteries, life's horrors, too. And not much love, I guessed.

"I can't help you," he said, his voice soft and wheezy. It sounded as if he couldn't breath properly, and I wondered why he would be out in the cold and snow. Alone.

Adam's body seemed to bounce nervously; his hands gestured wildly.

"There's an Indian woman. I've had . . . visions of her. Somewhere not far from here. I think she can heal me. But she's dying. There's not much time."

Pausing for several seconds, the Saturn Man eventually nodded.

"Mary Walks Lightly. A healer woman."

"Where is she? Can she get rid of the night touch? Where *is* she?"

The Saturn Man frowned.

Frustrated, I blurted out, "Do you know the street she lives on? The area?"

He looked at me and I stepped back reflexively; Andrea stayed at my shoulder, slightly behind me.

"Out there," he said, pointing north. "Many go to her."

"We have to find her right away," Adam persisted. "You have to tell us where she lives."

Again, he said, "Out there."

Then he rose. He faced Adam, an expression of deep sorrow in his eyes.

"God forgive me for what I've done to you."

And with that, he trudged away, across the ice and snow, moving slowly, stooped over, a man who appeared to be waiting only for death.

"Let's drive around," I said, "ask anybody we see if they know a person named 'Mary Walks Lightly.'"

Adam was down. I think he was ready to give up.

"We'll help you," said Andrea. "We promised you we would."

"We ain't gonna do it," Adam murmured.

"Sure we will," I insisted.

He shook his head.

"Lawrence knows the bear statue. He's been here."

"The snowstorm, Adam . . . that had to slow him up."

Again, Adam shook his head.

"I feel him, Rob. He's near."

CHAPTER 26

"She's thinking about me."

Behind the wheel of the Dodge, I looked for an indication of where the Saturn Man had gone. Disappeared. He had simply disappeared, having given us so little information. I turned to respond to Adam's comment.

"Mary Walks Lightly?"

"Yeah," said Adam.

Rubbing her arms to generate some warmth, Andrea bubbled with optimism somehow.

"It's such a pretty name . . . Mary Walks Lightly . . . she can help, can't she?"

"Adam," I said, "can you see . . . can you tell where she is?"

He put his hand to the side of his head.

"Drive. Drive in the direction the Saturn Man pointed."

So I did. I believe we were going north.

Minutes later, we passed a sign reading "Commerce City," and it appeared we had entered the Denver suburbs. Houses thinned out; some looked poor. Quite a few mobile homes.

"I feel something," said Adam.

I had to drive slowly, though the Dodge's snow tires held the road pretty well.

"She wouldn't be living among poor people, would she?" I muttered.

"Seems kind of desolate," Andrea followed.

We saw a sign for Brighton, 12 miles.

"Keep going a little ways," said Adam. "I've got something."

"Look up there at all those cars," Andrea exclaimed.

Adam blinked, then concentrated on the line of her finger.

"Yeah," I said, "a bunch of cars."

Leaning forward, Adam studied the gathering of cars, many parked along the side of the road, others hugged close to a long mobile home situated about forty yards from traffic.

"What's going on there?" Andrea prodded.

"I believe it's her. Rob, park out here. I believe she's in that mobile home."

Adam grabbed at the steering wheel to make certain I pulled over.

There must have been twenty or thirty cars scattered about—and people, a crowd of people up near the mobile home despite the cold air and the light snow falling.

"You really think this is it?" I asked Adam.

"Yeah . . . yeah, I do. She's thinking about me. She knows I'm coming."

Then he wheeled around and tried to look out the rear window. I don't think he could have seen much because it was iced over.

"Let's move," he said. "Lawrence is on our tails."

"Jesus," I murmured. "Why can't we shake him?"

We tumbled out of the Dodge and hustled across the road to join the mob.

I'd never come upon a group of people quite like this one.

It was a combination freak show and outdoor church meeting—you could hear hymns being sung, you could hear a man preaching loudly, you could hear someone playing a harmonica—and you could see all manner of sick and disabled people. Old folks in wheelchairs bundled up in blankets; folks on crutches; children crying and wailing.

As we approached, a small, thin man hideously marked

with a purplish growth on one side of his face thrust some sticks of wood at us.

"Ghostwood?" he exclaimed. "You needin' some special luck? These has been touched by Mary her ownself. Ghostwood—it's to keep bad and wicked things away."

They looked like pretty ordinary sticks to me.

Adam confronted the man as Andrea and I lagged back, unsure of what to make of everything.

"Mary? You mean, Mary Walks Lightly? She's in that mobile home, isn't she?"

The wisp of a man surveyed Adam suspiciously.

"She be. She's been uh havin' her Christmas healin' since yesterday mornin'. Not even uh blizzard keeps these down-on-their-luck types from comin' out. Ghostwood—it'll sure help 'em. One dollar a stick. You can afford one dollar, can't ya?"

Adam escaped the man, and we followed; the crowd, still noisy and animated, parted some as we pushed our way through. At the door to the mobile home stood two young men—both Indians—one must have been well over six feet and have weighed 300 pounds. The other was average in size with long black hair tied in double braids.

"Hold it right there," the braided one exclaimed.

"I've got to see Mary Walks Lightly," said Adam. "She's the only one who can take away the night touch. I've been cursed with it."

Adam held his hands out as if to show him, but the young man, wary and kind of nervous, said, "Stay back. Wait your turn. All of these people are ahead of you. You must wait."

"But I can't wait . . . there's someone after me . . . he's trying to kill me . . . and Mary Walks Lightly, I know . . . I know she's dying," Adam cried. "I've got to see her before she dies. Tell her I'm here."

Well, a moment or two after he said that all hell broke loose.

Hard to recall exactly what happened first; the noise,

the movement, the atmosphere of the place seemed to ignite all at once, detonated by Adam's words.

I heard a fat woman wail, "Mary's dying! Lord God help us! Mary's dying!"

And the man who had been preaching stopped momentarily, then admonished everyone to "pray for the spirit of Mary in its transition . . . pray that she may carry on her work a little longer. So many hunger for the food of her healing."

Loud and frightened murmurs rippled through the crowd like dominoes falling; and like some giant organism, it lurched forward, pressing us into the young man.

"Get back!" he yelled. "Everyone move back!"

"Is she dying? Tell us the God's truth," someone shouted.

We were almost trampled. I held onto Andrea.

The larger Indian braced himself, managing to shove a dozen people away from the door.

"No," said the other young man, "my mother is not dying. She is ill, but she is not dying. Not dying."

The commotion continued until something odd occurred. A peculiar sound thrummed out into the cold, dry Colorado air.

Drumbeats.

And an eerie, rhythmical chant.

I hadn't seen the old Indian man before; he seemed to have materialized from beneath the mobile home, walking defiantly into the pulsing mob, drumming upon a tom-tom with a long block of wood.

The crowd semicircled him, watching, listening.

He performed for ten minutes. Perhaps more.

Then he ceased abruptly, raised his arms to the sky, and chanted softly. His flowing, shoulder-length black hair was speckled with gray; he wore an old peacoat much like the one worn by the Saturn Man.

He quieted the crowd.

Three men and a woman entered the center of the crowd when the old Indian disappeared inside the mobile home; they had trays lined with styrofoam cups.

"We have coffee and hot chocolate. Come have a hot drink," they said.

They were from some church group; their voices were kind and warm.

Adam turned to me.

"Rob, I've got to get in to see her. Help me get around these guys at the door."

As I started to say something, someone touched my arm.

"Does your friend have powers?"

It was a small boy. He nodded toward Adam, and then I looked more closely at him—and my entire body tensed. The boy's face was ghastly white; gray circles hung around pinkish eyes that never blinked; he was frail, the top of his head too large for his facial structure and his horribly thin neck.

A woman, apparently his mother, edged near us. "We came from Texas. Is it true about Mary Walks Lightly? She's our last hope. He's got cancer. Doctors say . . ."

"I don't know," I replied.

Adam had slipped away.

The boy's birdlike fingers had clamped onto my wrist.

I glanced over my shoulder at Andrea. Her mouth gaped open almost comically.

At the front of the mobile home, Adam again was talking to the two young men; I couldn't hear what he was saying even though the noise level of the crowd had lowered considerably.

The woman and the grotesquely pale boy hovered by Andrea and me.

I felt sorry for them. Wanted to help them.

When Adam returned, he seemed very nervous.

Into my ear he whispered, "Watch for Lawrence. He's near. I can feel he's near."

Clay Lawrence stared at the statue of the bear.

Memory clawed at him. He avoided its reach for a moment.

And he thought: They must have stopped to sleep

during the night. How else would I have beaten them to Denver? The snow ... they probably won't make it through the snow.

What had Doc Newton said? The bear. Denver. A large building. It could only mean one place. A place which held memories. How many years ago had it been? Ten, maybe? He had met Hugh and Kristin Kelley in Denver for a couple of days of skiing. And on a Sunday afternoon, they had come to the museum—a gloriously bright and sunny day.

Hugh took our picture in front of this bear.

Kristin and me.

God, she had enjoyed herself skiing and had loved the museum.

She had never seen the skeleton of a dinosaur.

He returned to his car and waited. Drove around. Parked near the museum an hour later.

Then a stroke of good luck. He saw the Dodge easing away from the park and he followed it.

North of the city.

He watched them stop, certain it was the same old Dodge.

But why would they go into that mob of people? he wondered.

From his car he surveyed the scene.

Not the right place to finish the job.

Too many people around.

But then again, the crowd might hide me.

"This could be it," he muttered to himself as he checked his revolver, got out and crossed the road to merge with those seeking healing at the hands of Mary Walks Lightly.

"Adam, what did the guy say? Is he gonna let you in to see his mother?"

My friend, still eyeing the crowd apprehensively, shrugged.

"He said he'd go inside and ask her about me. No promises—no special favors."

"God, did you tell him to hurry?"

I was feeling tension coming off Adam's body; I wanted things to be resolved immediately. If Adam could get in to see the healer woman, then our trip, all the bad stuff, would have been worth it.

Behind me, Andrea was talking with the cancer boy's mother and another woman. I caught part of their conversation, and I felt like I'd been hit by a sledgehammer square in the chest. . . .

"Could he help my Allison?"

"I think he could . . . I've seen him heal himself and . . . and a cat. I can ask him for you."

I wheeled to meet Andrea's approach. I was mad and scared. Mostly scared.

"Goddamn it, Andrea, why did you tell that woman about Adam?"

Her face slackened.

Adam leaned between us; he'd been watching the crowd and the front door of the mobile home.

"Hey, what are you guys talking about? Andy, what is it?"

She swallowed and took a deep breath.

She fidgeted with her hands and frowned.

"That woman behind me there . . . her little girl . . ."

Adam glanced at me.

"Rob? What's going on?"

"Ask bigmouth," I growled.

Andrea threw her head back and closed her eyes and bit her lip.

"Her little girl's blind, Adam . . . and so I told her you might, you know. . . ."

At that instant the young Indian man stepped out and gestured for Adam to come.

Disregarding him a moment, Adam said to Andrea, "Blind? Where is she? Let me see her."

"Adam," I exclaimed, "damn it, there's no time for this. Mary Walks Lightly wants you inside."

A blond-haired girl, wrapped snugly in a parka, toddled

329

forward—she must have been around six and had no front teeth.

Adam bent down to her.

"What's your name?"

"Allison Carson. Allison LuAnn Carson."

She smiled shyly at Adam; Andrea clutched at my arm, hoping, I think, that I would let her off the hook for what she had done.

The young Indian man impatiently tapped me on the shoulder.

"My mother wants to meet your friend . . . now . . . she's failing fast."

"Adam, you can do this later," I said.

The girl's mother reached out at me as if to hold me away from Adam and her daughter.

"Please . . . oh, please give my little girl this chance."

God, I didn't know what to do.

"What about Adam's chance?" I said. "Lady, you don't understand."

Adam and Allison were talking; I heard her giggle.

And then I realized that the crowd had surrounded us, blocking us from the mobile home.

A man's voice echoed, "He's a healer! There's gonna be a healing!"

"No!" I exclaimed. "No, he has to get to Mary Walks Lightly. He has to."

But it was no use; the curiosity seekers, believers in miracles, formed a fortress around us.

"Oh, Jesus, look," I said to Andrea.

On the far side of the rough circle stood Lawrence.

I hoped Adam would see him and decide to run for the mobile home.

I started to warn him, but there was something in Lawrence's expression—a fascination—I don't know what. I watched him. He made no move to pull out his revolver.

The crowd grew silent.

Adam had sunk to his knees in front of the girl.

An intense hush covered the scene.

Raising his left hand to the side of her head, Adam said, "Just relax, Allison. I'm gonna touch your eyes. I won't do anything to hurt you."

"Will I be able to see the mountains when you're through?" she asked. "I've always wanted to see the mountains."

"I hope so, Allison. I really do."

Every nerve in me came alive as I witnessed what took place.

People all around the circle closed their eyes and appeared to be praying silently.

"Are there mountains around here?" the little girl asked. "Momma says there are."

"Yes," said Adam. "Big tall ones."

The girl smiled her toothless smile.

And Adam gently pressed his hands onto the bridge of her nose and stretched his fingers so that one touched her left eye and one her right.

"Shut your eyes, Allison."

He held his fingers there for perhaps a minute, though to me, all time had stopped.

To the east, sunlight threatened to cut through the snow clouds.

"Keep your eyes shut," Adam murmured.

He pushed to his feet and stood, looking down at her. Then he lifted her into his arms and gestured for people to back away. He turned so that he faced the mobile home and the stretch of the Rockies to the west. Through scattered clouds, you could see a peak or two.

Perched on Adam's shoulders, Allison said, "Can I open them now?"

And the crowd seemed to hold its breath.

"Yeah. Yeah, open them and take a look off in the distance."

For a moment, Allison said nothing.

Oh, Jesus, no . . . he couldn't heal her, I thought to myself.

"What do you think about those mountains?" said Adam.

The little girl let out a big sigh.

"Is that what those are? Well, I'll tell you this," she said, "they're pretty nice."

Her mother issued a joyful scream and the crowd buzzed and one or two shouted, "She can see! He healed her!" And some exclaimed, "Praise God!"

I searched the surrounding circle for Lawrence and saw him slip away.

He's given up! something within me cried out.

"He's given up," I said to Andrea, but she had pressed closer to Adam and the little girl, who was then laughing and asking about the names of various colors.

Then it started. The begging. The pathetic requests.

"Heal my boy! . . . Touch my daddy's crippled legs! . . . My friend has AIDS. Please save him!"

God, they were gonna crush Adam.

So I caught him by the elbow and drove people out of the way. I shoved them and swore at them and the young Indian man tried to help clear a path.

Hands. Everywhere I looked I saw hands . . . reaching out . . . reaching out for Adam . . . like some weird, tentacled monster, the crowd reached for him.

Someone snatched his orange stocking cap.

"It has powers!" a man yelled. "I have his cap!"

And part of the crowd pursued that voice and the blur of orange.

It was like hungry fish being tossed pieces of bread. Adam was the bread.

Then, in one final wrenching movement, the two Indians squeezed us inside the mobile home. Somehow Andrea made it, too.

Dazed and disoriented, Adam stumbled forward.

Andrea and I balanced him.

"It's okay now," I told him. "You're safe in here."

Suddenly excited and happy. Andrea pressed her face close to Adam's.

"This is where you get rid of the night touch," she exclaimed. "You'll be free of it. You'll be normal again."

Adam flashed a weak smile as Andrea hugged him.

"That's right," I added. "Mary Walks Lightly . . . she's here. We made it, friend."

There were tears in his eyes.

He shook his head and clutched at my shoulder.

The Indian with braided hair—his name was Jonathan—gestured hurriedly.

"This way. Come this way."

He led us down a long dark hallway. The walls of the mobile home were completely covered with photos and paintings and objects—some Christian, most Indian, it appeared: beads and small rugs, feathers, bones, pictures of the Virgin Mary and Christ and a massive painting of a white buffalo.

Jonathan was impatient; he guided us as quickly as he could into a small room filled with candles.

God, it was eerie.

Deep in the shadows, on a pallet on the floor, you could see a huge dark object. A person.

Jonathan leaned down.

"Mother, he's here."

"Adam made it," Andrea whispered in my ear. "Rob, he made it."

Yeah, I realized it was all gonna work out, just like my dad used to say—somehow things will work out.

If you looked closely, you could see the smooth outline of Mary Walks Lightly's round face. Her eyes were shut. But there was this . . . aura, I guess the word is, about her. Not really a color. Something powerful there.

She stirred. I think one of her hands moved.

Adam stepped forward and Jonathan stood aside to let him draw near.

It was awesome. All those candles. The silence.

Adam reached down and touched her hand.

And he paused and lowered his head kinda like he was praying.

I remember wondering how he would react when the night touch was removed—would he jump around and cheer? Or just be quietly thankful to be relieved of his curse?

Then Adam spoke, and at first, I thought I had misunderstood—his words confused me.

"Goodbye," he said. "Goodbye, Mary Walks Lightly."

"Why do you say that?" Jonathan asked him.

"Your mother is dead," said Adam. "A moment ago. And I was too late."

It's an awful thing to admit, but right then I hated that little blind girl Adam had healed. If he hadn't taken the time to heal her . . . and if Andrea . . . I just couldn't accept it.

Andrea embraced him.

We all sorta staggered out of that room, stunned, no idea what to do next.

Stoic, very solemn, Jonathan guided us to the front room.

"You better leave out the back way unless you want to stay and serve the crowd. You could carry on my mother's work . . . you have the power. I saw you work."

Adam shook his head.

"Cold," he said. "The night touch is turning on me . . . cold like ice."

"What is he saying, Rob?" Andrea demanded.

But I had no real idea. Everything seemed so mystifying.

"Come on," I said. "Let's go."

We circled beyond several other mobile homes, eventually tracking our way to the Dodge. Out of habit, I looked around for Lawrence. Didn't see him. At least Adam wouldn't have to worry about being hunted down.

We helped our friend into the front seat; WaKeeney immediately jumped into his lap and began to purr.

Disappointment hung in the air.

"Adam, we'll find another way. We'll find a way to get rid of the night touch. Don't give up, man."

I glanced at Andrea, wanting her to offer some encouragement, but she was stone silent.

"I'm cold," Adam mumbled. "Freezing."

Andrea felt his face.

"Rob!"

I touched his cheek and his left hand. They were so cold they almost burned my fingers.

"God, oh, God . . . we have to find a warm place."

I drove west. Had no idea where I was going. Had vague thoughts of locating a hospital.

We had gone about a mile or so when it started snowing again. On top of that, I caught sight of a car I recognized: Lawrence's.

He had stopped at a service station.

And I hoped and prayed that he hadn't seen us . . . that he hadn't changed his mind about not killing Adam.

"Watch out the back," I ordered Andrea. "I saw Lawrence at that station there at the intersection."

Andrea was silent for a moment.

I stole a glance at Adam. His face had grayed; his body seemed to curl up and grow smaller.

"God, Andrea, I think Adam's pretty sick. And this heater is just blowing cold air."

"Rob?"

"Is he following us? What do you see?"

"He is."

"Damn it. Damn, oh damn. Why won't he stop?"

Andrea reached over the seat and placed a hand on Adam's cheek.

"Rob, we gotta get him inside somewhere."

It was early afternoon; dark gray snow clouds lowered upon us and it began to snow harder—big, soft flakes. In any other situation, it would have been a beautiful scene.

"Where are we, Rob?"

"In some suburb north of Denver. I think maybe I'm gonna pull into one of these apartment complexes. See if someone will let us get warmed up."

"Hurry, Rob. Adam's bad. And Lawrence is still back there."

"How far away?"

"Quarter mile or so. I don't know."

I turned onto a road flanked by an open field to the north; on the other side was a row of blue-gray apart-

335

ments—few cars around.

"I'm trying some of these," I said. "Hang on to WaKeeney when I get out. Keep one eye peeled for Lawrence, too."

Well, I banged on several doors and got no response.

Just when I was about ready to give up, I tried one more and this Mexican guy greeted me. Seemed friendly. His dog barked and jumped around eagerly.

"Chico. Hey, stay down."

"Please, mister," I said, "the heater's gone out in our car, and my friends and I are 'bout to freeze. We drove here from Kansas and . . . could you let us come in a minute and warm ourselves?"

"Kansas? Where in Kansas you from? I grew up in Kansas."

Lucky break for us, I thought to myself.

"From Warrior Stand. It's north of Emporia."

"Well, hey, bring your friends in."

His smile made me feel super.

"We'll just stop a minute," I followed. "Thanks. Thanks, this is great. I'll tell 'em to come on in."

I knew we had no right to put the guy in the path of danger—Lawrence might choose the time to go for Adam—I had no way of knowing.

Helping Adam out of the storm and the cold was my only concern. Andrea's too.

CHAPTER 27

"You okay, buddy?"

Our good samaritan helped Adam into a chair, studied him, and smiled.

"He got real cold," I explained. "Like I said, the heater in our old car went out."

"His arm's been hurt, too," Andrea added. "He'll be better once he gets some warmth."

"Listen," said our host, "we've got a big pot of vegetable soup on the stove. You guys want some? I bet you're hungry."

Well, in fact, we were.

"Oh, we didn't plan on anybody feedin' us. We can go to a restaurant . . . I mean, we have money. It's just that Adam here, you know, . . . we needed to stop."

I hoped that the guy wouldn't be too suspicious. Andrea and I both occasionally glanced at the front door, half expecting Lawrence to barge in and open up on Adam.

"My wife's upstairs asleep, and Chico doesn't eat soup. So there's plenty."

On the way to the kitchen, he switched on the television.

"You guys Bronco fans?"

I thought maybe he was talking about a rodeo.

"Not exactly," I replied. "We have a friend back home who is."

When the picture locked in place, I realized that he was referring to football.

A worried look on her face, Andrea bent down in front of Adam and rubbed his left arm. He grew a little more alert. Even smiled weakly.

Over steaming bowls of soup, we relaxed and watched the football game, and during commercials our host had his dog do tricks for us. Smart dog.

Adam revived. He slurped down his soup as if he hadn't eaten in days. And he picked up on the flow of the game and soon was cheering for the Denver team. I believe they were winning.

At halftime, I got to thinking we ought to leave. Thing is, though, I had no idea where we should go. What was going to happen to Adam? We had failed to get rid of the night touch, and, apparently, Lawrence remained on our trail.

Was he outside waiting for us?

There was a sliding glass door beyond the television set leading into a small backyard area. It really bugged me because it would have been easy for Lawrence to sneak around and . . . well, anyway, I finished my soup and found myself mesmerized by the wind swirling the soft flakes of snow.

"You guys come out to go skiing?"

Our new friend's question set off alarms in me.

"Yes," I said. But at just that same moment, Andrea said, "No."

I frowned at her; through the awkwardness and embarrassment, I tried to explain.

"We came out to ski, but . . . the storm . . . we couldn't make it to the ski areas. So . . . so we visited a friend of Adam's in town. And then we were driving around and our heater went on the blink and we got sorta lost . . . and . . . here we are."

I don't think he swallowed my story, but he didn't jump on it. Thank goodness. Instead, he started talking about Kansas, about growing up in some little town I'd never heard of, about playing football and having good friends. He told us that was the best thing you could have—friends you have good memories of.

338

He seemed real interested in Adam. They hit it off great. After the game—Denver won—Andrea and I kinda faded—a warm apartment, warm food in our stomachs, we dozed off for a few minutes—maybe it was an hour.

When I woke up, Adam and the guy were laughing, and the guy's wife had come downstairs.

"You think we should go?" I whispered to Andrea.

She shrugged.

"I suppose we should."

But when I announced it, our host said he wanted to talk to us some more. I began to panic just a little.

"Look," he said, "I've got a feeling you didn't come out to Denver to ski. You can't be any older than sixteen, are you?"

"Fifteen," Adam muttered.

Our host surveyed us pretty closely.

"You guys in some kind of trouble?"

Oh, Jesus.

Andrea started crying softly. I hugged her to me.

Adam came to the rescue.

"We didn't steal a car or rob a bank."

"What'd you do? Are you running away from home?"

"You could say that . . . yeah, we are . . . because . . . there's this man who's after us. After me."

"And, for some reason, you don't want the cops involved."

Adam nodded.

At that point, I joined the conversation.

"We wouldn't want to get you in hot water on this. So maybe it's better if we don't tell you all the details. Okay?"

The guy glanced at his wife and then back at us.

"Hey, listen, you seem like good kids to me. I won't call the cops if you don't want me to."

"I wish we could give you the truth," I said. "But . . . it's a pretty hard story to believe. A strange story."

And then the guy said, "I have a friend who writes strange stories."

"Not this strange," I remarked.

There was an awkward pause before the guy kind of smiled.

"So where you going from here?"

I shrugged, but suddenly Adam surprised us all.

"California," he exclaimed. "I think it's the best place for me. It's where I'll need to go. But my friends . . . they'll take a bus back to Kansas. They've helped me enough."

Andrea and I said nothing. We didn't want to put a damper on Adam's mood; he seemed as happy and contented as we'd seen him in a long time.

"How's a good way to California from Denver?" Adam asked.

And he and the guy talked about routes; I just sat and listened, realizing the journey had reached a new stage. Adam would be moving on without me and Andrea.

I felt sad. At the same time, Adam appeared hopeful.

About then, the guy's dog acted as if it heard something beyond the sliding glass door, and my thoughts shifted to Lawrence. Was he still out there, waiting, watching . . . ?

Lucky star.

Clay Lawrence leaned against the back fence of the apartment complex and stared into the night sky. Snowflakes drifted onto his eyelids and hair. He had stood out in the cold for several hours, thinking about lucky stars.

"Perky has one," he murmured.

He inched closer to the sliding glass door.

"I could shoot all of them. What does it matter? Hubie would. He'd shoot Curry. Perky would praise God."

He gently stamped his feet to remove the snow.

His hands were so cold he couldn't clutch his revolver. In his thoughts, snow fell softly.

He couldn't recall, for a fleeting moment, why he wanted to kill the young man inside the warm apartment.

340

It had something to do with a song—no, a saying—like a proverb. How did it go?

March will search, April will try,
And May will tell if you live or die.

"Shoot all of them," he whispered. "For making me cold. Hubie would. But he doesn't have a lucky star."

It was a slow and deliberate letting go. Of reality.

He could feel it, sense it taking place.

But couldn't stop it.

March will search. . . .

And he straightened his back against the wall and the swirl of snow in his thoughts ceased. He saw a crowd. He saw Adam Dodd touching the eyes of the blind girl . . . and the crowd . . . "Praise God" . . . lucky stars . . . and . . . *April will try* . . . Hubie's gonna get his man . . . she could see the mountains . . . *And May will tell if you live or die.*

Healed the little girl.

But he killed Kristin.

Yes, that was it.

. . . live or die.

Lawrence slipped the revolver out of its holster and edged to the glass door.

"Chico! Chico, come away from there!"

The guy had to lift the dog and wrestle with it playfully to stop it from whining.

A chill raced down my spine. Can't say exactly why.

Except that I could see the sudden terror in Adam's eyes.

He stood up.

"We've got to go," he exclaimed. "Now."

We said goodbye to our good samaritan and his wife—people who had taken us in out of the cold.

Funny, but I don't even remember their names.

Maybe Andrea does.

Hot soup and a place for Adam to recover himself. And a dog named "Chico." And a fear that at any moment

Lawrence would ambush us. That's what I remember.

It was cold but clear as we rattled around until we found the interstate running south toward Colorado Springs. The only good thing about our repeatedly getting lost was that we seemed to have ditched Lawrence.

"He'd been waiting all the time," I said.

Adam drove along, WaKeeney snuggled up in his lap, both appearing to be oblivious to the threat of our pursuer. WaKeeney, having been locked in the Dodge, had heard Nature's call, and so the aroma of cat shit filled the darkness.

Andrea tried rolling down a window. Not much help.

I told her to lie back and get some sleep if she could.

"If we're lucky, we'll have lost Lawrence by the time we make it to Colorado Springs. You and me'll buy a bus ticket home and Adam can . . ."

I couldn't finish the sentence.

Andrea crawled within herself. I was hoping she wouldn't cry.

"Hey," said Adam. "Hey, you guys, don't give me this hangdog crap. Things are gonna be okay. Yeah, okay. California. It's where all the weirdos are. Bound to be one weirdo who can fix the night touch."

I was doubtful. I mean, I wanted to believe . . . just couldn't quite do it.

As we skated atop the snowy road, Adam began to sing.

"Cal-ah-forn-yah, here I come! Right back where I started from! Open up your Golden Gate, Cal-ah-forn-yah, here I come!"

He really belted it out. Like a madman. . . .

The lights flanking the interstate through Denver flashed diamond and ice in Lawrence's eyes. Like stars.

Lucky stars.

Vaguely he realized that his left hand was frostbitten.

He laid it against the heater vent, but the fiery tingle in his fingers would not relent.

He couldn't be certain whether the taillights of the old Dodge were still up ahead.

Some dark imperative pulled him on.

At moments, he heard the voice of a little girl singing a song especially for him.

Slowly, slowly letting go.

But a part of him wouldn't let go.

It insisted that he finish the job.

Finish the job.

Finish the job.

He switched on the radio.

And the little girl's voice flooded out all other sounds.

"Tell me you like me/And I'll do you no wrong . . . do you no wrong . . . do you no wrong."

"It's gonna work," said Adam. "You guys, ding damn it." He laughed. "It's gonna work. Caly-forny is the place I ought-ee be. I could be the Beverly Hills Jayhawker. Or . . . or maybe go to San Francisco . . . I left my hear-ar-ar-art in San Francisco."

Well, finally, I had to chuckle at the guy. His silly songs and all.

Damnit, I wanted to go on with him even though it was a crazy idea.

In the next few miles something happened. My sudden good feeling evaporated. I remember an exit sign for "Castle Rock" and I remember how warm it was getting inside the Dodge.

WaKeeney felt it first and scrambled out of Adam's lap.

Andrea stuck her head into the front seat and said, "Look at the windows! The car's fogging up. Why is it so warm?"

"Roll down the back windows," I exclaimed.

Adam's face had tightened; sweat coated it.

I leaned closer to him.

343

"Jesus, man, what is it?"

He carefully pulled off onto the shoulder.

"It's my left hand and arm. Burning up. Night touch. You better drive."

I traded places with him.

Concerned, Andrea hovered, needing to say something to him or do something for him. But helpless.

"You guys," Adam murmured. "Don't worry. The next rest area, turn in. I think I can maybe pack it in snow and cool it down."

Andrea reached forward and touched his arm at about the elbow.

"Adam! My God!"

"Hey, no problem," he responded. "We've got a bigger one than this."

We exchanged glances. I didn't want to hear what he had to say.

"Lawrence is behind us. He's not gonna give up."

I had to grip the wheel hard because I felt like I was falling into a deep, black pit or that the cold, snow-glistened Colorado landscape was about to swallow us.

There was so little traffic, the hour close to midnight, that I felt we were stranded. I wanted to see cars. People.

Suddenly Adam moaned.

"Rob, hurry! We have to do something!"

"Jesus, Andrea, I'm trying."

I hit the exit ramp for the rest area so fast that we fishtailed, and because of the fogged windows, I could barely see.

Before I could bring the Dodge to a stop, Adam pushed himself out, staggering toward a pair of picnic tables.

"Rob, where's he going?"

"Leave him alone. Just leave him alone."

He plunged past the tables, falling to his knees in a snowdrift.

As we approached, in the shadowy darkness, we could see steam mushrooming up around Adam's body.

"Rob, oh God, is he dying?"

I grabbed her and shook her.

"No. Don't say that. He's not. He's gonna be okay."
God almighty, I wanted to believe that.
Then we heard Adam chuckling, and it gave me chills.
Time seemed to accelerate.
In my thoughts we were speeding through a dark tunnel, drawn by an intensely bright light at the end.
"You guys . . . it's all right. Come on over here."
Cautiously we hunkered down beside him.
"Oh, Adam, don't die. Don't die, please."
Andrea embraced his neck.
"How are you feeling?" I asked.
"Like a million bucks, asshole," he joked.
I took a handful of snow and tossed it at him.
"What can we do, man?"
"Stop being so damned morbid. I'm just a little weak. That's all. Need some strength."
We fell silent for awhile.
WaKeeney, having escaped from the car, sauntered up, meowing.
Adam reached out and petted him.
"I've been thinking," said Andrea, "of maybe a way we could help."
I was skeptical before she even explained.
She took my hand.
"If we concentrated real hard . . . maybe we could draw strength from each other. Because . . . because we care about each other."
Then something strange happened.
Adam clasped his right hand over hers.
"Andrea," he said, "I'll try it."
He had called her "Andrea," not "Andy"—made me feel funny.
It was the closest the three of us had ever been.
It was like we knew each other's thoughts.
We stood, and there in the snow, we held hands. Closed our eyes.
No one said a word. No one needed to.
After a few seconds, I felt something.
Adam's left hand seemed normal—cooled way down;

345

his body gave off a glow.

But then suddenly he took his hand away.

I opened my eyes.

Andrea screamed and put her hands to her mouth.

Not twenty feet from us Lawrence drew a bead on Adam with a two-hand hold on his revolver.

"No lucky star for you," Lawrence muttered, gesturing for Andrea and me to move to one side.

Adam said nothing. It was as if he knew this confrontation was inevitable.

The tension finally got to me.

"Use the night touch, Adam," I exclaimed. "Use it to save yourself."

He shook his head.

"No. Never again."

"Hubie would do it," said Lawrence.

We had no idea what he was talking about. There was a fierce blankness in his expression.

He's gone crazy, a voice within me whispered. *Gone crazy*.

"I have something for you," said Adam.

"A lucky star?" Lawrence murmured.

"I understand . . . if you have to kill me . . . I understand."

"Kill you? Why would I kill you?"

Andrea moved closer to me. A surge of hope connected us.

"I have this for you," said Adam.

He reached into his pocket and retrieved something which picked up glints of light.

"It belonged to Kristin Kelley."

He handed the wildcat figurine toward Lawrence, who took it and stared at it.

"Kristin?"

"I want you . . . to forgive me," said Adam. "For what I did. I swear to God, I never meant to hurt her. It was the night touch."

Lawrence held the figurine up close to his eyes.

He began whispering. I couldn't make out what he was saying at first. Then I realized he was singing something—softly, to begin with, becoming louder until we could hear the words.

> Tell me you like me
> And I'll do you no wrong.
> Tell me you love me
> And I'll sing you a song.

Adam raised his hands out to his side.

"Will you forgive me?"

Lawrence stared at him, and for a moment that fierce blankness disappeared, and I saw the face of a determined hunter.

It happened in the blink of an eye.

No way to have stopped it.

"Coach Hugh," he exclaimed, "rest in peace."

The night exploded twice.

"No-o-o-o!" I screamed.

Slammed backward, Adam clutched at his right shoulder, stumbled, and fell heavily upon the snow.

Instantly Andrea and I ran to him.

A bright light whirl of confusion held the scene.

Andrea and I must have cried in our shocked bewilderment—I don't remember. What I do recall was turning to find Lawrence gone. And then I ran to find a pay phone only to discover that it didn't work.

Blood gushing from his shoulder and chest wounds, Adam lay there, motionless, a kind of peaceful expression on his face.

"I'm taking the Dodge back toward Denver for help. You go to the road and try to flag down someone, anyone."

Andrea wouldn't move; she just hovered over Adam's body. So I pulled her to her feet.

"Go on," I yelled. "We can't let it end like this."

Through her tears, she said, "He told me he loved me,

Rob. Loved me so much. And I couldn't love him back . . . not that way."

She lowered herself beside him again and held his hand.

I pushed myself away, knowing I couldn't watch the final moments.

CHAPTER 28

It won't be long before our cottonwood leafs out.

From here in the cemetery, I can watch the March wind toy with its branches. Wonder why it has to be so windy in Kansas? At least it's warm today. Two days ago we had a cold rain and a spitting of snow and sleet which reminded me of the Denver odyssey.

Everything reminds me of that journey.

Andrea is here next to me, lying on our snuggle blanket.

I can smell strawberry licorice.

She and I come up to the cemetery a lot these days— our refuge from the world. The police investigation of Adam and the deaths of Karl Dodd, Brian Gunnellson, and Kristin Kelley continues. We learned that Doyle and Ranger Man did not survive the burning tire shed. There's apparently a separate investigation of their deaths.

I'm tired of going over the same story again and again.

They say that next month they'll decide what to do about me and Andrea for our role in everything. Leah got us a lawyer. I think most of Warrior Stand supports us, but the kids at school just sorta leave us alone. Sometimes that hurts. Hurts Andrea more than me.

Pudge said I could have the old Dodge. Adam's Dodge. I don't really think of it as mine—not like I own it—more like I'm keeping it until Adam . . . well, that car holds a lot of memories. And still smells a little like cat shit.

Andrea and I go out to visit Mrs. Dodd every so often.

She decided not to leave the home place. Whenever we sit with her, she traps us into a marathon prayer session for Adam.

Last week Leah and I allowed some salvage workers to bulldoze the blackened remains of Sunset House. To my mind, they should have bulldozed the whole downtown, including the hardware.

I haven't forgiven Doc Newton. Maybe never will.

And no one has seen or heard from Detective Lawrence since Christmas.

WaKeeney is sleeping on Andrea's stomach.

I think he misses Adam.

Andrea is stirring, so WaKeeney will have to find another spot.

I'm looking down the slope from the cemetery as I usually do. Can't help it. It's just a habit.

"Rob, you know what I keep thinking?"

She's sitting up, Indian style, the wind mussing her hair. God, she's becoming a beautiful woman.

"No, what?"

"If I could see into the future, you know, and see how everything turns out, then I wouldn't sit around and mope so much. And cry. It's such a waste, it seems. If I could look ahead and see that we're married and have children and you're a famous painter and we live to be eighty or ninety or a hundred. You know, the women in my family live to be real old."

"Why don't you just hold on to the moment," I say to her, "and the good memories. Shouldn't always want more."

"I could be happy, Rob, if I only knew. Will we ever see him again?"

I feel a hot spear in my chest. I always do when anybody mentions Adam.

We listen to the eager, yet mournful Kansas wind, and eventually I say, "Tell me again . . . tell me everything you remember."

"Oh, Rob, . . . you know the story."

"Please."

She has to brace herself because it's such a difficult memory.

"When you left in the Dodge that night, I ran to the road and tried to flag down somebody. A highway patrolman stopped . . . maybe ten minutes later. I took him to where Adam was . . . but Adam was gone."

"And the patrolman looked all around the area? Wasn't there a trail of blood?"

She shakes her head.

"Very little blood except right where he fell."

"You think he healed himself again?"

"Yes. I put his hand on his chest before I ran to the road . . . and I guess . . . it's the only thing I can figure. Where do you think he is, Rob?"

"God, I don't know. Maybe California."

"Could he make it on foot? It was so cold."

"He had the night touch."

"It was making him sick."

"We got to believe he'll be okay," I tell her.

And so we sit quietly and let our thoughts ghost out to him.

One of these days maybe we'll see him coming up the slope. If not, well, it's like that guy out in Denver said— the important thing is to have good memories of your friends.

I wish that could be enough for Andrea and me.

I've come to the end of our strange story. There's an old Kansas saying about the mysteries of the seasons, of life and of death. I reach for Andrea, and I hold her, and I think of that old saying:

March will search, April will try
And May will tell if you live or die.